RAINBOW BRIDGE

STEVE ORLANDO
& STEVE FOXE
writers

VALENTINA BRANCATI
artist

MANUEL PUPPO colors
HASSAN OTSMANE-ELHAOU letters
VALENTINA BRANCATI with **MANUEL PUPPO** cover
CHARLES PRITCHETT logo & book design
MIKE MARTS editor

CREATED BY STEVE ORLANDO & STEVE FOXE

SEISMIC PRESS IS AN IMPRINT OF

MIKE MARTS - Editor-in-Chief • JOE PRUETT - Publisher/CCO • LEE KRAMER - President • JON KRAMER - Chief Executive Officer

STEVE ROTTERDAM - SVP, Sales & Marketing • DAN SHIRES - VP, Film & Television UK • CHRISTINA HARRINGTON - Managing Editor

TEDDY LEO - Associate Editor • MARC HAMMOND - Sr. Retail Sales Development Manager • RUTHANN THOMPSON - Sr. Retailer Relations Manager

KATHERINE JAMISON - Marketing Manager • KELLY DIODATI - Ambassador Outreach Manager • BLAKE STOCKER - Director of Finance

AARON MARION - Publicist • LISA MOODY - Finance • RYAN CARROLL - Director, Comics/Film/TV Liaison • JAWAD QURESHI - Technology Advisor/Strategist

RACHEL PINNELAS - Social Community Manager • CHARLES PRITCHETT - Design & Production Manager • COREY BREEN - Collections Production

STEPHANIE CASEBIER & SARAH PRUETT - Publishing Assistants

AfterShock and Seismic Logo Designs by COMICRAFT

Publicity: contact AARON MARION (aaron@publichausagency.com) & RYAN CROY (ryan@publichausagency.com) at PUBLICHAUS

Special thanks to: ATOM! FREEMAN, IRA KURGAN, MARINE KSADZHIKYAN, KEITH MANZELLA,
ANTONIA LIANOS, ANTHONY MILITANO, STEPHAN NILSON & ED ZAREMBA

AFTERSHOCKCOMICS.COM Follow us on social media 🐦 📷 f

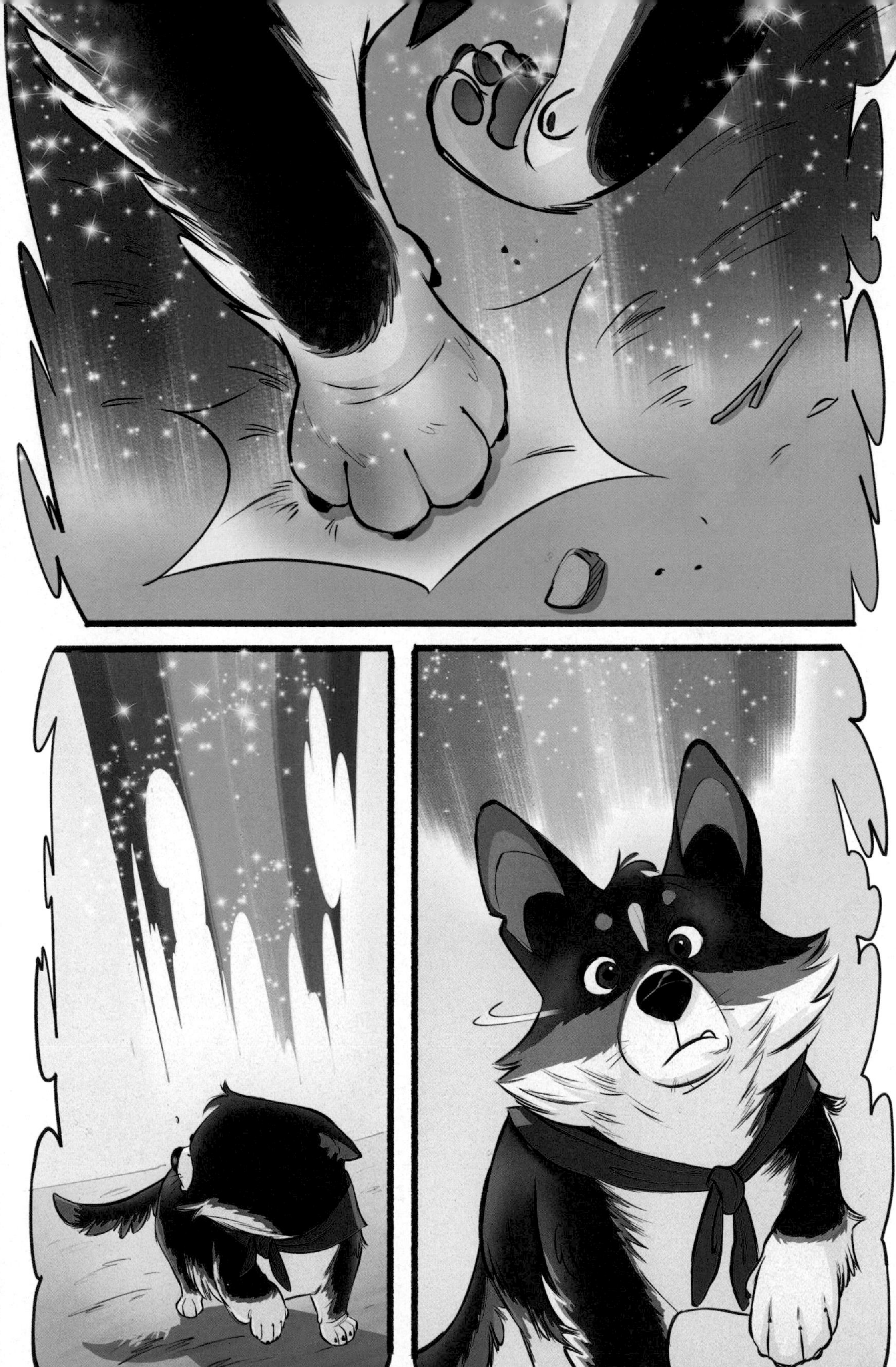

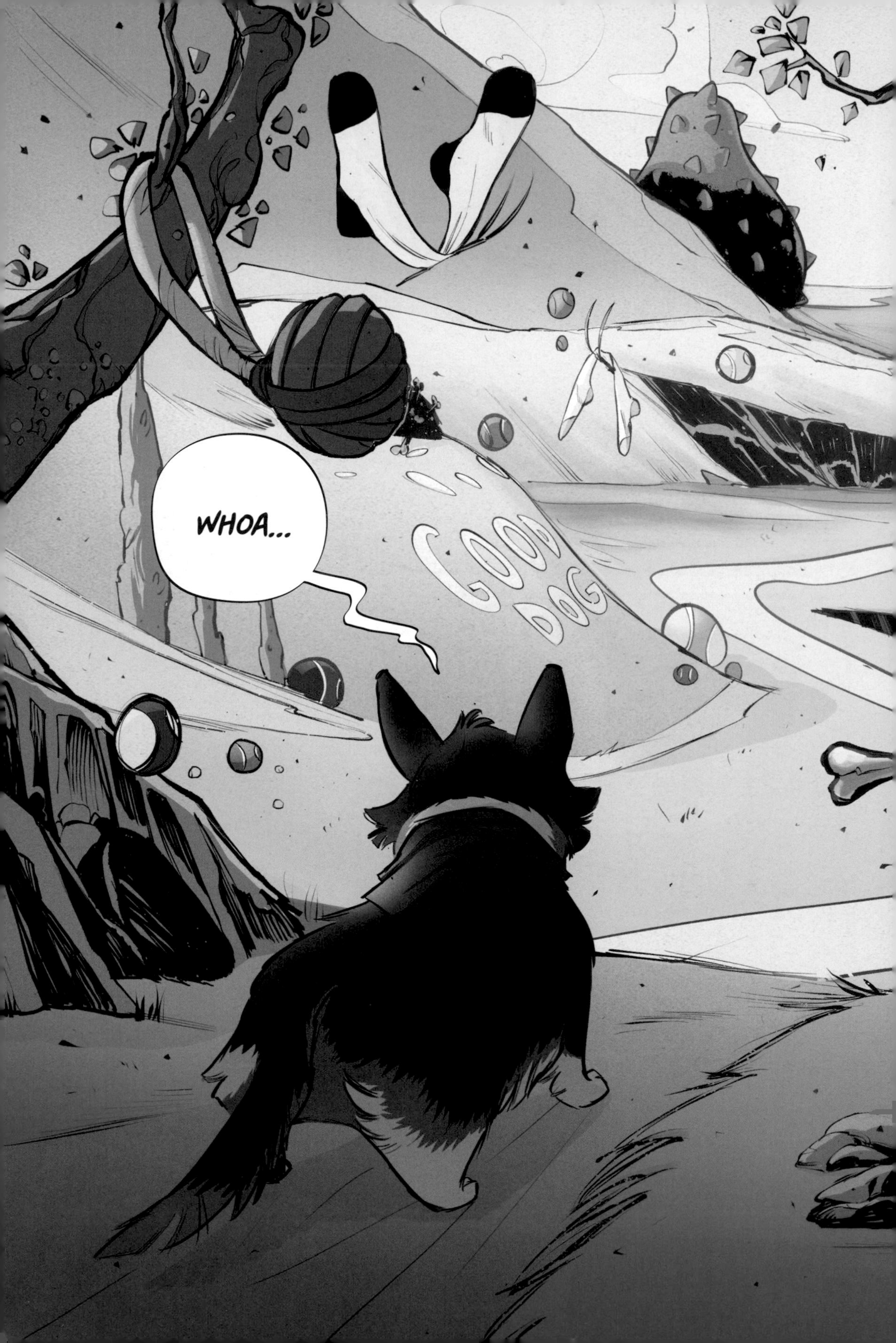
WHOA...
GOOD DOG

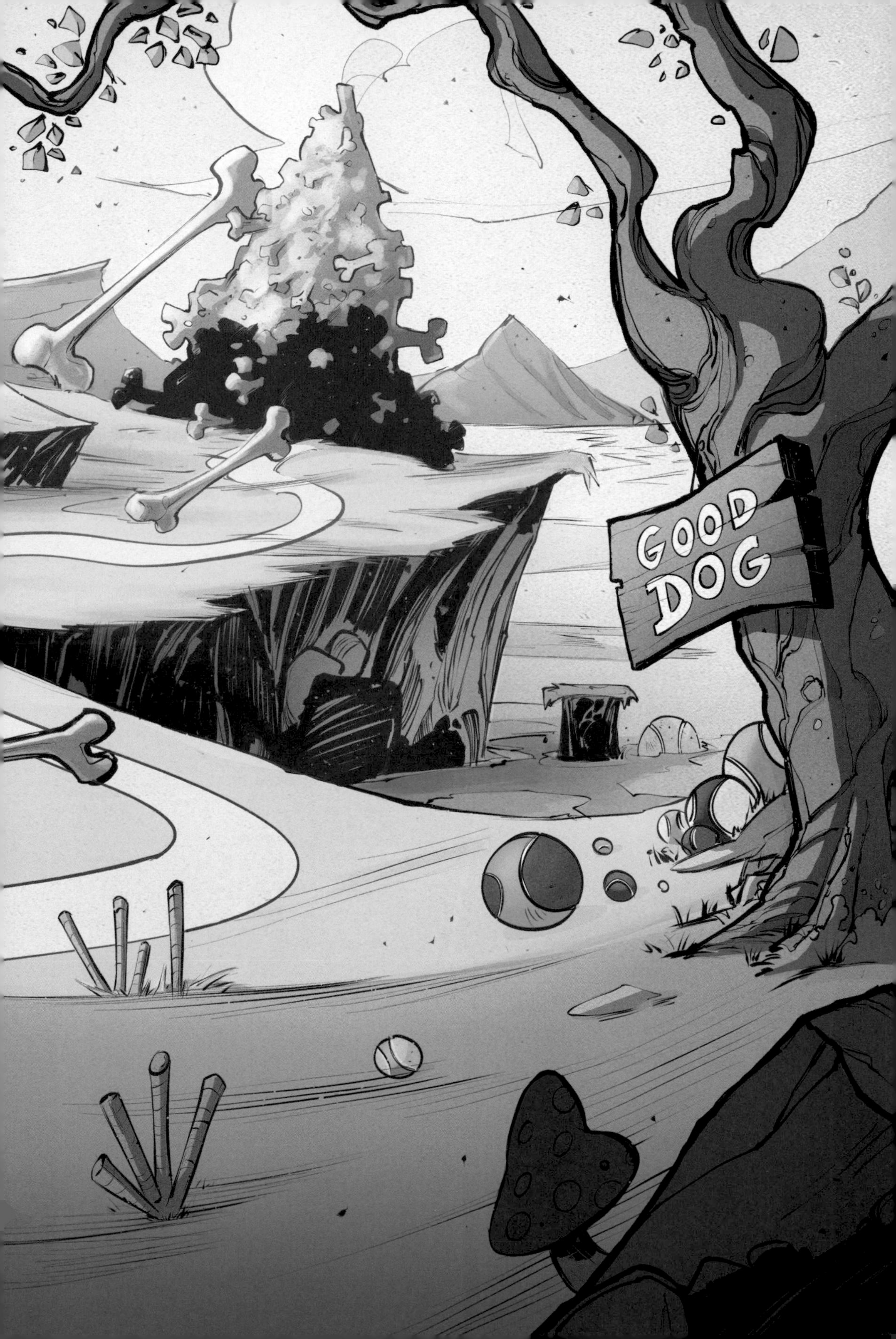
GOOD DOG

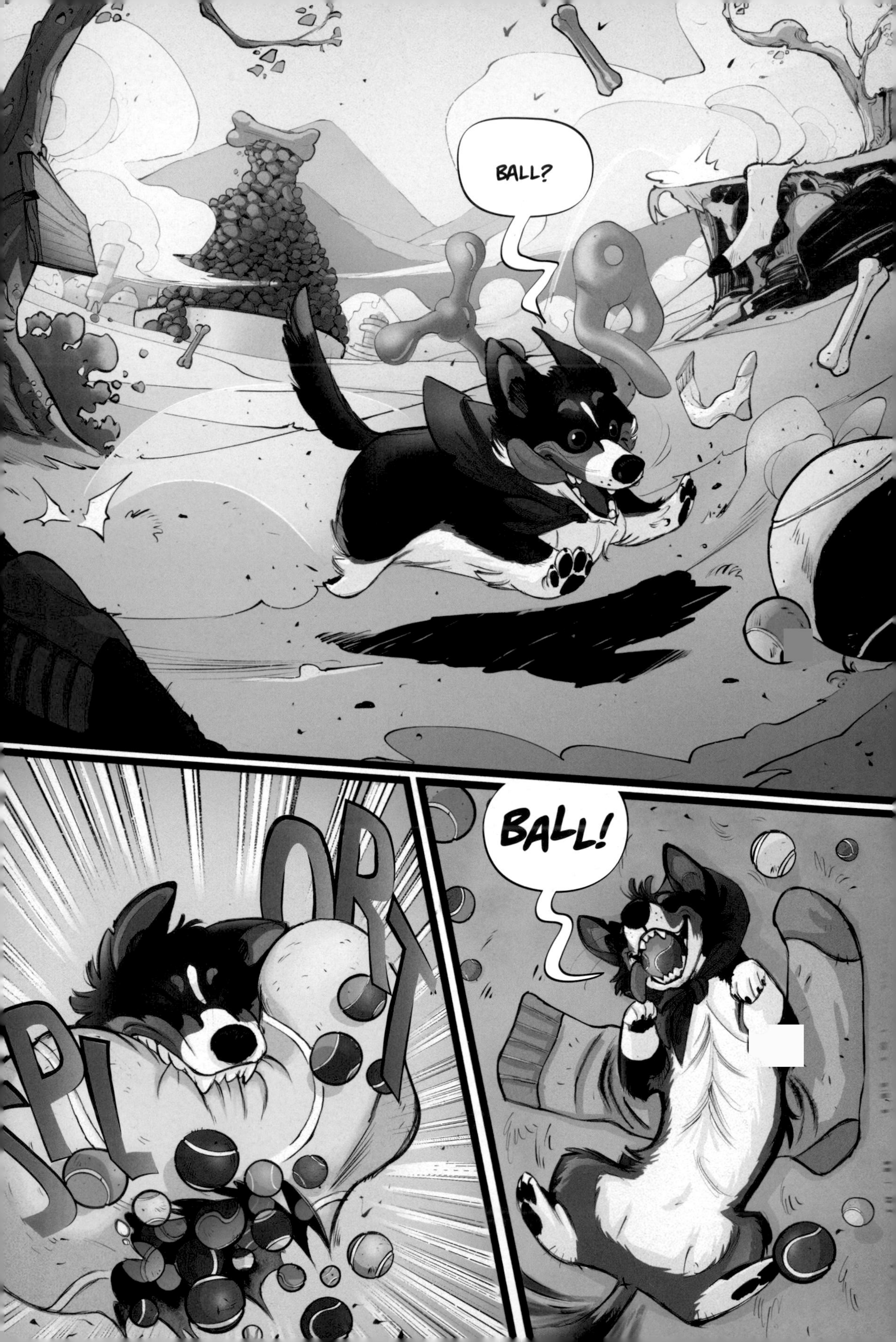
BALL?
BALL!

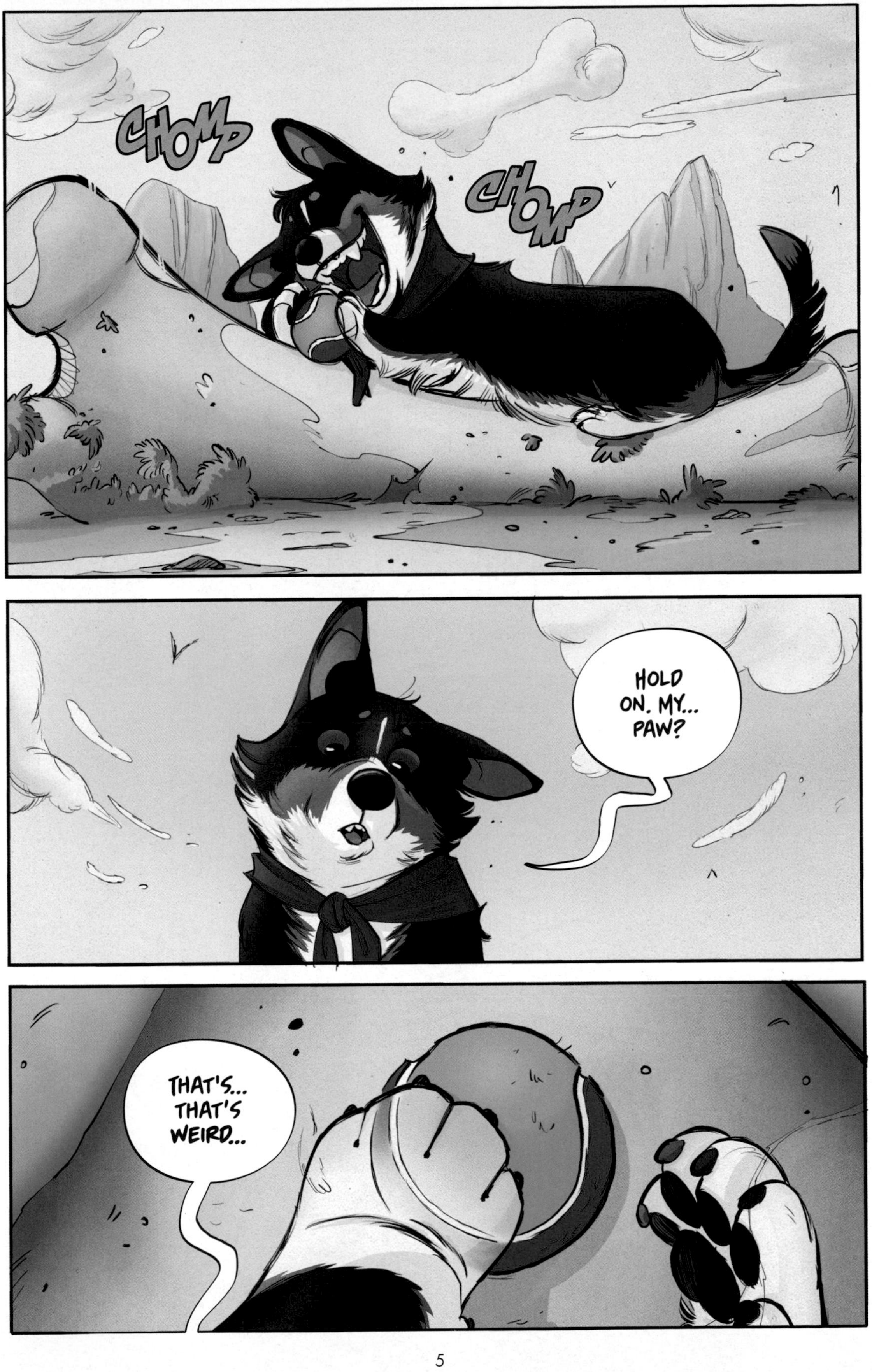
CHOMP
CHOMP
HOLD ON. MY... PAW?
THAT'S... THAT'S WEIRD...

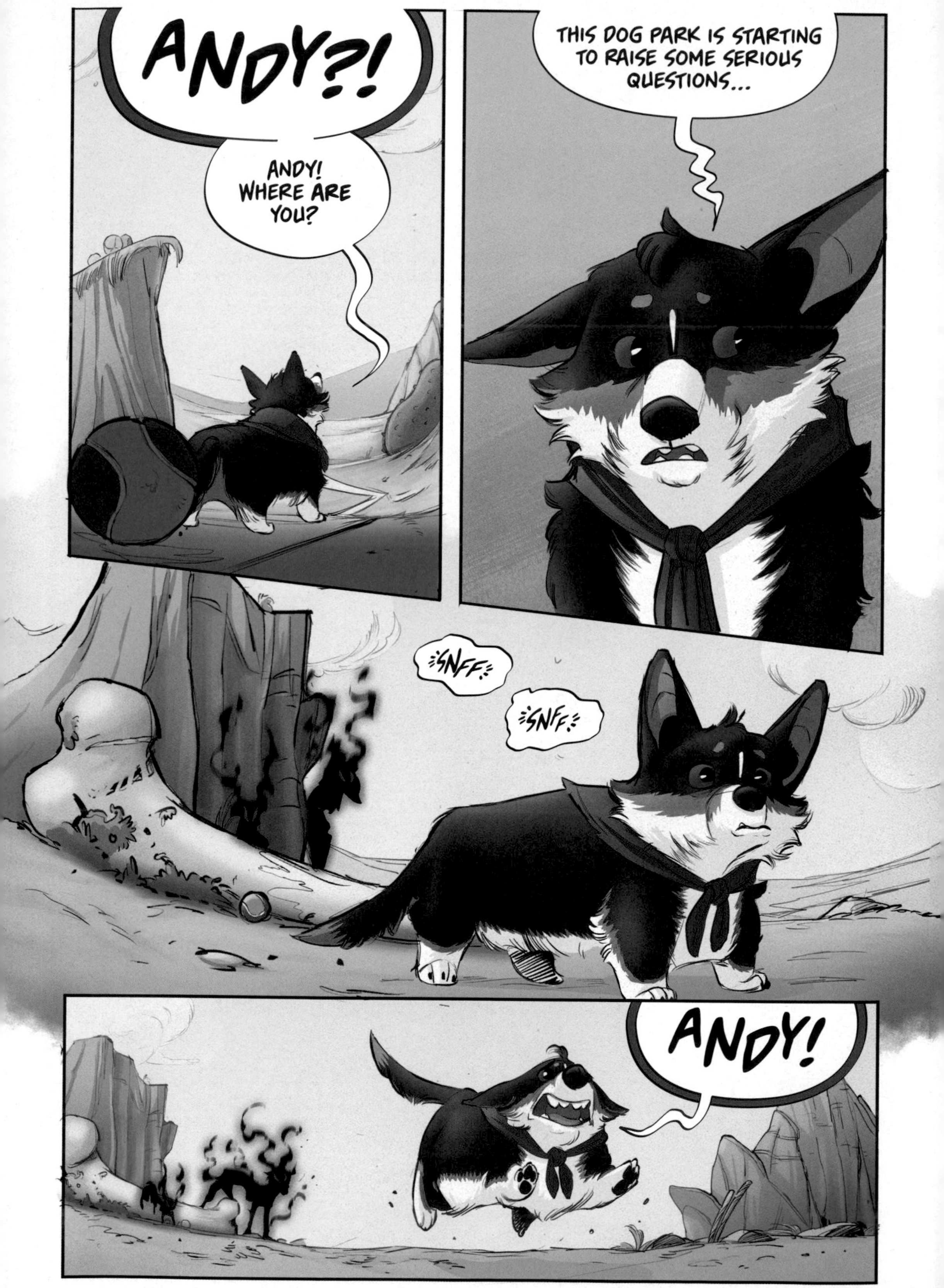
ANDY?!
ANDY! WHERE ARE YOU?
THIS DOG PARK IS STARTING TO RAISE SOME SERIOUS QUESTIONS...
SNFF
SNFF
ANDY!

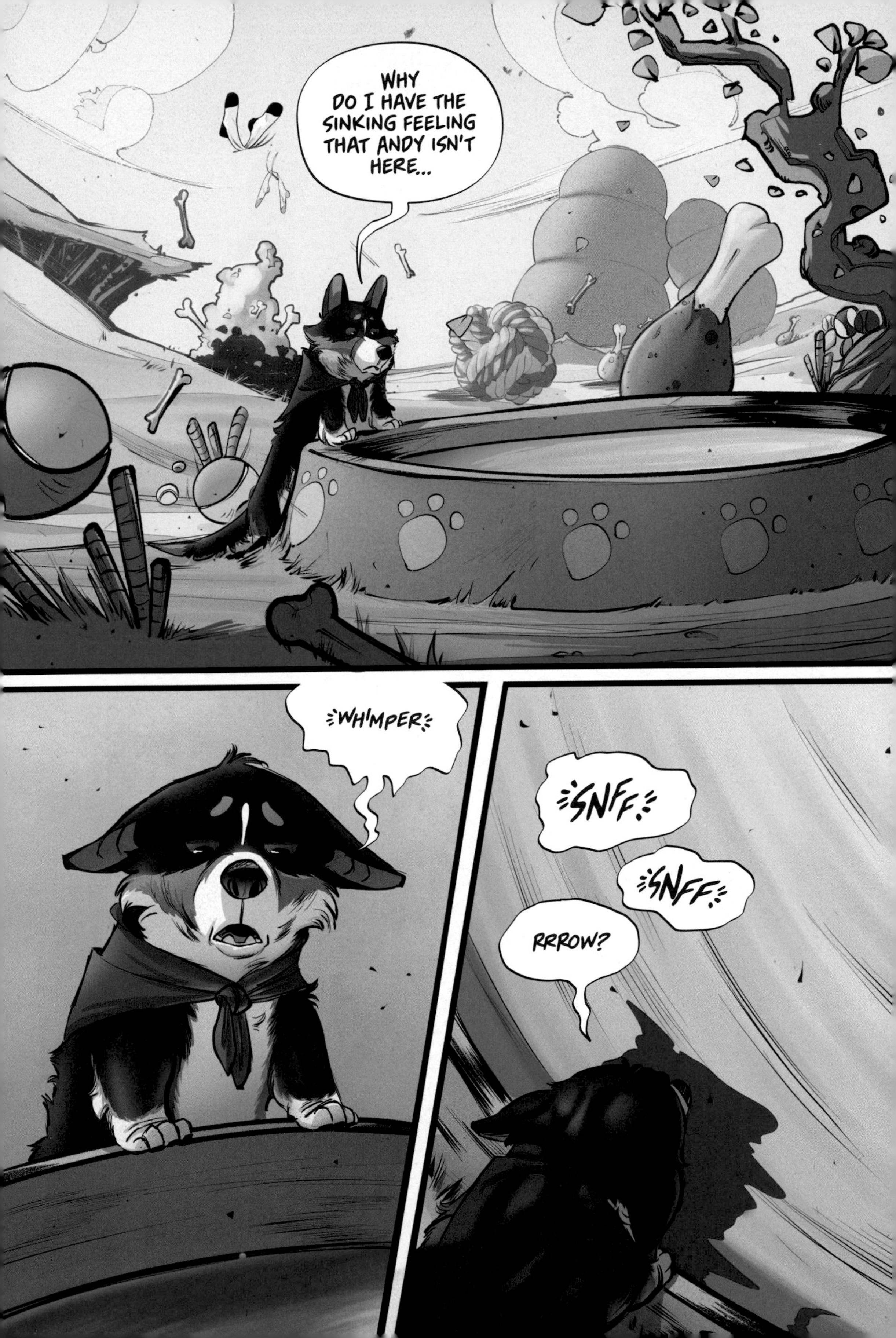
WHY DO I HAVE THE SINKING FEELING THAT ANDY ISN'T HERE...
WHIMPER
SNFF
SNFF
RRROW?

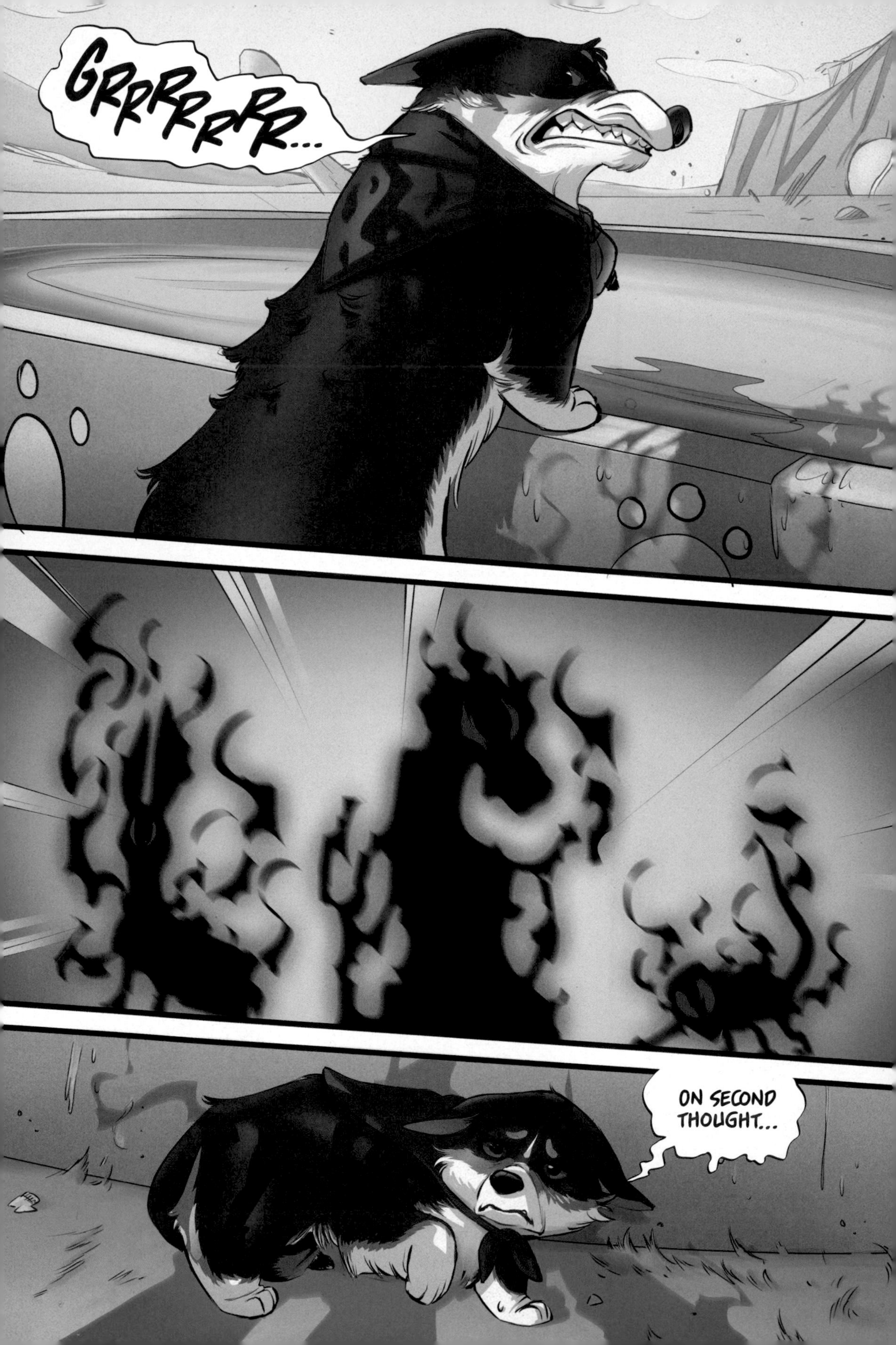
GRRRRRRR...
ON SECOND THOUGHT...

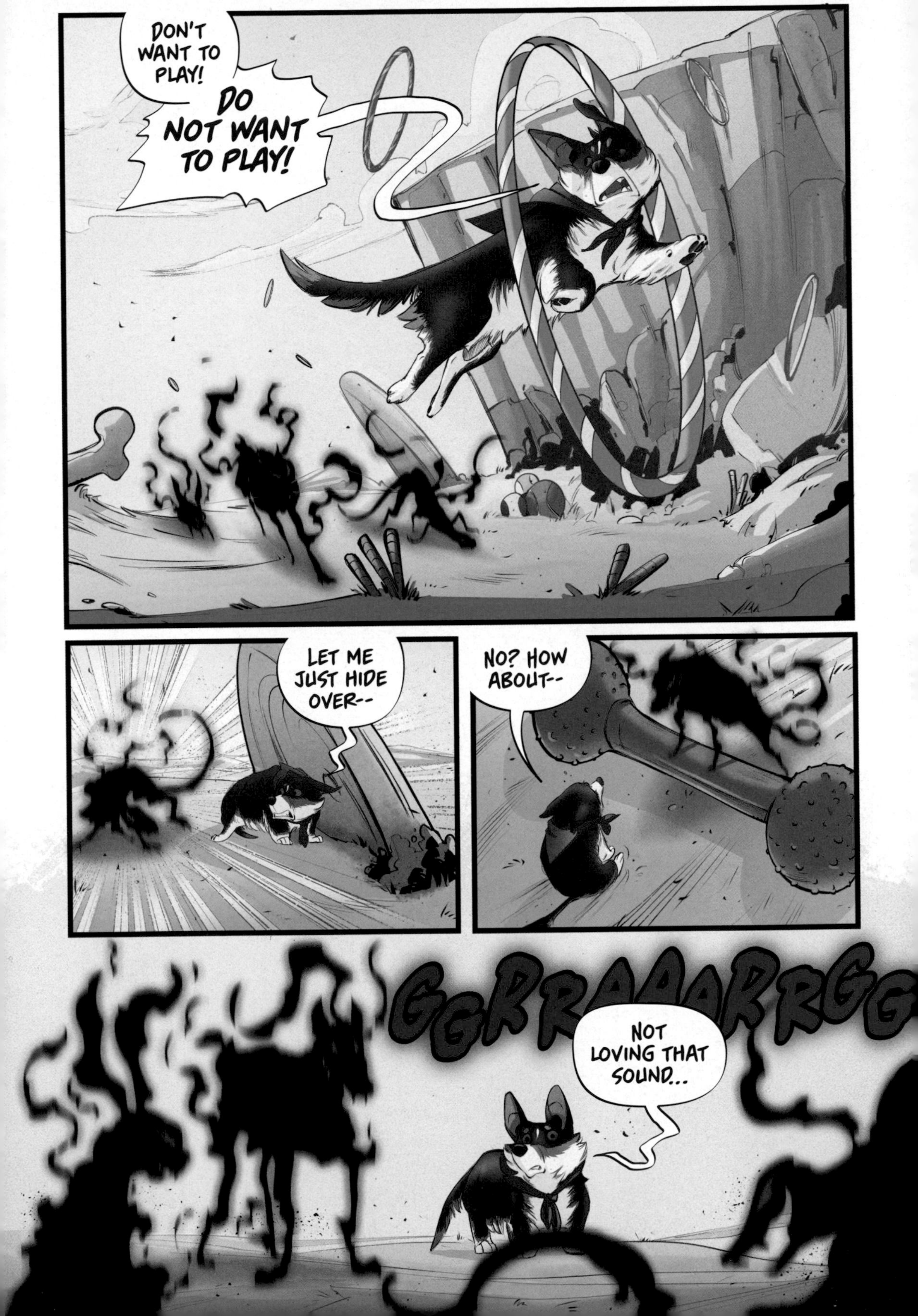
DON'T WANT TO PLAY!
DO NOT WANT TO PLAY!
LET ME JUST HIDE OVER--
NO? HOW ABOUT--
GGRRAAARRGG
NOT LOVING THAT SOUND...

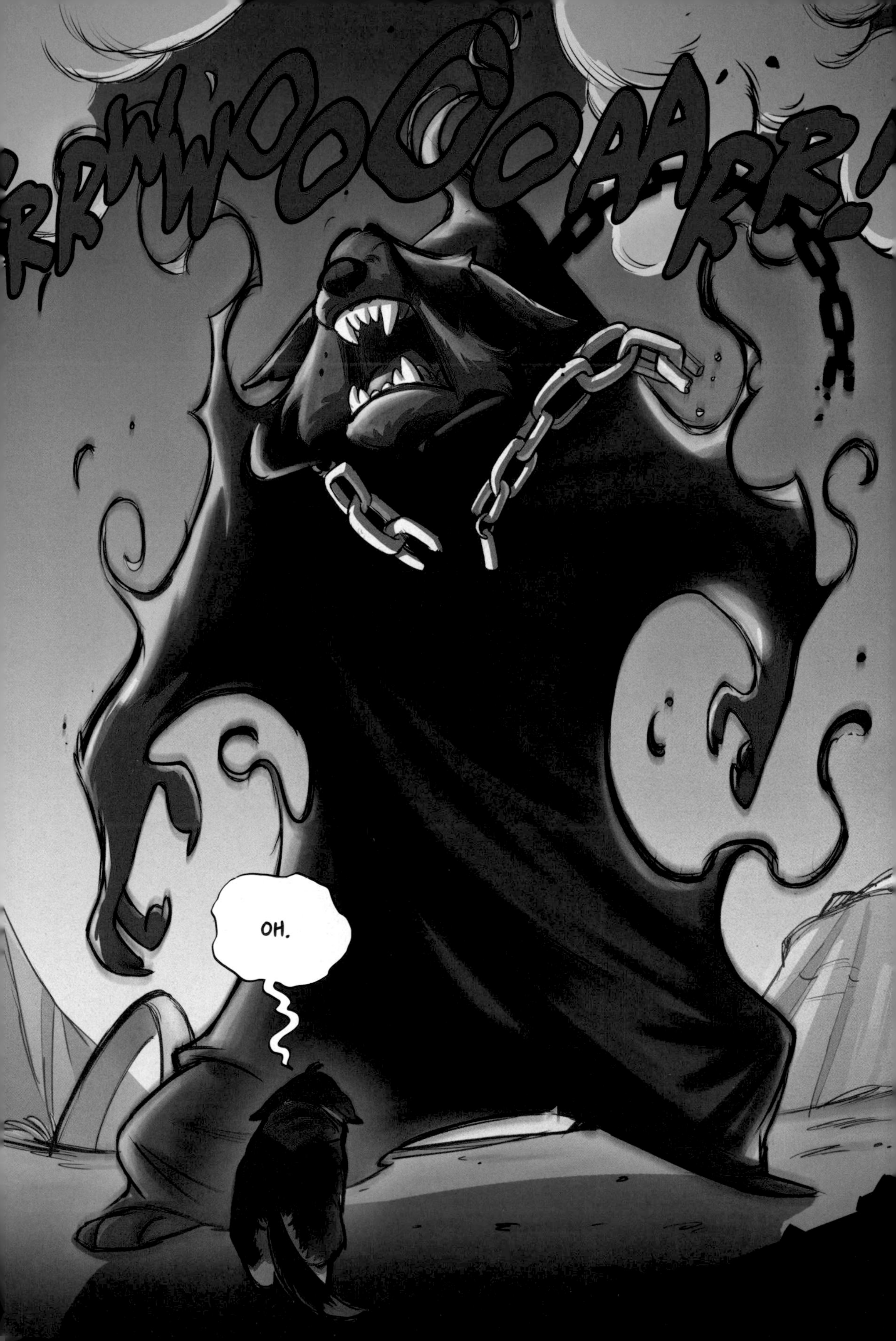
RRRWOOOOAARR!
OH.

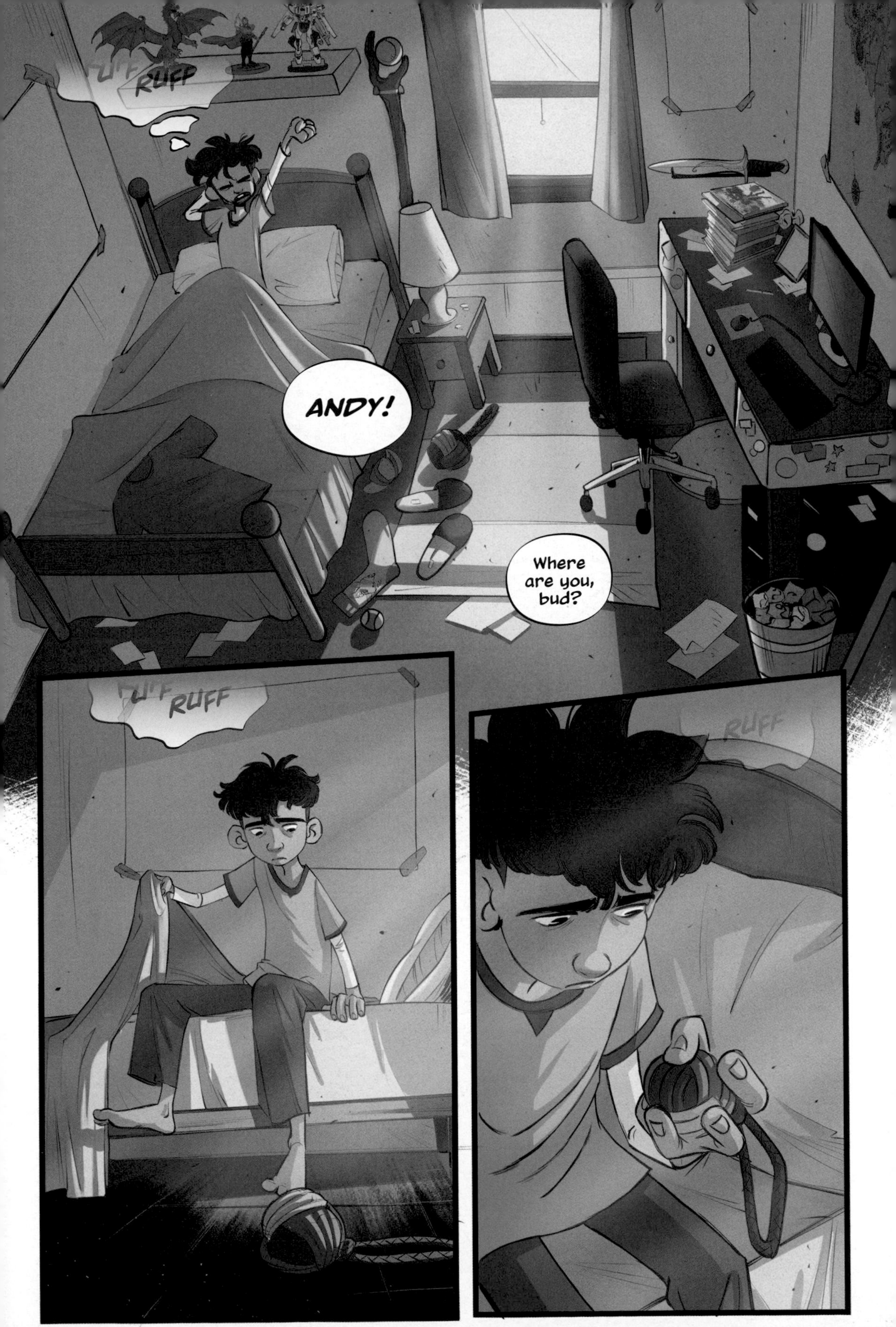
RUFF RUFF
ANDY!
Where are you, bud?
RUFF RUFF
RUFF

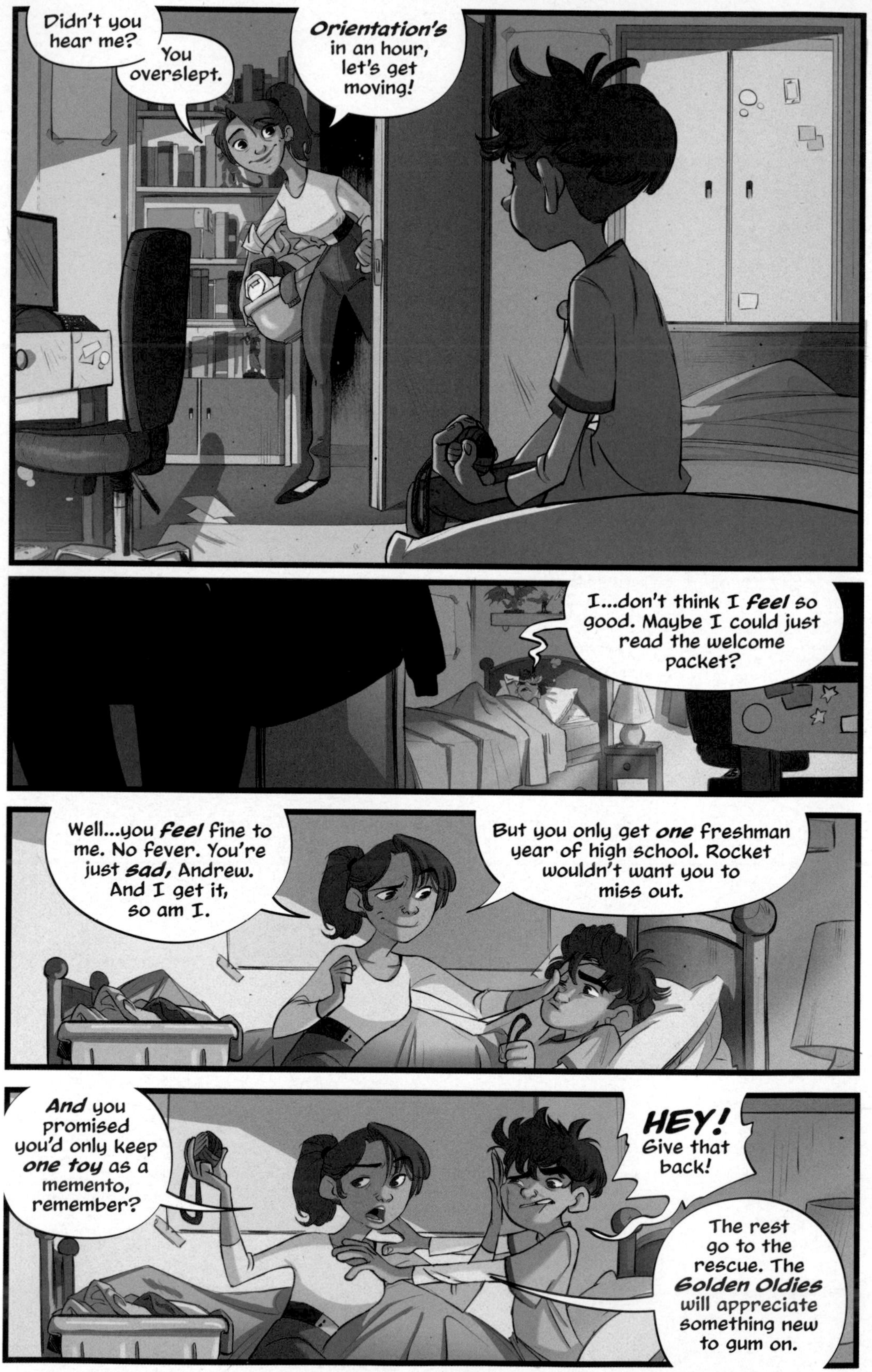
Didn't you hear me?
You overslept.
Orientation's in an hour, let's get moving!
I...don't think I feel so good. Maybe I could just read the welcome packet?
Well...you feel fine to me. No fever. You're just sad, Andrew. And I get it, so am I.
But you only get one freshman year of high school. Rocket wouldn't want you to miss out.
And you promised you'd only keep one toy as a memento, remember?
HEY! Give that back!
The rest go to the rescue. The Golden Oldies will appreciate something new to gum on.

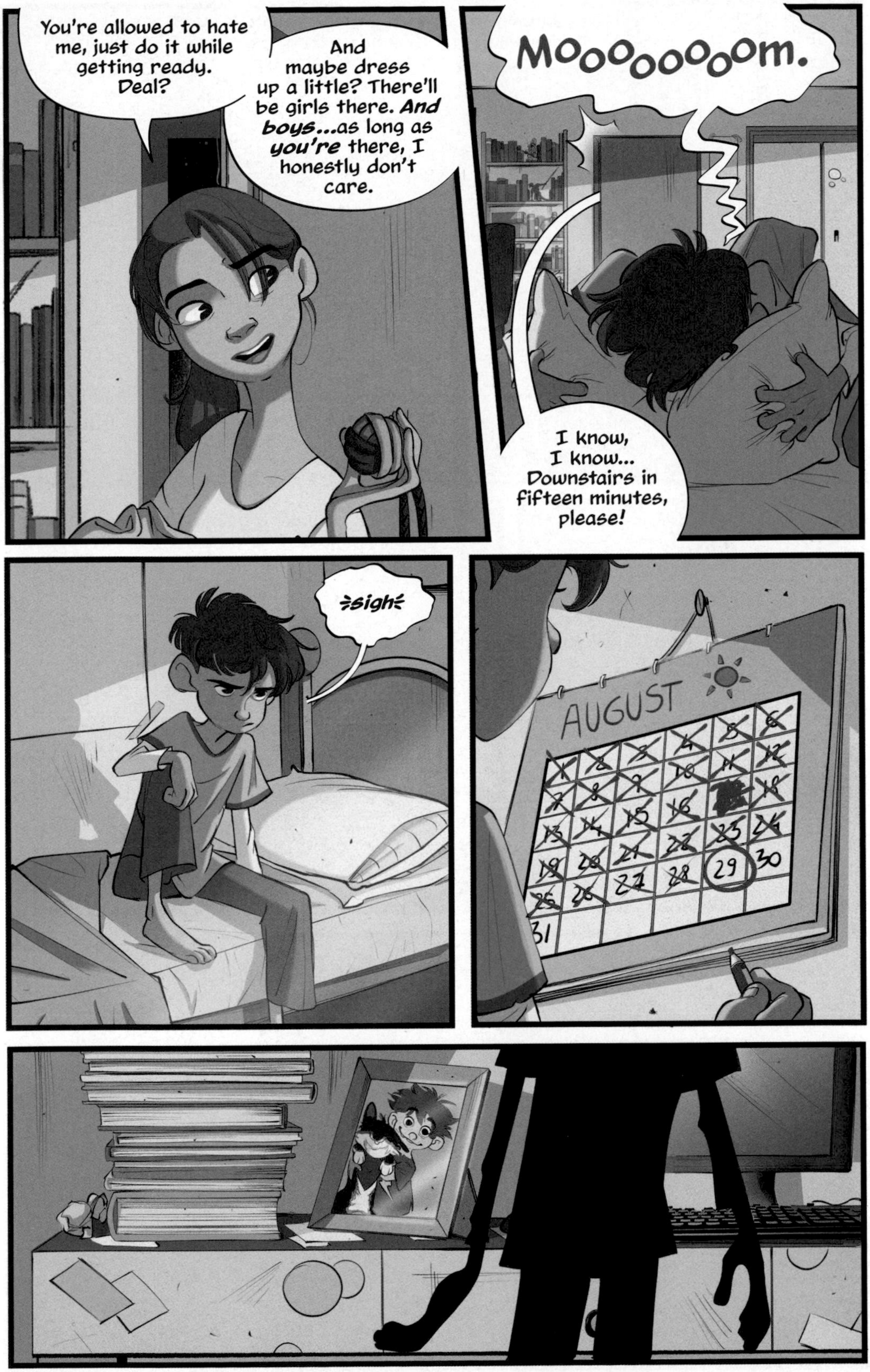
You're allowed to hate me, just do it while getting ready. Deal?
And maybe dress up a little? There'll be girls there. ***And boys...***as long as ***you're*** there, I honestly don't care.
Mooooooom.
I know, I know... Downstairs in fifteen minutes, please!
sigh
AUGUST
1 2 3 4 5 6
7 8 9 10 11 12
13 14 15 16 18
19 20 21 22 23 24
25 26 27 28 29 30
31

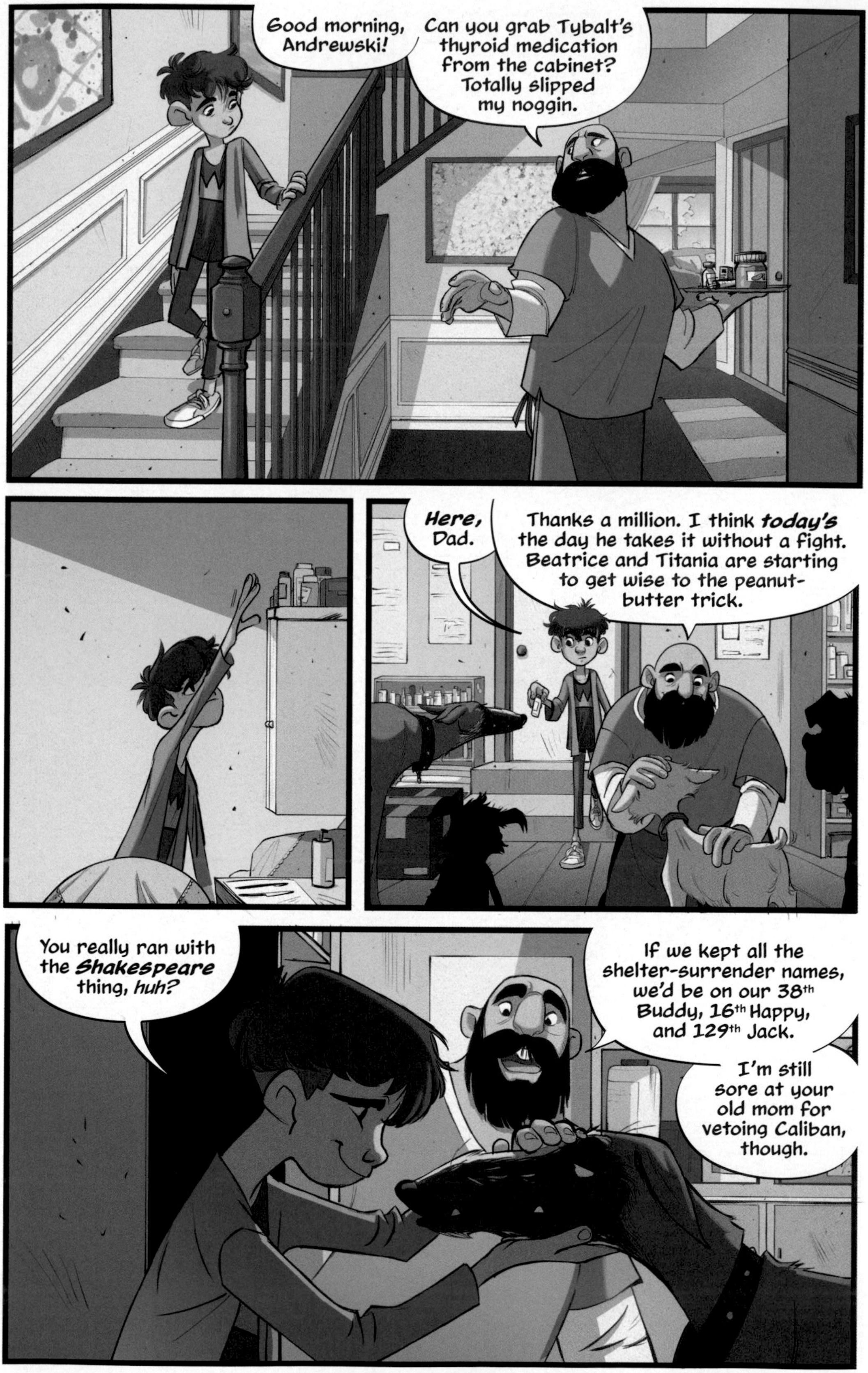
Good morning, Andrewski!
Can you grab Tybalt's thyroid medication from the cabinet? Totally slipped my noggin.
Here, Dad.
Thanks a million. I think *today's* the day he takes it without a fight. Beatrice and Titania are starting to get wise to the peanut-butter trick.
You really ran with the *Shakespeare* thing, *huh?*
If we kept all the shelter-surrender names, we'd be on our 38th Buddy, 16th Happy, and 129th Jack.
I'm still sore at your old mom for vetoing Caliban, though.

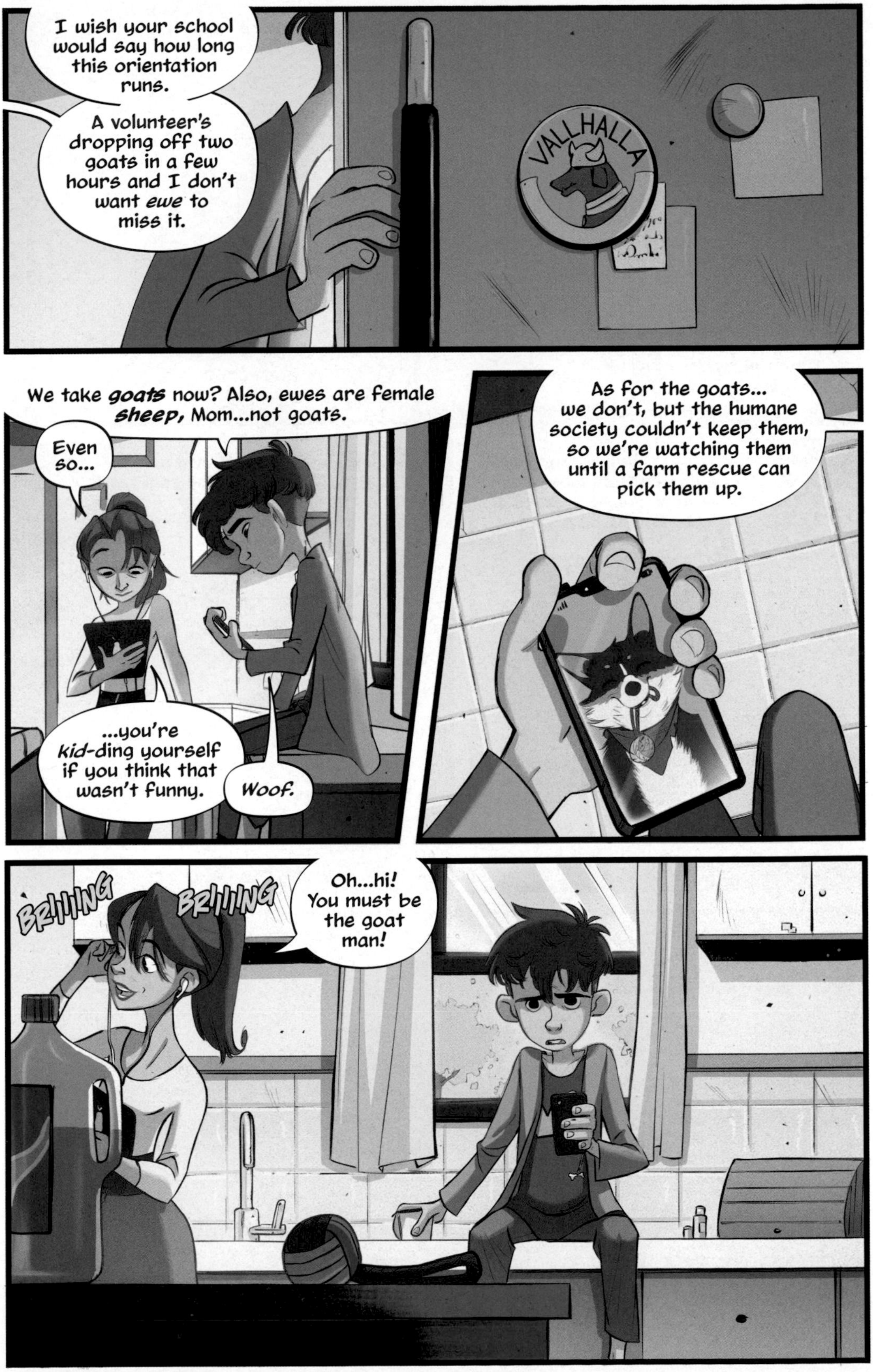
I wish your school would say how long this orientation runs.
A volunteer's dropping off two goats in a few hours and I don't want *ewe* to miss it.
VALLHALLA
We take **goats** now? Also, ewes are female **sheep,** Mom...not goats.
Even so...
...you're *kid*-ding yourself if you think that wasn't funny.
Woof.
As for the goats... we don't, but the humane society couldn't keep them, so we're watching them until a farm rescue can pick them up.
BRIIIING
BRIIIING
Oh...hi! You must be the goat man!

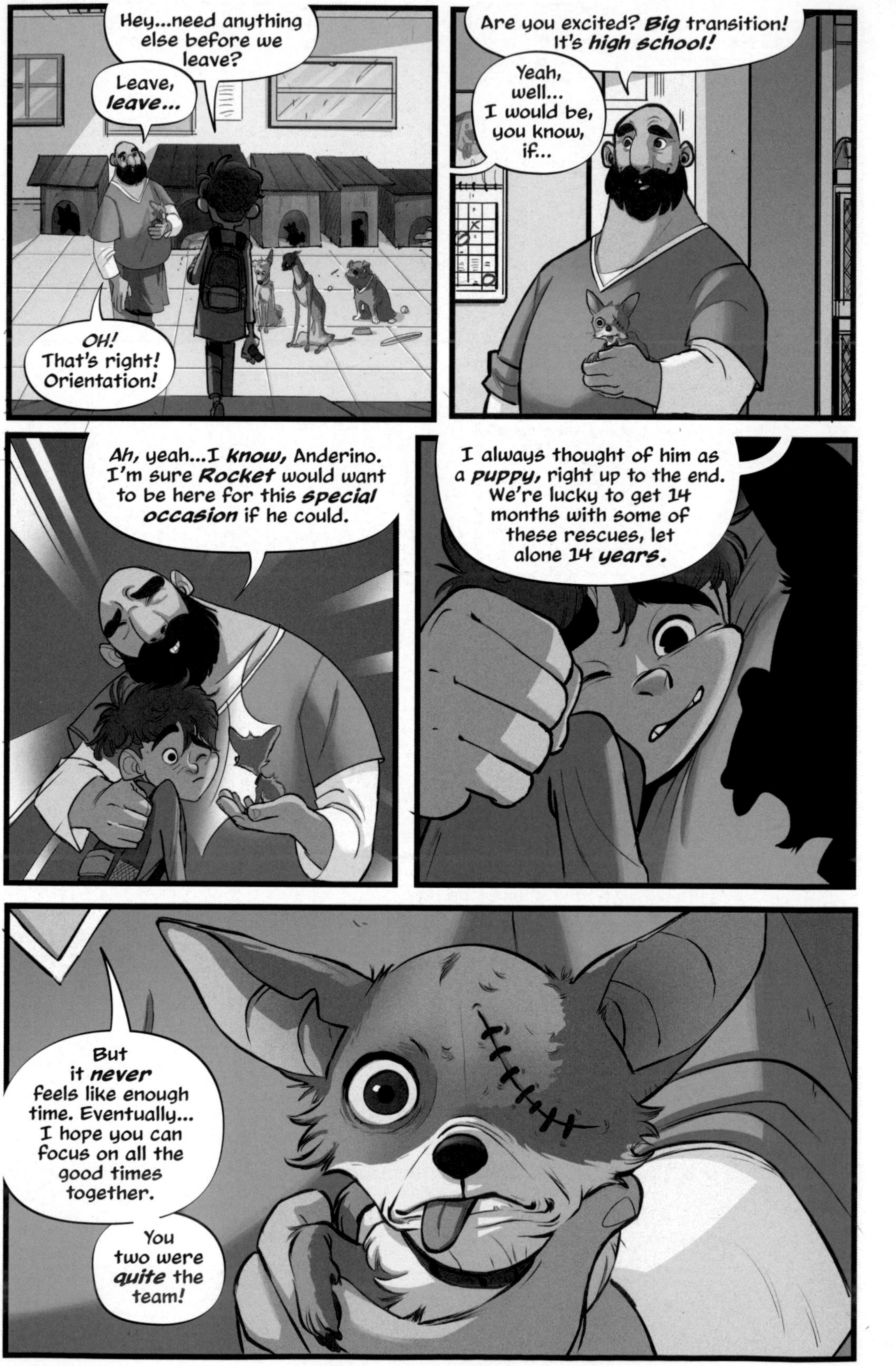

Hey...need anything else before we leave?
Leave, *leave...*
OH! That's right! Orientation!
Are you excited? *Big* transition! It's *high school!*
Yeah, well... I would be, you know, if...
Ah, yeah...I *know,* Anderino. I'm sure *Rocket* would want to be here for this *special occasion* if he could.
I always thought of him as a *puppy,* right up to the end. We're lucky to get 14 months with some of these rescues, let alone 14 *years.*
But it *never* feels like enough time. Eventually... I hope you can focus on all the good times together.
You two were *quite* the team!

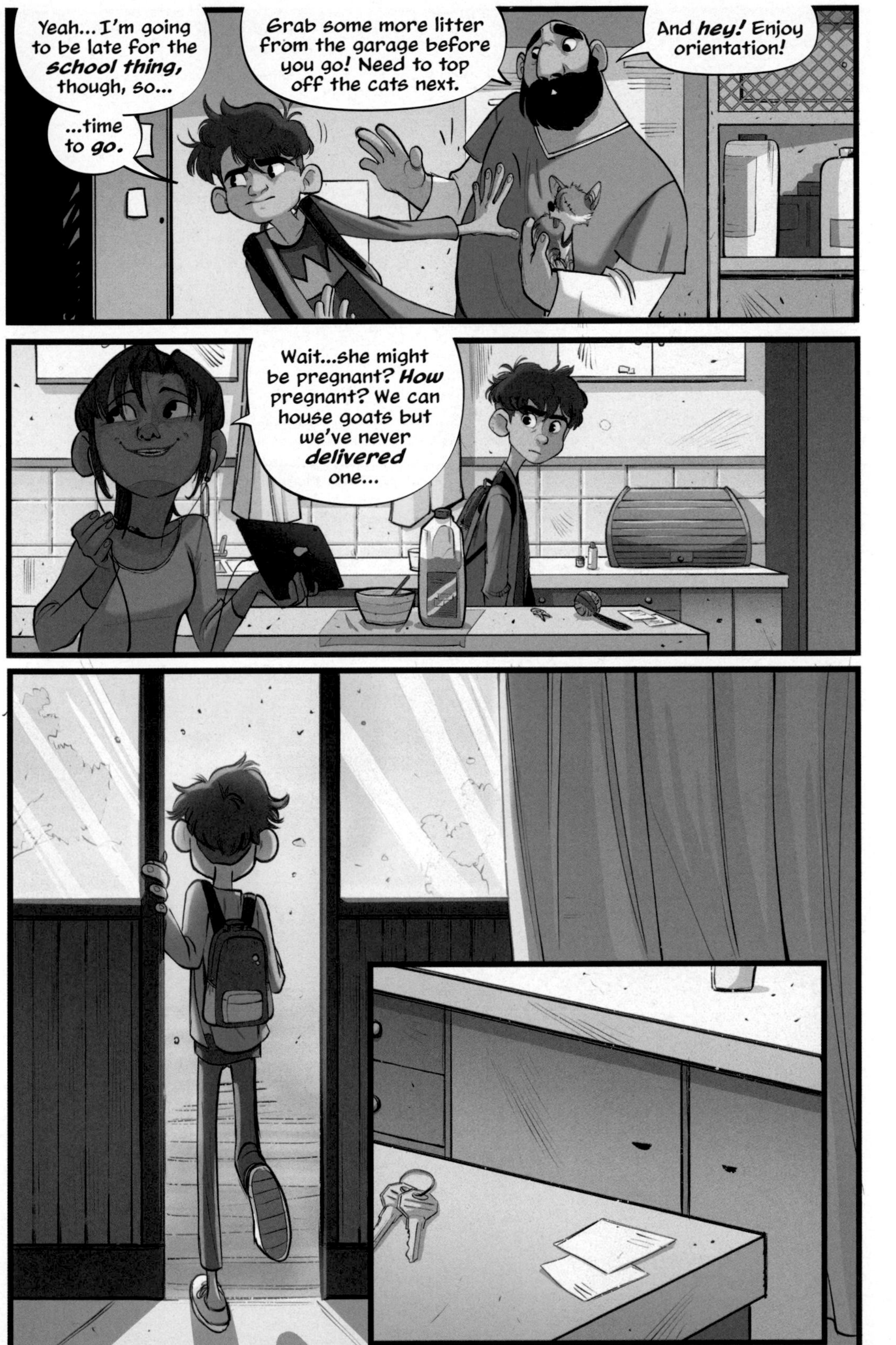
Yeah... I'm going to be late for the *school thing,* though, so...
...time to *go.*
Grab some more litter from the garage before you go! Need to top off the cats next.
And *hey!* Enjoy orientation!
Wait...she might be pregnant? *How* pregnant? We can house goats but we've never *delivered* one...

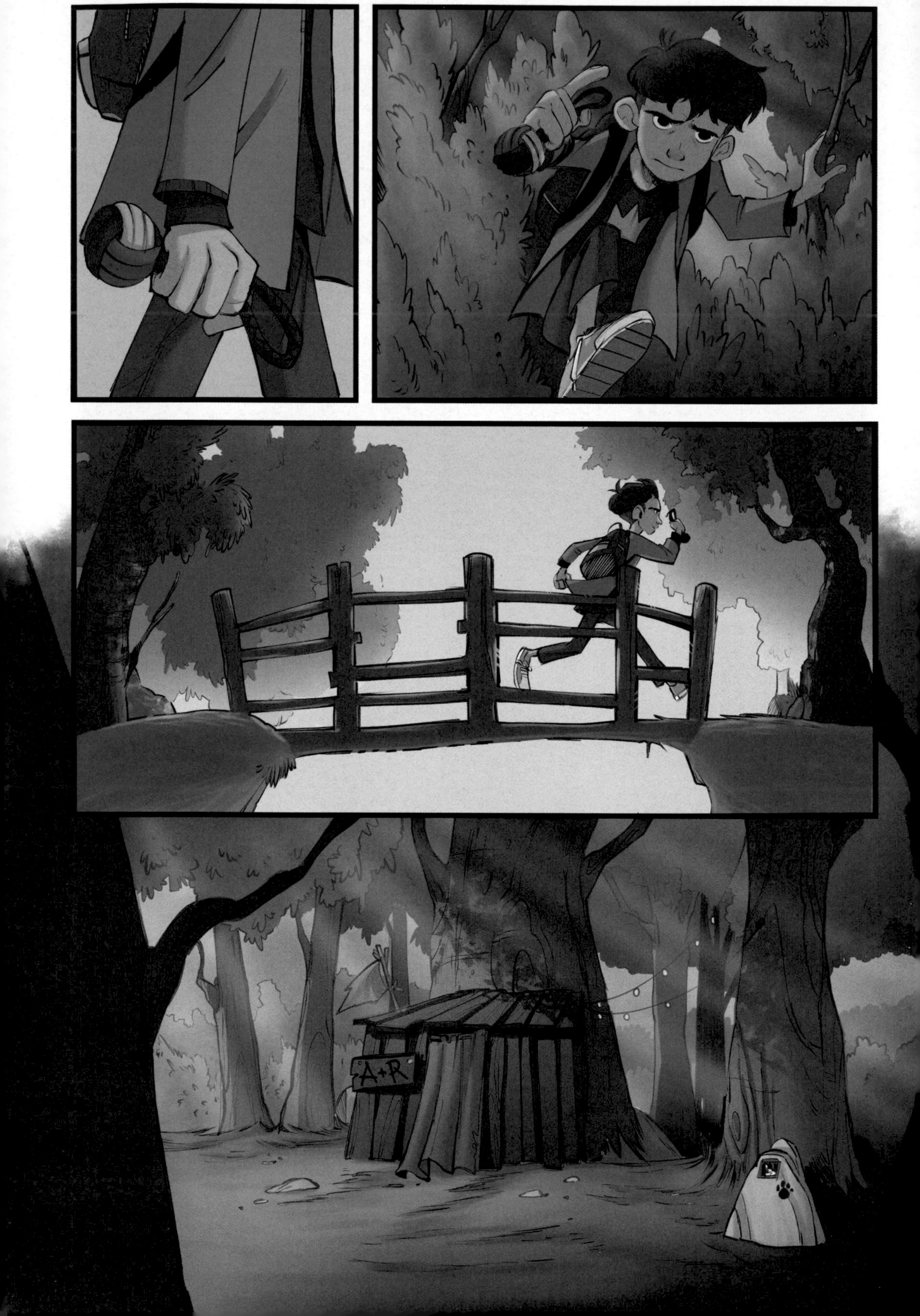
A+R

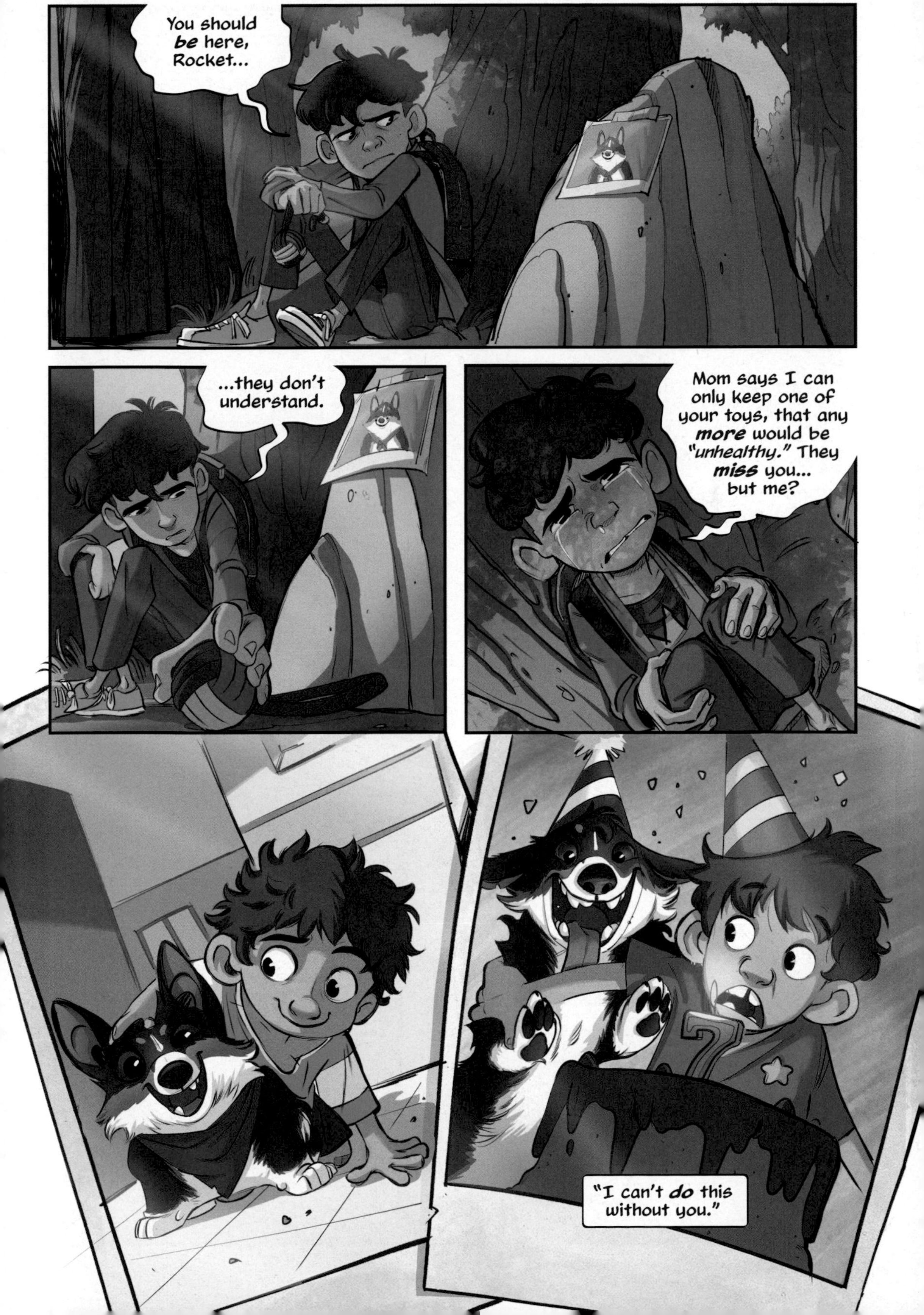
You should be here, Rocket...
...they don't understand.
Mom says I can only keep one of your toys, that any more would be "unhealthy." They miss you... but me?
"I can't do this without you."

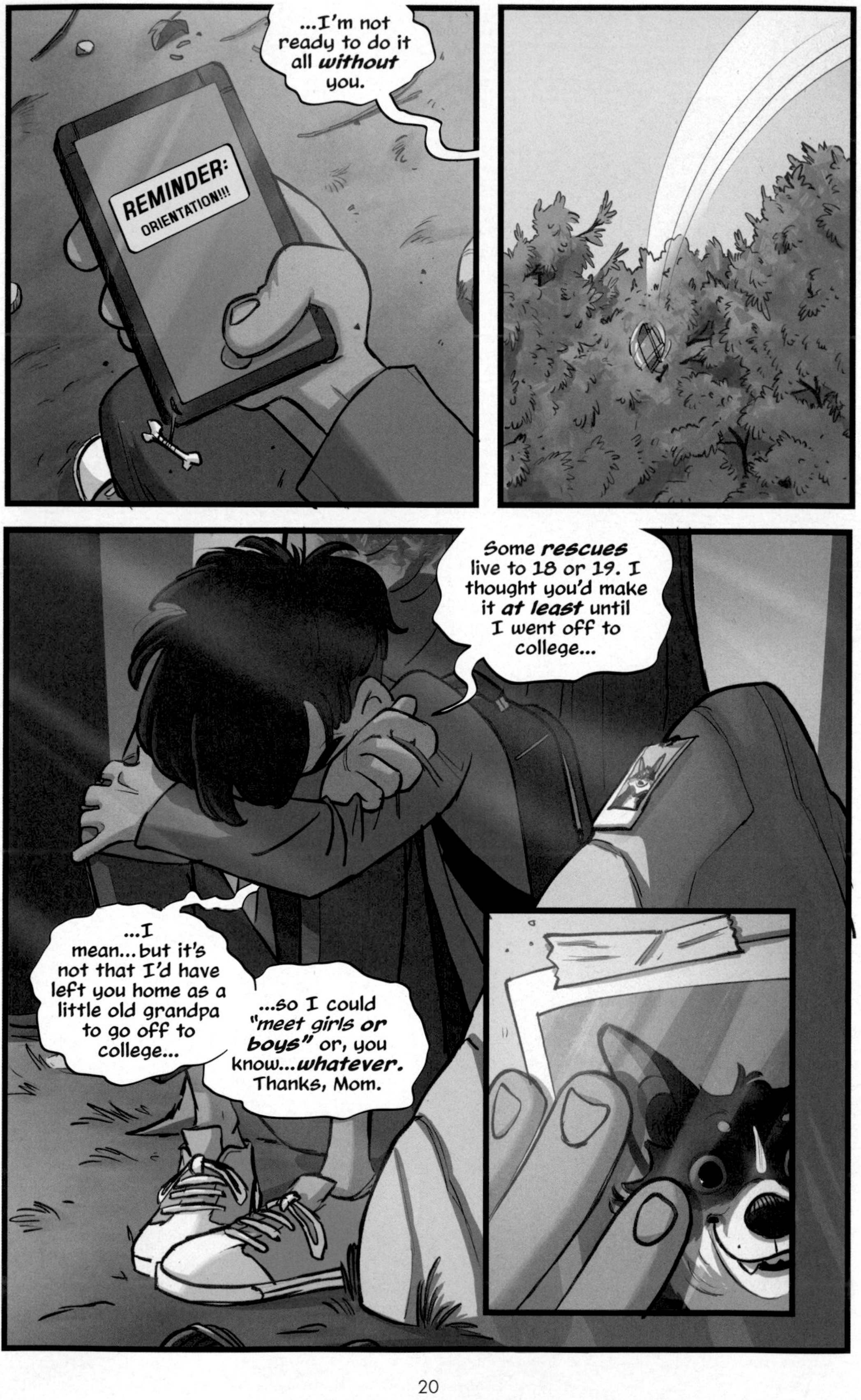
...I'm not ready to do it all *without* you.
REMINDER:
ORIENTATION!!!
Some *rescues* live to 18 or 19. I thought you'd make it *at least* until I went off to college...
...I mean...but it's not that I'd have left you home as a little old grandpa to go off to college...
...so I could *"meet girls or boys"* or, you know...*whatever.* Thanks, Mom.

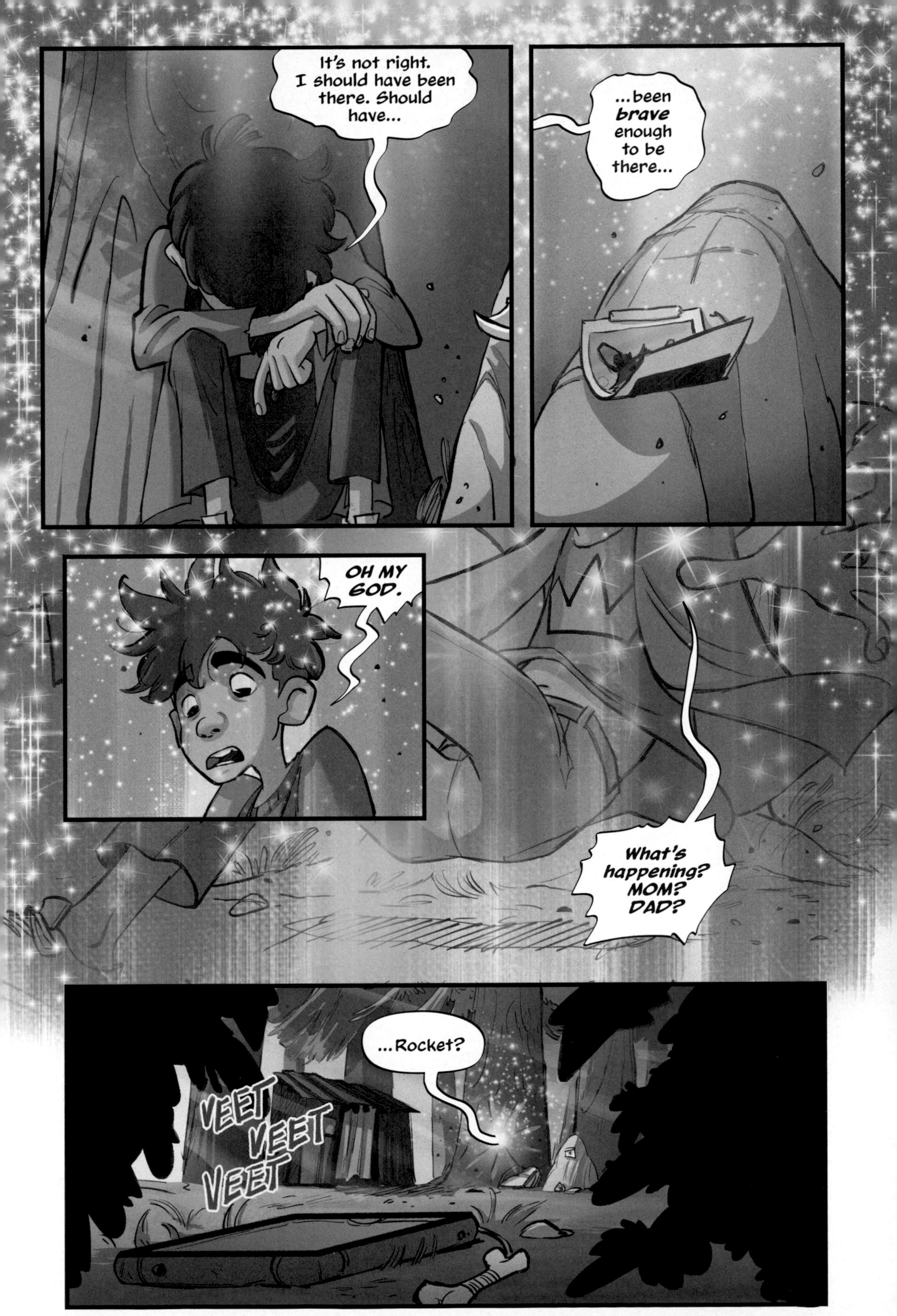
It's not right. I should have been there. Should have...
...been brave enough to be there...
OH MY GOD.
What's happening? MOM? DAD?
...Rocket?
VEET VEET VEET

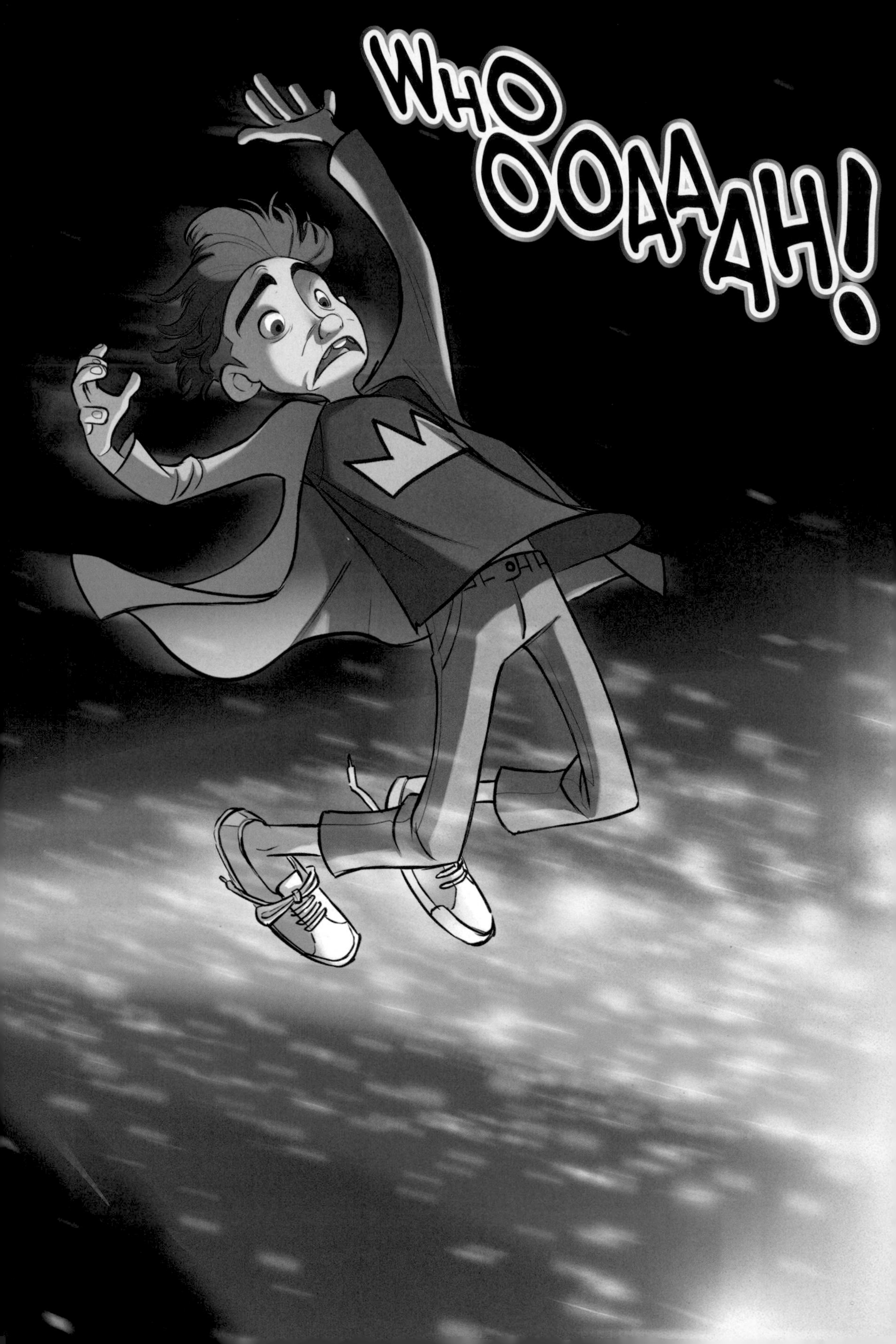
WHOOOAAAH!

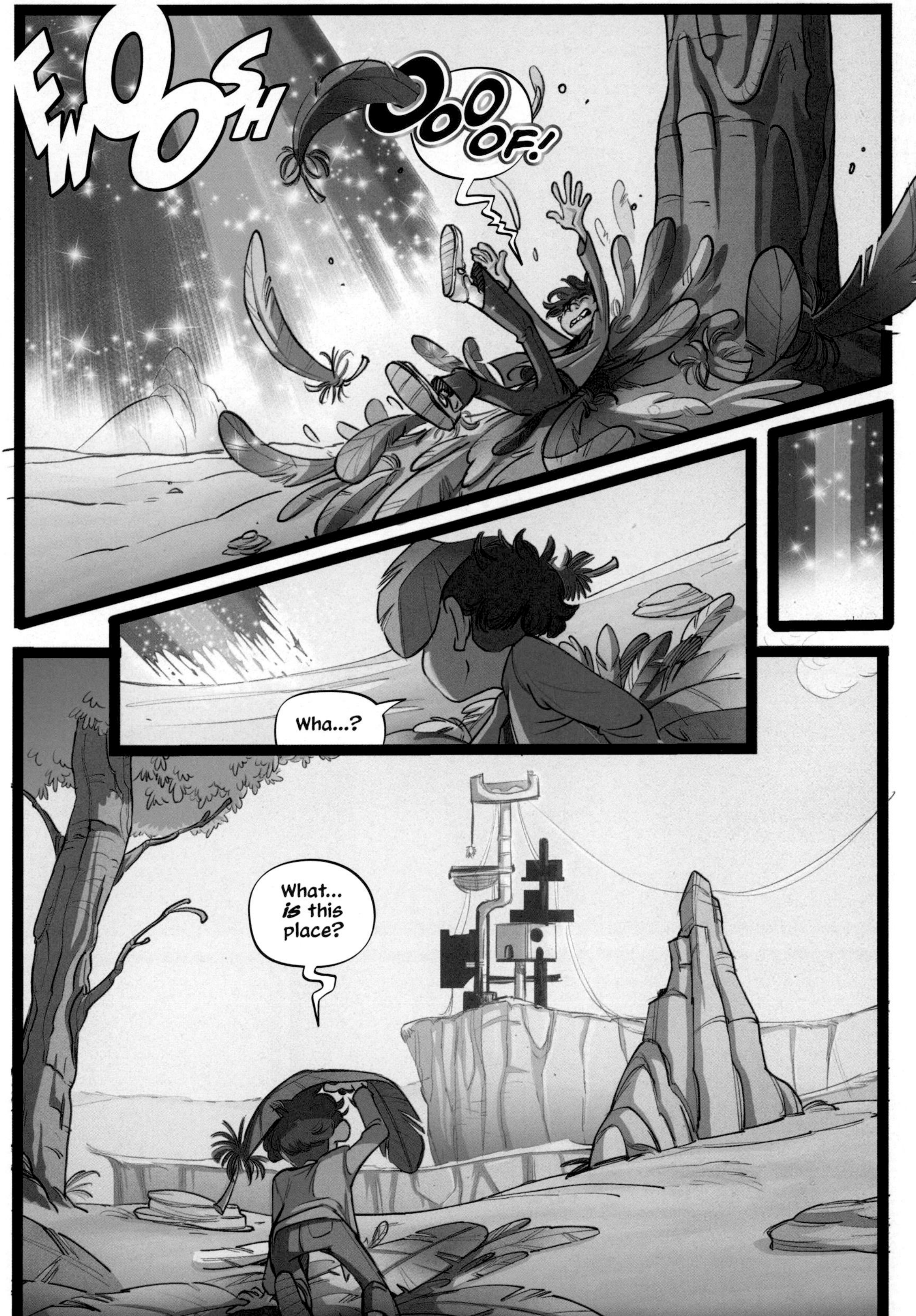
FWOOOSH
OOOOOF!
Wha...?
What...
is this
place?

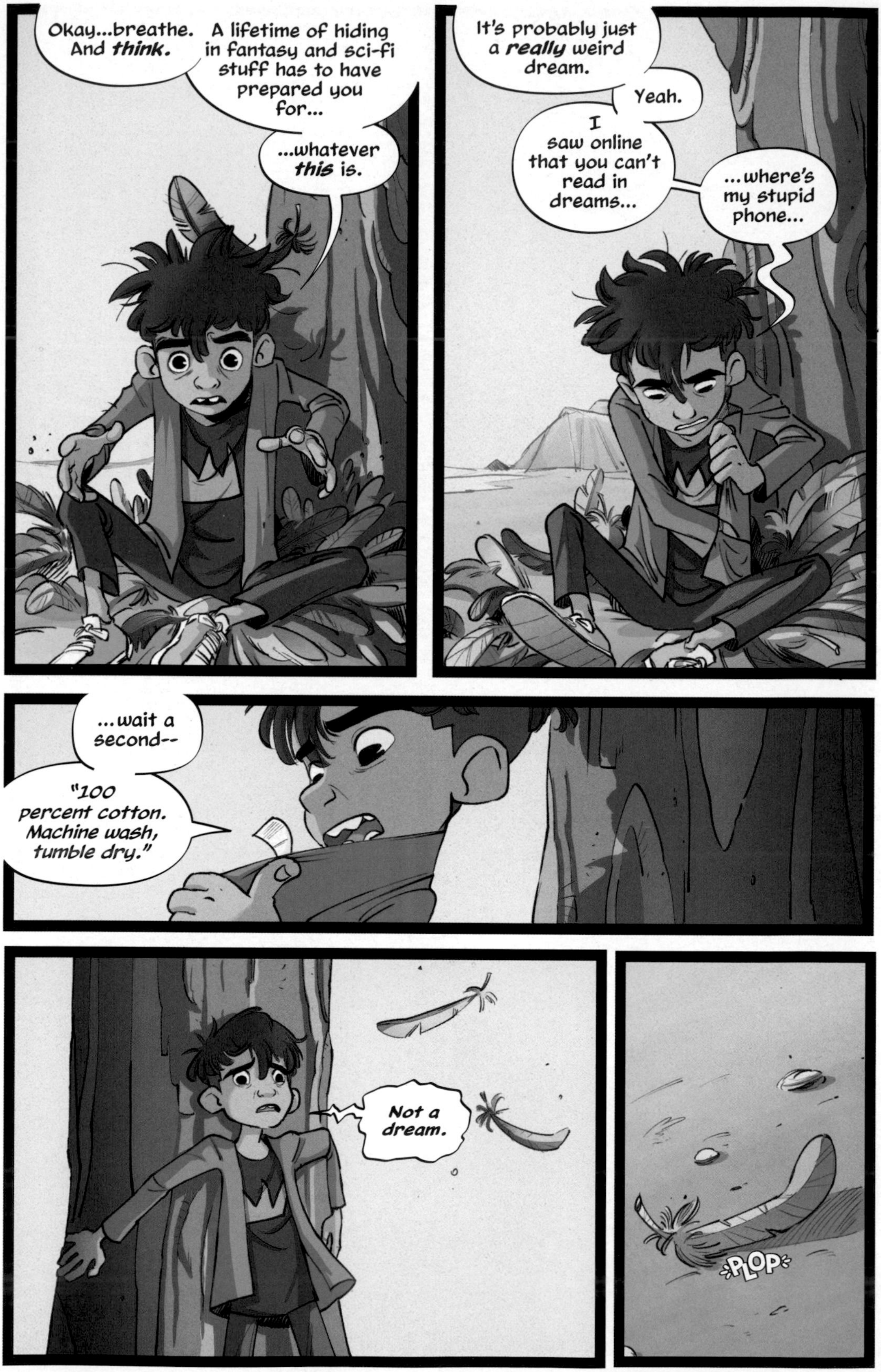
Okay...breathe. And *think.*
A lifetime of hiding in fantasy and sci-fi stuff has to have prepared you for...
...whatever *this* is.
It's probably just a *really* weird dream.
Yeah.
I saw online that you can't read in dreams...
...where's my stupid phone...
...wait a second--
"100 percent cotton. Machine wash, tumble dry."
Not a dream.
PLOP

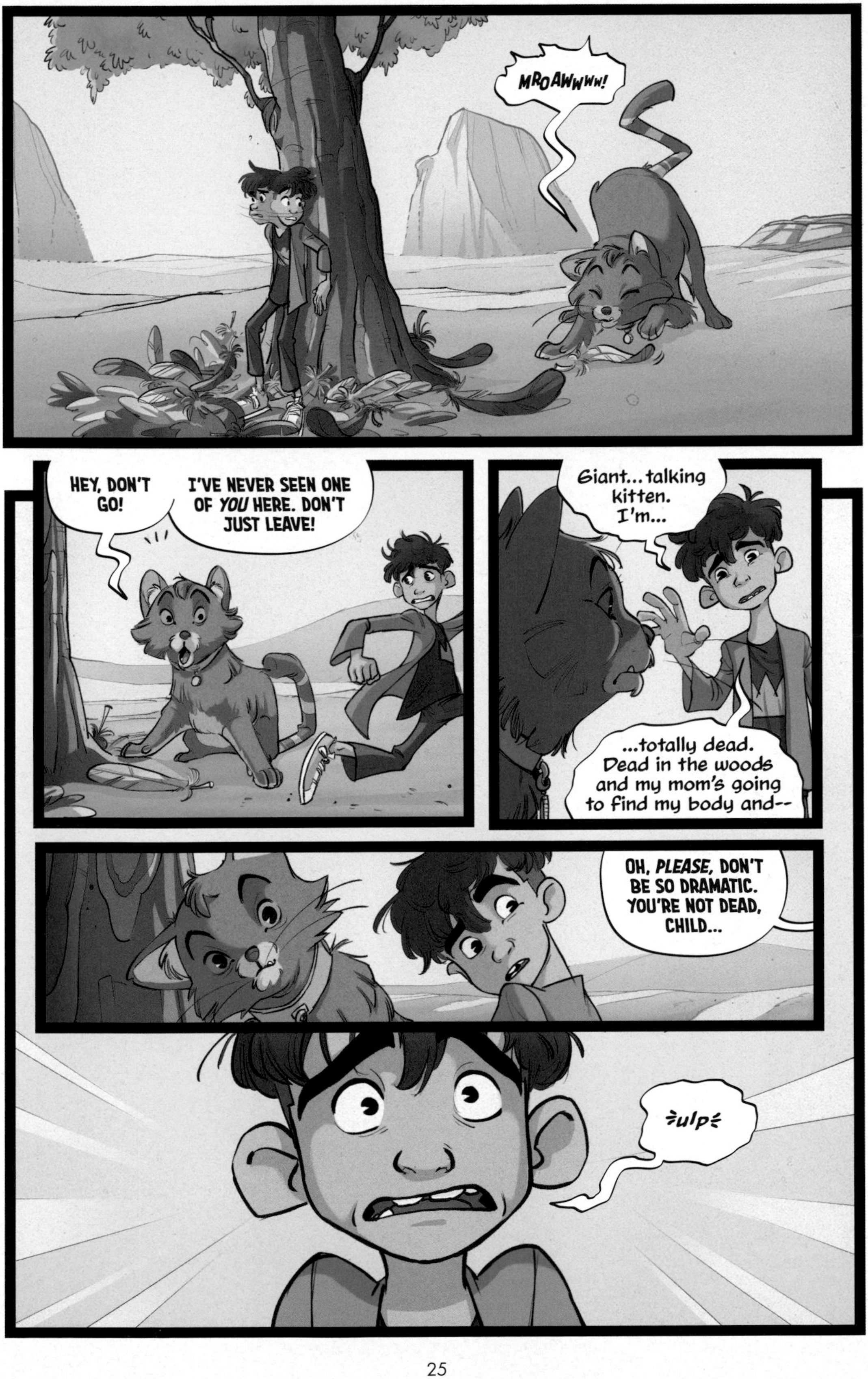
MROAWWWW!
HEY, DON'T GO!
I'VE NEVER SEEN ONE OF *YOU* HERE. DON'T JUST LEAVE!
Giant... talking kitten. I'm...
...totally dead. Dead in the woods and my mom's going to find my body and--
OH, *PLEASE,* DON'T BE SO DRAMATIC. YOU'RE NOT DEAD, CHILD...
ulp

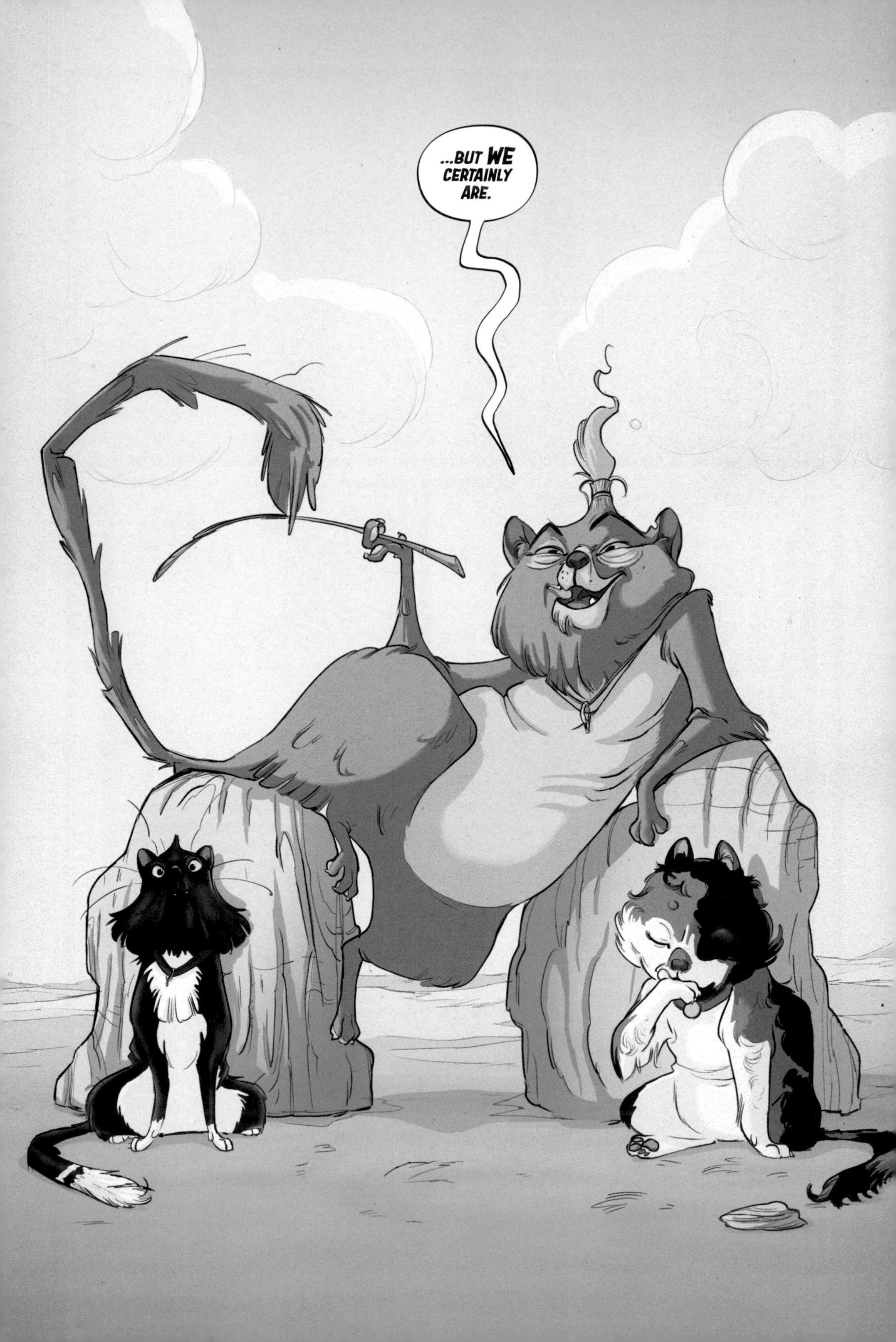
...BUT WE CERTAINLY ARE.

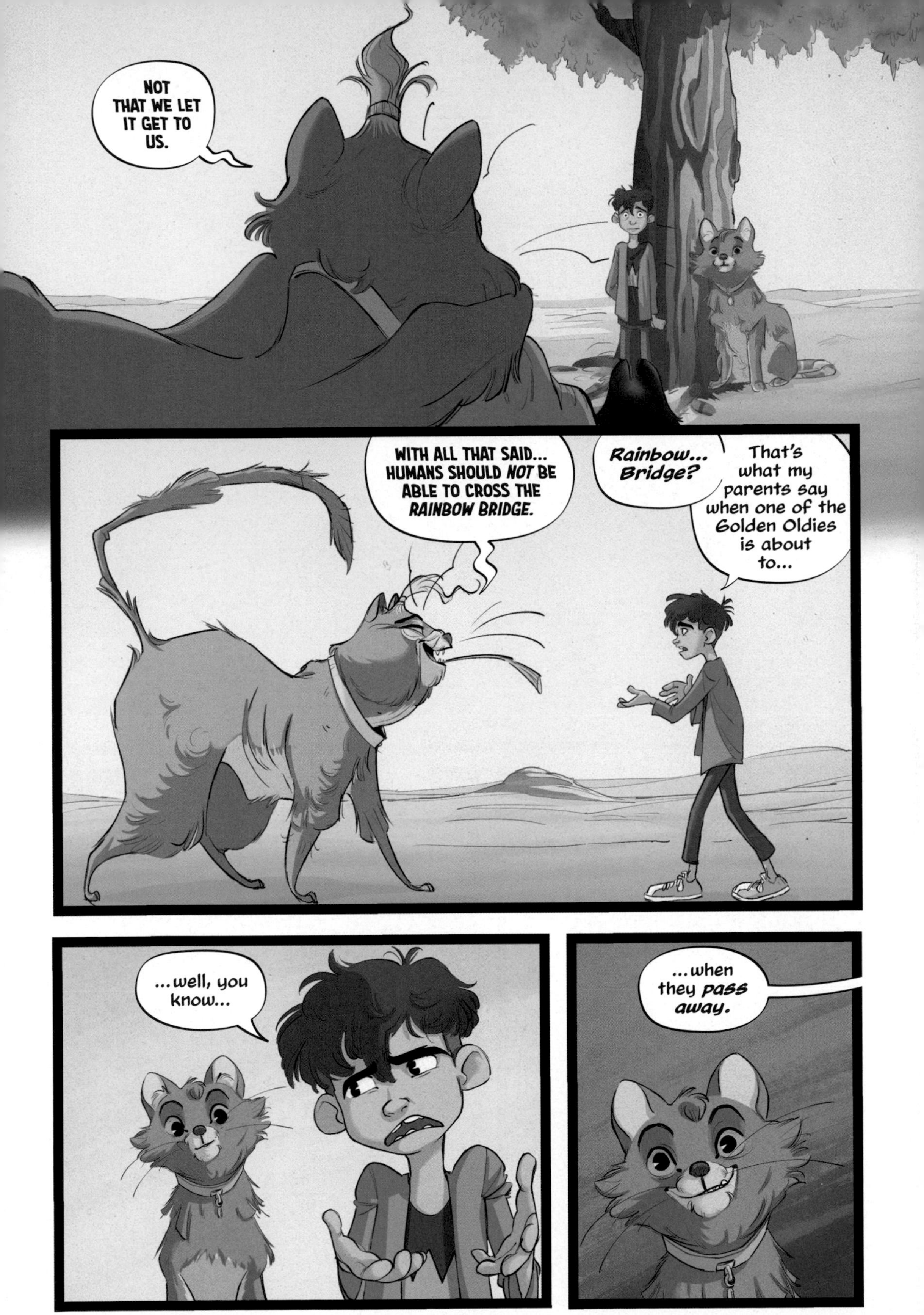
NOT THAT WE LET IT GET TO US.
WITH ALL THAT SAID... HUMANS SHOULD NOT BE ABLE TO CROSS THE RAINBOW BRIDGE.
Rainbow... Bridge?
That's what my parents say when one of the Golden Oldies is about to...
...well, you know...
...when they pass away.

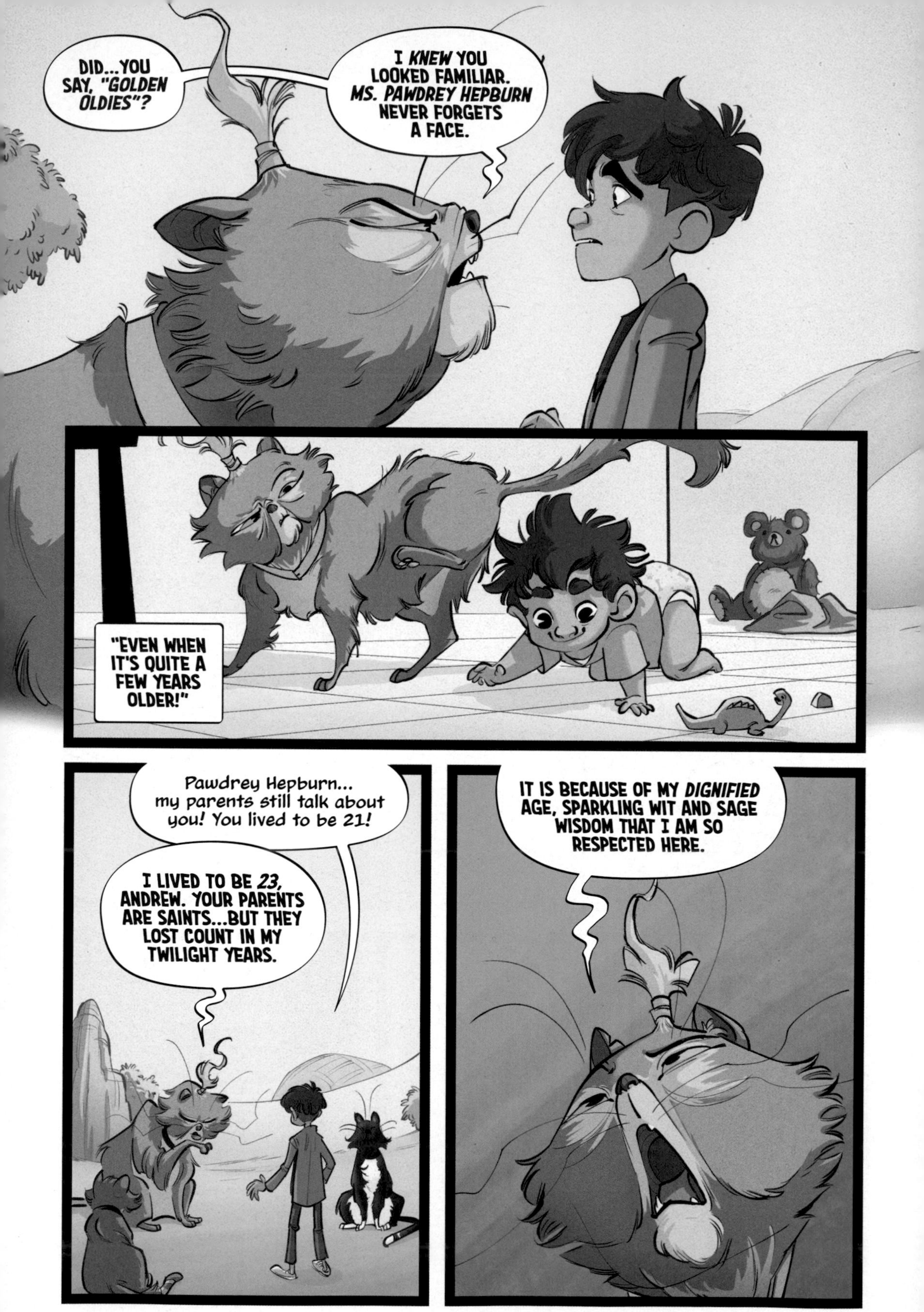
DID...YOU SAY, "GOLDEN OLDIES"?
I KNEW YOU LOOKED FAMILIAR. MS. PAWDREY HEPBURN NEVER FORGETS A FACE.
"EVEN WHEN IT'S QUITE A FEW YEARS OLDER!"
Pawdrey Hepburn... my parents still talk about you! You lived to be 21!
I LIVED TO BE 23, ANDREW. YOUR PARENTS ARE SAINTS...BUT THEY LOST COUNT IN MY TWILIGHT YEARS.
IT IS BECAUSE OF MY DIGNIFIED AGE, SPARKLING WIT AND SAGE WISDOM THAT I AM SO RESPECTED HERE.

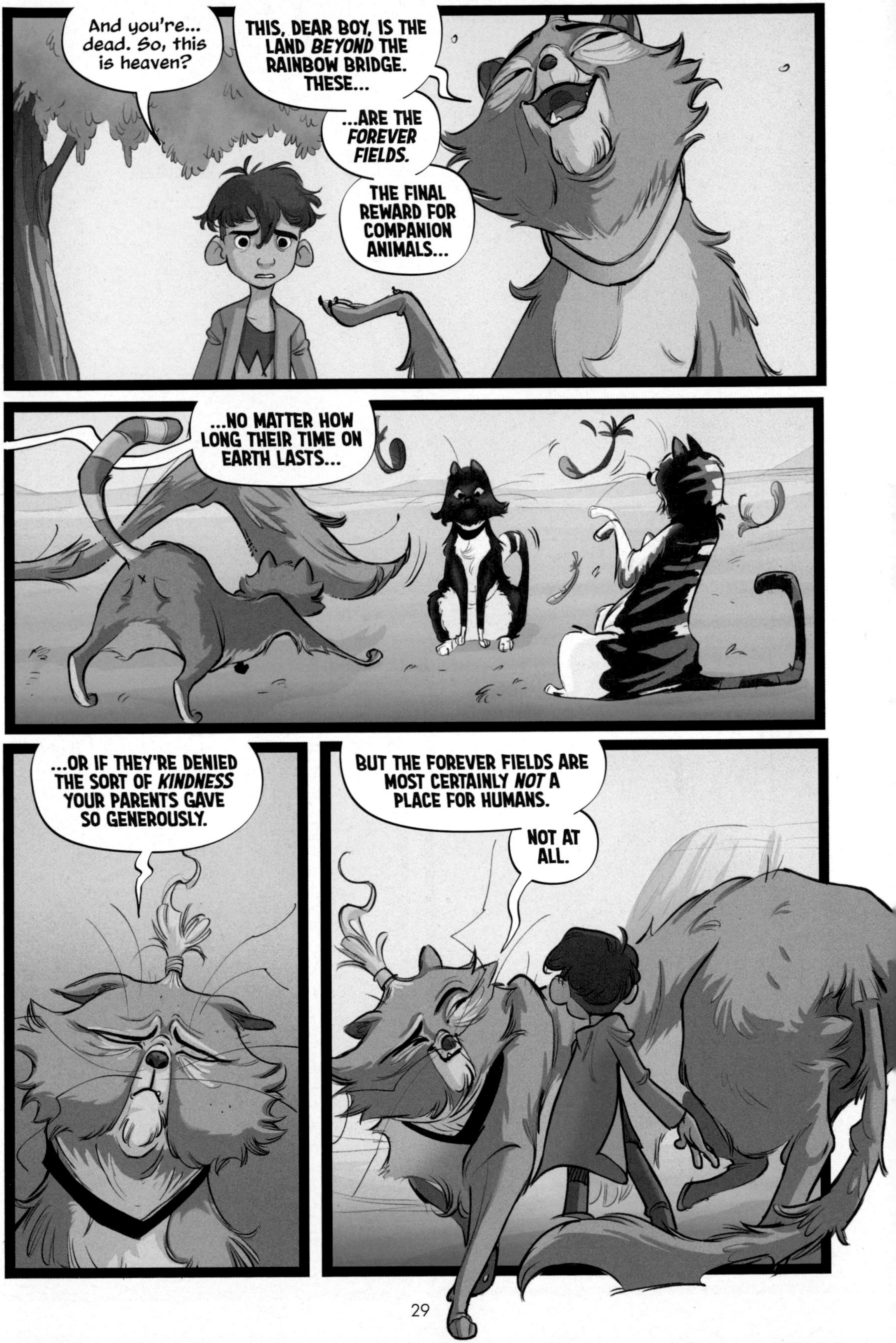
And you're... dead. So, this is heaven?
THIS, DEAR BOY, IS THE LAND *BEYOND* THE RAINBOW BRIDGE. THESE...
...ARE THE *FOREVER FIELDS.*
THE FINAL REWARD FOR COMPANION ANIMALS...
...NO MATTER HOW LONG THEIR TIME ON EARTH LASTS...
...OR IF THEY'RE DENIED THE SORT OF *KINDNESS* YOUR PARENTS GAVE SO GENEROUSLY.
BUT THE FOREVER FIELDS ARE MOST CERTAINLY *NOT* A PLACE FOR HUMANS.
NOT AT ALL.

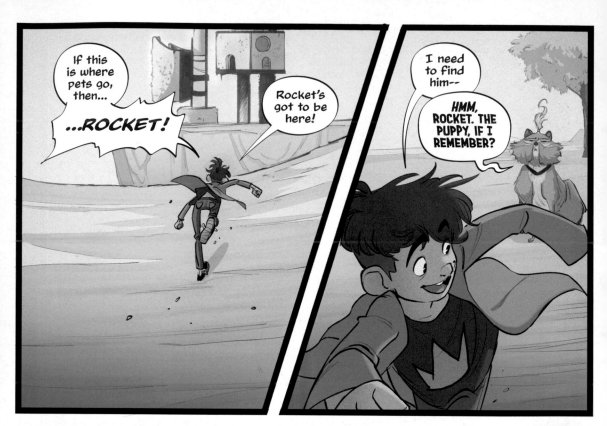

If this is where pets go, then...

...ROCKET!

Rocket's got to be here!

I need to find him--

HMM, ROCKET. THE PUPPY, IF I REMEMBER?

'WHO COULD FORGET A CREATURE OF SUCH...SPIRIT?'

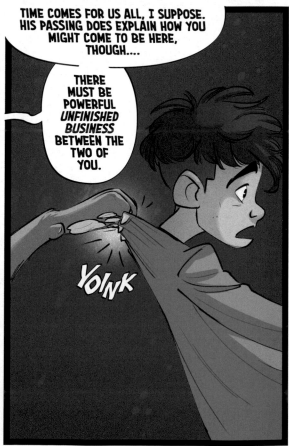

TIME COMES FOR US ALL, I SUPPOSE. HIS PASSING DOES EXPLAIN HOW YOU MIGHT COME TO BE HERE, THOUGH....

THERE MUST BE POWERFUL UNFINISHED BUSINESS BETWEEN THE TWO OF YOU.

YOINK

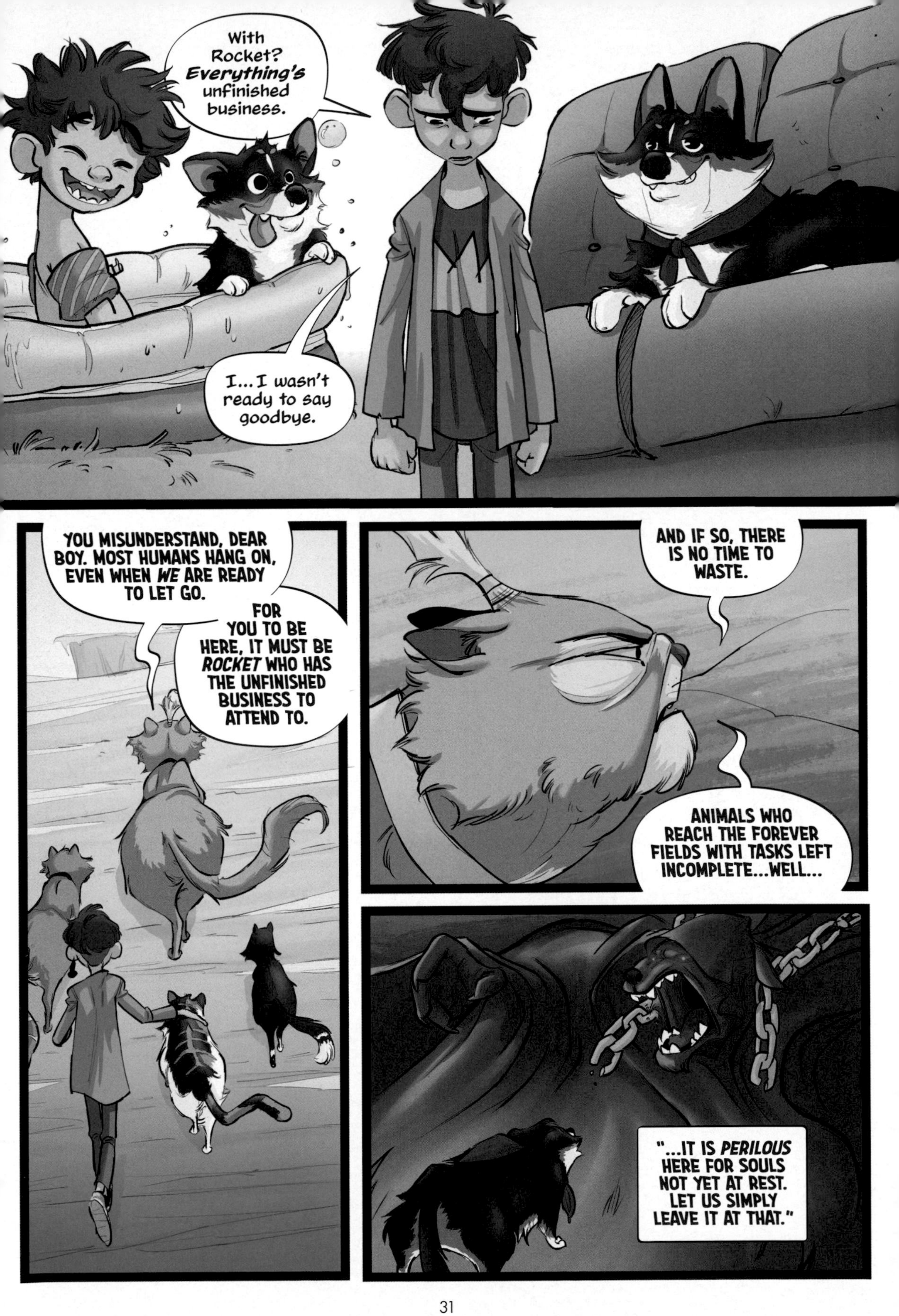
With Rocket? *Everything's* unfinished business.
I...I wasn't ready to say goodbye.
YOU MISUNDERSTAND, DEAR BOY. MOST HUMANS HANG ON, EVEN WHEN *WE* ARE READY TO LET GO.
FOR YOU TO BE HERE, IT MUST BE *ROCKET* WHO HAS THE UNFINISHED BUSINESS TO ATTEND TO.
AND IF SO, THERE IS NO TIME TO WASTE.
ANIMALS WHO REACH THE FOREVER FIELDS WITH TASKS LEFT INCOMPLETE...WELL...
"...IT IS *PERILOUS* HERE FOR SOULS NOT YET AT REST. LET US SIMPLY LEAVE IT AT THAT."

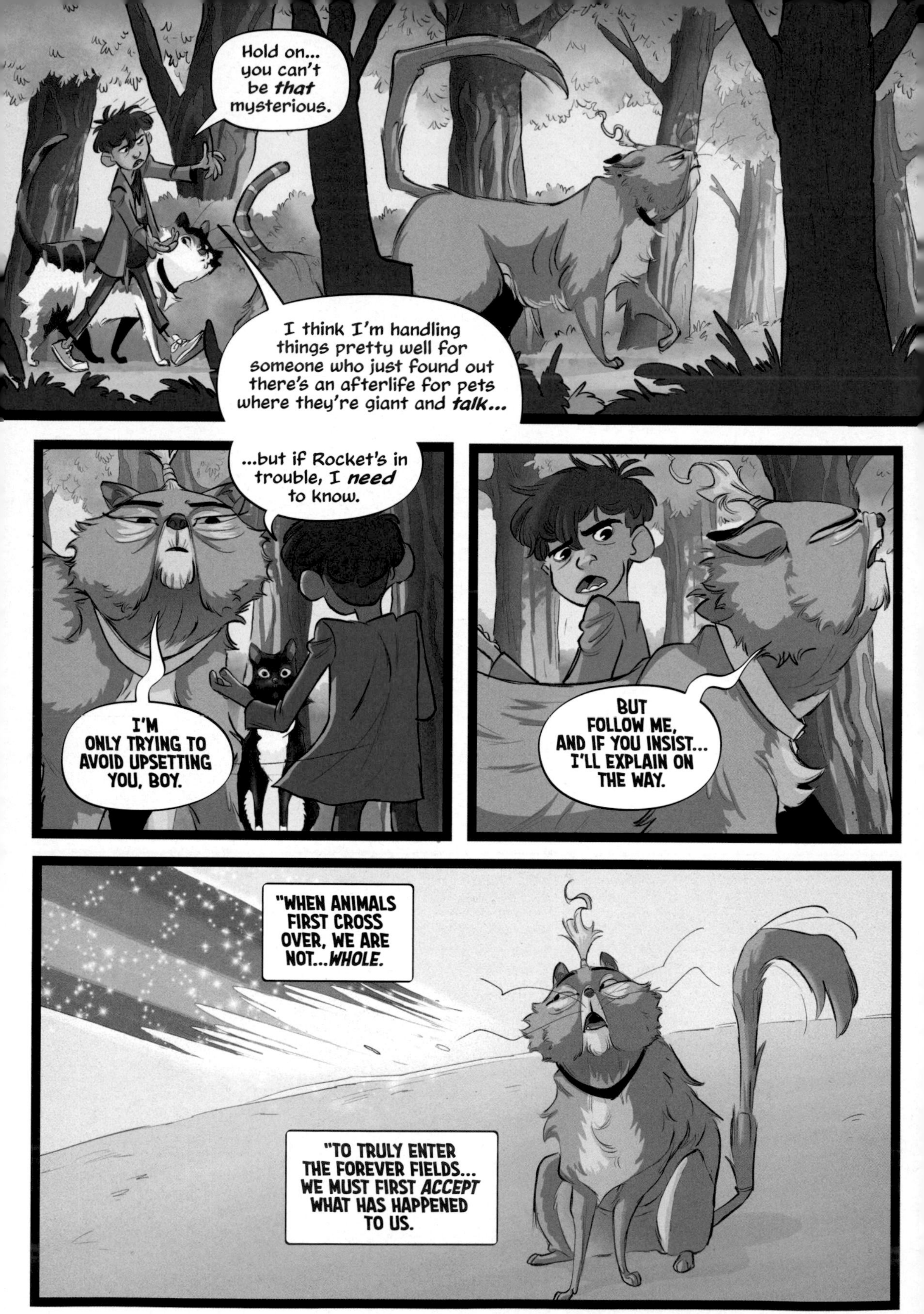
Hold on... you can't be *that* mysterious.
I think I'm handling things pretty well for someone who just found out there's an afterlife for pets where they're giant and *talk...*
...but if Rocket's in trouble, I *need* to know.
I'M ONLY TRYING TO AVOID UPSETTING YOU, BOY.
BUT FOLLOW ME, AND IF YOU INSIST... I'LL EXPLAIN ON THE WAY.
"WHEN ANIMALS FIRST CROSS OVER, WE ARE NOT...*WHOLE.*
"TO TRULY ENTER THE FOREVER FIELDS... WE MUST FIRST *ACCEPT* WHAT HAS HAPPENED TO US.

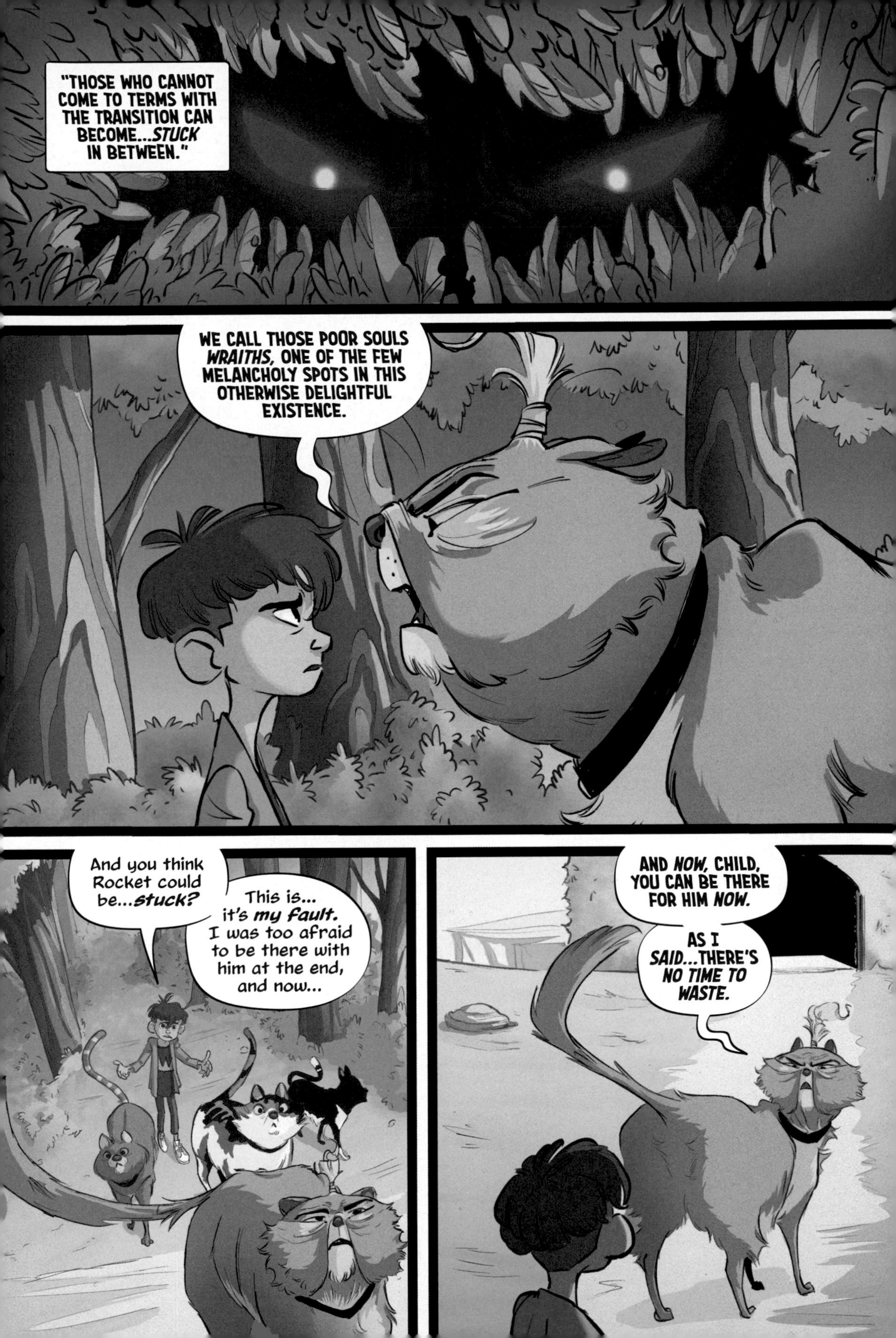
"THOSE WHO CANNOT COME TO TERMS WITH THE TRANSITION CAN BECOME...*STUCK* IN BETWEEN."
WE CALL THOSE POOR SOULS *WRAITHS,* ONE OF THE FEW MELANCHOLY SPOTS IN THIS OTHERWISE DELIGHTFUL EXISTENCE.
And you think Rocket could be...*stuck?*
This is... it's *my fault.* I was too afraid to be there with him at the end, and now...
AND *NOW,* CHILD, YOU CAN BE THERE FOR HIM *NOW.*
AS I *SAID*...THERE'S *NO TIME TO WASTE.*

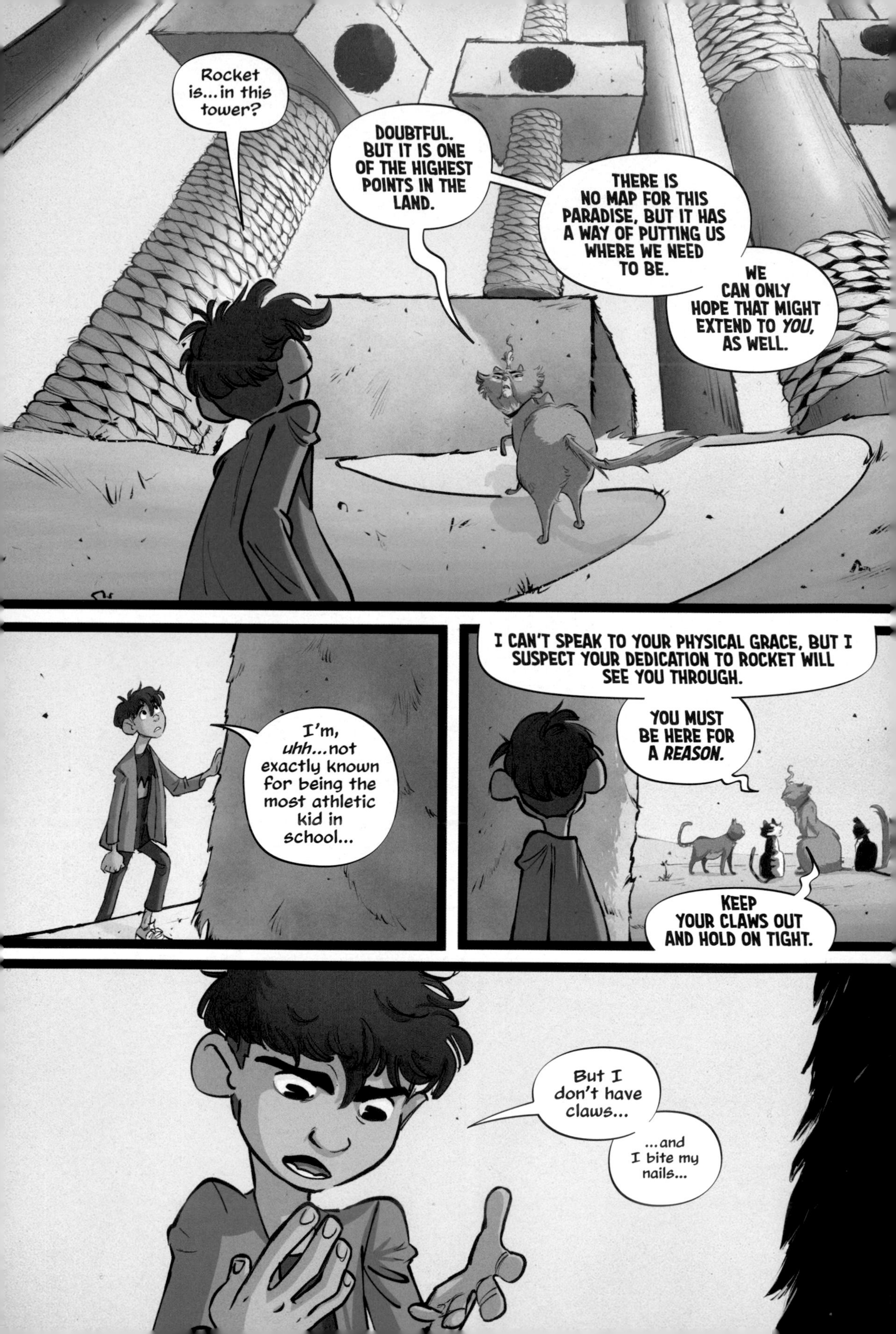
Rocket is...in this tower?
DOUBTFUL. BUT IT IS ONE OF THE HIGHEST POINTS IN THE LAND.
THERE IS NO MAP FOR THIS PARADISE, BUT IT HAS A WAY OF PUTTING US WHERE WE NEED TO BE.
WE CAN ONLY HOPE THAT MIGHT EXTEND TO *YOU,* AS WELL.
I'm, *uhh*...not exactly known for being the most athletic kid in school...
I CAN'T SPEAK TO YOUR PHYSICAL GRACE, BUT I SUSPECT YOUR DEDICATION TO ROCKET WILL SEE YOU THROUGH.
YOU MUST BE HERE FOR A *REASON.*
KEEP YOUR CLAWS OUT AND HOLD ON TIGHT.
But I don't have claws...
...and I bite my nails...

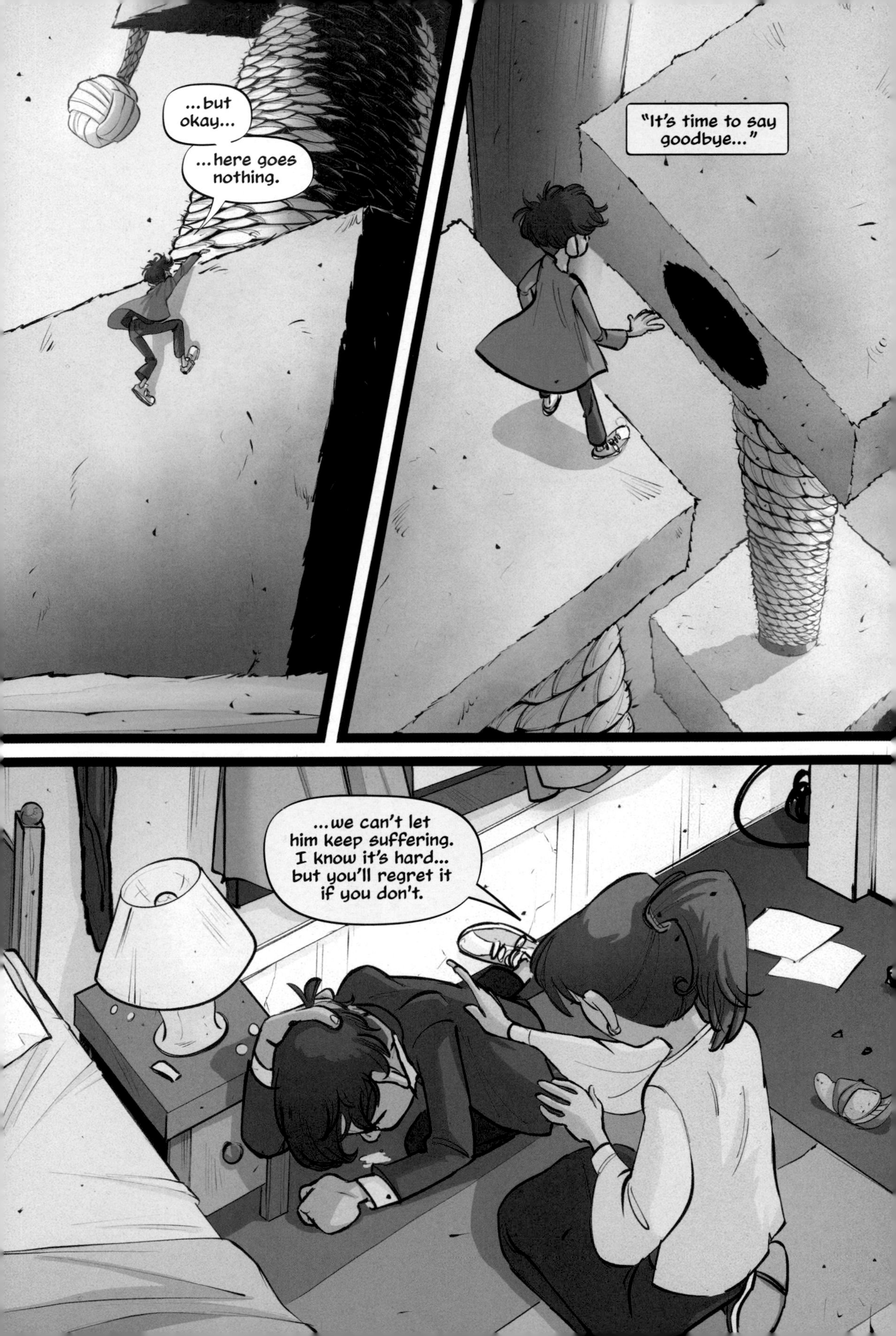
...but okay...
...here goes nothing.
"It's time to say goodbye..."
...we can't let him keep suffering. I know it's hard... but you'll regret it if you don't.

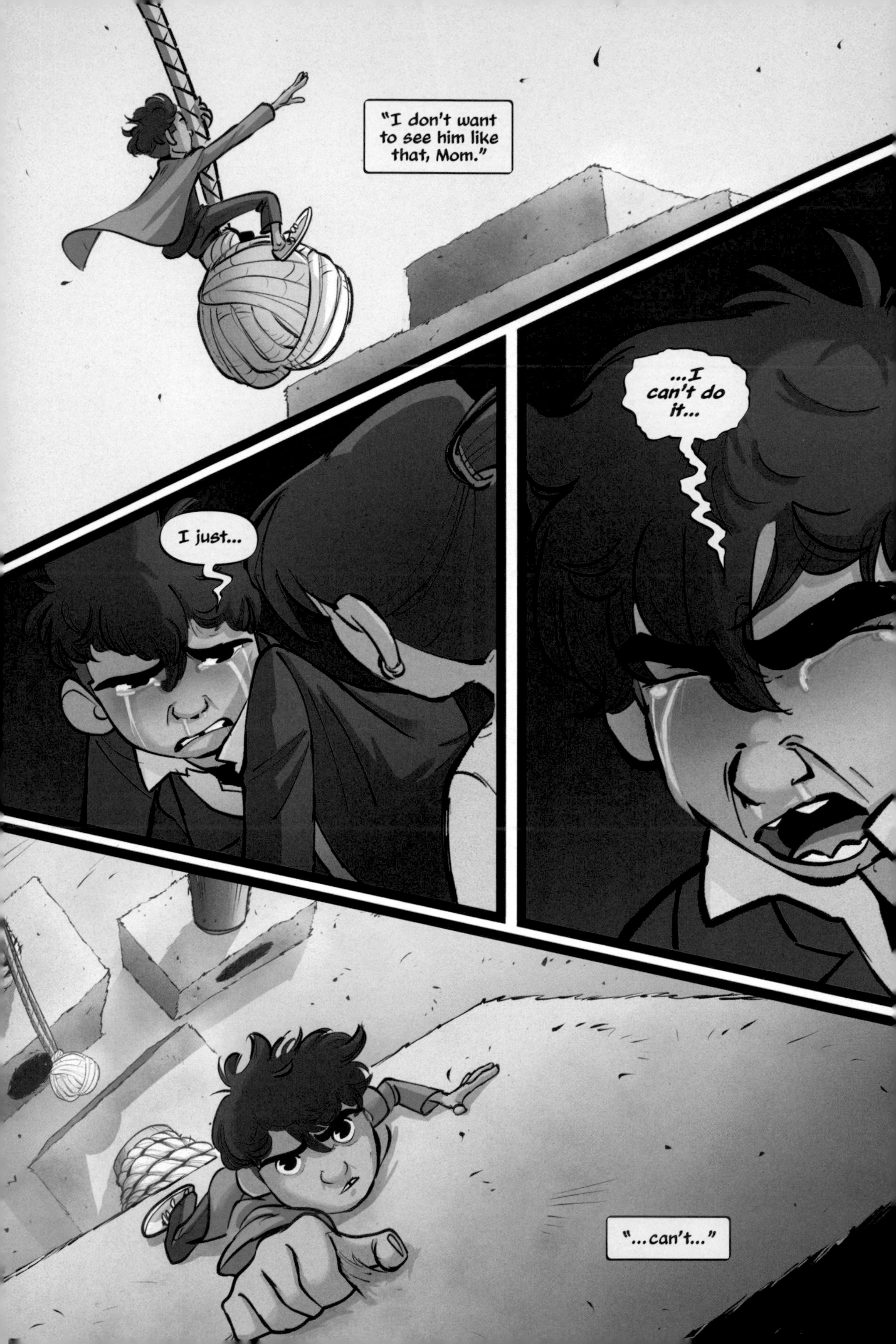
"I don't want to see him like that, Mom."
I just...
...I can't do it...
"...can't..."

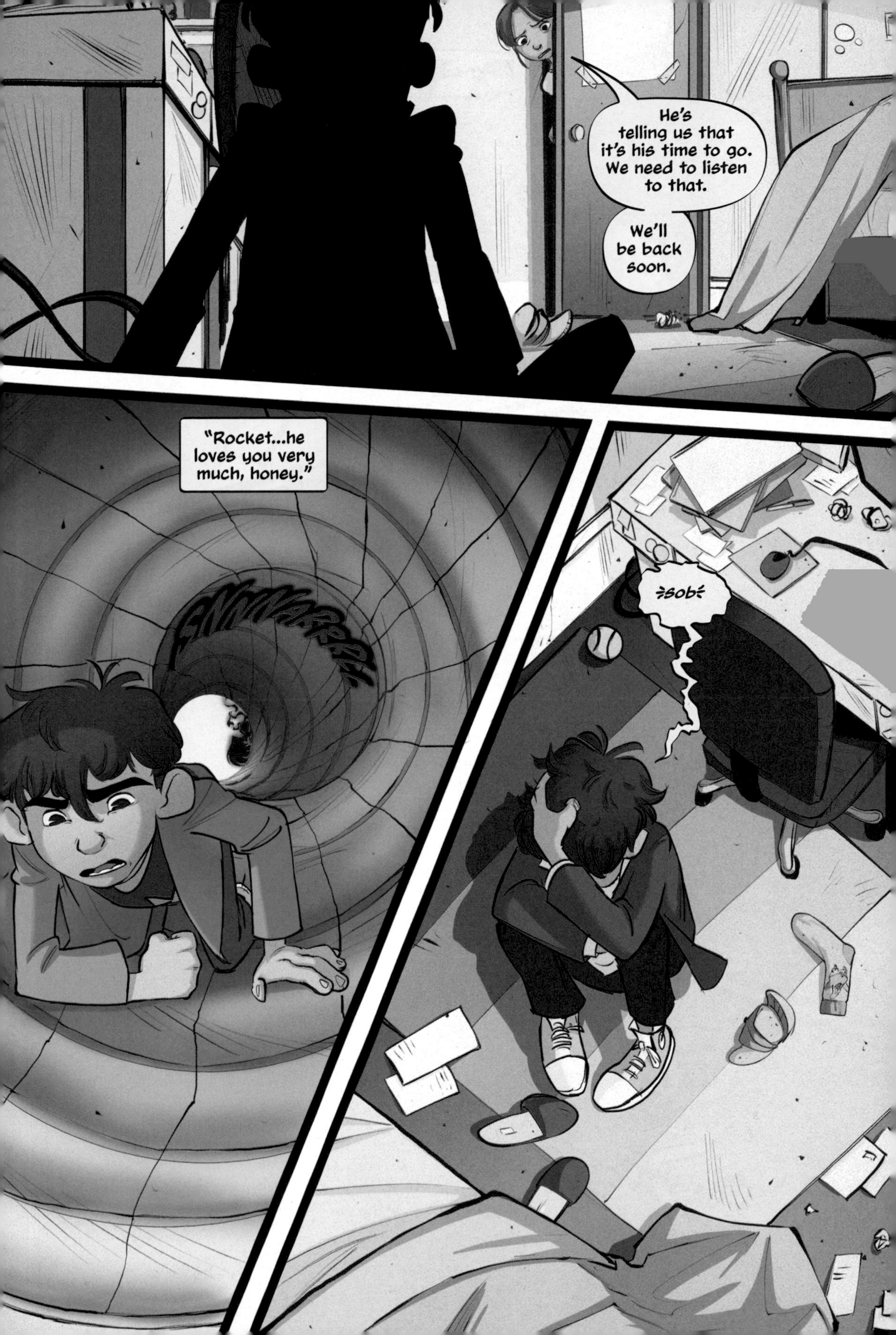

He's telling us that it's his time to go. We need to listen to that.
We'll be back soon.
"Rocket...he loves you very much, honey."
SNWARRR!
sob

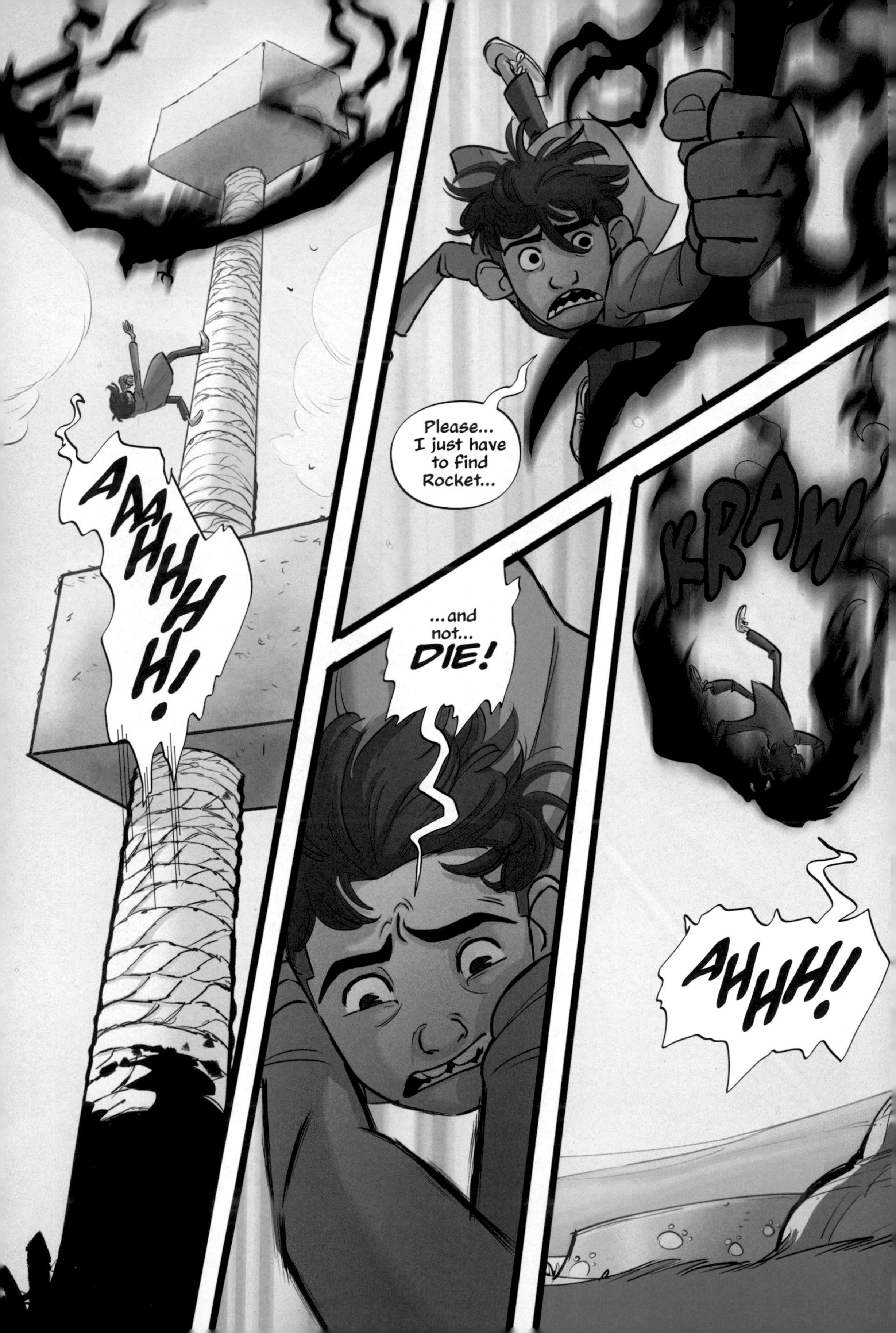
AAAHHHH!
Please... I just have to find Rocket...
KRAW
...and not... DIE!
AHHH!

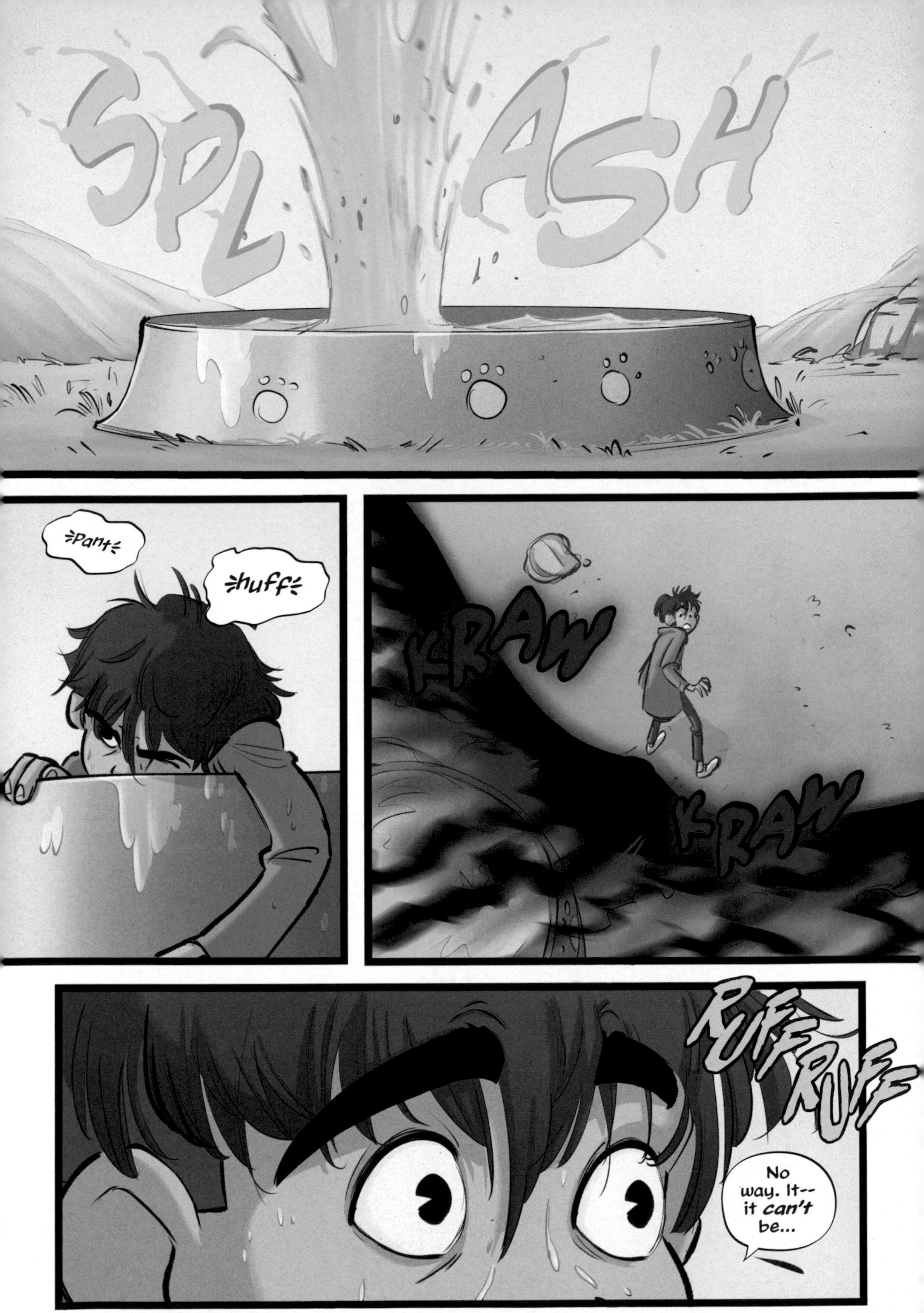
SPLASH
Pant
huff
KRAW
KRAW
RUFF RUFF
No way. It-- it can't be...

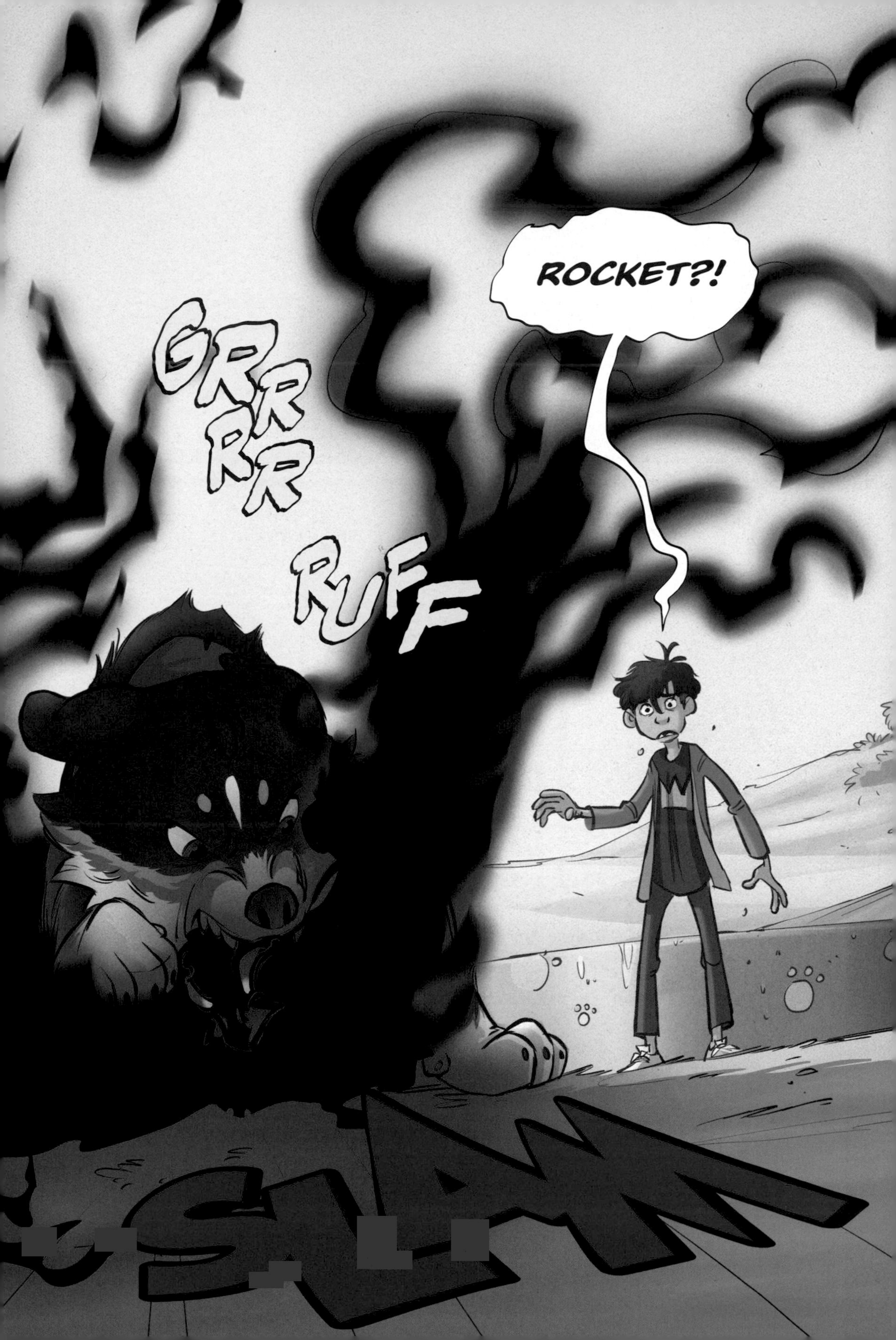
GRRRR
RUFF
ROCKET?!
SLAM

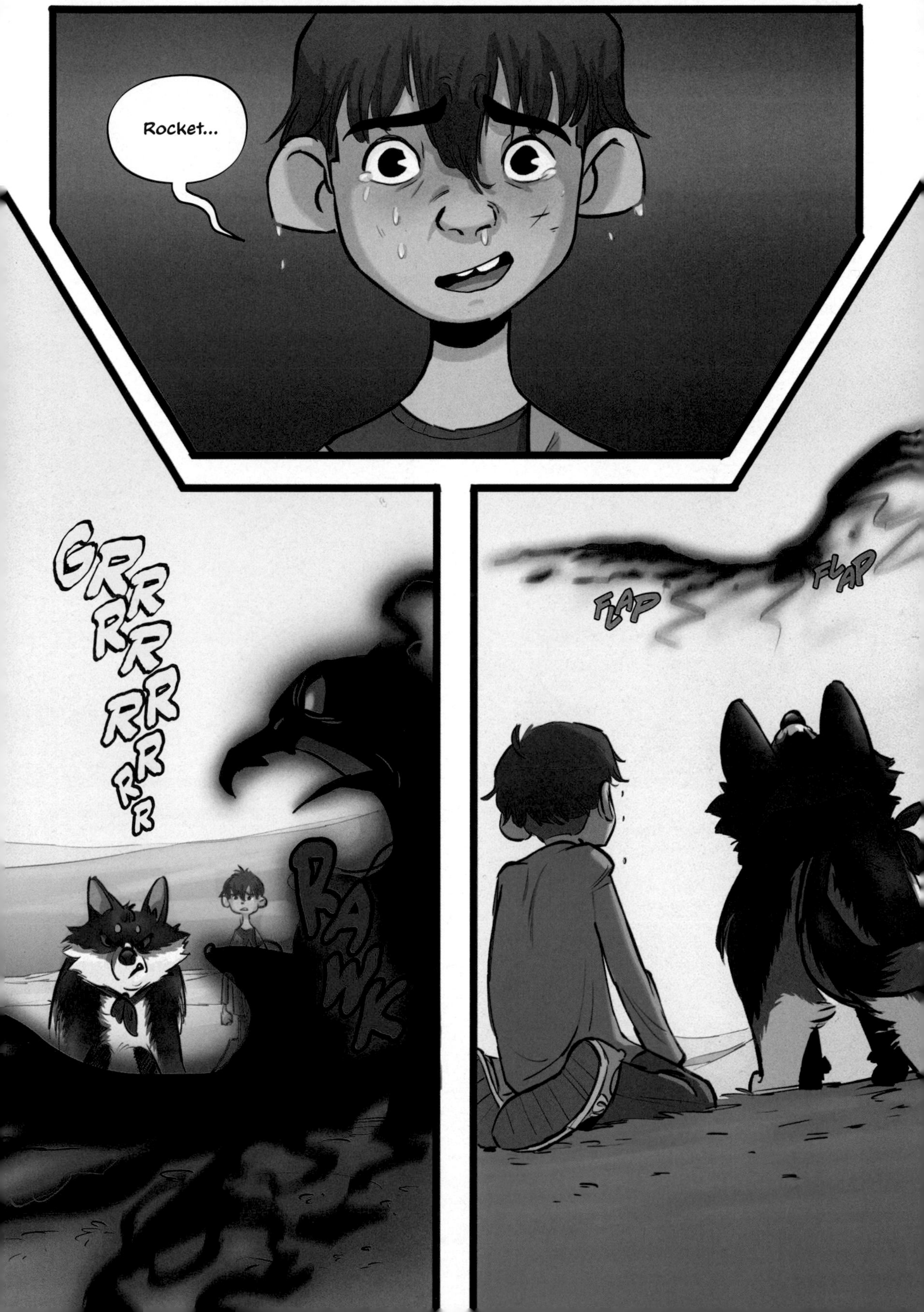
Rocket...
GRRRRRRRRRR
RAWK
FLAP
FLAP

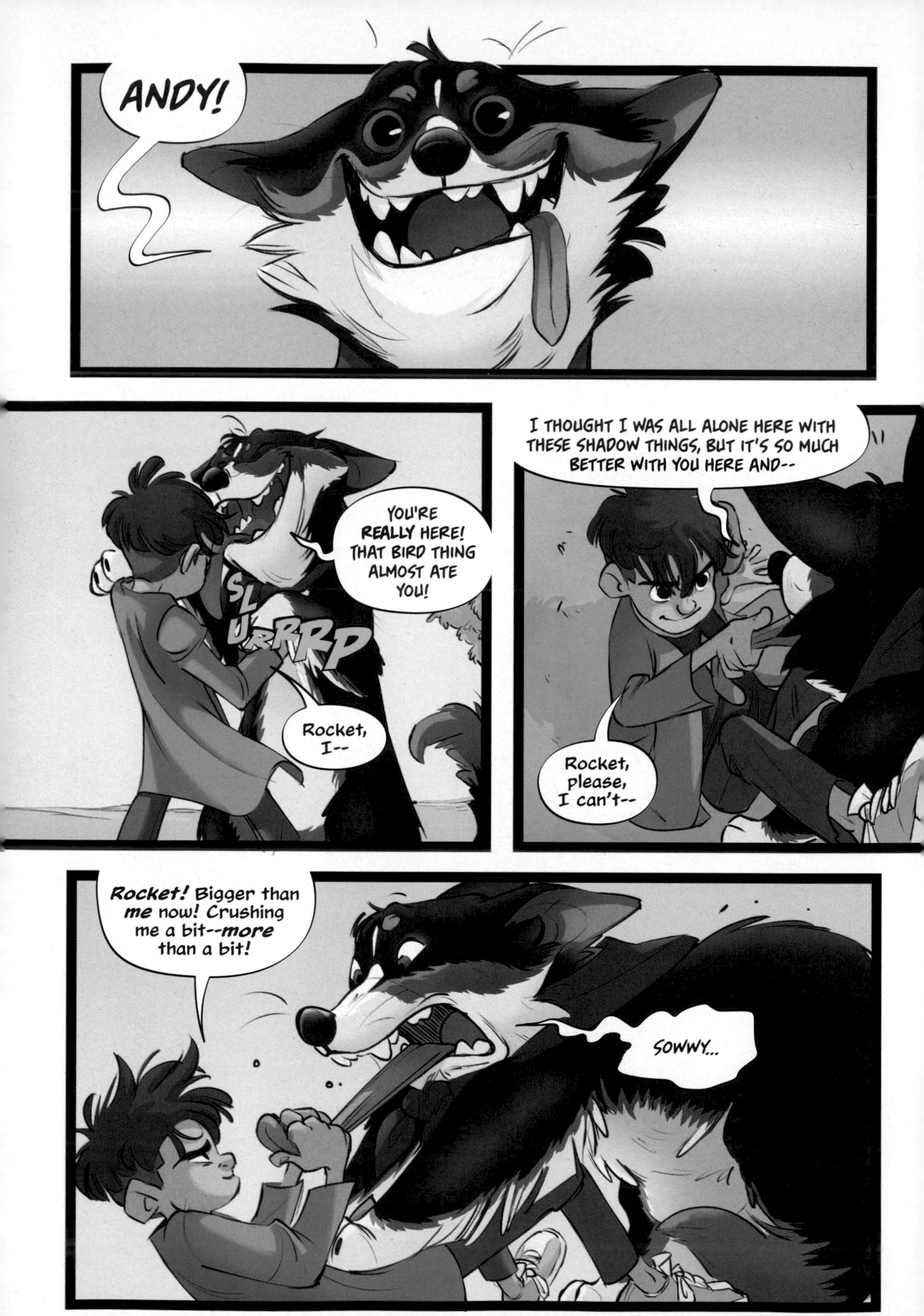
ANDY!
YOU'RE REALLY HERE! THAT BIRD THING ALMOST ATE YOU!
SLURRRP
Rocket, I--
I THOUGHT I WAS ALL ALONE HERE WITH THESE SHADOW THINGS, BUT IT'S SO MUCH BETTER WITH YOU HERE AND--
Rocket, please, I can't--
Rocket! Bigger than ***me*** now! Crushing me a bit--***more*** than a bit!
SOWWY...

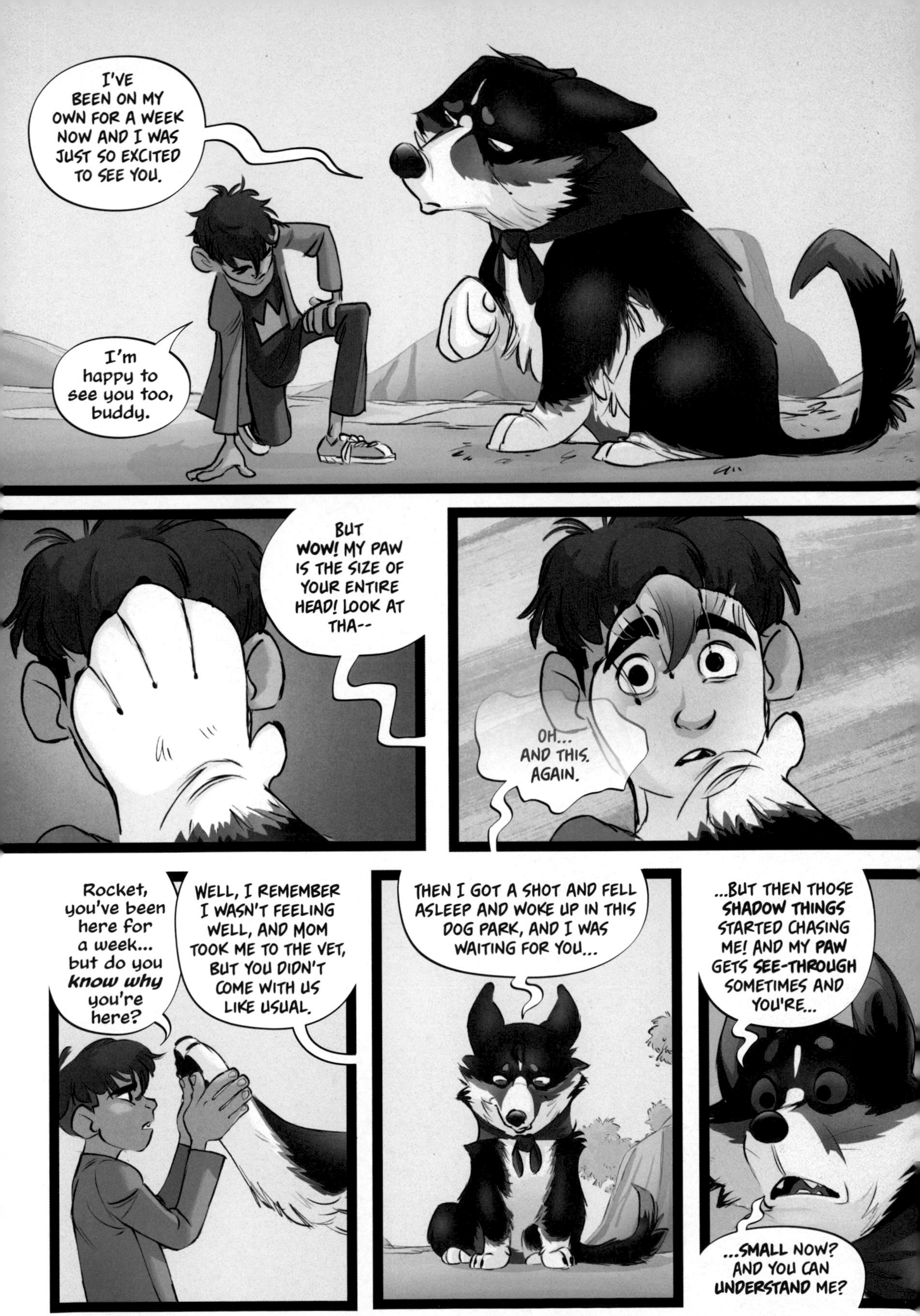
I'VE BEEN ON MY OWN FOR A WEEK NOW AND I WAS JUST SO EXCITED TO SEE YOU.
I'm happy to see you too, buddy.
BUT WOW! MY PAW IS THE SIZE OF YOUR ENTIRE HEAD! LOOK AT THA--
OH... AND THIS. AGAIN.
Rocket, you've been here for a week... but do you *know why* you're here?
WELL, I REMEMBER I WASN'T FEELING WELL, AND MOM TOOK ME TO THE VET, BUT YOU DIDN'T COME WITH US LIKE USUAL.
THEN I GOT A SHOT AND FELL ASLEEP AND WOKE UP IN THIS DOG PARK, AND I WAS WAITING FOR YOU...
...BUT THEN THOSE SHADOW THINGS STARTED CHASING ME! AND MY PAW GETS SEE-THROUGH SOMETIMES AND YOU'RE...
...SMALL NOW? AND YOU CAN UNDERSTAND ME?

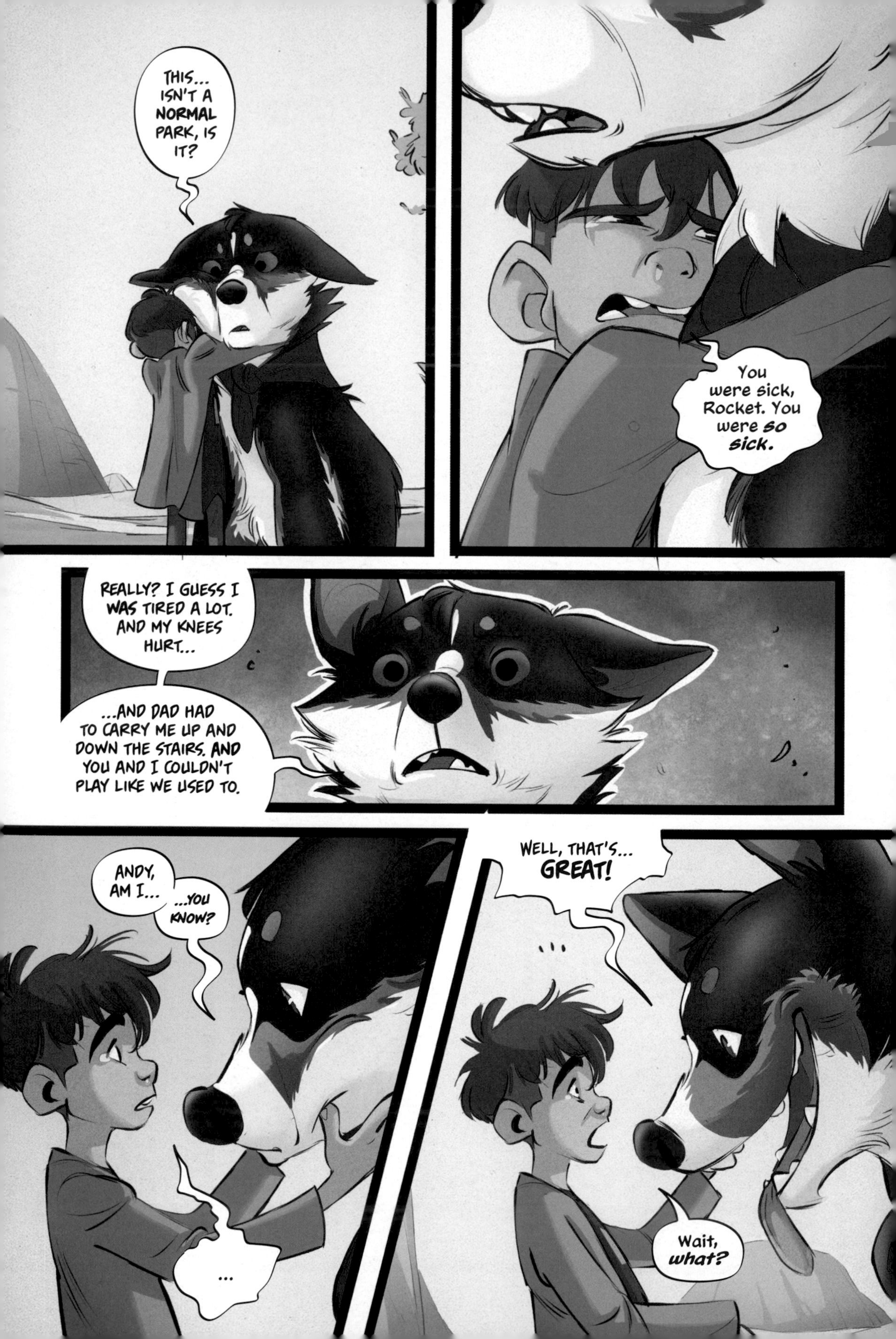
THIS... ISN'T A NORMAL PARK, IS IT?
You were sick, Rocket. You were so sick.
REALLY? I GUESS I WAS TIRED A LOT. AND MY KNEES HURT...
...AND DAD HAD TO CARRY ME UP AND DOWN THE STAIRS. AND YOU AND I COULDN'T PLAY LIKE WE USED TO.
ANDY, AM I...
...YOU KNOW?
...
WELL, THAT'S... GREAT!
Wait, what?

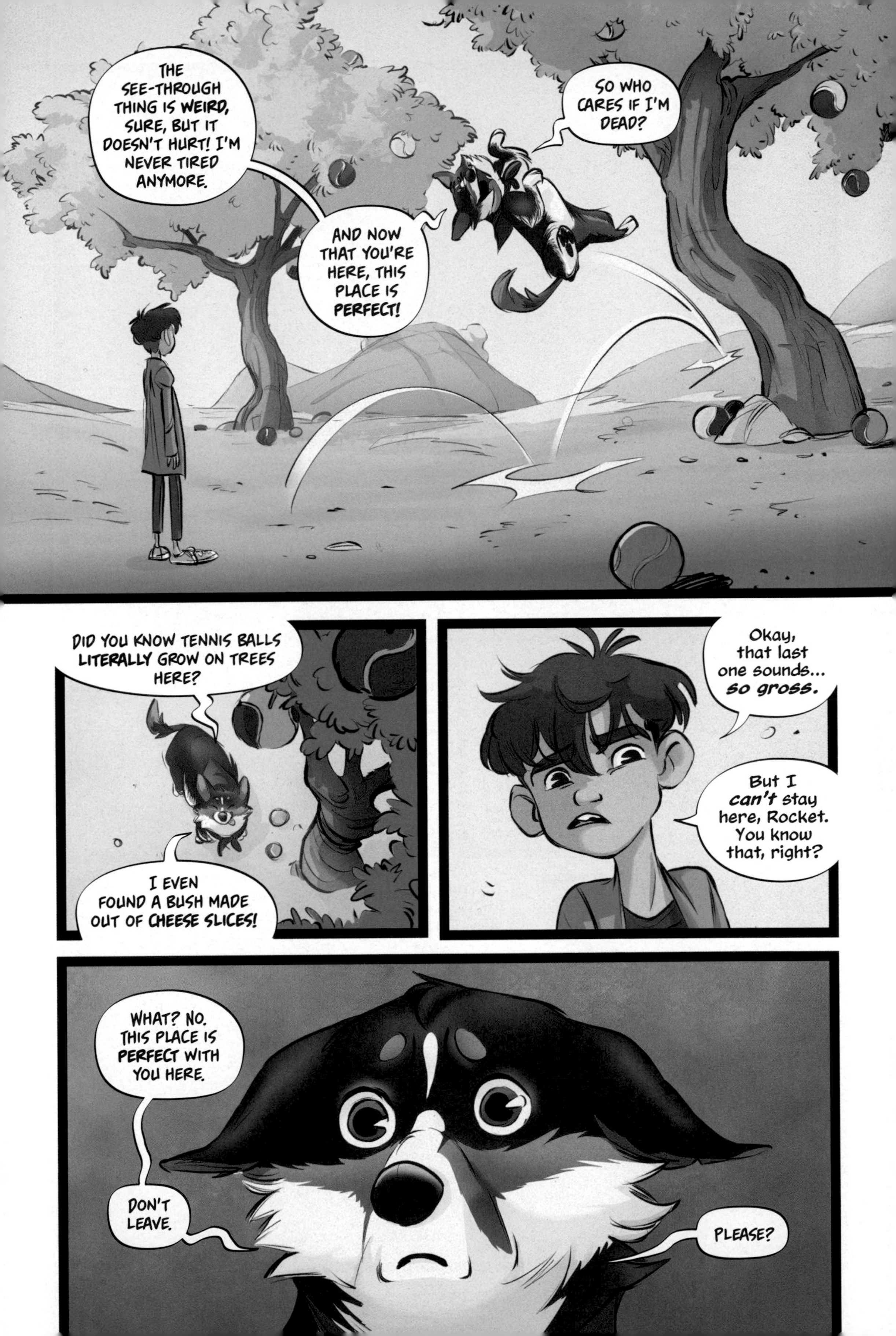
THE SEE-THROUGH THING IS WEIRD, SURE, BUT IT DOESN'T HURT! I'M NEVER TIRED ANYMORE.
AND NOW THAT YOU'RE HERE, THIS PLACE IS PERFECT!
SO WHO CARES IF I'M DEAD?
DID YOU KNOW TENNIS BALLS LITERALLY GROW ON TREES HERE?
I EVEN FOUND A BUSH MADE OUT OF CHEESE SLICES!
Okay, that last one sounds... *so gross.*
But I *can't* stay here, Rocket. You know that, right?
WHAT? NO. THIS PLACE IS PERFECT WITH YOU HERE.
DON'T LEAVE.
PLEASE?

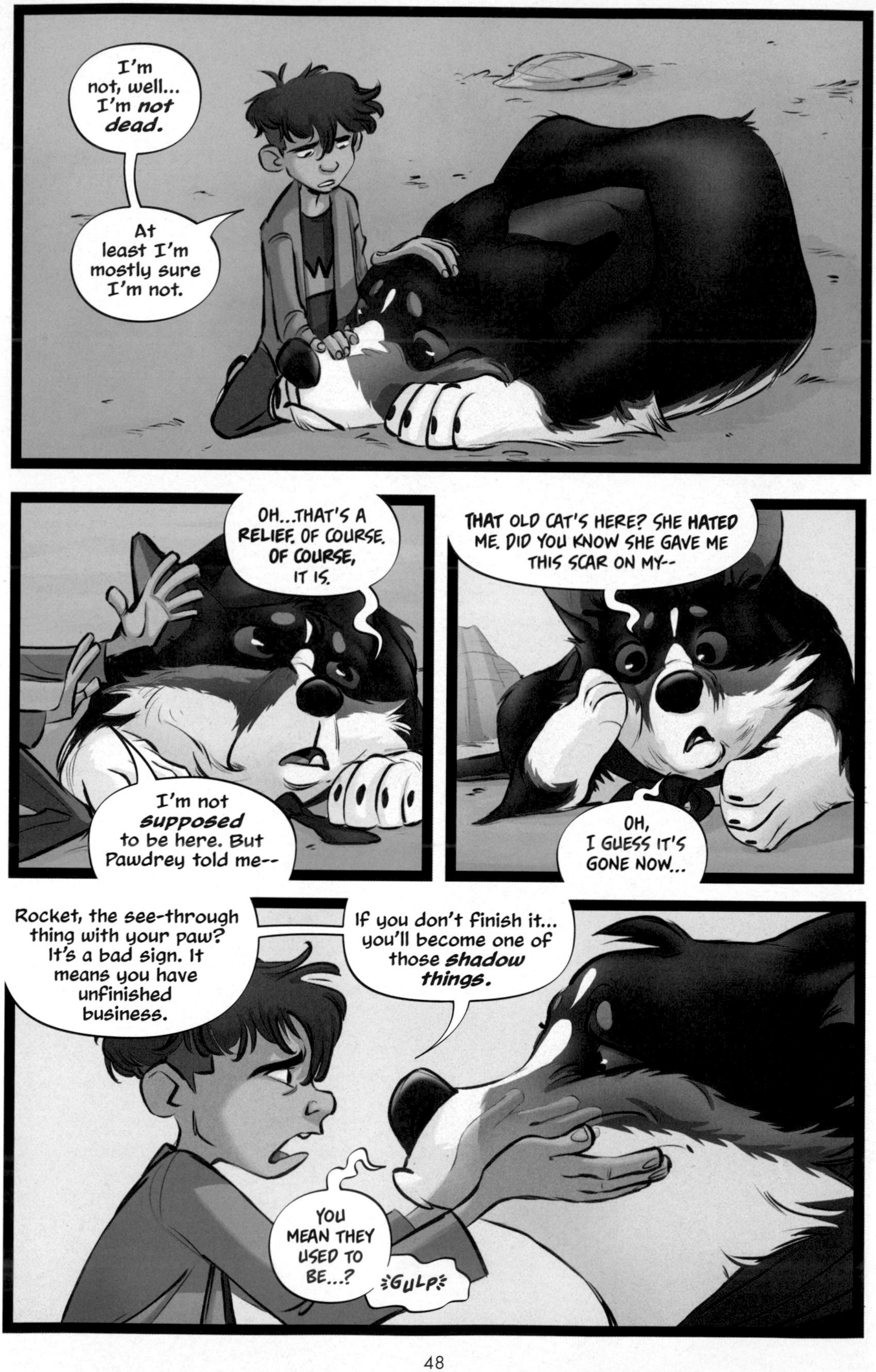
I'm not, well... I'm ***not dead.***
At least I'm mostly sure I'm not.
OH...THAT'S A RELIEF. OF COURSE. OF COURSE, IT IS.
I'm not ***supposed*** to be here. But Pawdrey told me--
THAT OLD CAT'S HERE? SHE HATED ME. DID YOU KNOW SHE GAVE ME THIS SCAR ON MY--
OH, I GUESS IT'S GONE NOW...
Rocket, the see-through thing with your paw? It's a bad sign. It means you have unfinished business.
If you don't finish it... you'll become one of those ***shadow things.***
YOU MEAN THEY USED TO BE...?
GULP

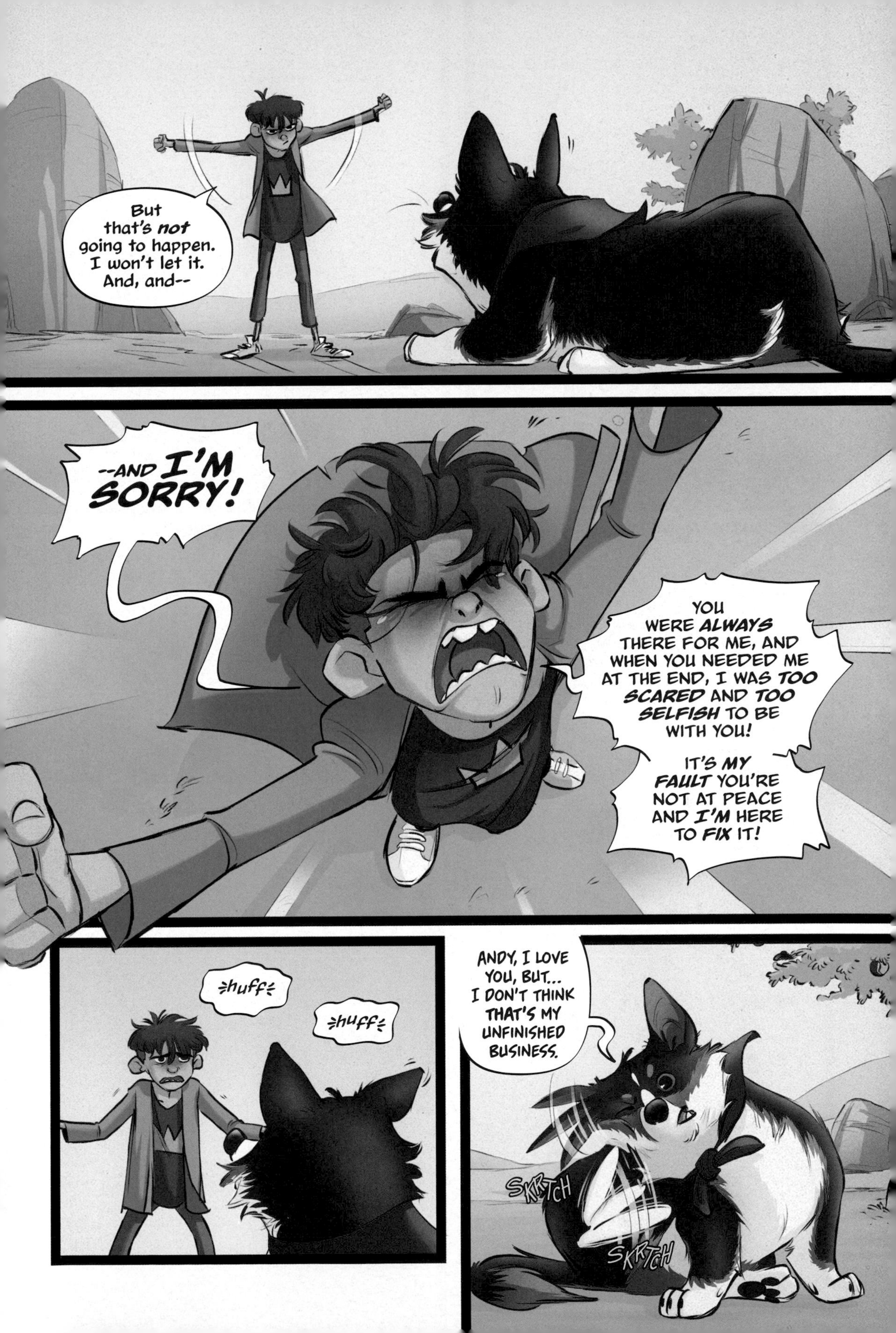
But that's *not* going to happen. I won't let it. And, and--
--AND **I'M SORRY!**
YOU WERE ***ALWAYS*** THERE FOR ME, AND WHEN YOU NEEDED ME AT THE END, I WAS ***TOO SCARED*** AND ***TOO SELFISH*** TO BE WITH YOU!
IT'S ***MY FAULT*** YOU'RE NOT AT PEACE AND ***I'M*** HERE TO ***FIX*** IT!
huff
huff
ANDY, I LOVE YOU, BUT... I DON'T THINK **THAT'S** MY UNFINISHED BUSINESS.
SKRTCH
SKRTCH

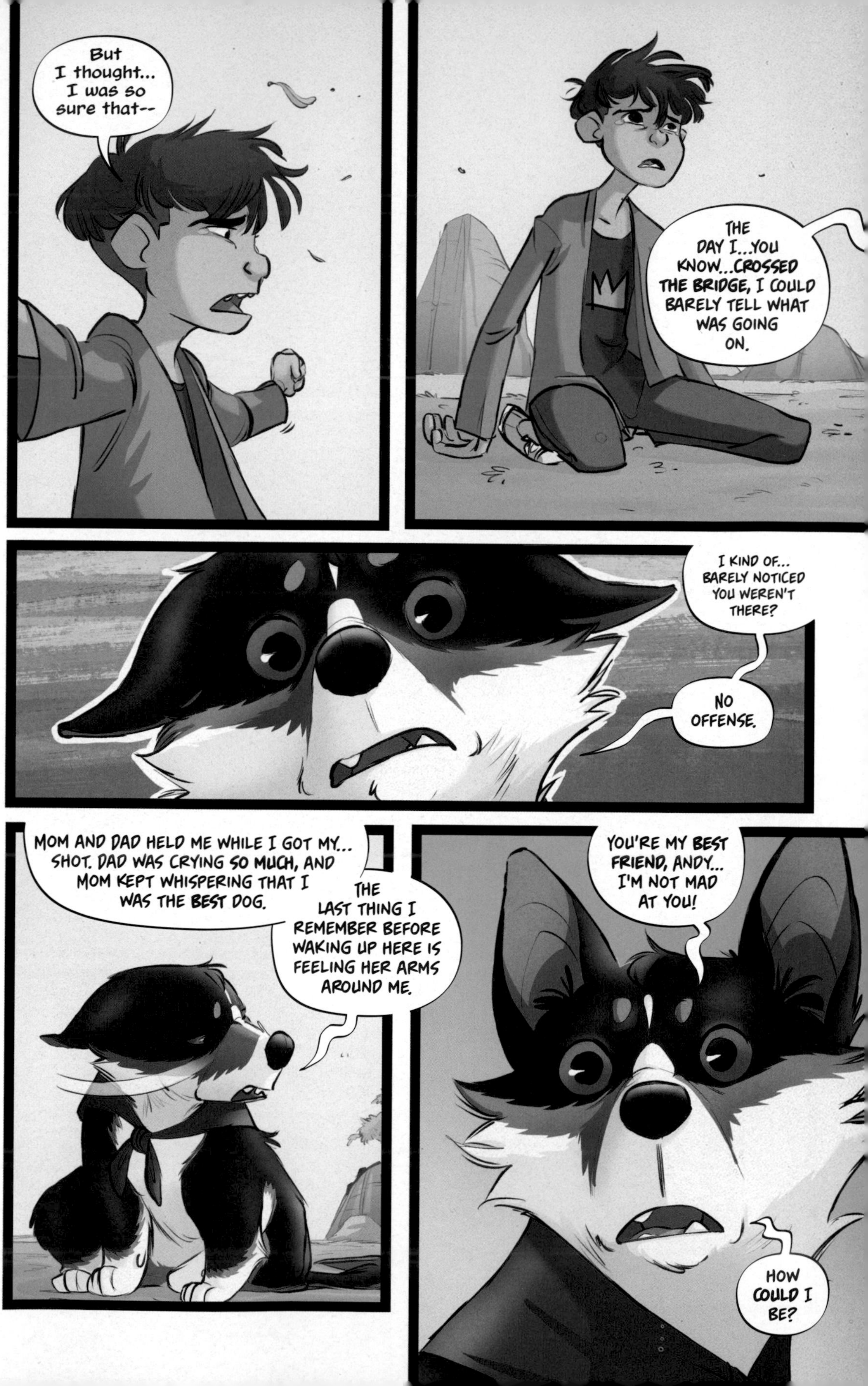
But I thought... I was so sure that--
THE DAY I...YOU KNOW...CROSSED THE BRIDGE, I COULD BARELY TELL WHAT WAS GOING ON.
I KIND OF... BARELY NOTICED YOU WEREN'T THERE?
NO OFFENSE.
MOM AND DAD HELD ME WHILE I GOT MY... SHOT. DAD WAS CRYING SO MUCH, AND MOM KEPT WHISPERING THAT I WAS THE BEST DOG.
THE LAST THING I REMEMBER BEFORE WAKING UP HERE IS FEELING HER ARMS AROUND ME.
YOU'RE MY BEST FRIEND, ANDY... I'M NOT MAD AT YOU!
HOW COULD I BE?

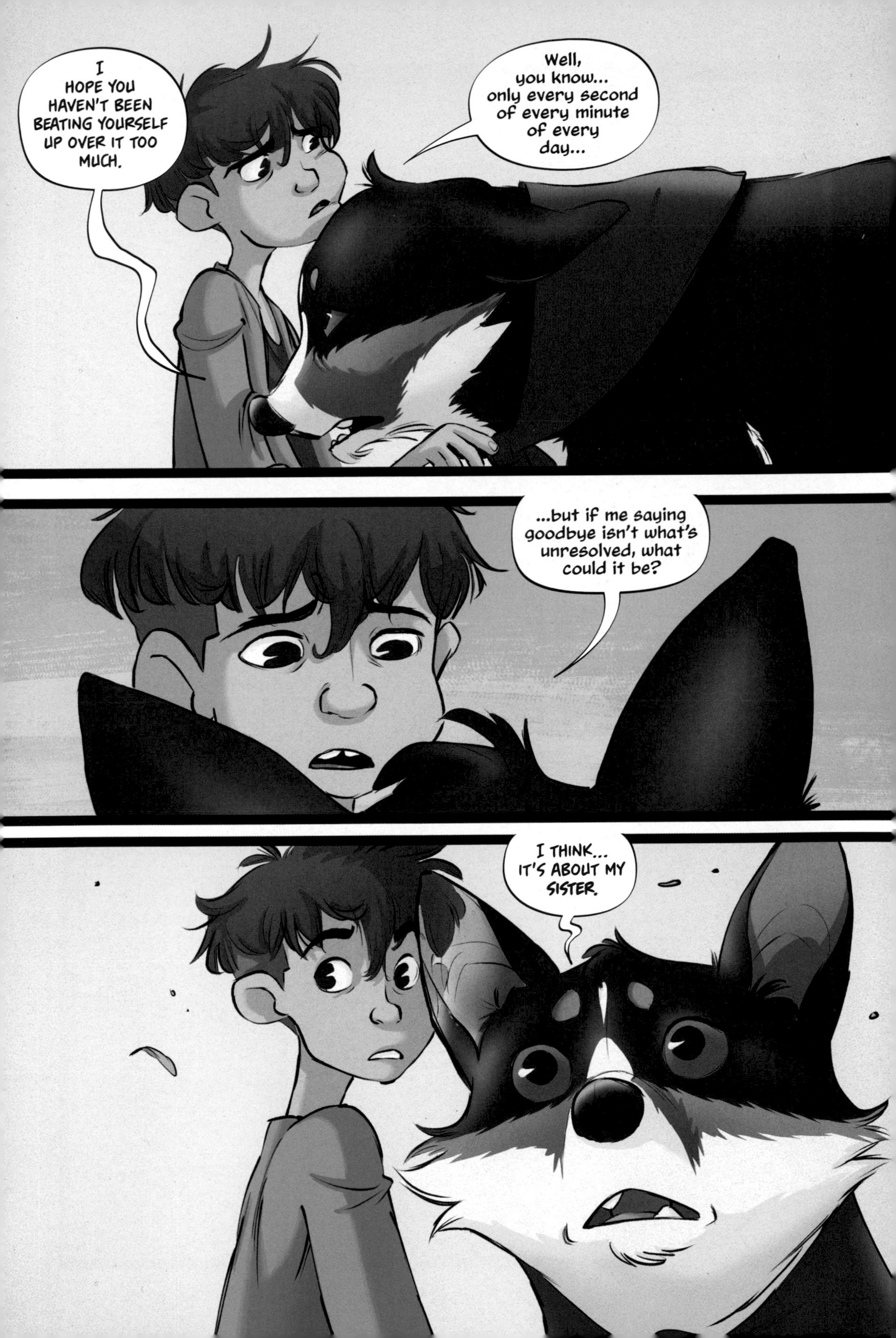
I HOPE YOU HAVEN'T BEEN BEATING YOURSELF UP OVER IT TOO MUCH.
Well, you know... only every second of every minute of every day...
...but if me saying goodbye isn't what's unresolved, what could it be?
I THINK... IT'S ABOUT MY SISTER.

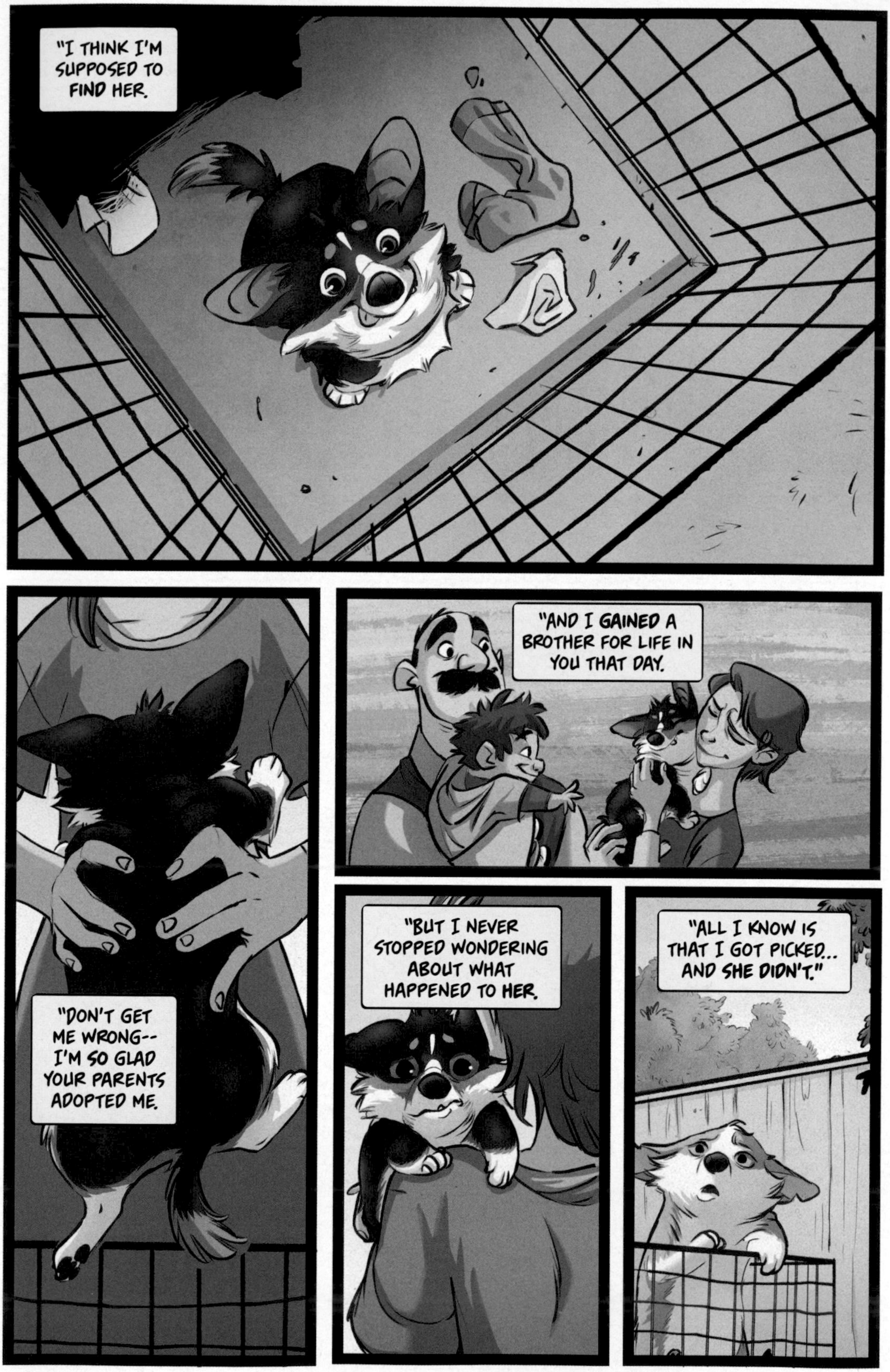
"I THINK I'M SUPPOSED TO FIND HER.
"DON'T GET ME WRONG-- I'M SO GLAD YOUR PARENTS ADOPTED ME.
"AND I GAINED A BROTHER FOR LIFE IN YOU THAT DAY.
"BUT I NEVER STOPPED WONDERING ABOUT WHAT HAPPENED TO HER.
"ALL I KNOW IS THAT I GOT PICKED... AND SHE DIDN'T."

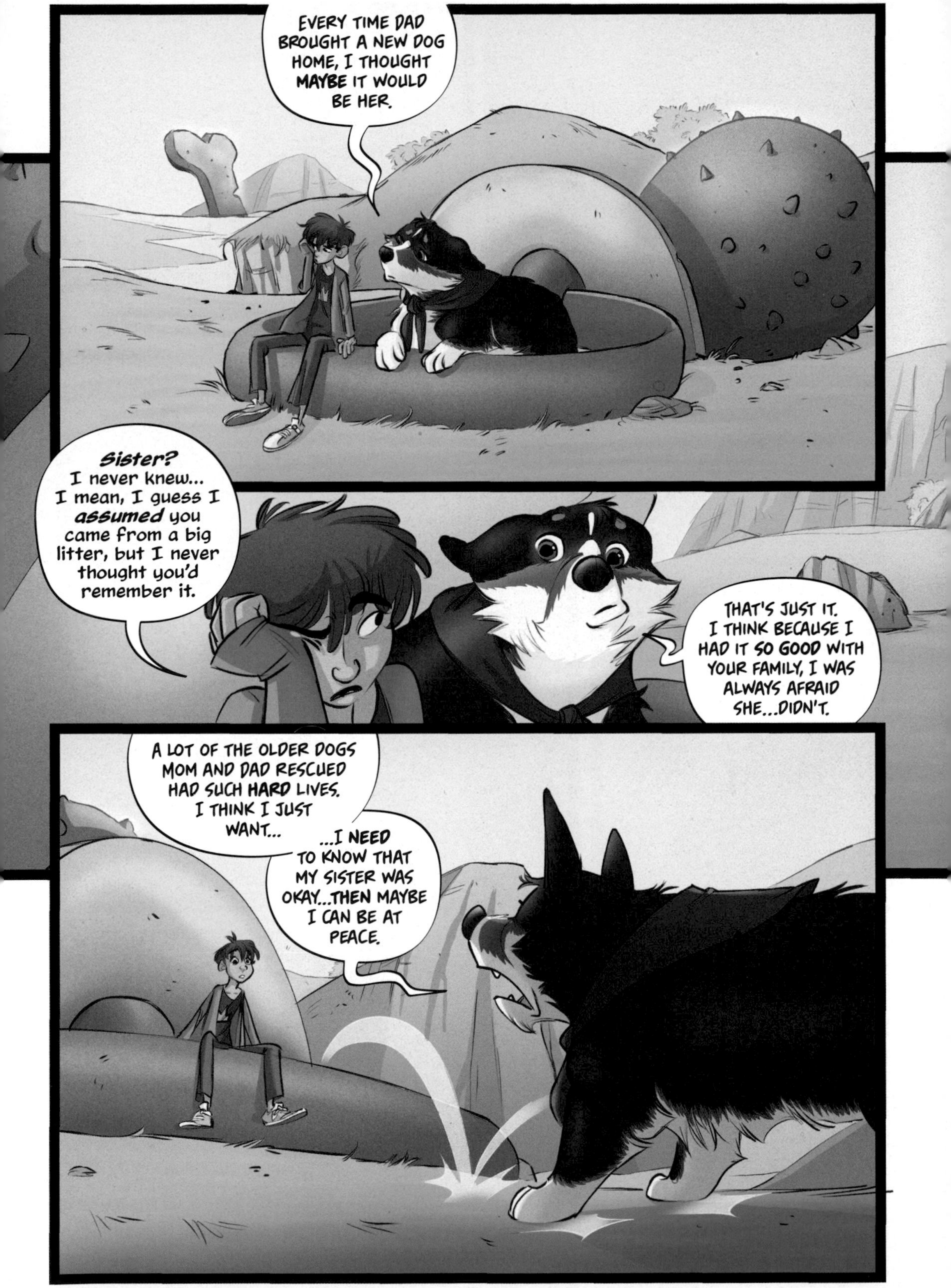
EVERY TIME DAD BROUGHT A NEW DOG HOME, I THOUGHT **MAYBE** IT WOULD BE HER.
Sister? I never knew... I mean, I guess I ***assumed*** you came from a big litter, but I never thought you'd remember it.
THAT'S JUST IT. I THINK BECAUSE I HAD IT SO **GOOD** WITH YOUR FAMILY, I WAS ALWAYS AFRAID SHE...DIDN'T.
A LOT OF THE OLDER DOGS MOM AND DAD RESCUED HAD SUCH **HARD** LIVES. I THINK I JUST WANT...
...I **NEED** TO KNOW THAT MY SISTER WAS OKAY...THEN MAYBE I CAN BE AT PEACE.

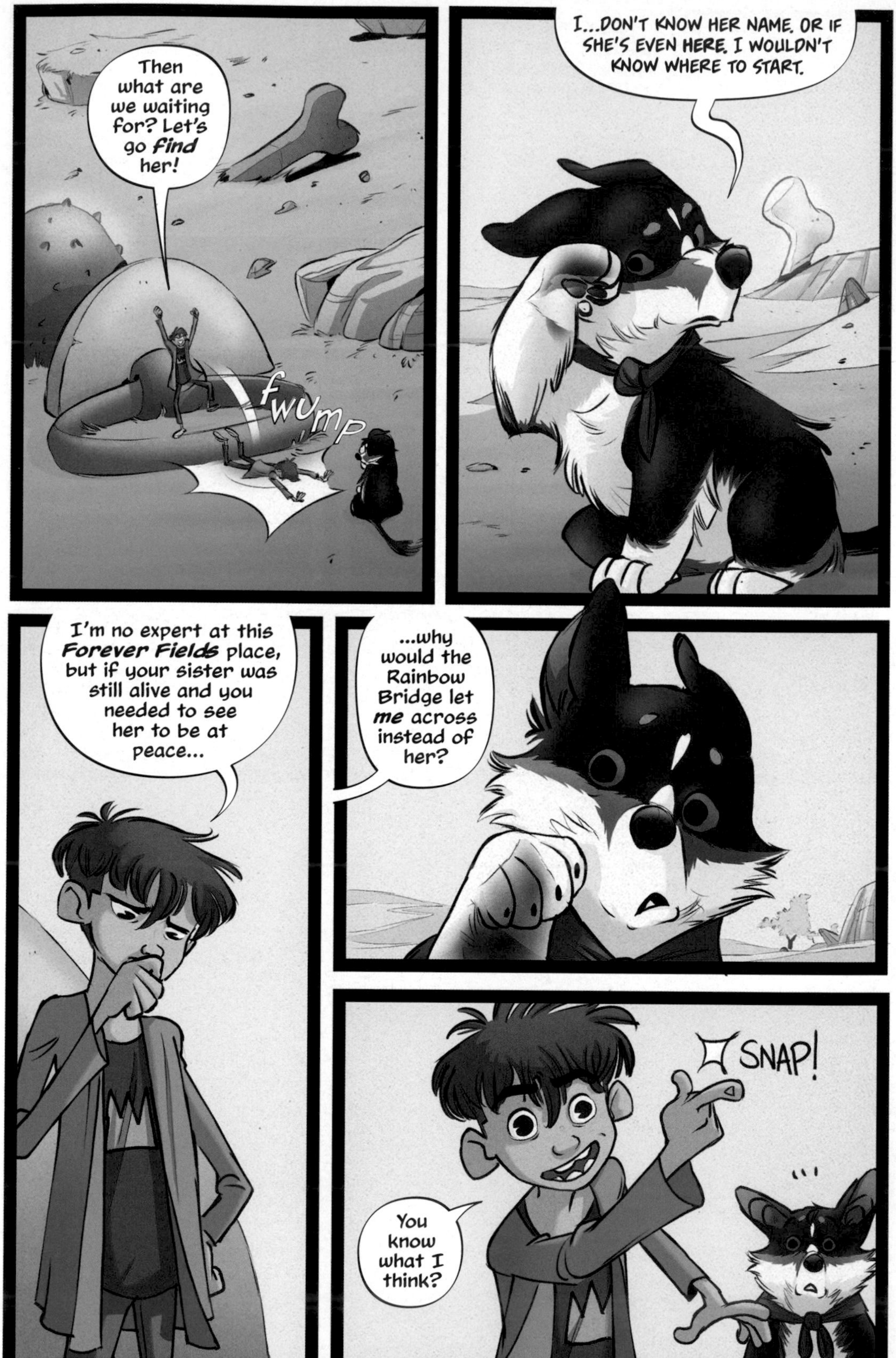
Then what are we waiting for? Let's go *find* her!
fwump
I...DON'T KNOW HER NAME. OR IF SHE'S EVEN HERE. I WOULDN'T KNOW WHERE TO START.
I'm no expert at this *Forever Fields* place, but if your sister was still alive and you needed to see her to be at peace...
...why would the Rainbow Bridge let *me* across instead of her?
SNAP!
You know what I think?

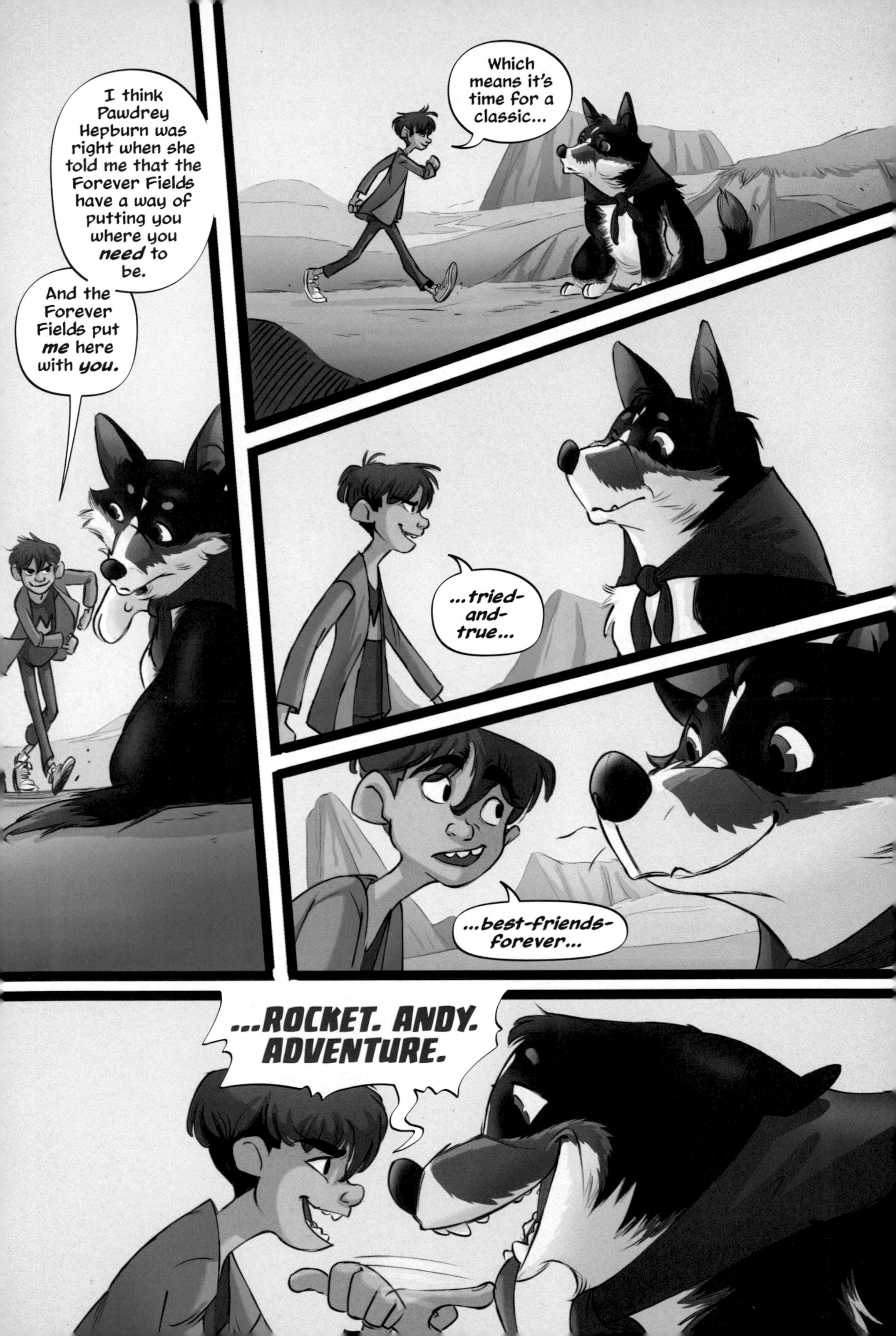
I think Pawdrey Hepburn was right when she told me that the Forever Fields have a way of putting you where you *need* to be.
And the Forever Fields put *me* here with *you.*
Which means it's time for a classic...
...tried-and-true...
...best-friends-forever...
...ROCKET. ANDY. ADVENTURE.

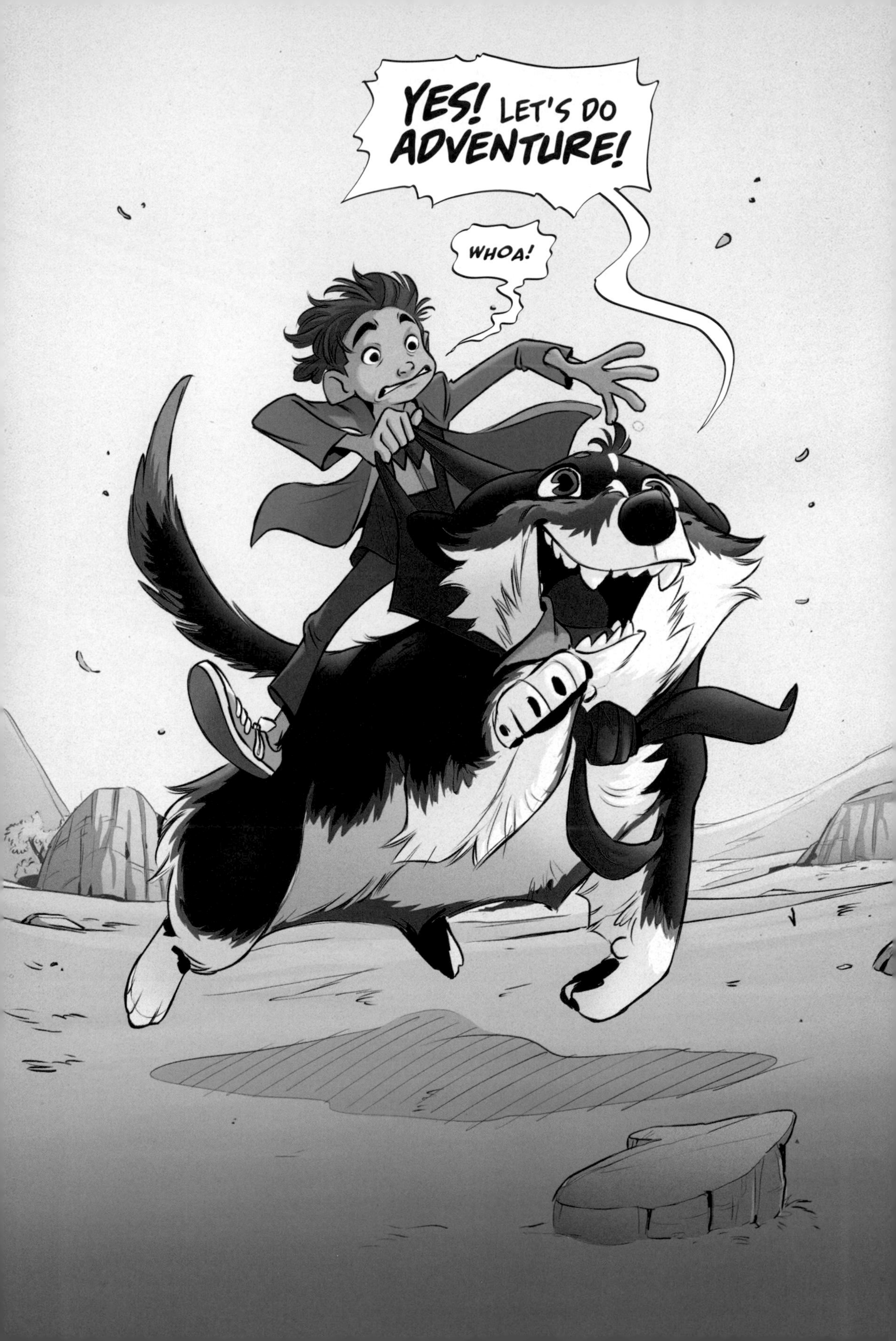
YES! LET'S DO ADVENTURE!
WHOA!

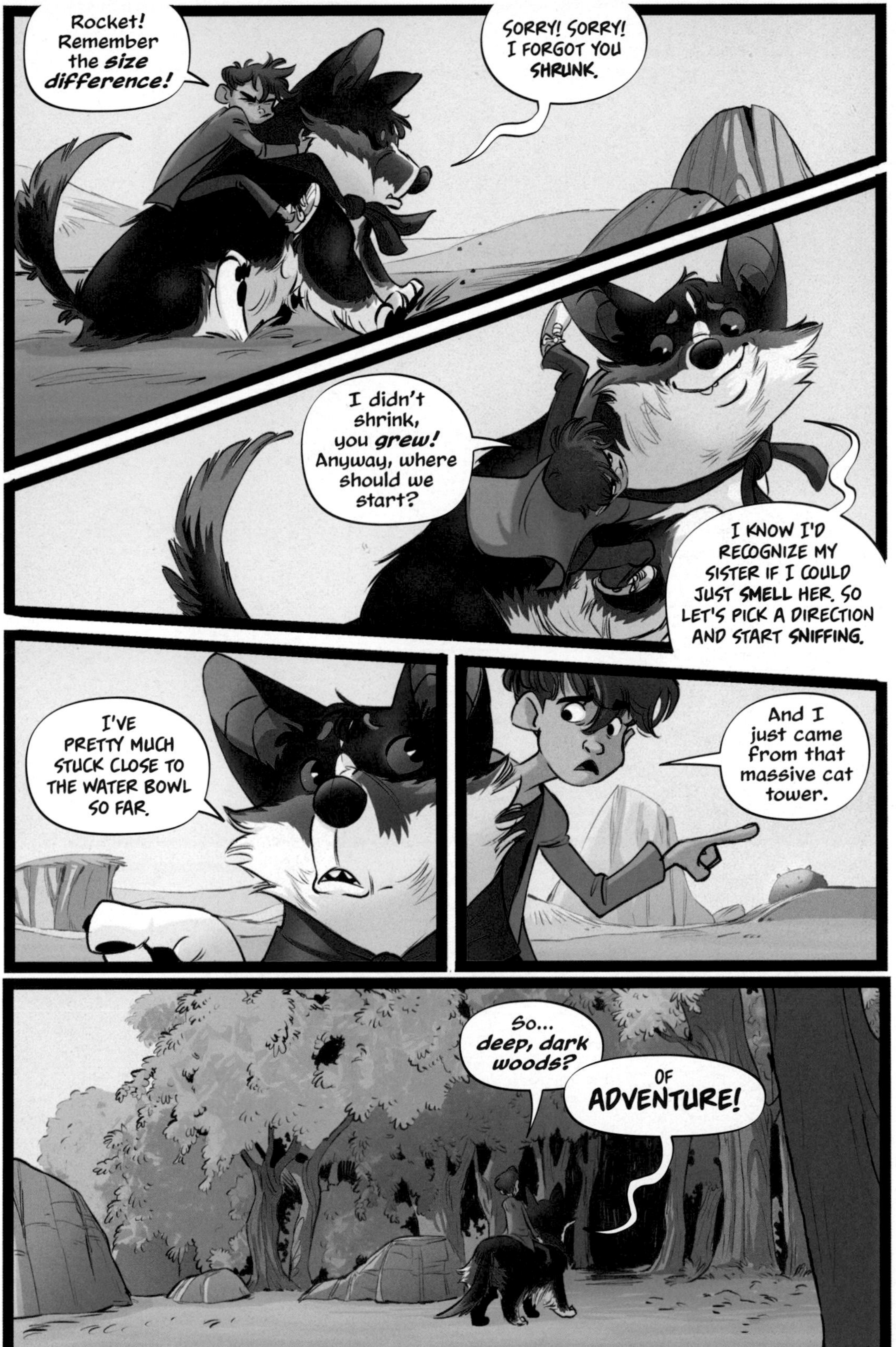
Rocket! Remember the *size difference!*
SORRY! SORRY! I FORGOT YOU **SHRUNK**.
I didn't shrink, you ***grew!*** Anyway, where should we start?
I KNOW I'D RECOGNIZE MY SISTER IF I COULD JUST **SMELL** HER. SO LET'S PICK A DIRECTION AND START **SNIFFING**.
I'VE PRETTY MUCH STUCK CLOSE TO THE WATER BOWL SO FAR.
And I just came from that massive cat tower.
So... ***deep, dark woods?***
OF **ADVENTURE!**

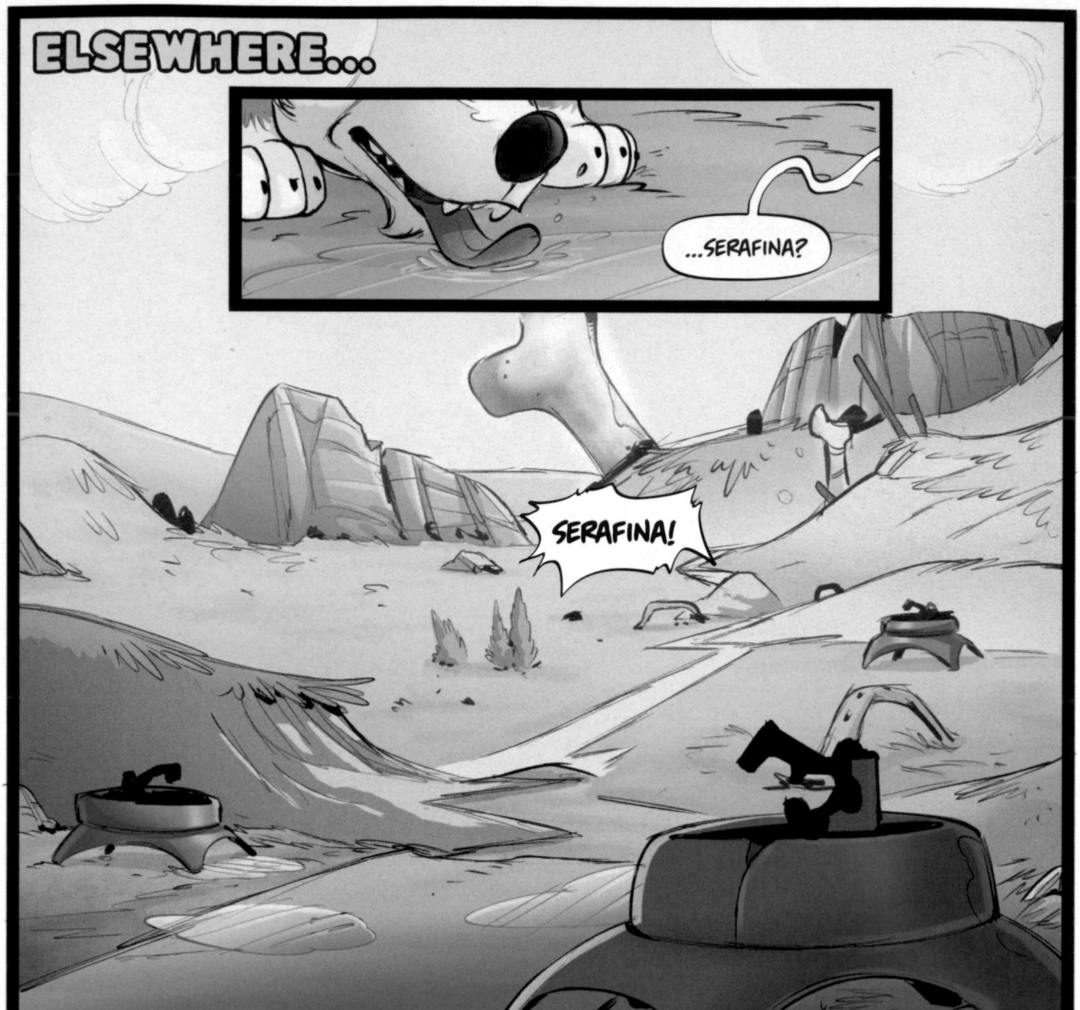
ELSEWHERE...
...SERAFINA?
SERAFINA!

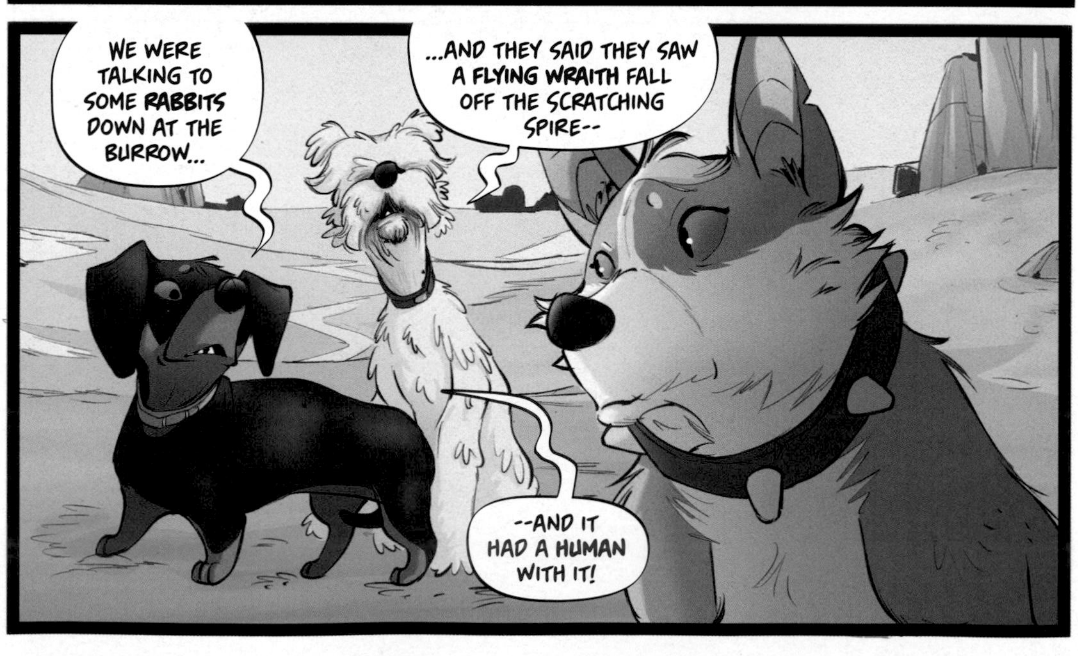
WE WERE TALKING TO SOME RABBITS DOWN AT THE BURROW...
...AND THEY SAID THEY SAW A FLYING WRAITH FALL OFF THE SCRATCHING SPIRE--
--AND IT HAD A HUMAN WITH IT!

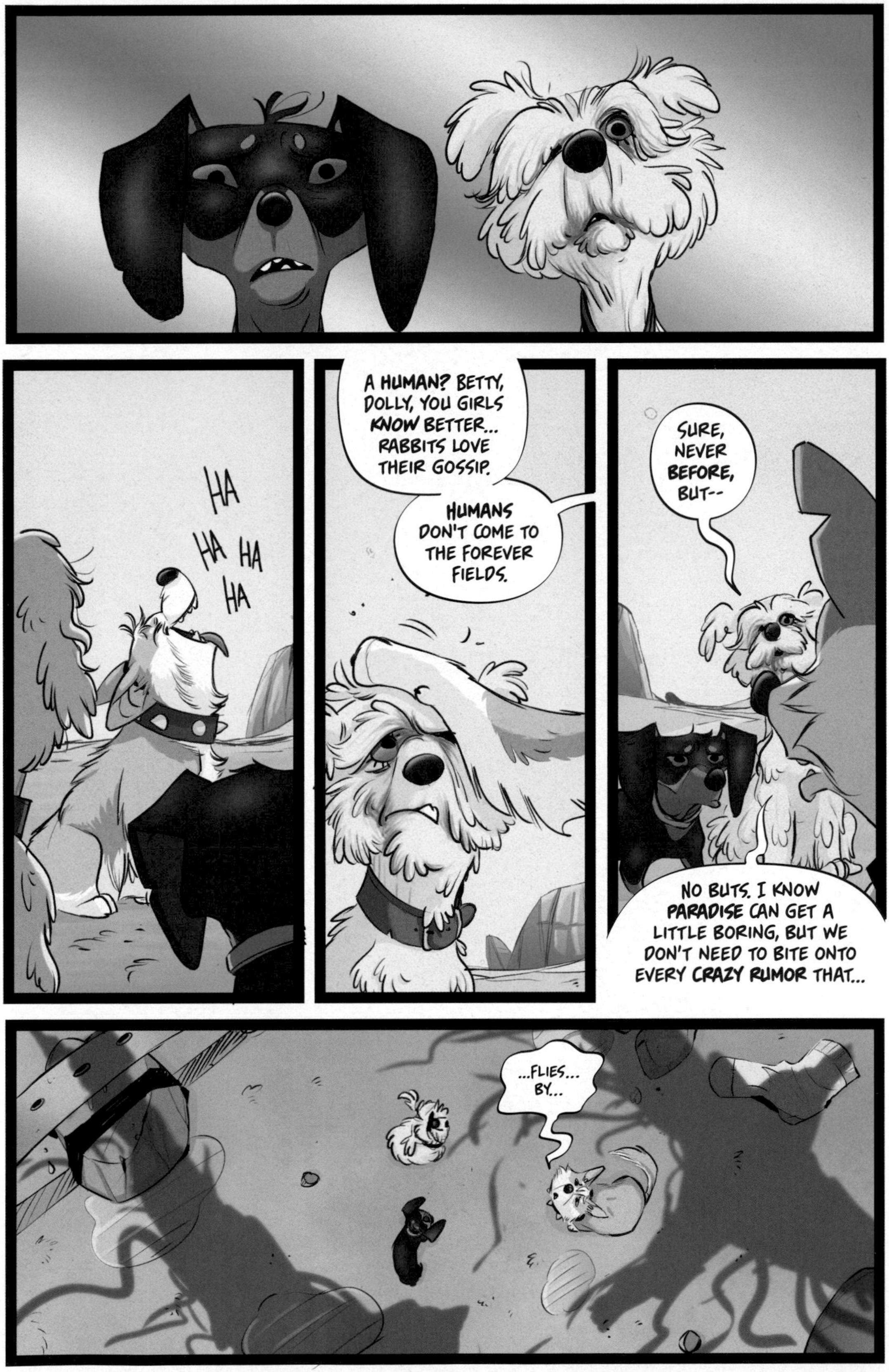
HA
HA HA
HA
A HUMAN? BETTY, DOLLY, YOU GIRLS KNOW BETTER... RABBITS LOVE THEIR GOSSIP.
HUMANS DON'T COME TO THE FOREVER FIELDS.
SURE, NEVER BEFORE, BUT--
NO BUTS. I KNOW PARADISE CAN GET A LITTLE BORING, BUT WE DON'T NEED TO BITE ONTO EVERY CRAZY RUMOR THAT...
...FLIES... BY...

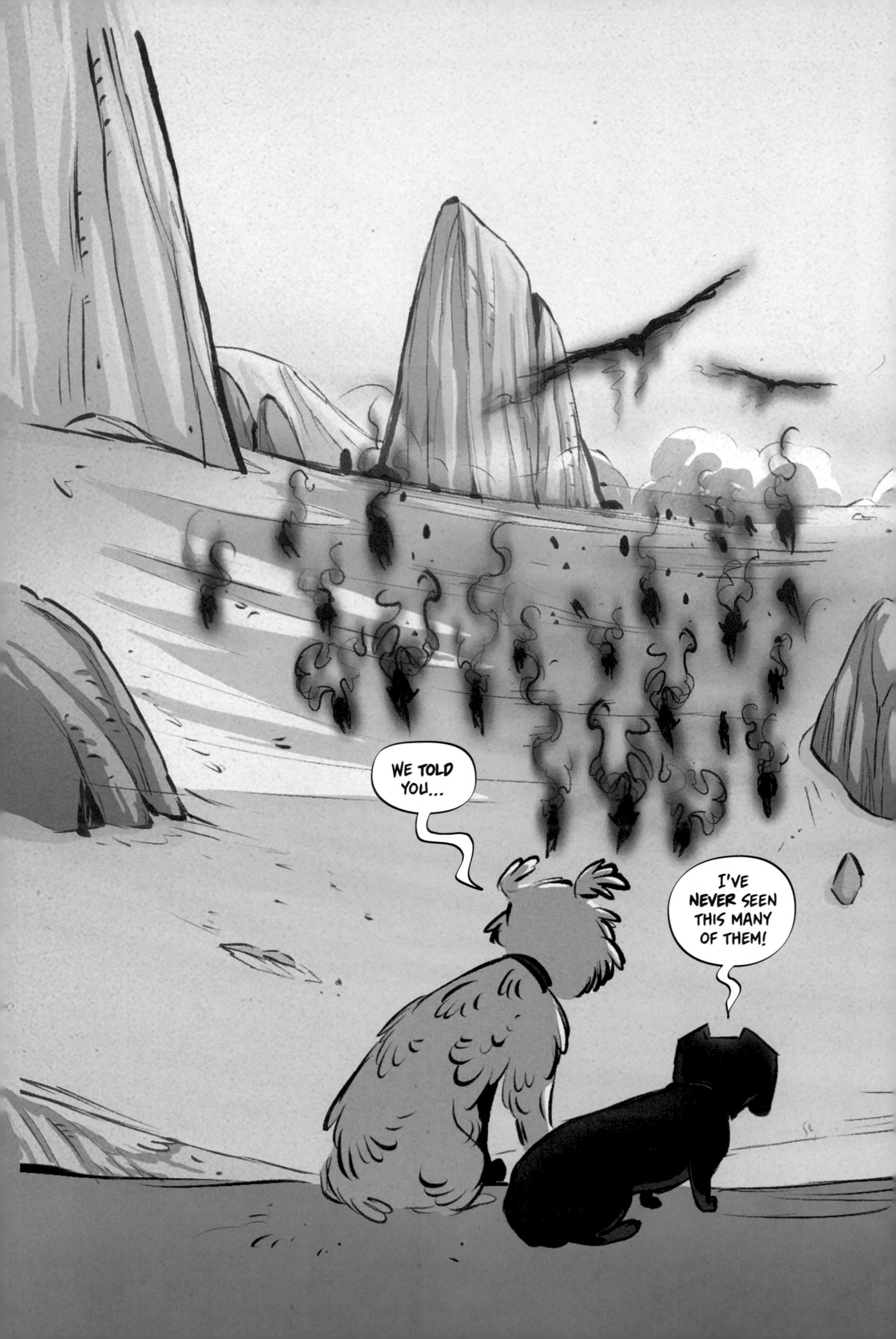
WE TOLD YOU...
I'VE NEVER SEEN THIS MANY OF THEM!

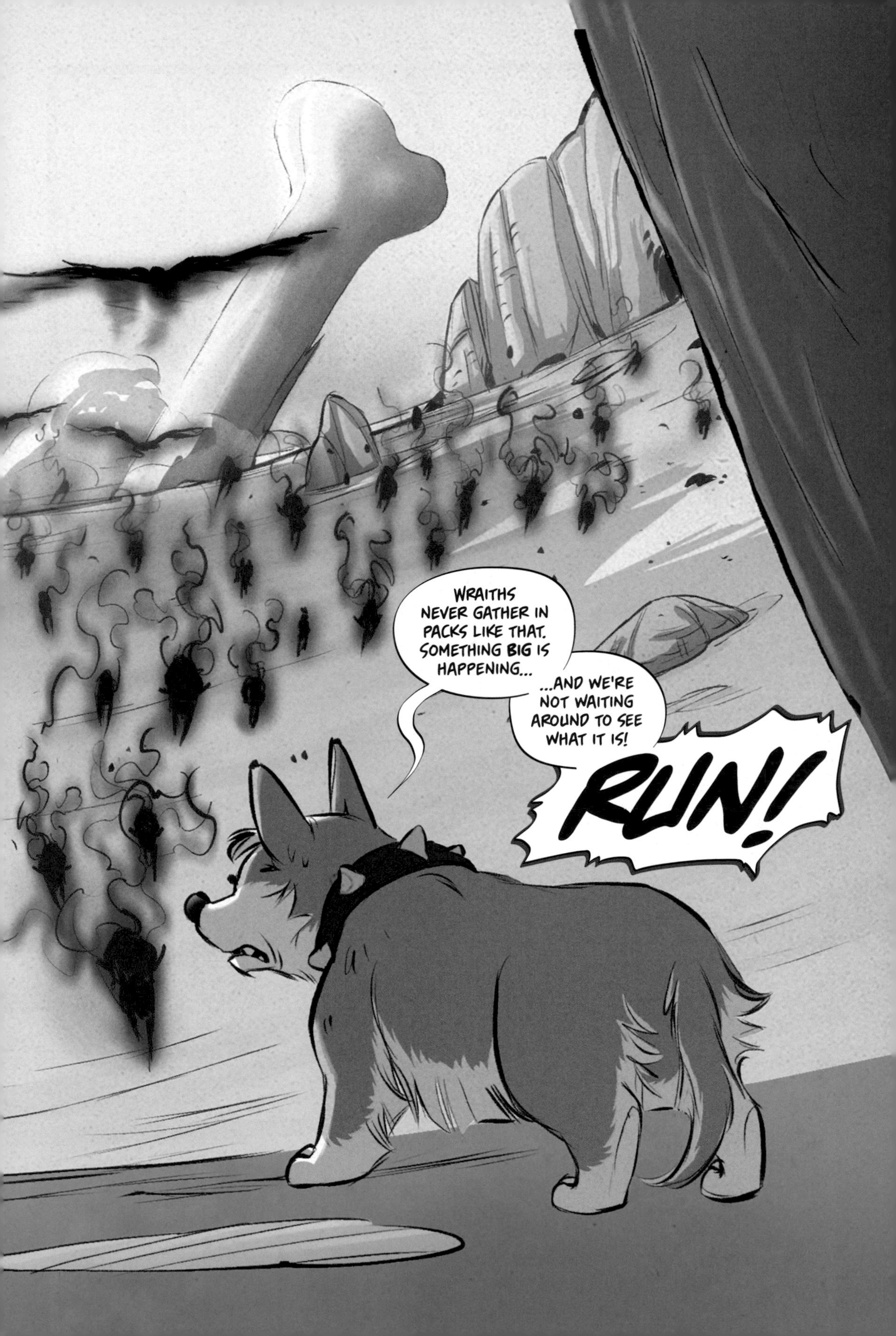
WRAITHS NEVER GATHER IN PACKS LIKE THAT. SOMETHING BIG IS HAPPENING...
...AND WE'RE NOT WAITING AROUND TO SEE WHAT IT IS!
RUN!

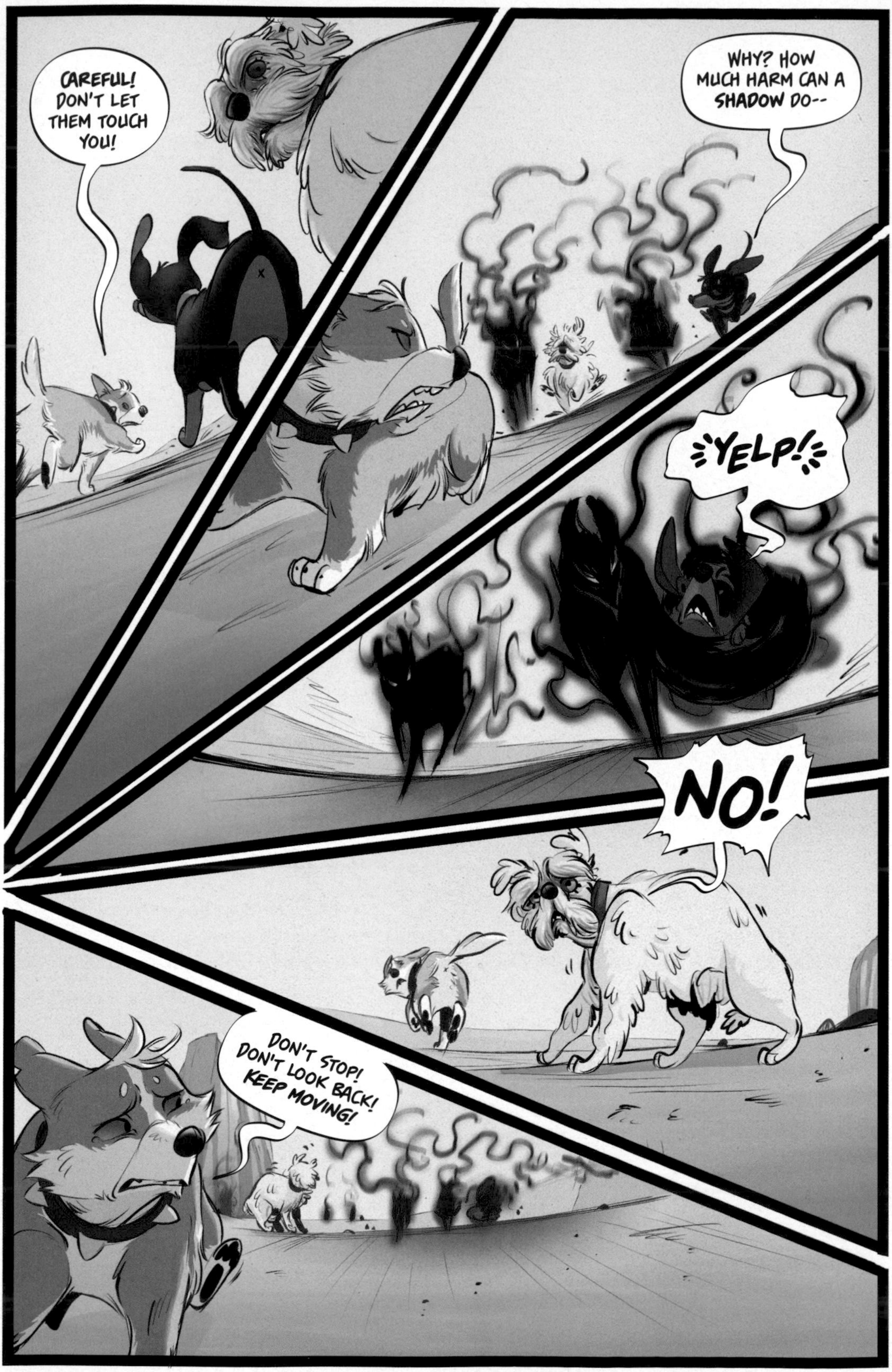
CAREFUL! DON'T LET THEM TOUCH YOU!
WHY? HOW MUCH HARM CAN A SHADOW DO--
YELP!
NO!
DON'T STOP! DON'T LOOK BACK! KEEP MOVING!

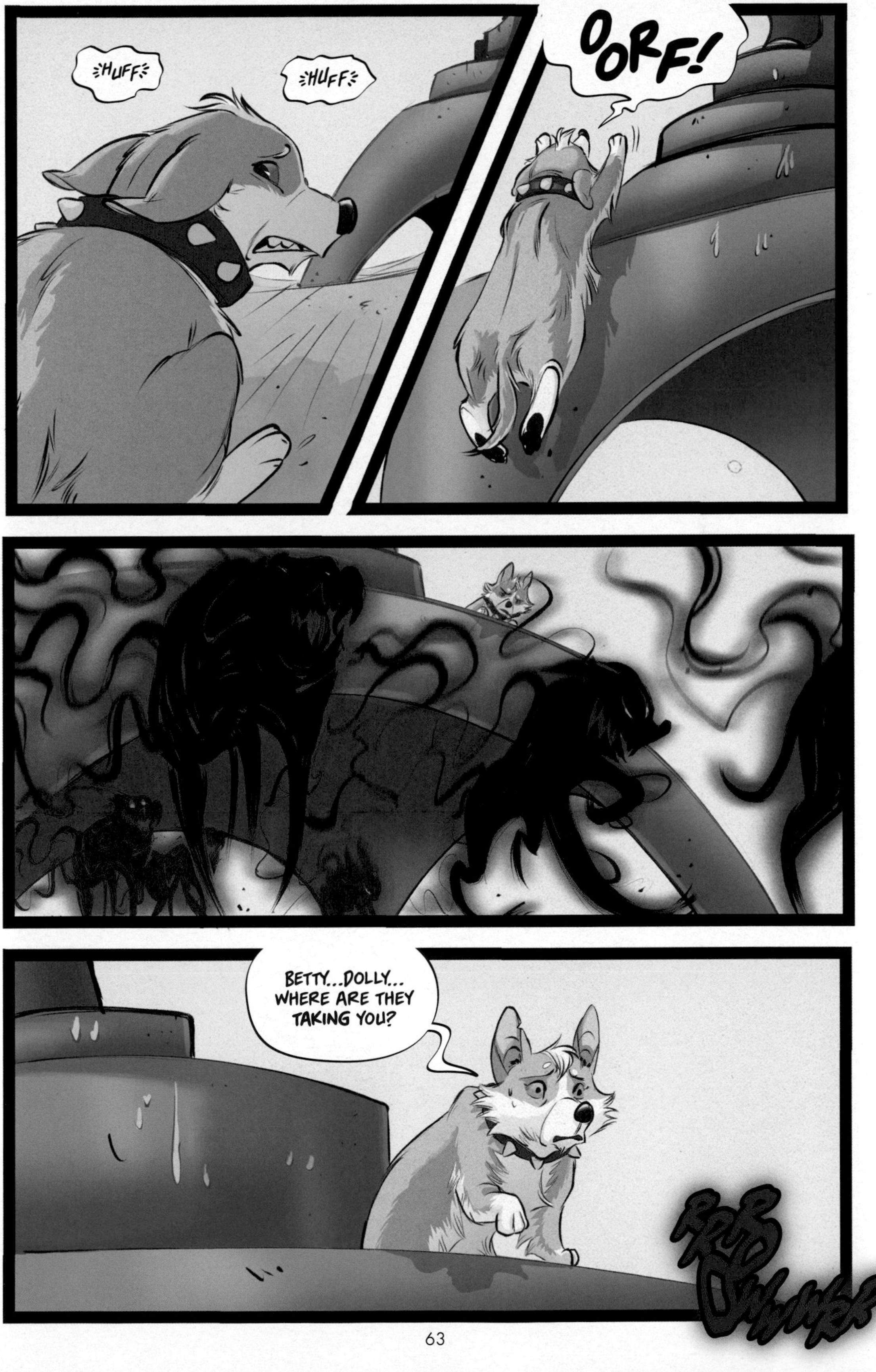
HUFF
HUFF
OOORF!
BETTY...DOLLY... WHERE ARE THEY TAKING YOU?

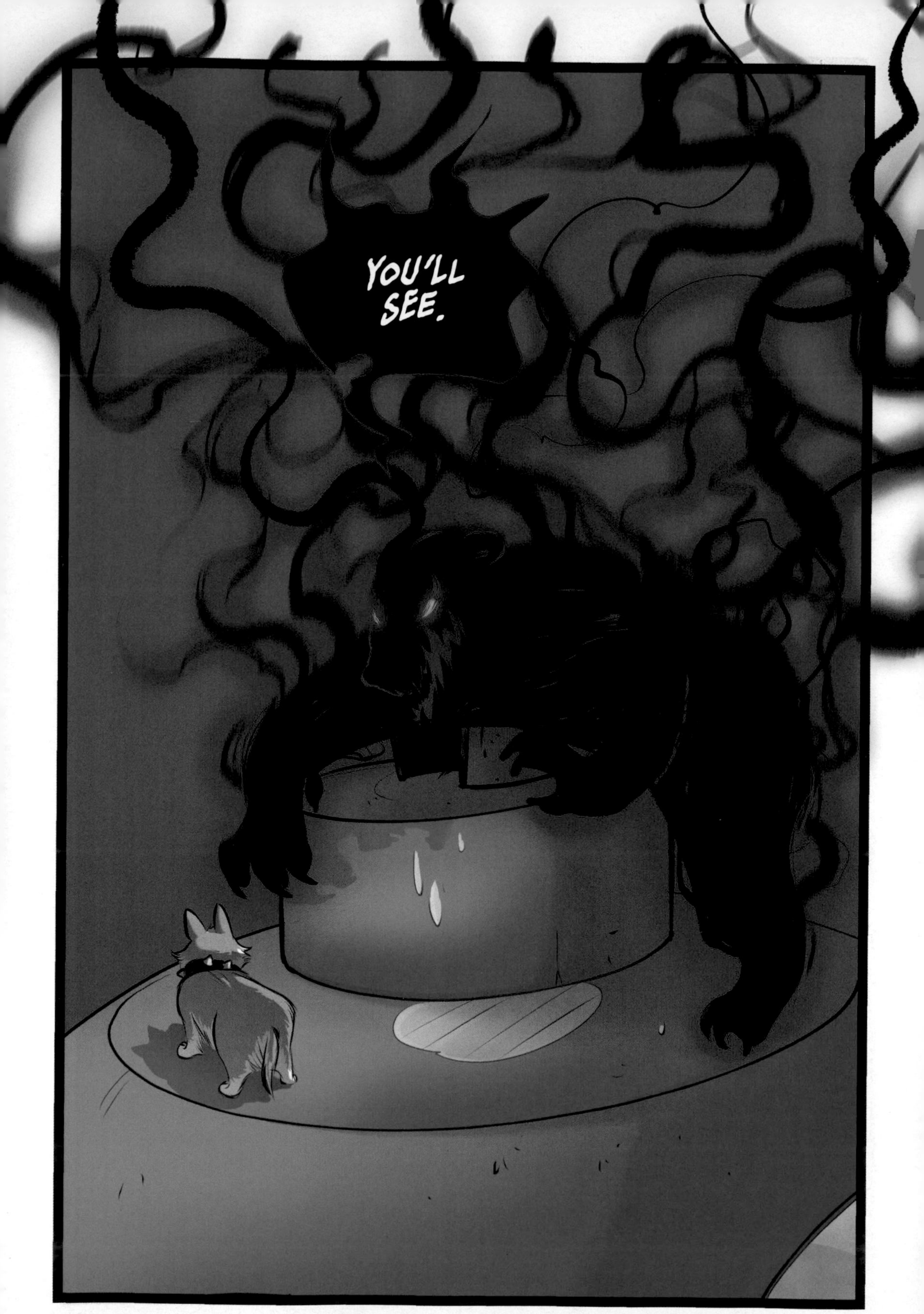
YOU'LL SEE.

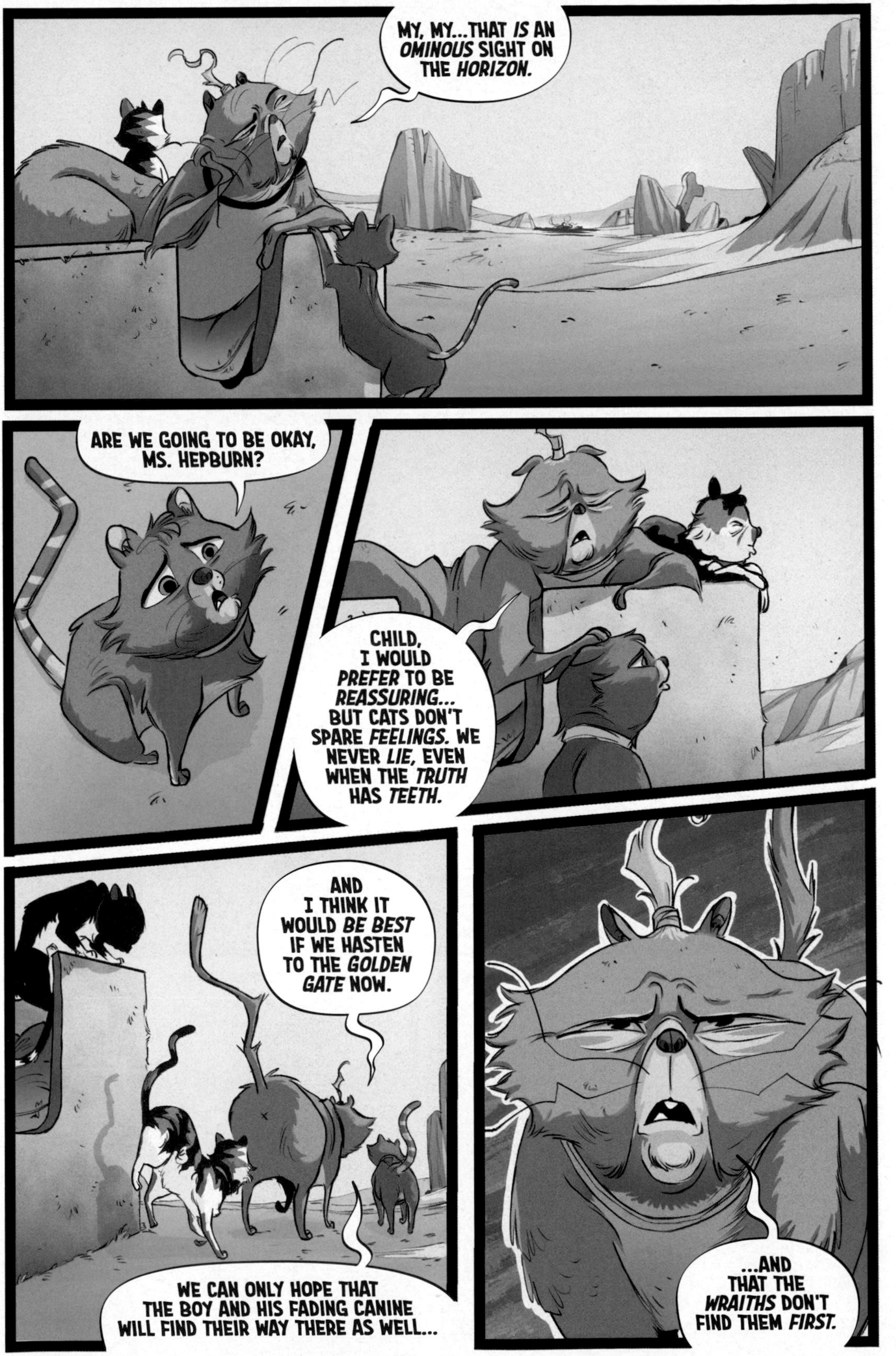
MY, MY...THAT IS AN OMINOUS SIGHT ON THE HORIZON.
ARE WE GOING TO BE OKAY, MS. HEPBURN?
CHILD, I WOULD PREFER TO BE REASSURING... BUT CATS DON'T SPARE FEELINGS. WE NEVER LIE, EVEN WHEN THE TRUTH HAS TEETH.
AND I THINK IT WOULD BE BEST IF WE HASTEN TO THE GOLDEN GATE NOW.
WE CAN ONLY HOPE THAT THE BOY AND HIS FADING CANINE WILL FIND THEIR WAY THERE AS WELL...
...AND THAT THE WRAITHS DON'T FIND THEM FIRST.

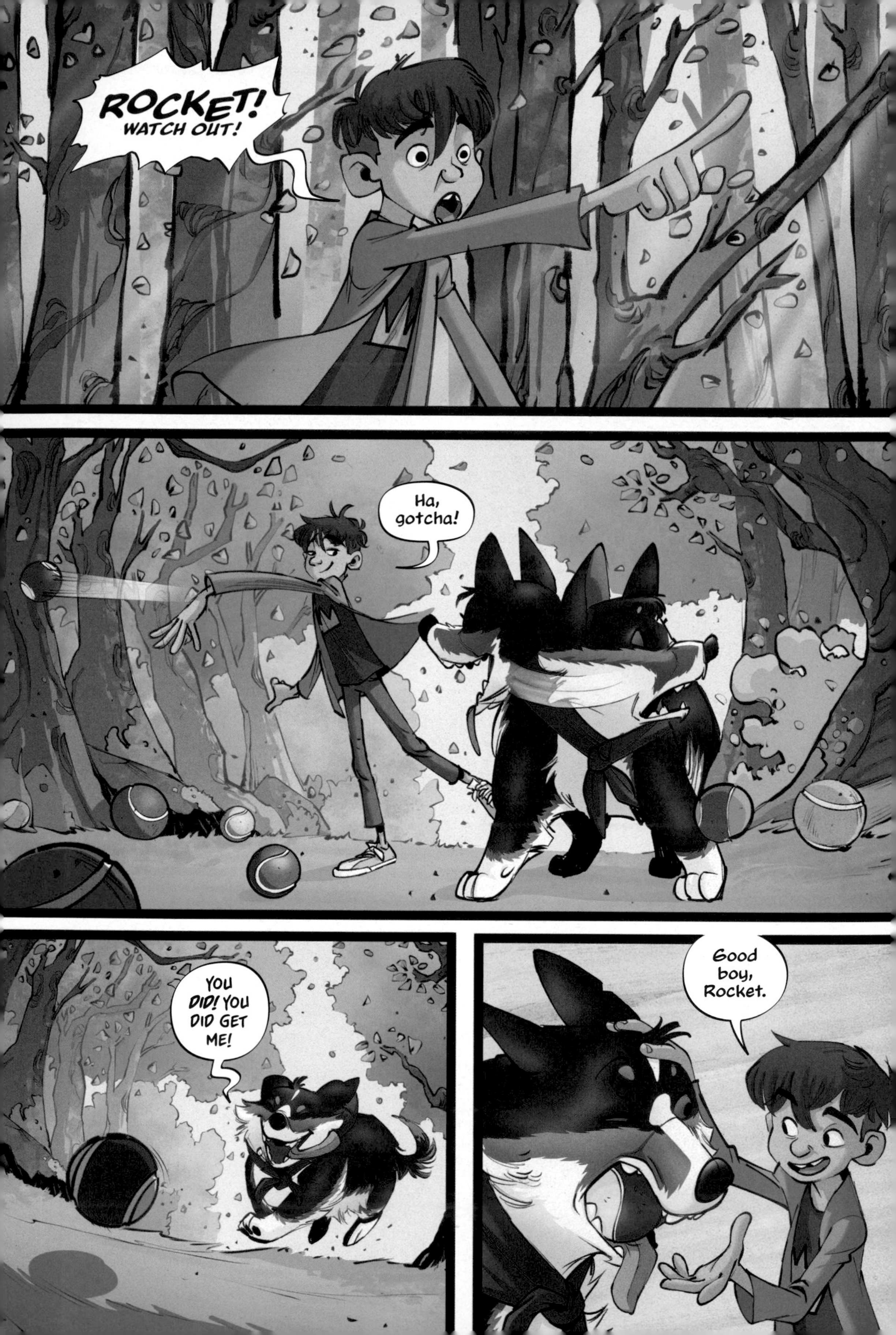
ROCKET!
WATCH OUT!
Ha, gotcha!
YOU DID! YOU DID GET ME!
Good boy, Rocket.

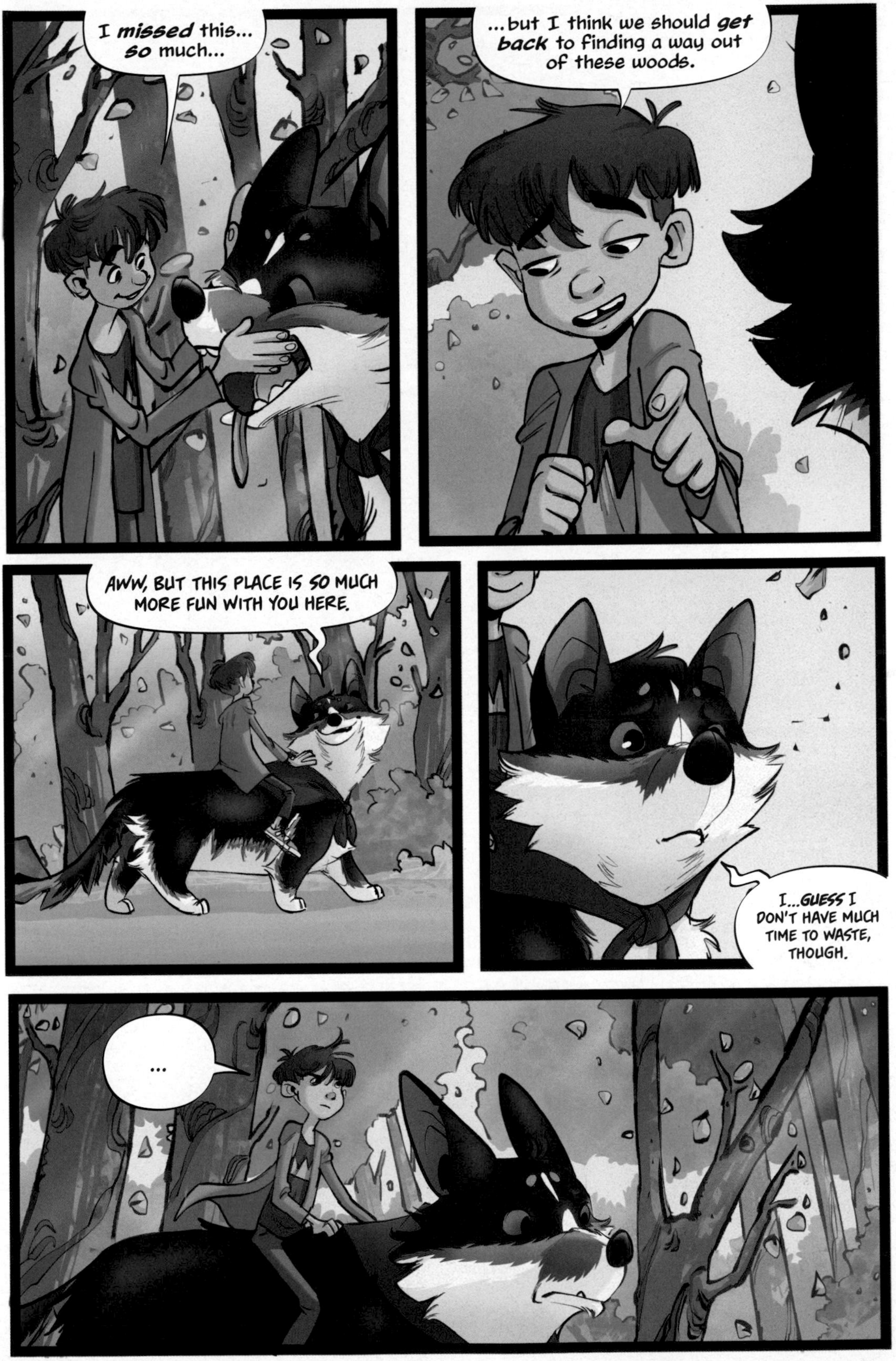
I missed this... so much...
...but I think we should get back to finding a way out of these woods.
AWW, BUT THIS PLACE IS SO MUCH MORE FUN WITH YOU HERE.
I...GUESS I DON'T HAVE MUCH TIME TO WASTE, THOUGH.
...

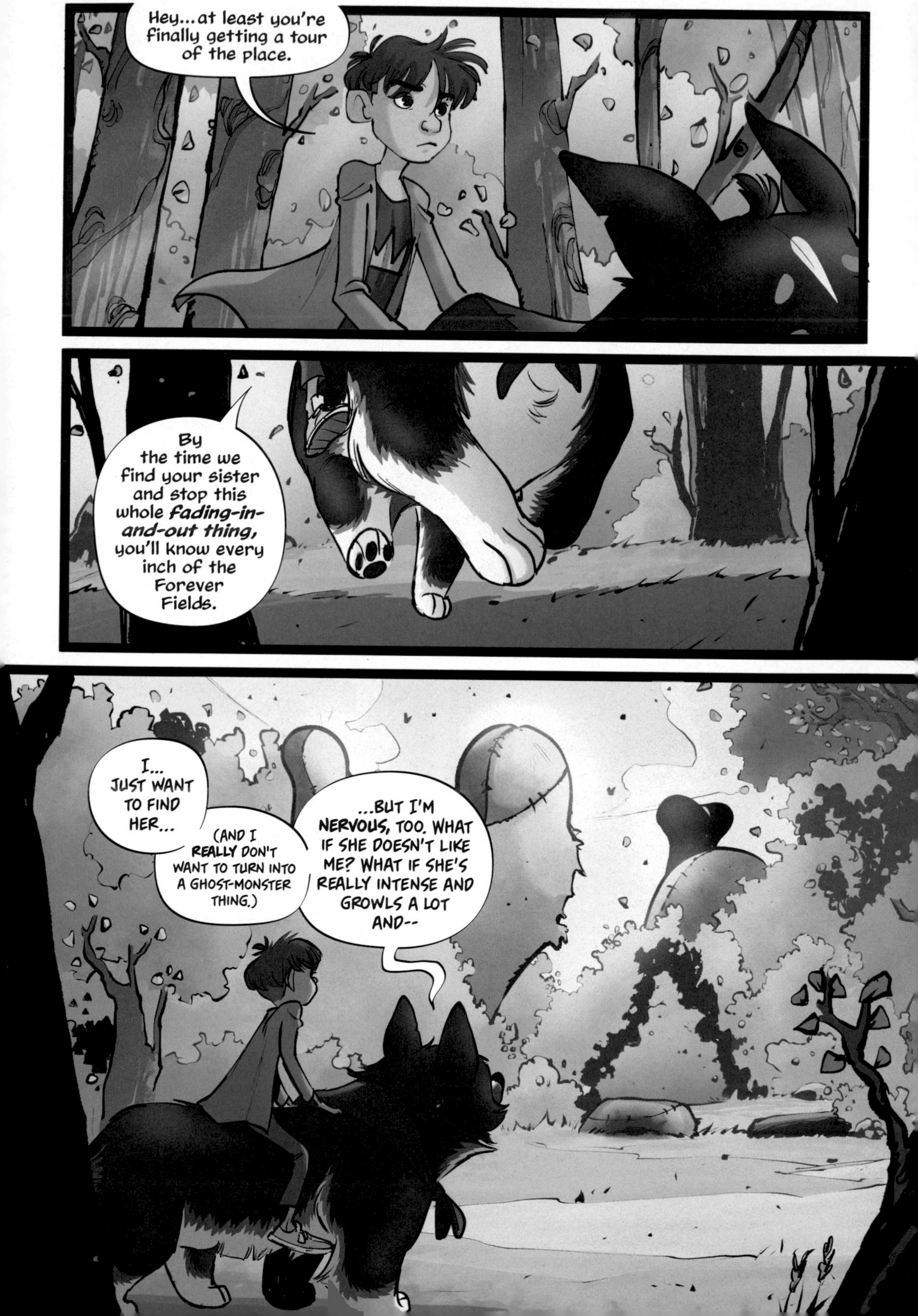
Hey... at least you're finally getting a tour of the place.
By the time we find your sister and stop this whole *fading-in-and-out thing,* you'll know every inch of the Forever Fields.
I... JUST WANT TO FIND HER...
(AND I **REALLY** DON'T WANT TO TURN INTO A GHOST-MONSTER THING.)
...BUT I'M **NERVOUS,** TOO. WHAT IF SHE DOESN'T LIKE ME? WHAT IF SHE'S REALLY INTENSE AND GROWLS A LOT AND--

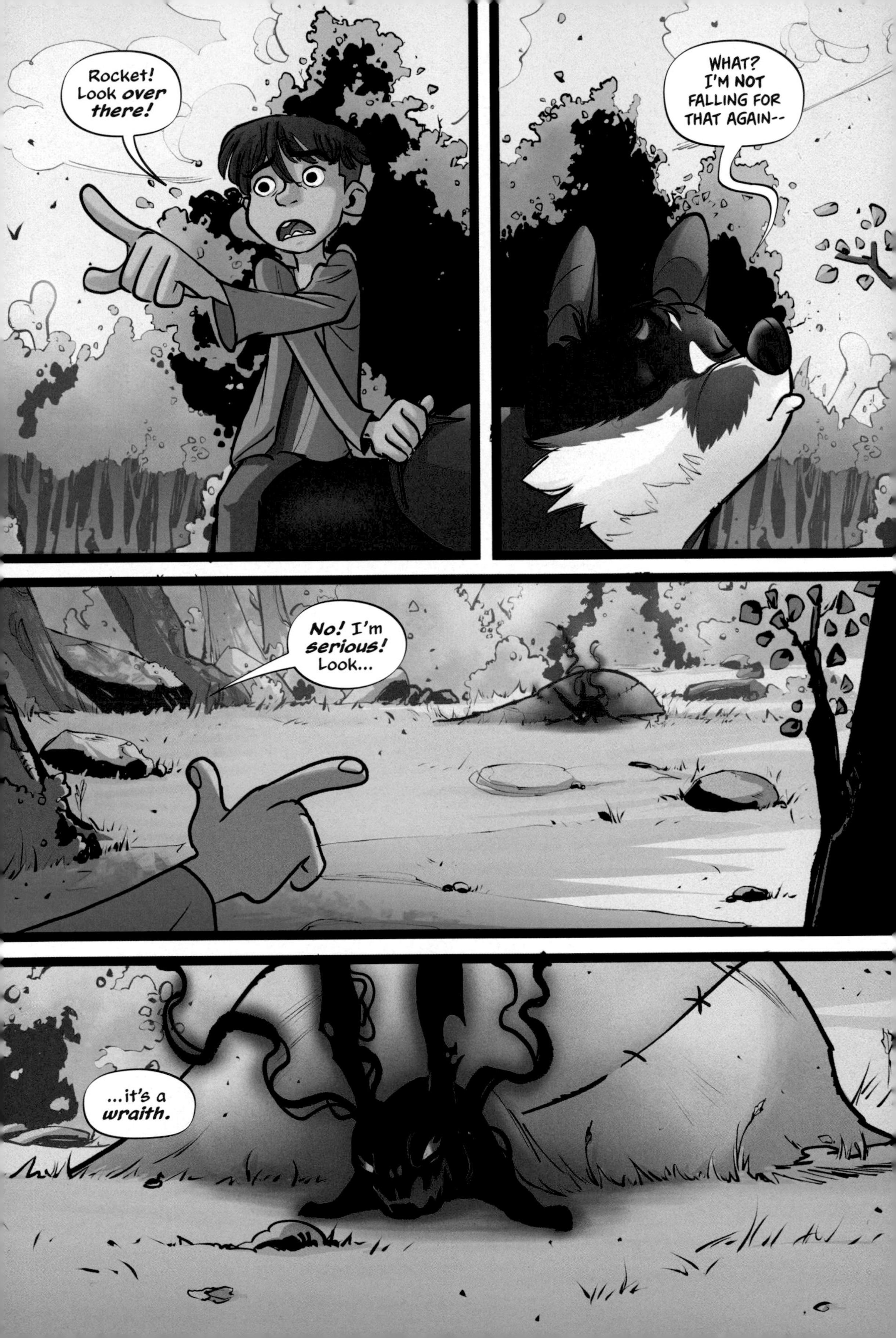
Rocket! Look *over there!*
WHAT? I'M NOT FALLING FOR THAT AGAIN--
No! I'm *serious!* Look...
...it's a *wraith.*

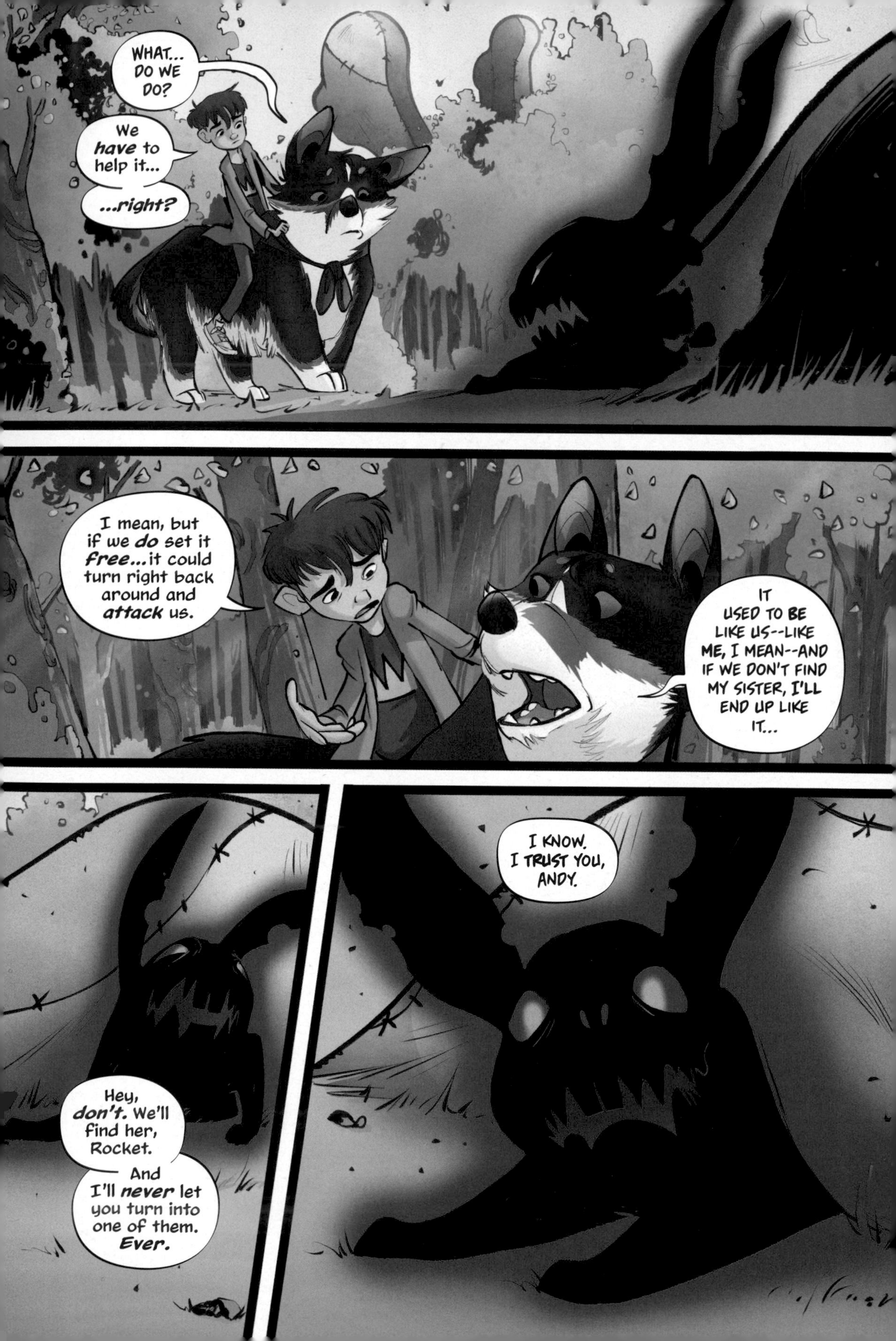
WHAT... DO WE DO?
We *have* to help it...
...right?
I mean, but if we *do* set it *free...* it could turn right back around and *attack* us.
IT USED TO BE LIKE US--LIKE ME, I MEAN--AND IF WE DON'T FIND MY SISTER, I'LL END UP LIKE IT...
I KNOW. I TRUST YOU, ANDY.
Hey, *don't.* We'll find her, Rocket.
And I'll *never* let you turn into one of them. *Ever.*

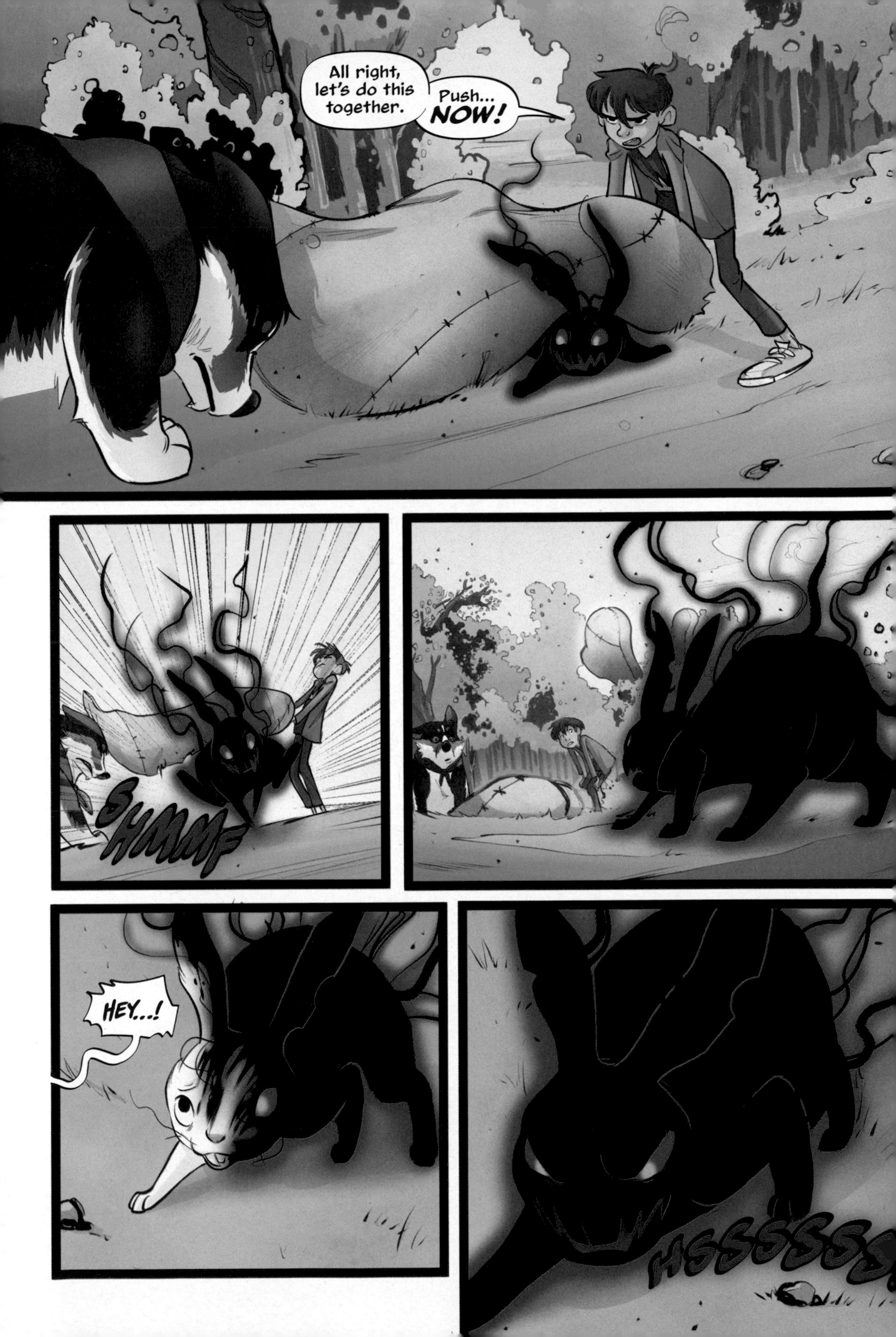
All right, let's do this together.
Push... NOW!
SHMMF
HEY...!
HSSSSSS

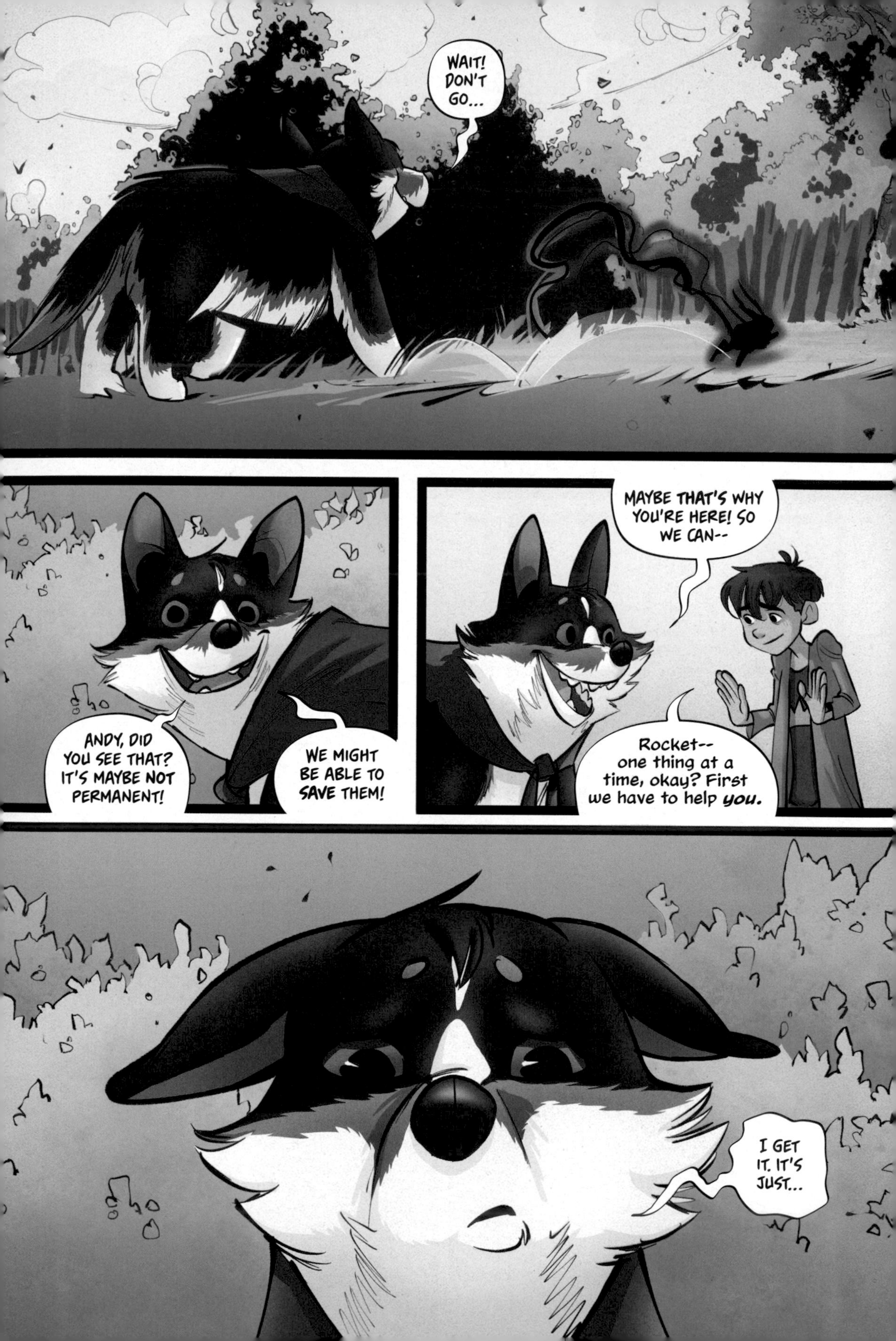
WAIT! DON'T GO...
ANDY, DID YOU SEE THAT? IT'S MAYBE NOT PERMANENT!
WE MIGHT BE ABLE TO SAVE THEM!
MAYBE THAT'S WHY YOU'RE HERE! SO WE CAN--
Rocket-- one thing at a time, okay? First we have to help you.
I GET IT. IT'S JUST...

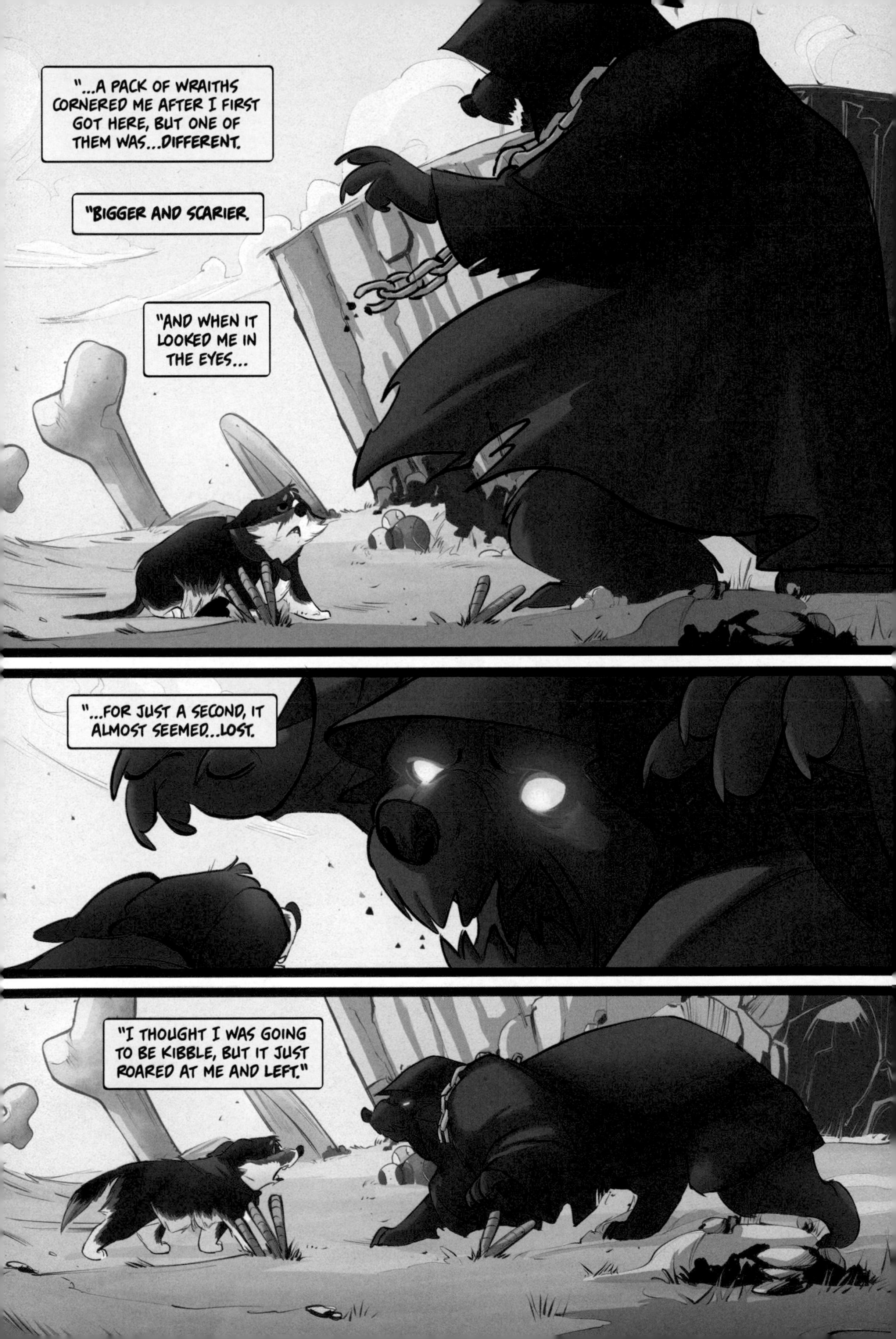
"...A PACK OF WRAITHS CORNERED ME AFTER I FIRST GOT HERE, BUT ONE OF THEM WAS...DIFFERENT.
"BIGGER AND SCARIER.
"AND WHEN IT LOOKED ME IN THE EYES...
"...FOR JUST A SECOND, IT ALMOST SEEMED...LOST.
"I THOUGHT I WAS GOING TO BE KIBBLE, BUT IT JUST ROARED AT ME AND LEFT."

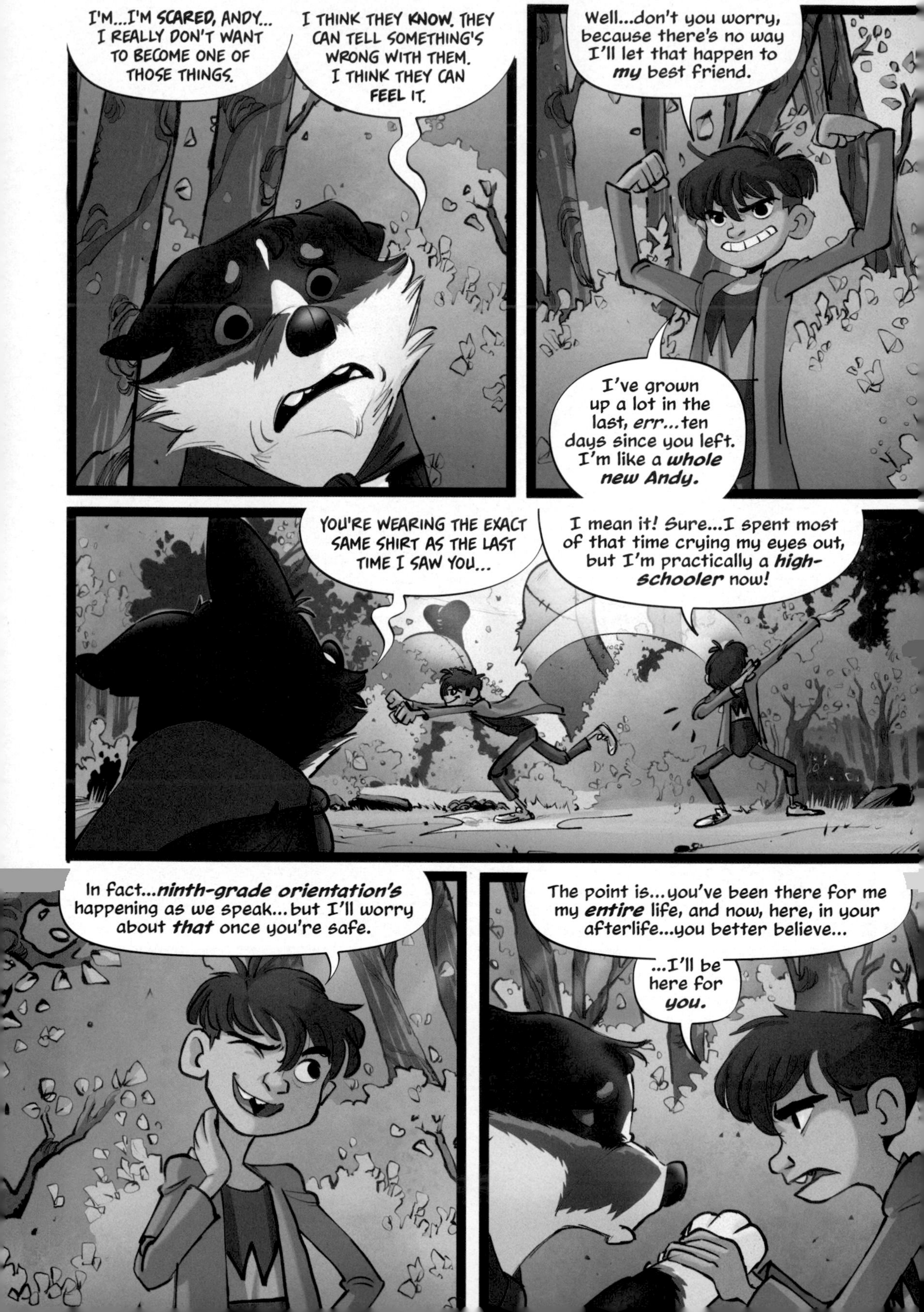
I'M...I'M SCARED, ANDY... I REALLY DON'T WANT TO BECOME ONE OF THOSE THINGS.
I THINK THEY KNOW. THEY CAN TELL SOMETHING'S WRONG WITH THEM. I THINK THEY CAN FEEL IT.
Well...don't you worry, because there's no way I'll let that happen to my best friend.
I've grown up a lot in the last, err...ten days since you left. I'm like a whole new Andy.
YOU'RE WEARING THE EXACT SAME SHIRT AS THE LAST TIME I SAW YOU...
I mean it! Sure...I spent most of that time crying my eyes out, but I'm practically a high-schooler now!
In fact...ninth-grade orientation's happening as we speak...but I'll worry about that once you're safe.
The point is...you've been there for me my entire life, and now, here, in your afterlife...you better believe...
...I'll be here for you.

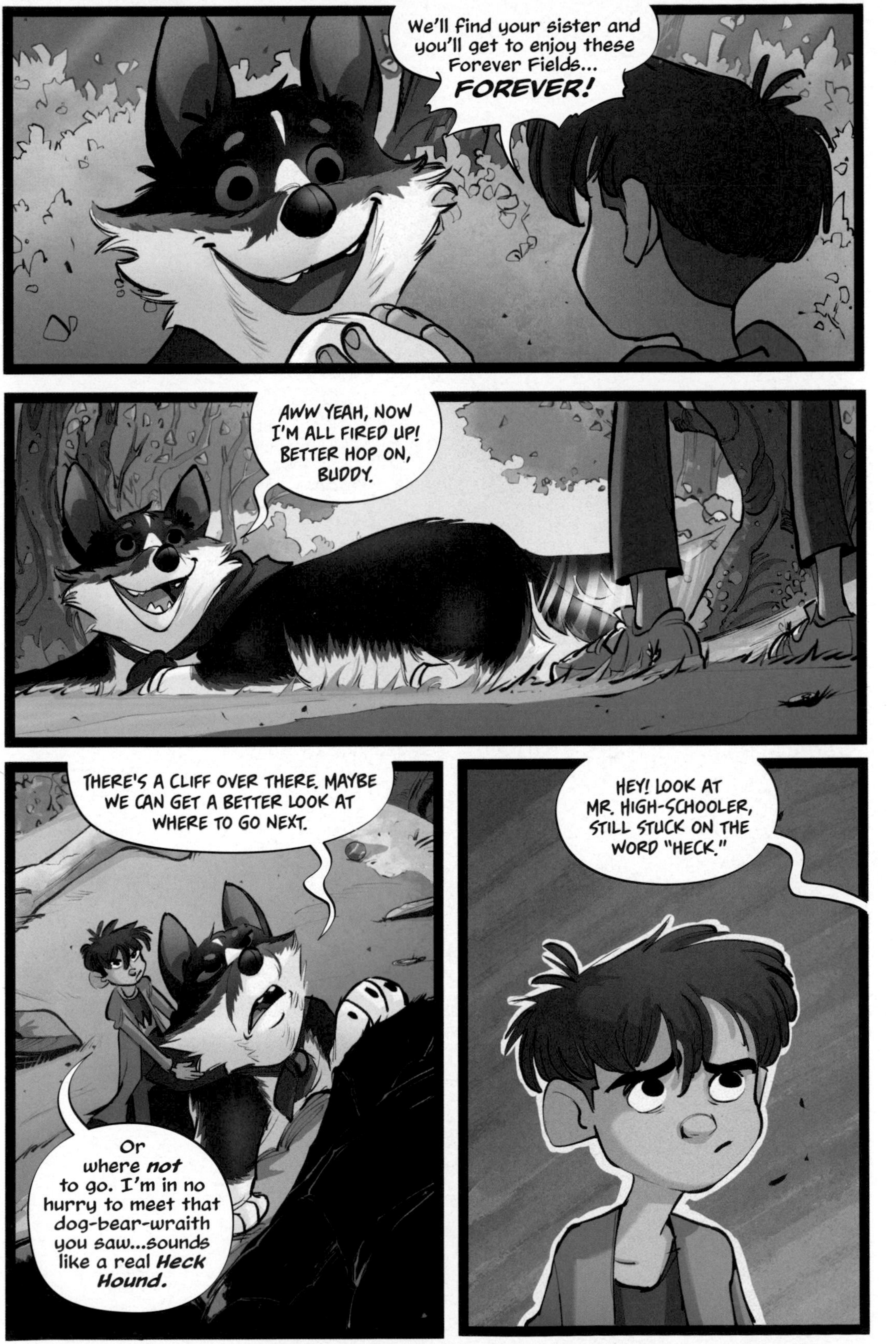

We'll find your sister and you'll get to enjoy these Forever Fields... **FOREVER!**
AWW YEAH, NOW I'M ALL FIRED UP! BETTER HOP ON, BUDDY.
THERE'S A CLIFF OVER THERE. MAYBE WE CAN GET A BETTER LOOK AT WHERE TO GO NEXT.
Or where ***not*** to go. I'm in no hurry to meet that dog-bear-wraith you saw...sounds like a real ***Heck Hound.***
HEY! LOOK AT MR. HIGH-SCHOOLER, STILL STUCK ON THE WORD "HECK."

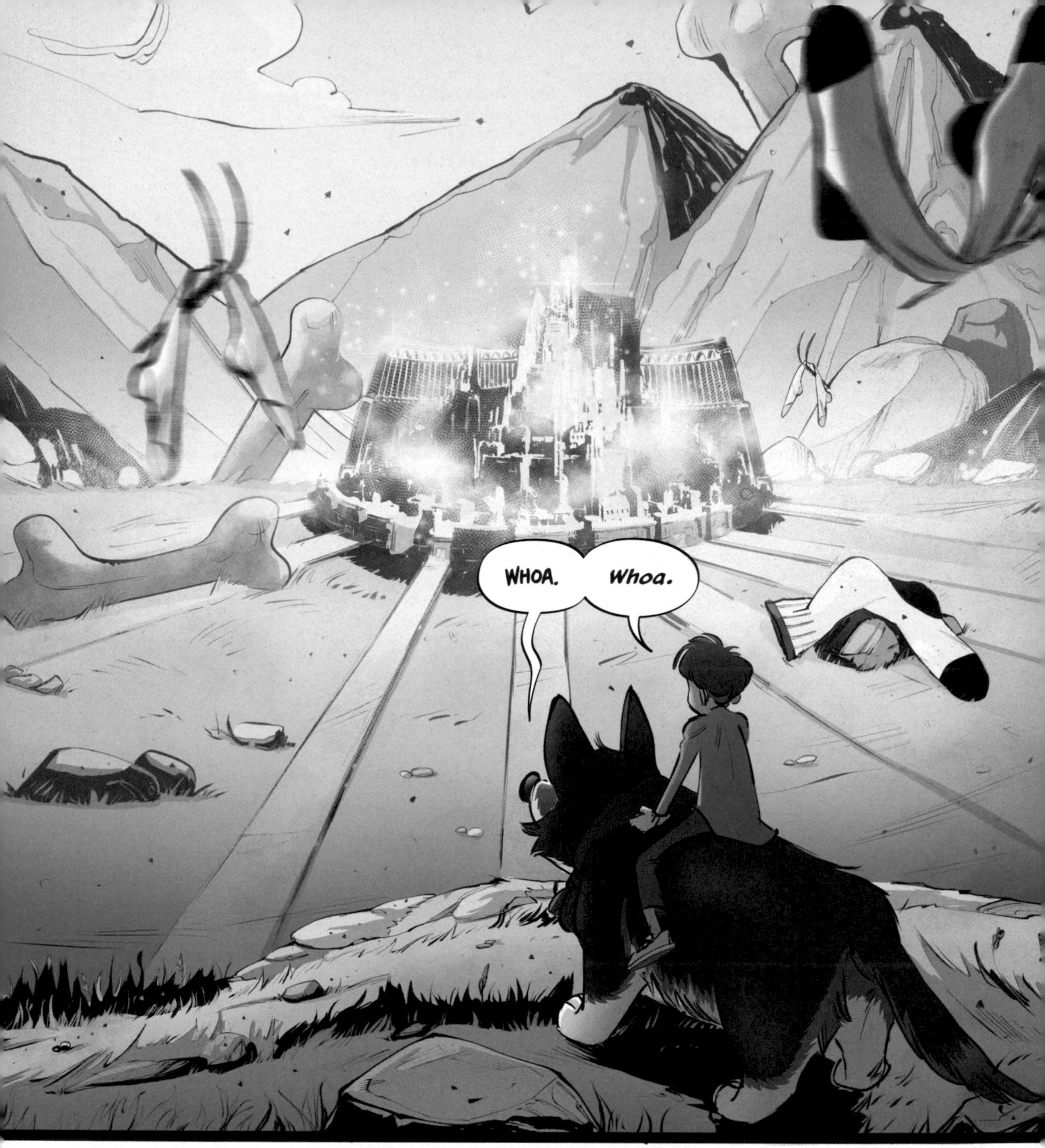
WHOA.
Whoa.

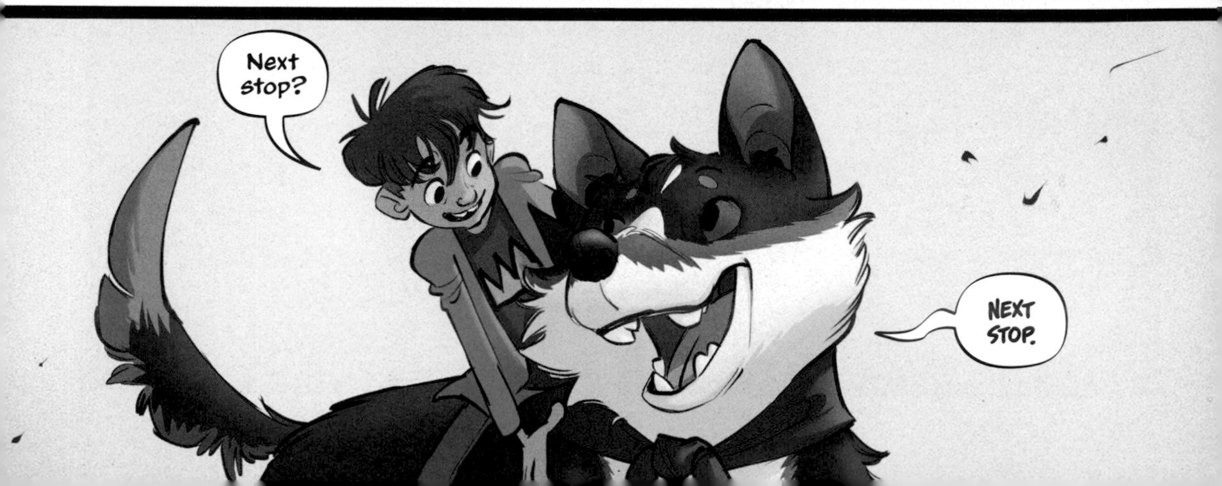
Next stop?
NEXT STOP.

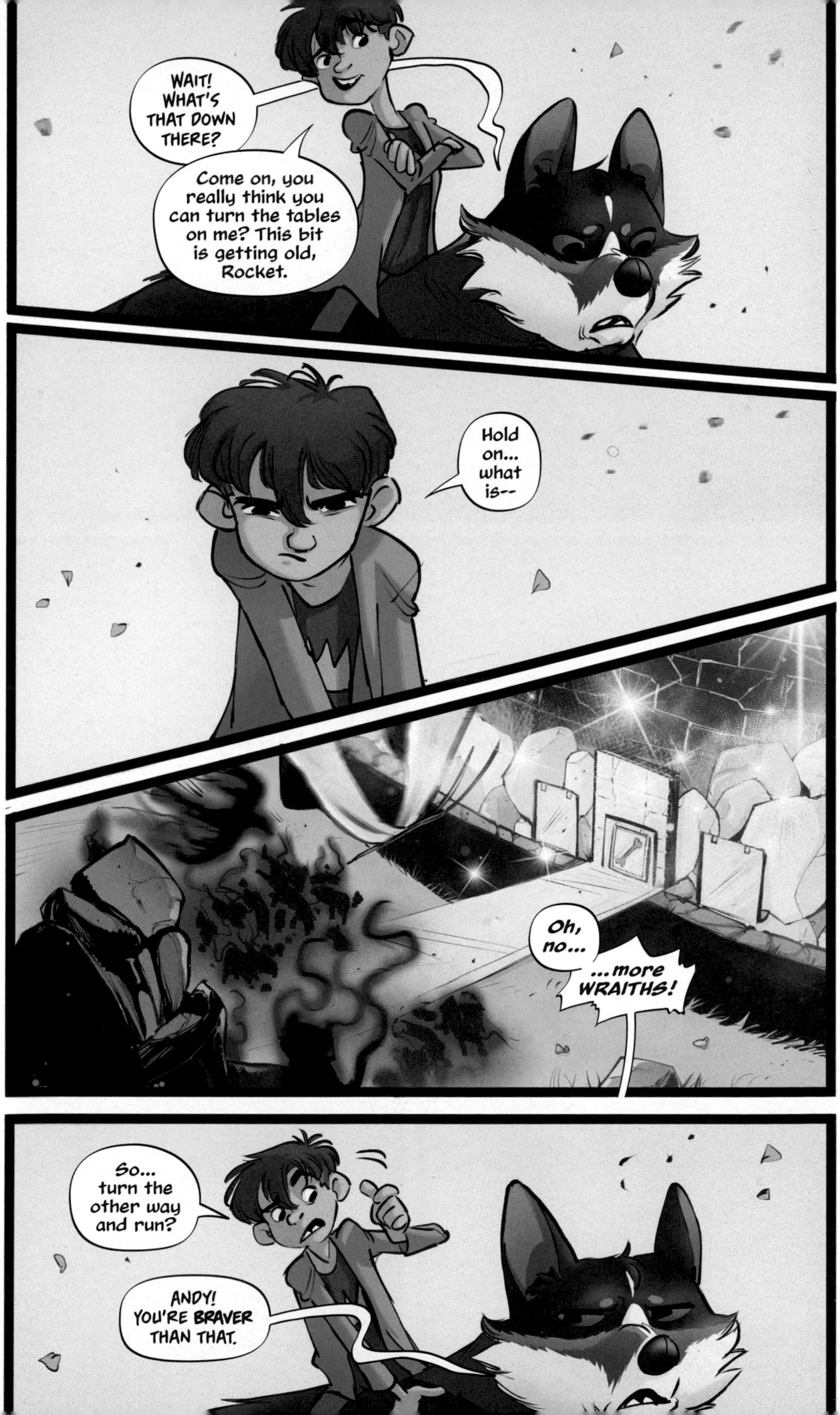
WAIT! WHAT'S THAT DOWN THERE?
Come on, you really think you can turn the tables on me? This bit is getting old, Rocket.
Hold on... what is--
Oh, no...
...more WRAITHS!
So... turn the other way and run?
ANDY! YOU'RE BRAVER THAN THAT.

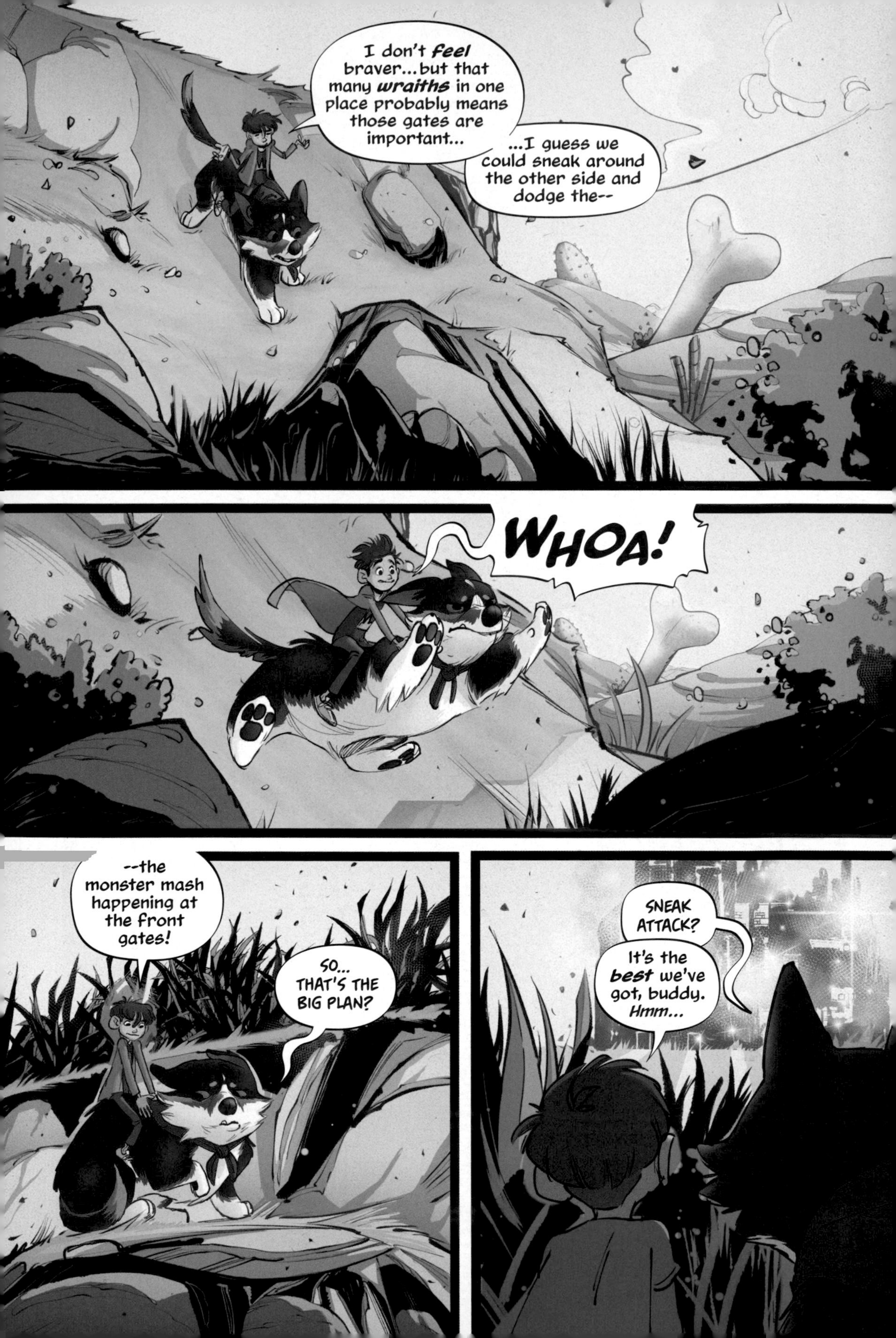
I don't *feel* braver...but that many *wraiths* in one place probably means those gates are important...
...I guess we could sneak around the other side and dodge the--
WHOA!
--the monster mash happening at the front gates!
SO... THAT'S THE BIG PLAN?
SNEAK ATTACK?
It's the *best* we've got, buddy. *Hmm...*

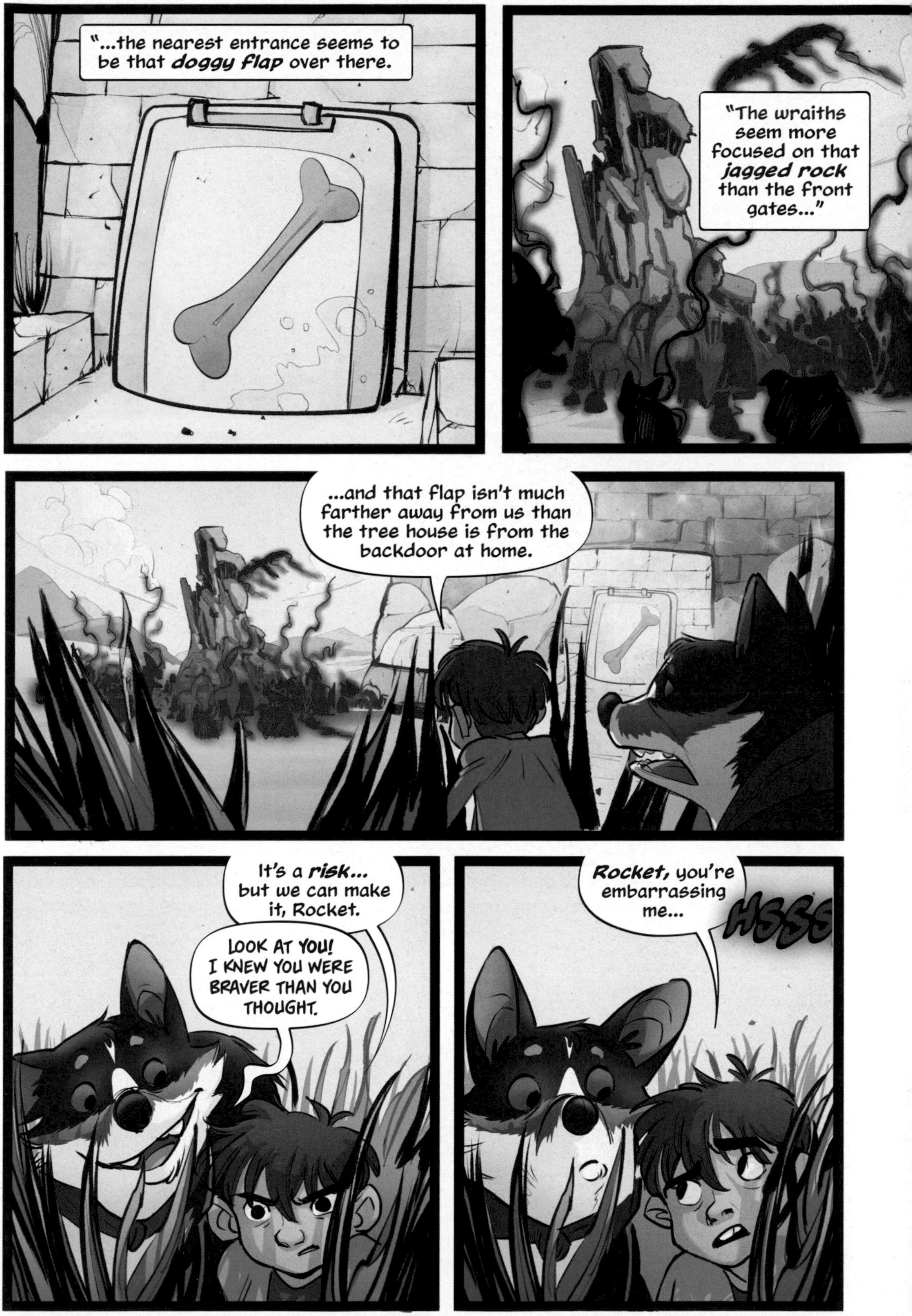
"...the nearest entrance seems to be that doggy flap over there.
"The wraiths seem more focused on that jagged rock than the front gates..."
...and that flap isn't much farther away from us than the tree house is from the backdoor at home.
It's a risk... but we can make it, Rocket.
LOOK AT YOU! I KNEW YOU WERE BRAVER THAN YOU THOUGHT.
Rocket, you're embarrassing me...
HSSS

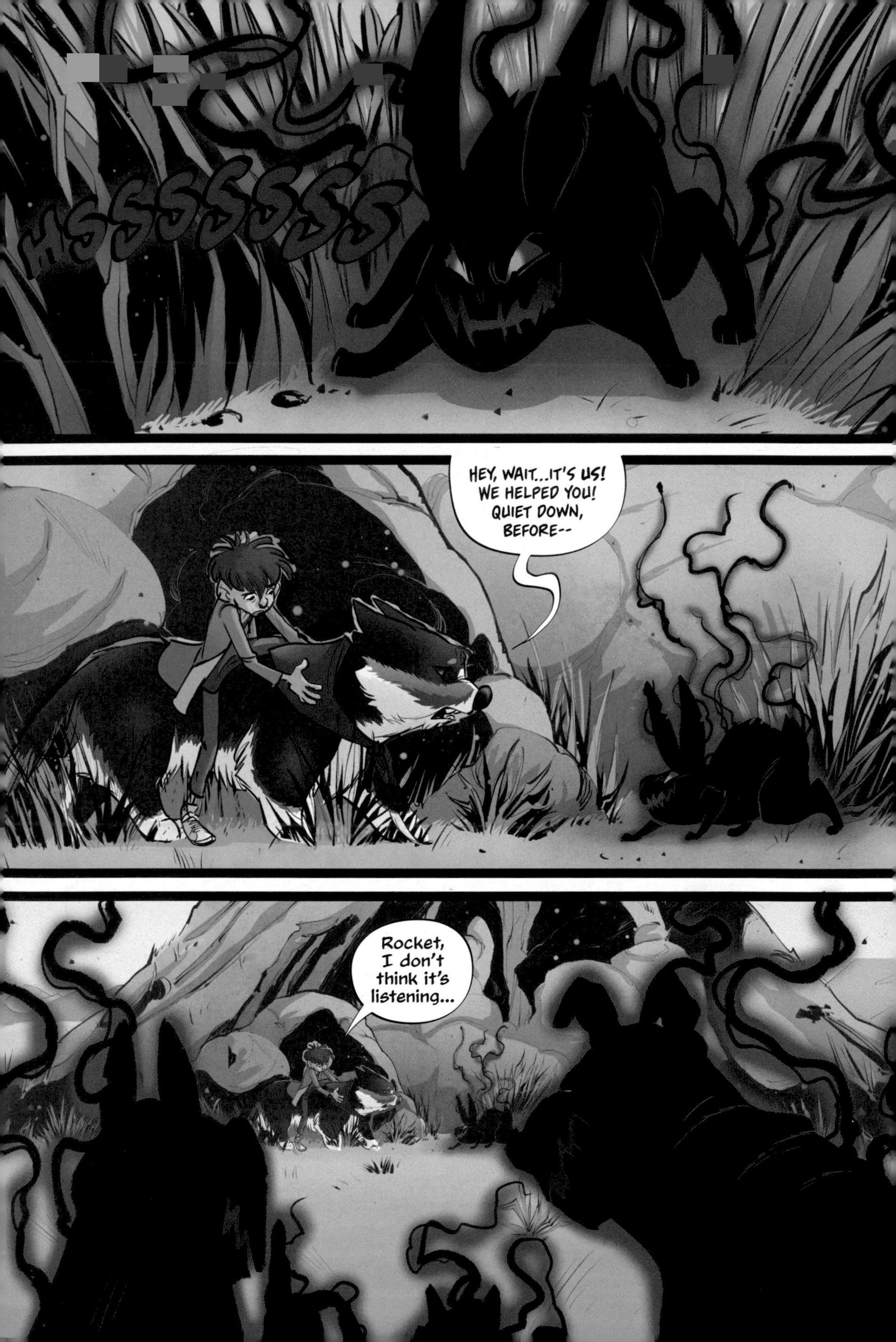
HSSSSSSS
HEY, WAIT...IT'S US! WE HELPED YOU! QUIET DOWN, BEFORE--
Rocket, I don't think it's listening...

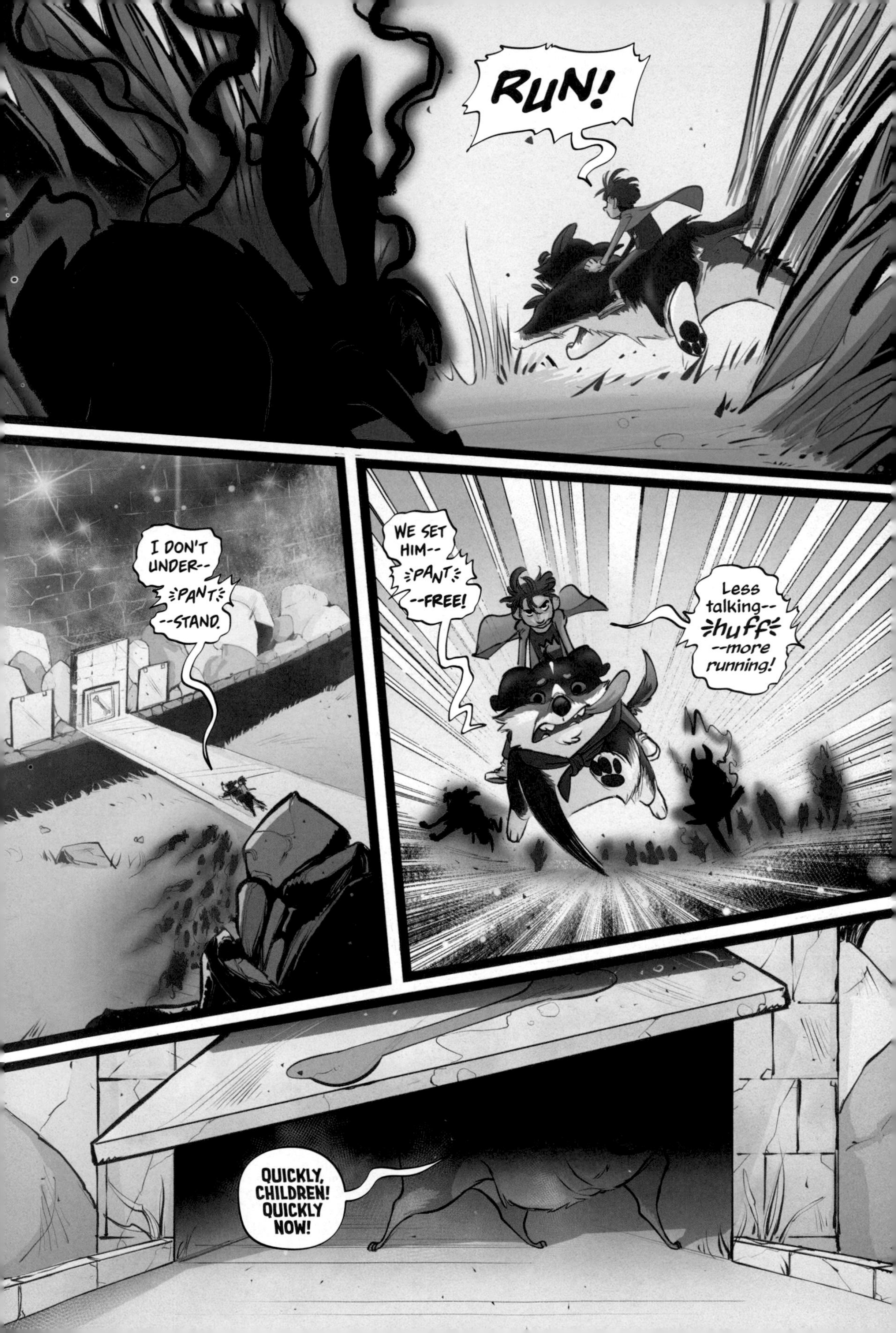
RUN!
I DON'T UNDER-- PANT --STAND.
WE SET HIM-- PANT --FREE!
Less talking-- huff --more running!
QUICKLY, CHILDREN! QUICKLY NOW!

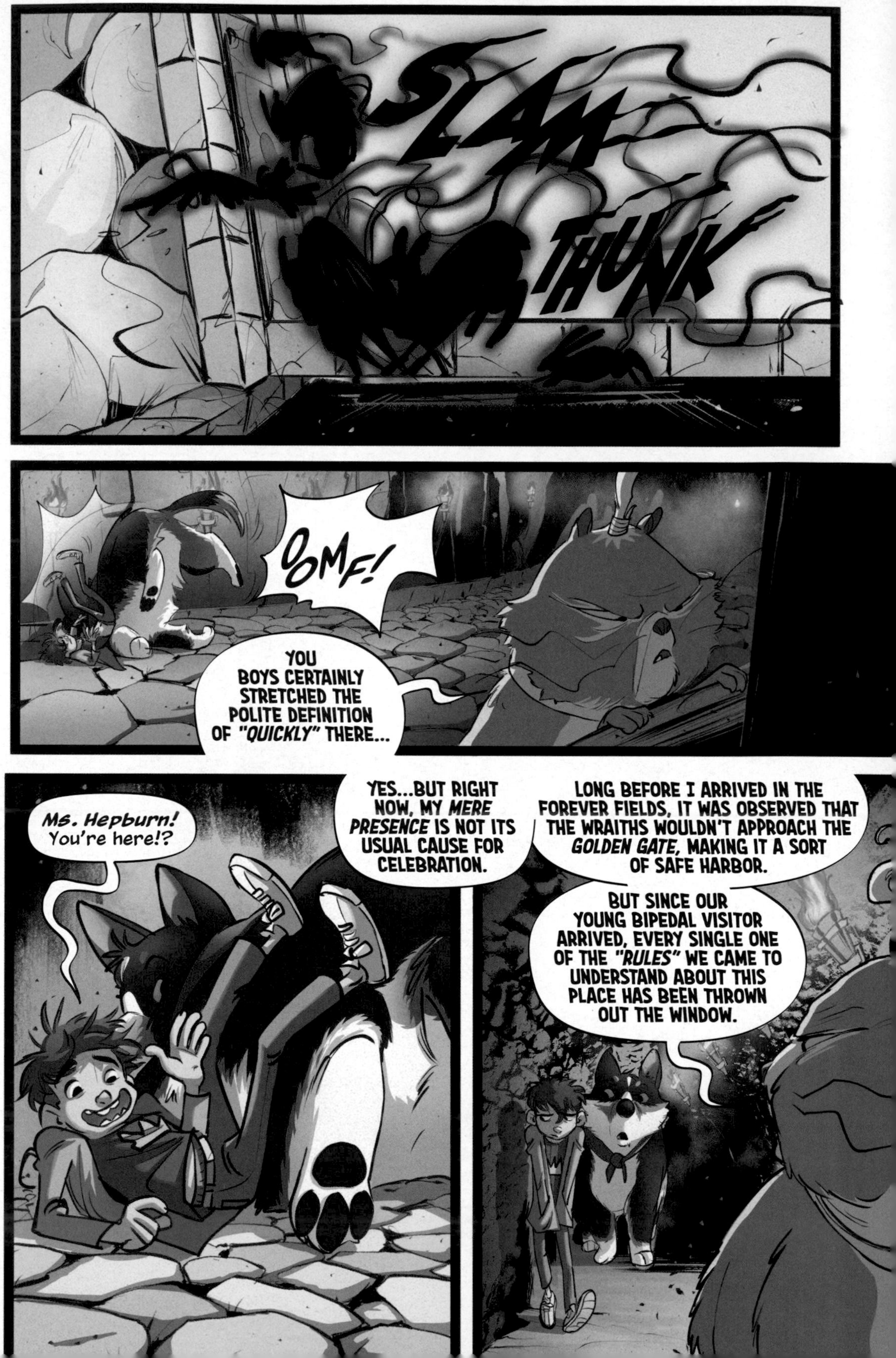
SLAM
THUNK
OOMF!
YOU BOYS CERTAINLY STRETCHED THE POLITE DEFINITION OF "QUICKLY" THERE...
Ms. Hepburn! You're here!?
YES...BUT RIGHT NOW, MY MERE PRESENCE IS NOT ITS USUAL CAUSE FOR CELEBRATION.
LONG BEFORE I ARRIVED IN THE FOREVER FIELDS, IT WAS OBSERVED THAT THE WRAITHS WOULDN'T APPROACH THE GOLDEN GATE, MAKING IT A SORT OF SAFE HARBOR.
BUT SINCE OUR YOUNG BIPEDAL VISITOR ARRIVED, EVERY SINGLE ONE OF THE "RULES" WE CAME TO UNDERSTAND ABOUT THIS PLACE HAS BEEN THROWN OUT THE WINDOW.

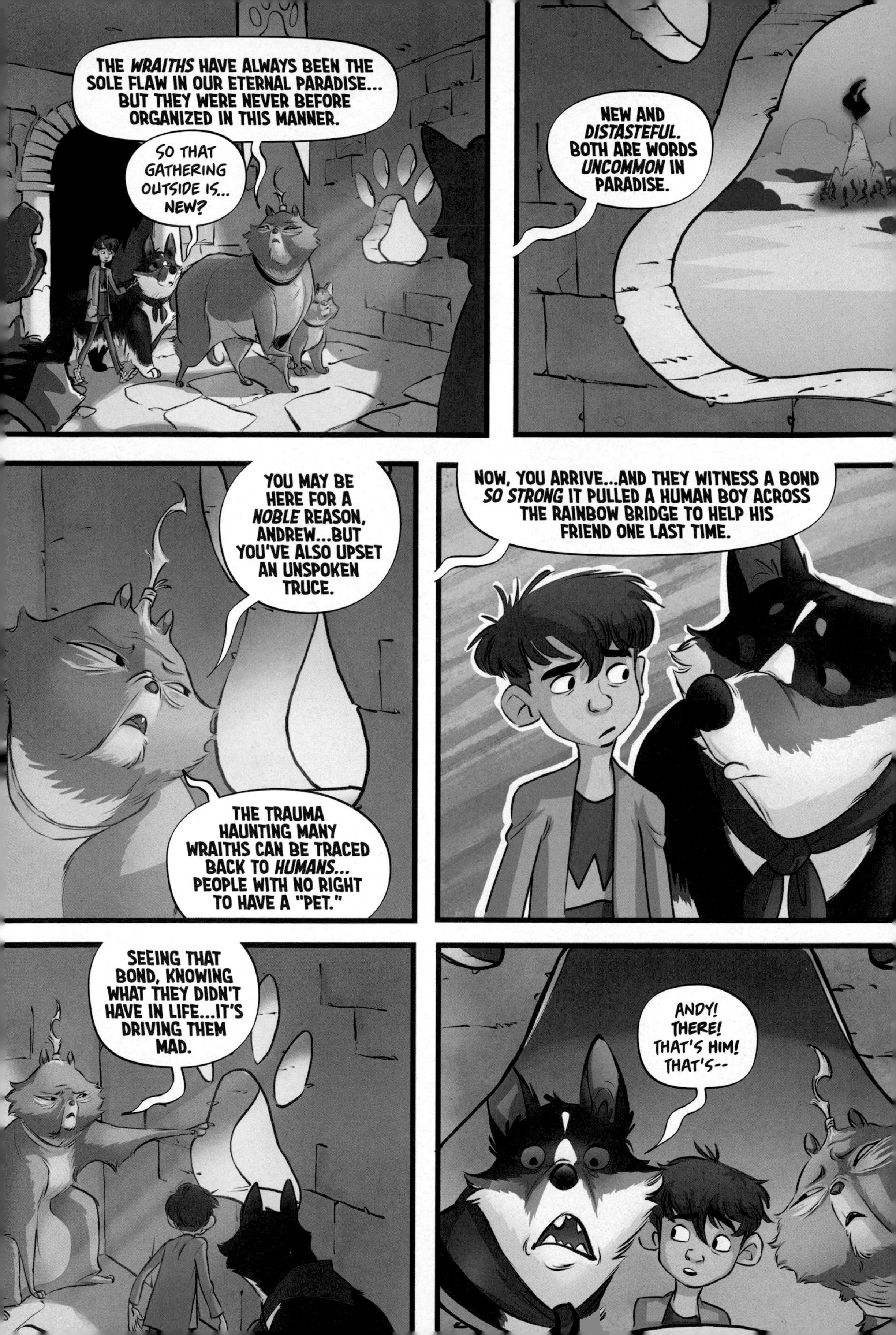
THE *WRAITHS* HAVE ALWAYS BEEN THE SOLE FLAW IN OUR ETERNAL PARADISE... BUT THEY WERE NEVER BEFORE ORGANIZED IN THIS MANNER.
SO THAT GATHERING OUTSIDE IS... NEW?
NEW AND *DISTASTEFUL.* BOTH ARE WORDS *UNCOMMON* IN PARADISE.
YOU MAY BE HERE FOR A *NOBLE* REASON, ANDREW...BUT YOU'VE ALSO UPSET AN UNSPOKEN TRUCE.
THE TRAUMA HAUNTING MANY WRAITHS CAN BE TRACED BACK TO *HUMANS...* PEOPLE WITH NO RIGHT TO HAVE A "PET."
NOW, YOU ARRIVE...AND THEY WITNESS A BOND *SO STRONG* IT PULLED A HUMAN BOY ACROSS THE RAINBOW BRIDGE TO HELP HIS FRIEND ONE LAST TIME.
SEEING THAT BOND, KNOWING WHAT THEY DIDN'T HAVE IN LIFE...IT'S DRIVING THEM MAD.
ANDY! THERE! THAT'S HIM! THAT'S--

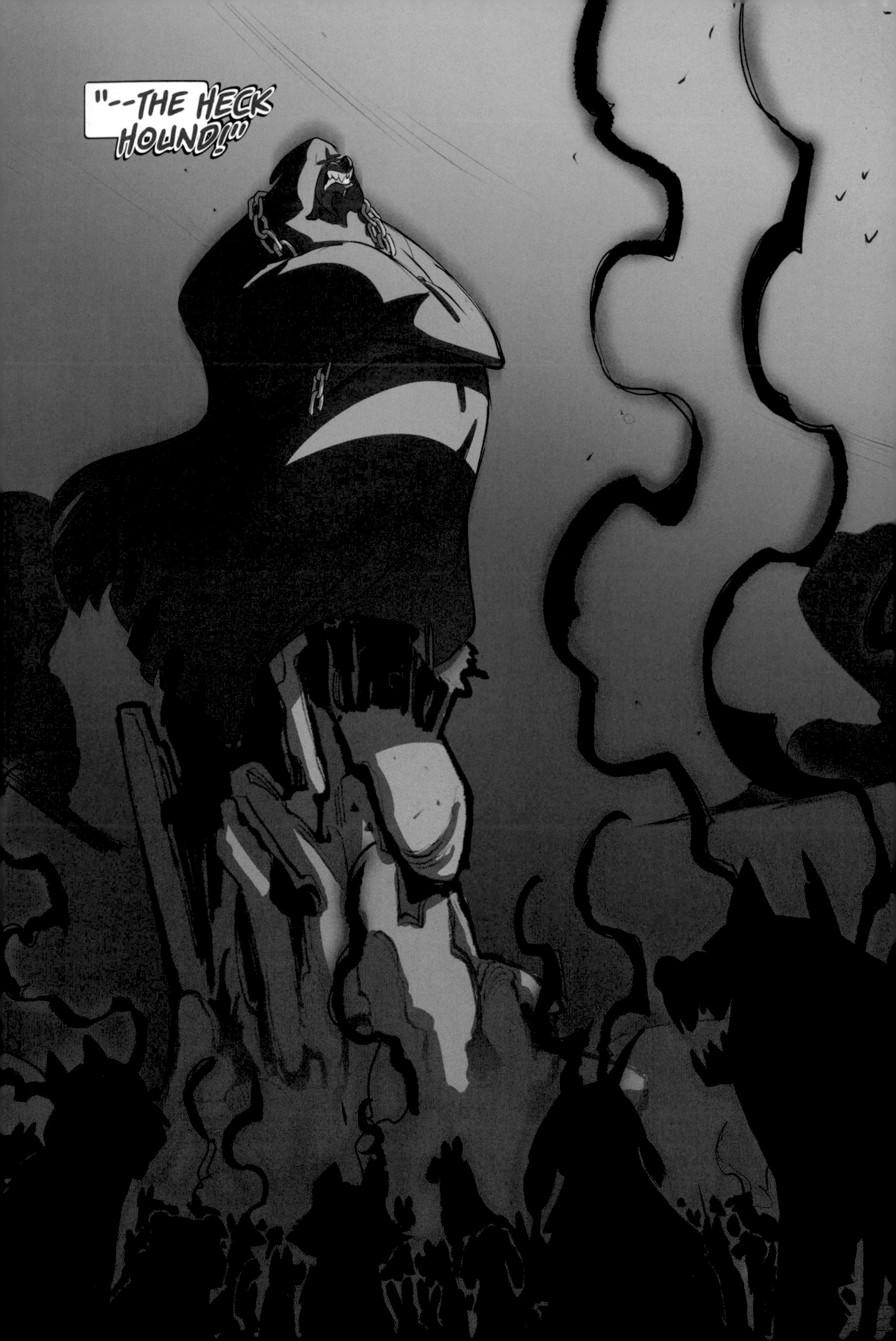
"--THE HECK HOUND!"

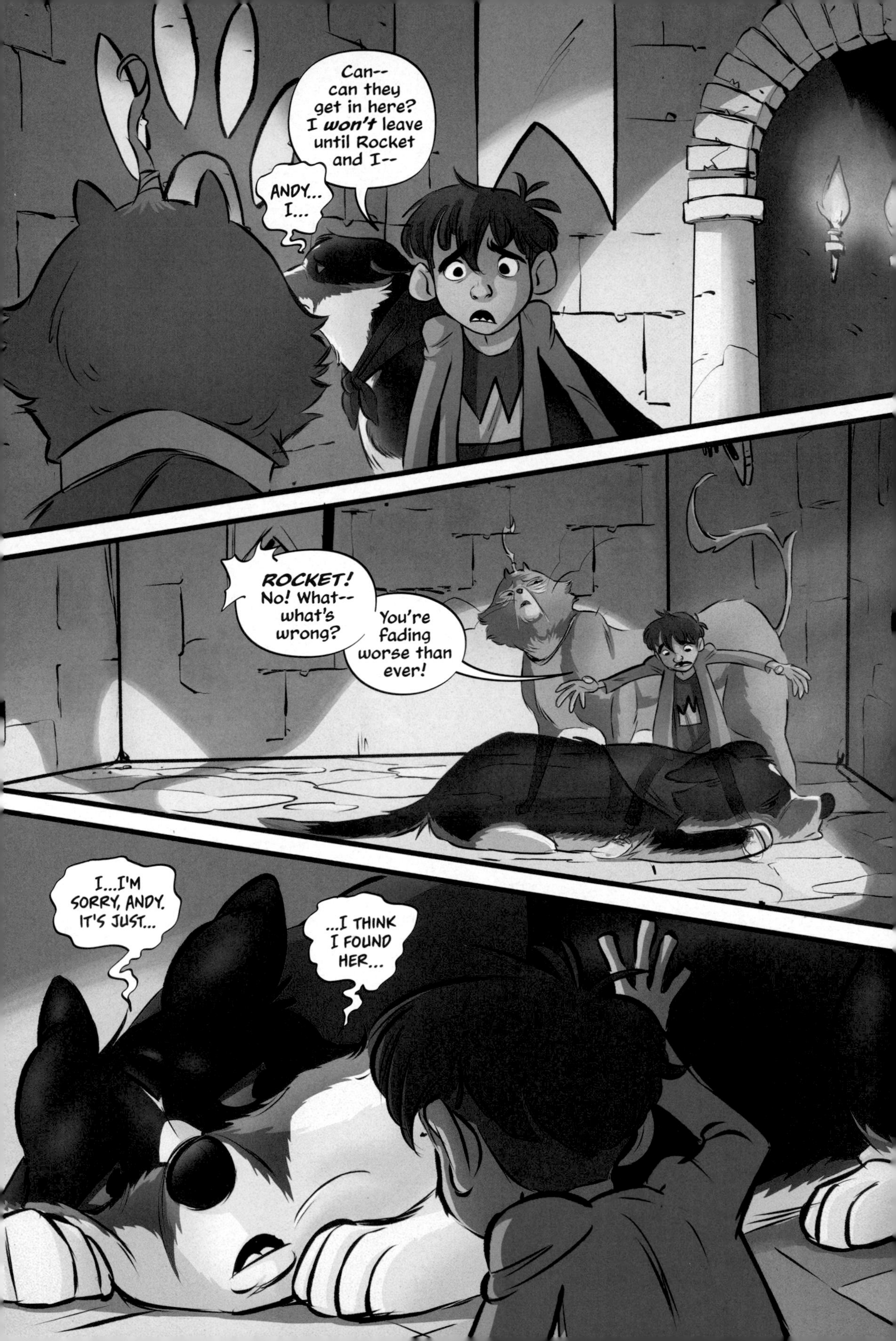
Can-- can they get in here? I *won't* leave until Rocket and I--
ANDY... I...
ROCKET! No! What-- what's wrong?
You're fading worse than ever!
I...I'M SORRY, ANDY. IT'S JUST...
...I THINK I FOUND HER...

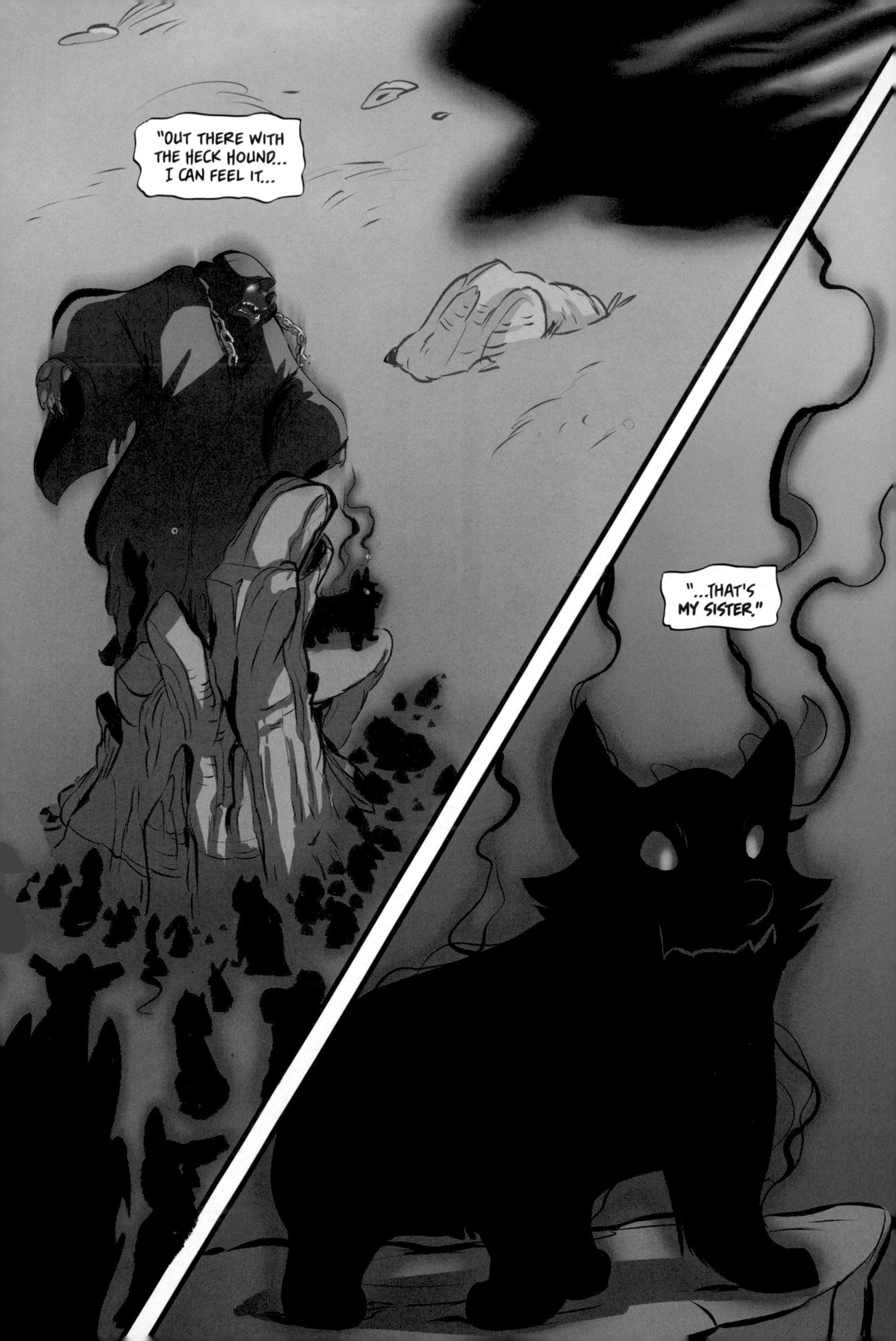
"OUT THERE WITH THE HECK HOUND... I CAN FEEL IT...
"...THAT'S MY SISTER."

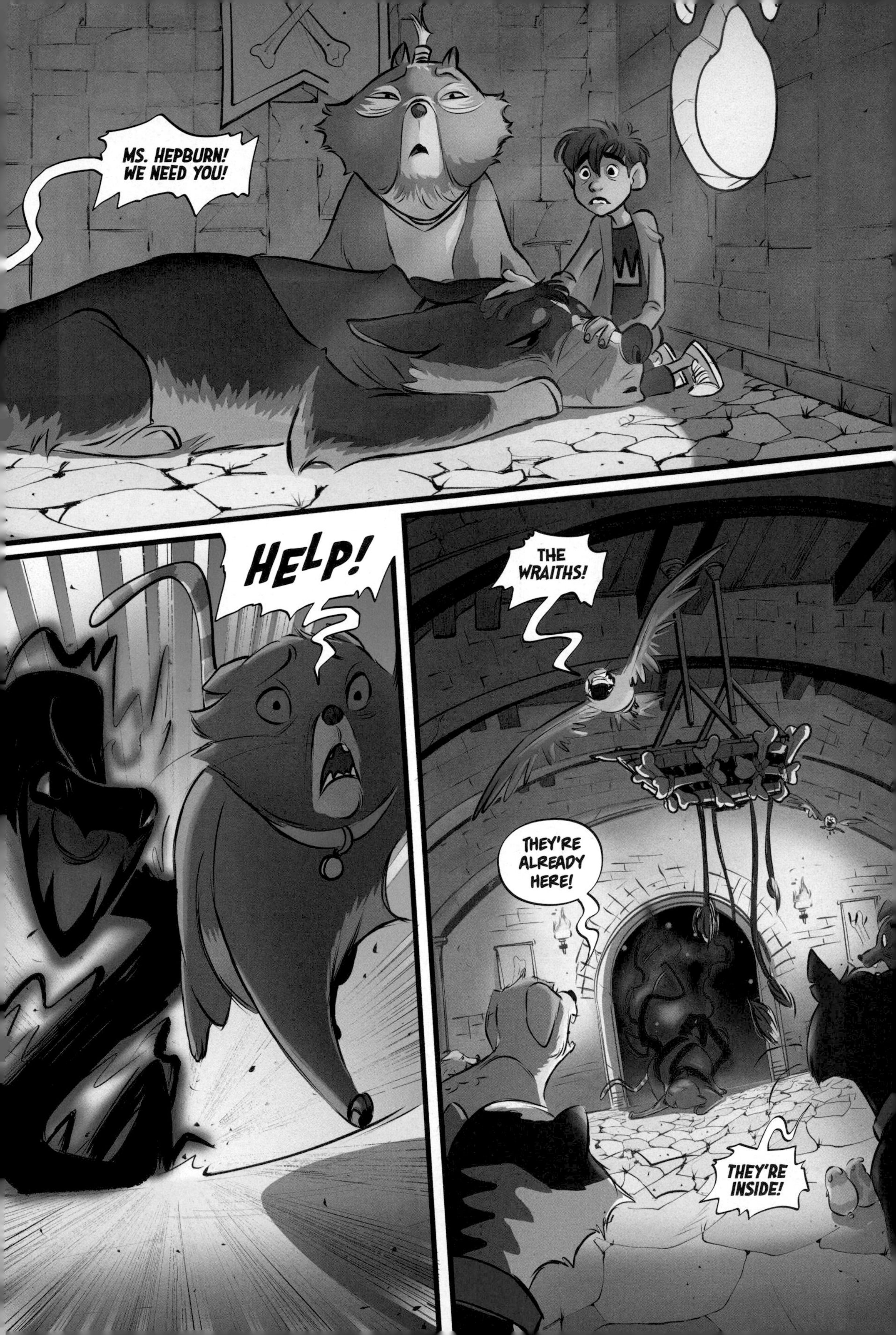
MS. HEPBURN! WE NEED YOU!
HELP!
THE WRAITHS!
THEY'RE ALREADY HERE!
THEY'RE INSIDE!

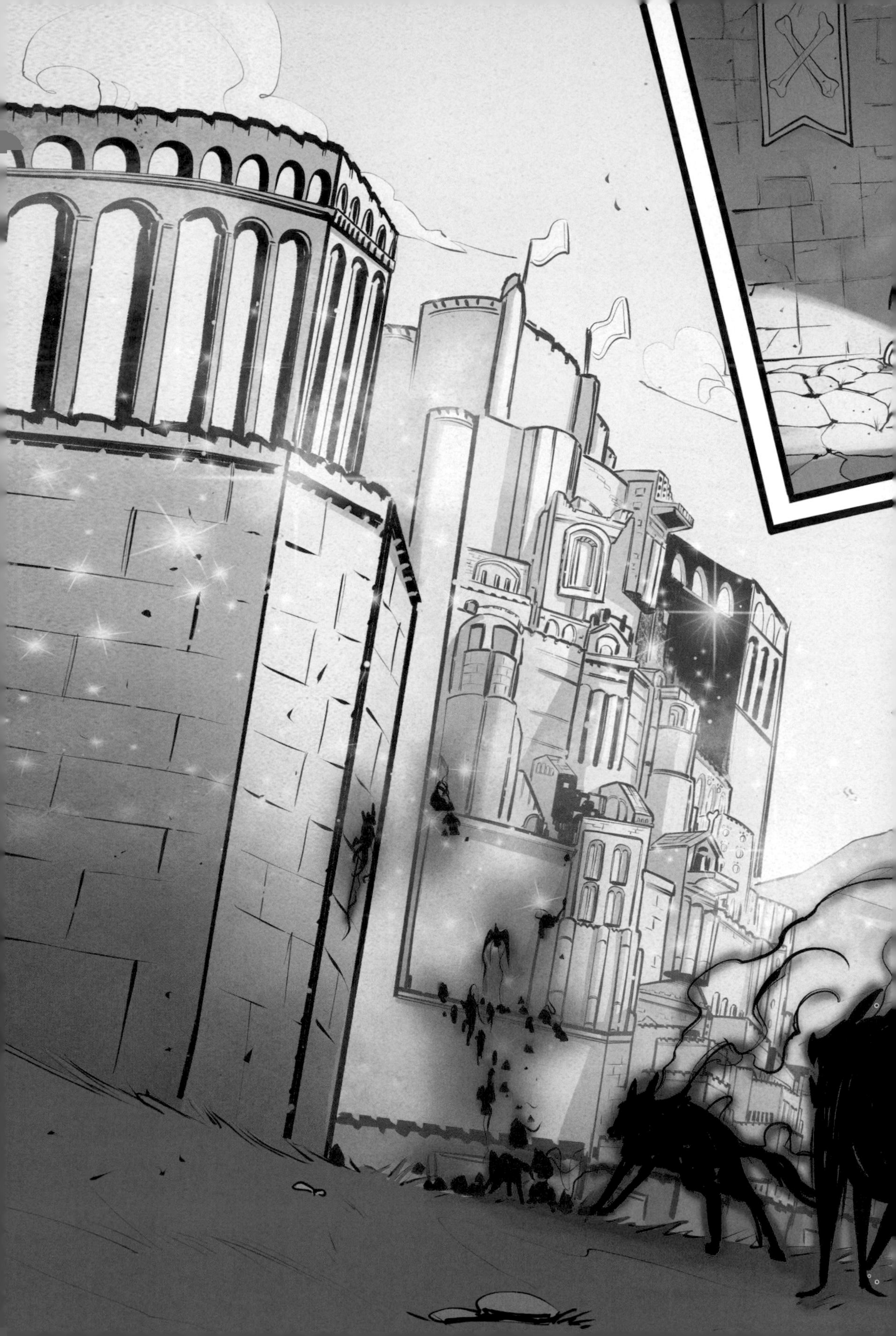

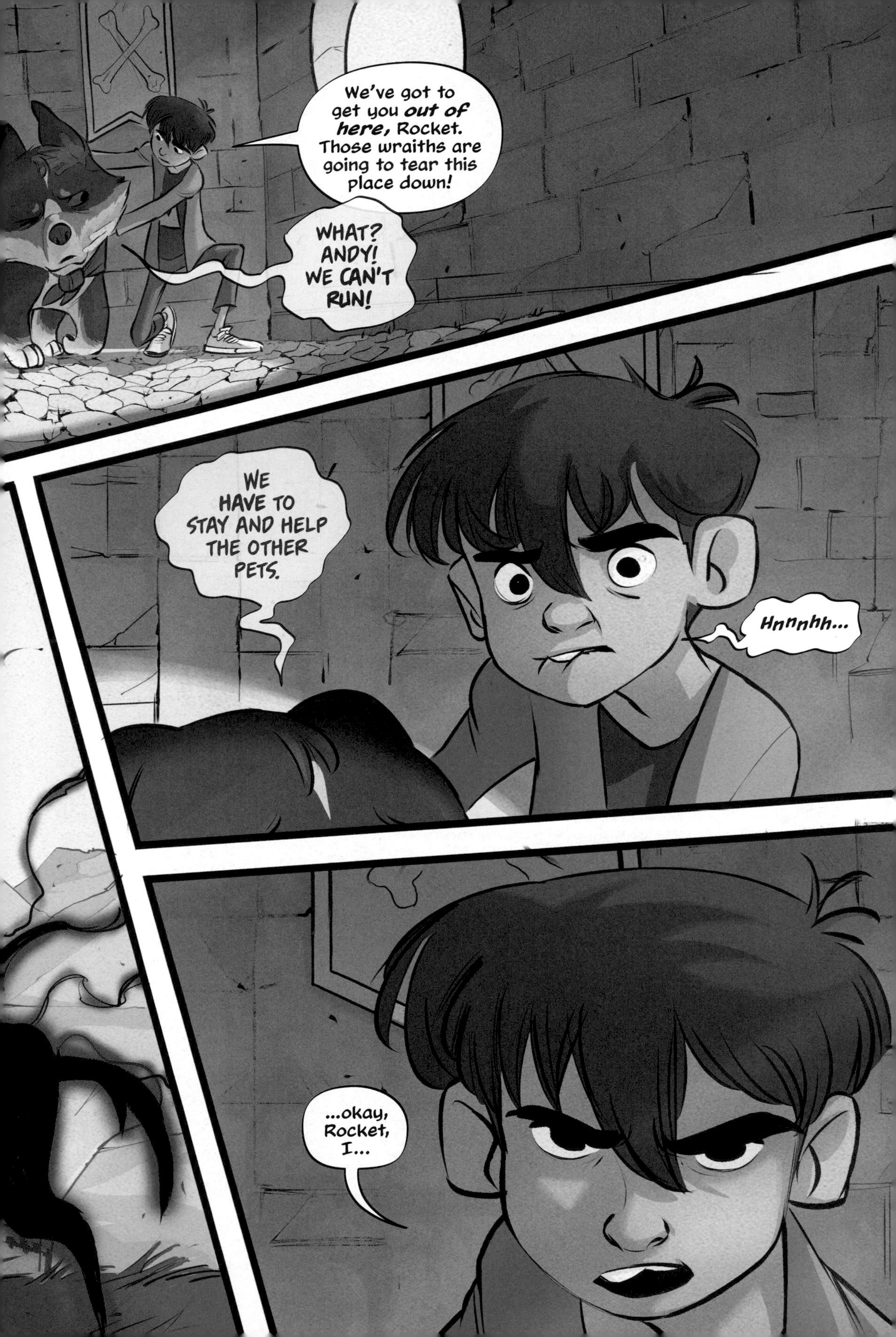
We've got to get you *out of here,* Rocket. Those wraiths are going to tear this place down!
WHAT? ANDY! WE CAN'T RUN!
WE HAVE TO STAY AND HELP THE OTHER PETS.
Hnnnhh...
...okay, Rocket, I...

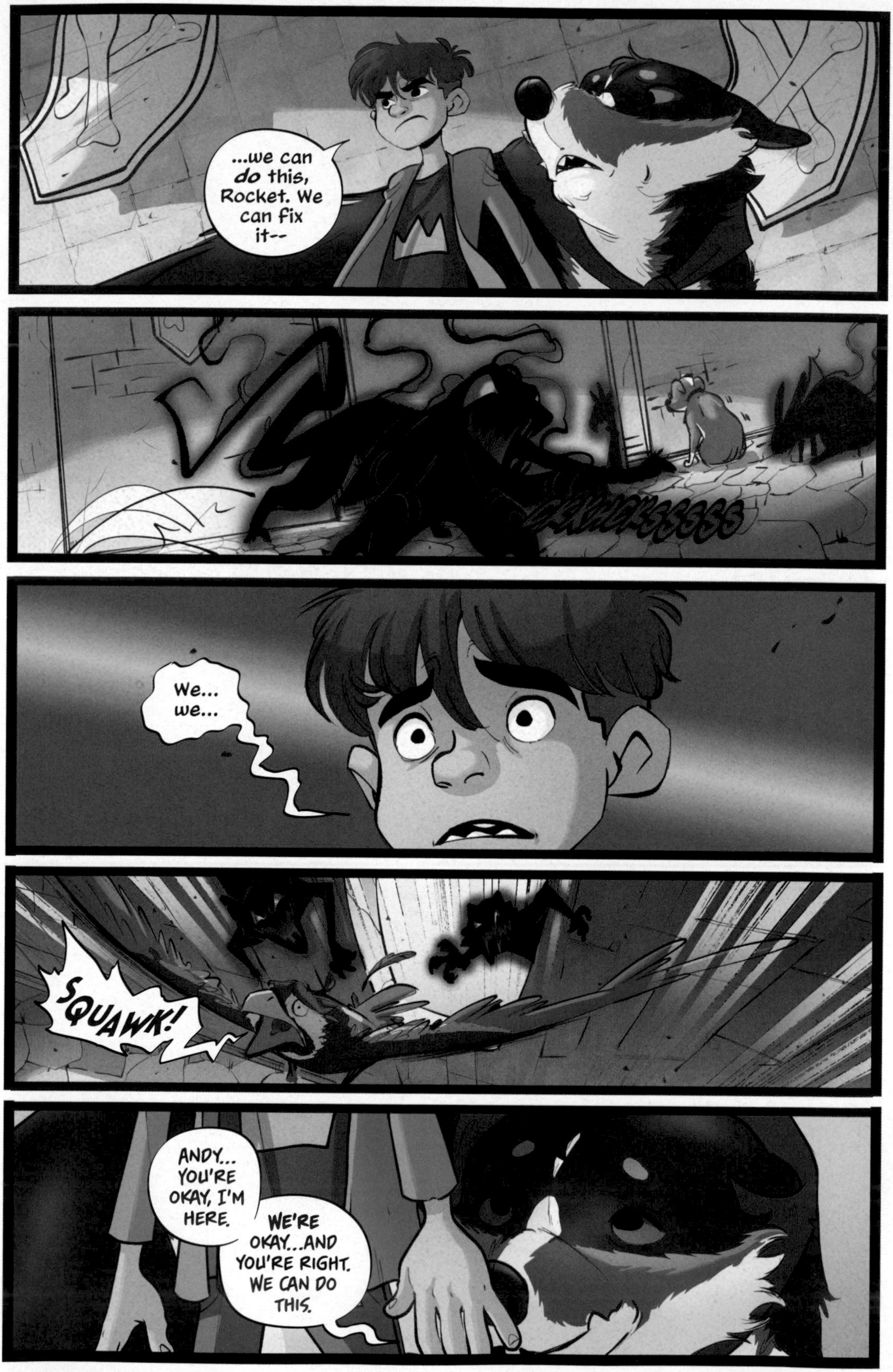
...we can do this, Rocket. We can fix it--
We... we...
SQUAWK!
ANDY... YOU'RE OKAY, I'M HERE.
WE'RE OKAY...AND YOU'RE RIGHT. WE CAN DO THIS.

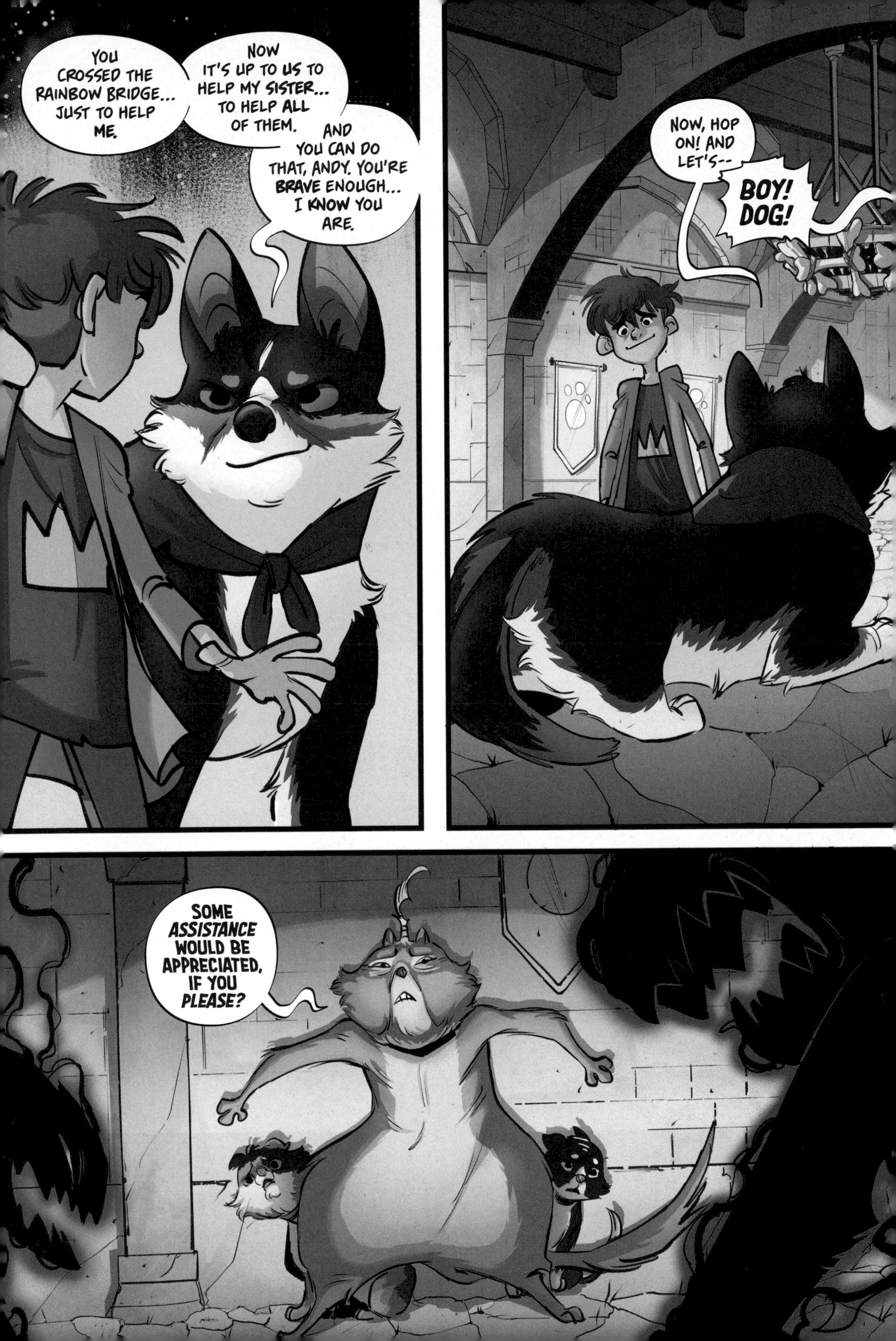
YOU CROSSED THE RAINBOW BRIDGE... JUST TO HELP ME.
NOW IT'S UP TO US TO HELP MY SISTER... TO HELP ALL OF THEM.
AND YOU CAN DO THAT, ANDY. YOU'RE BRAVE ENOUGH... I KNOW YOU ARE.
NOW, HOP ON! AND LET'S--
BOY! DOG!
SOME ASSISTANCE WOULD BE APPRECIATED, IF YOU PLEASE?

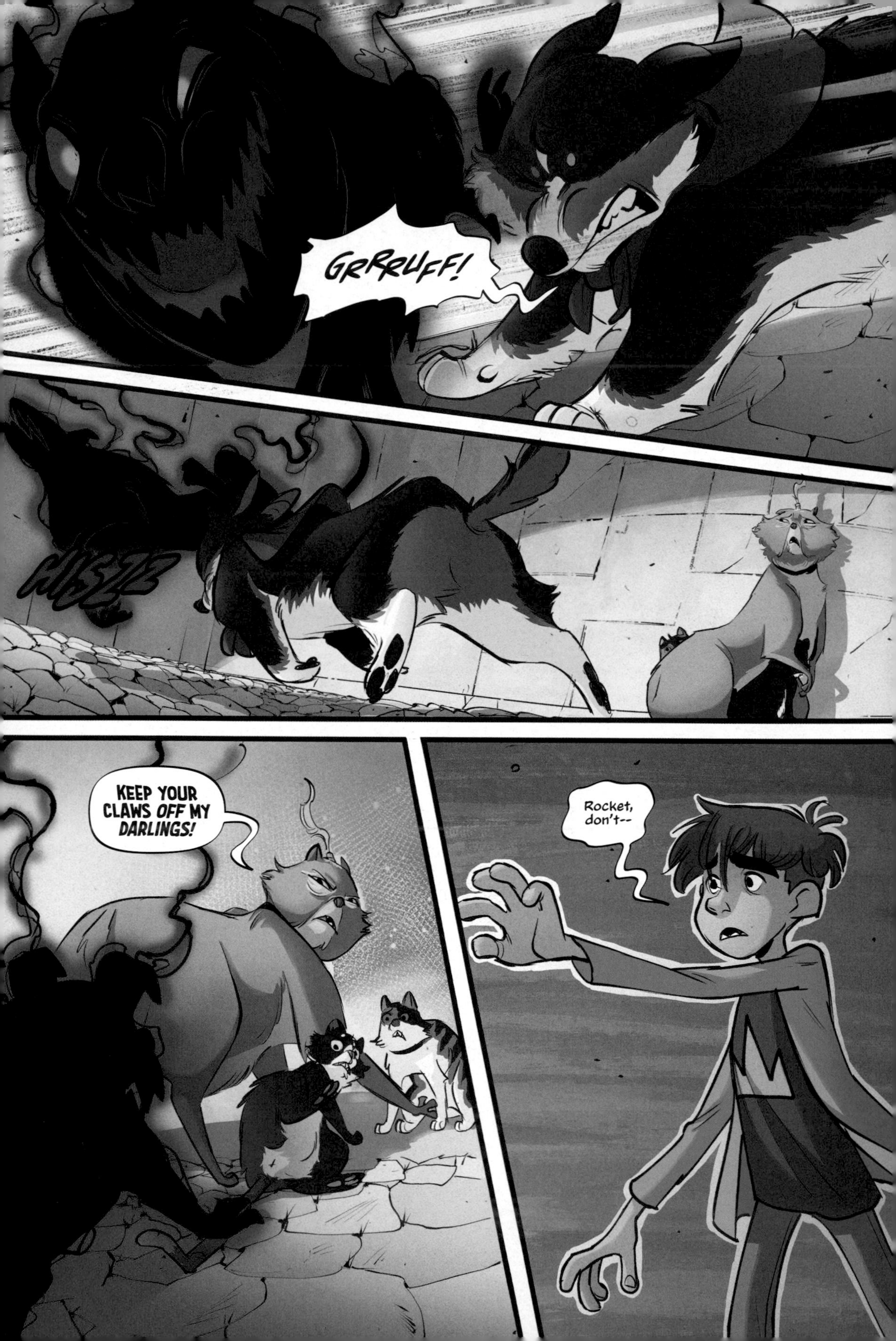
GRRRUFF!
KEEP YOUR CLAWS OFF MY DARLINGS!
Rocket, don't--

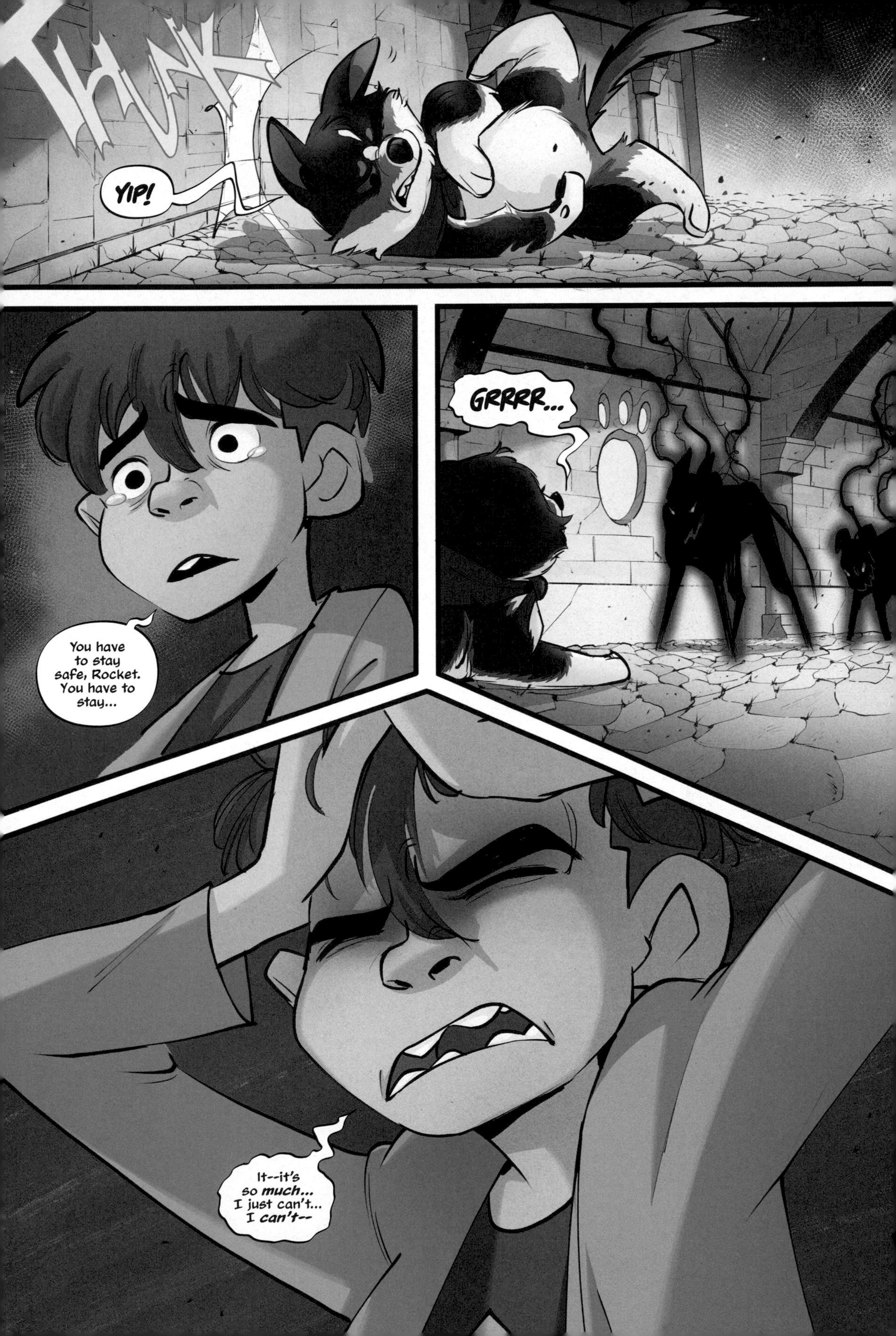
THUNK
YIP!
You have to stay safe, Rocket. You have to stay...
GRRRR...
It--it's so *much*... I just can't... I *can't*--

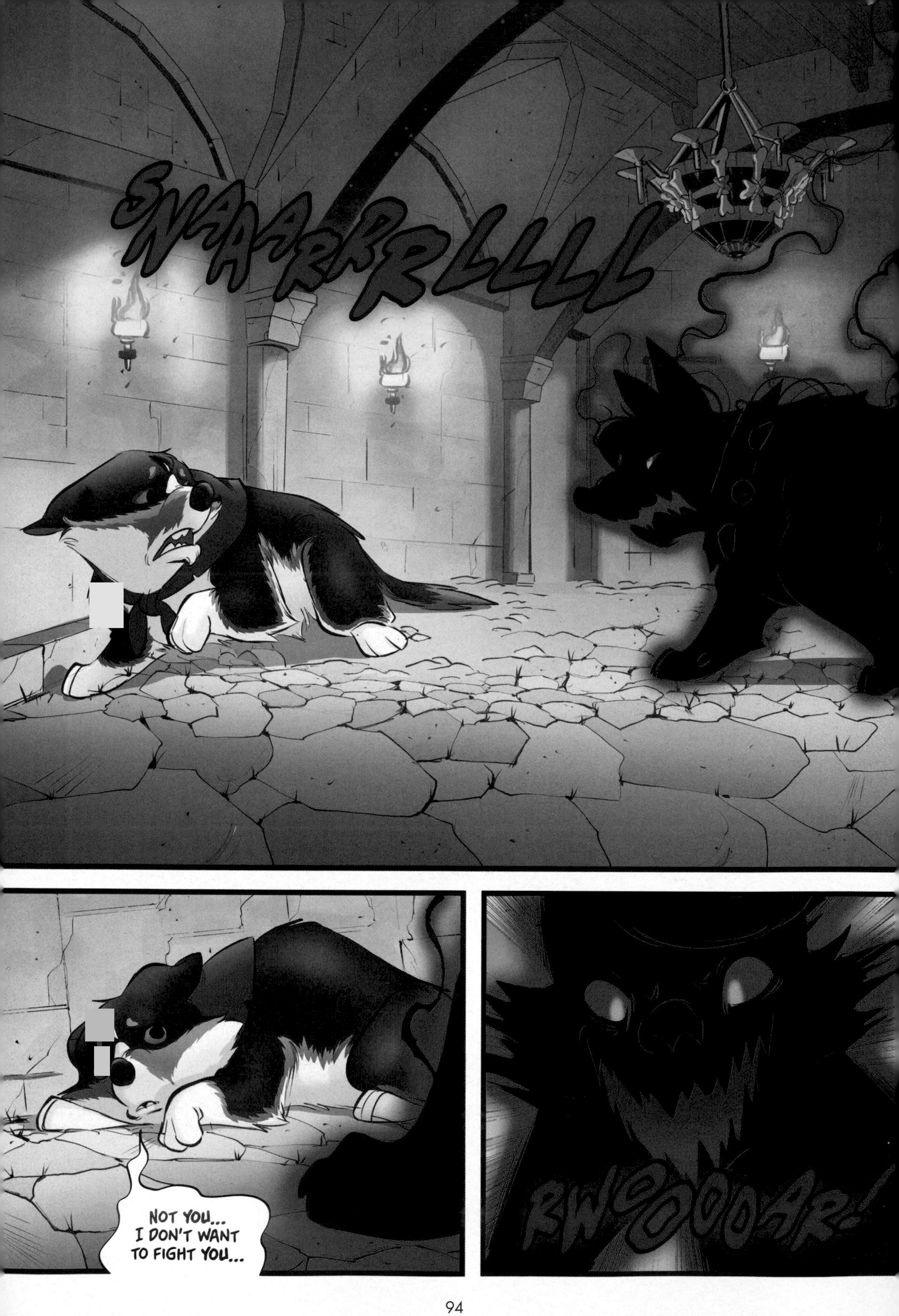
SNAARRRLLLL
NOT YOU... I DON'T WANT TO FIGHT YOU...
RWOOOOAR!

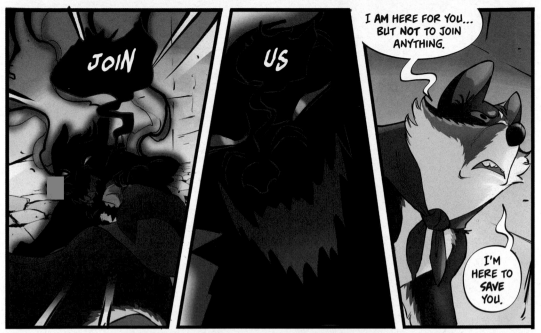

JOIN

US

I AM HERE FOR YOU... BUT NOT TO JOIN ANYTHING.

I'M HERE TO SAVE YOU.

THEN

PERISH

This is *too much*...

These wraiths... they're all so scared, so angry, even angrier than before--

--wait... *before*.

The rabbit.

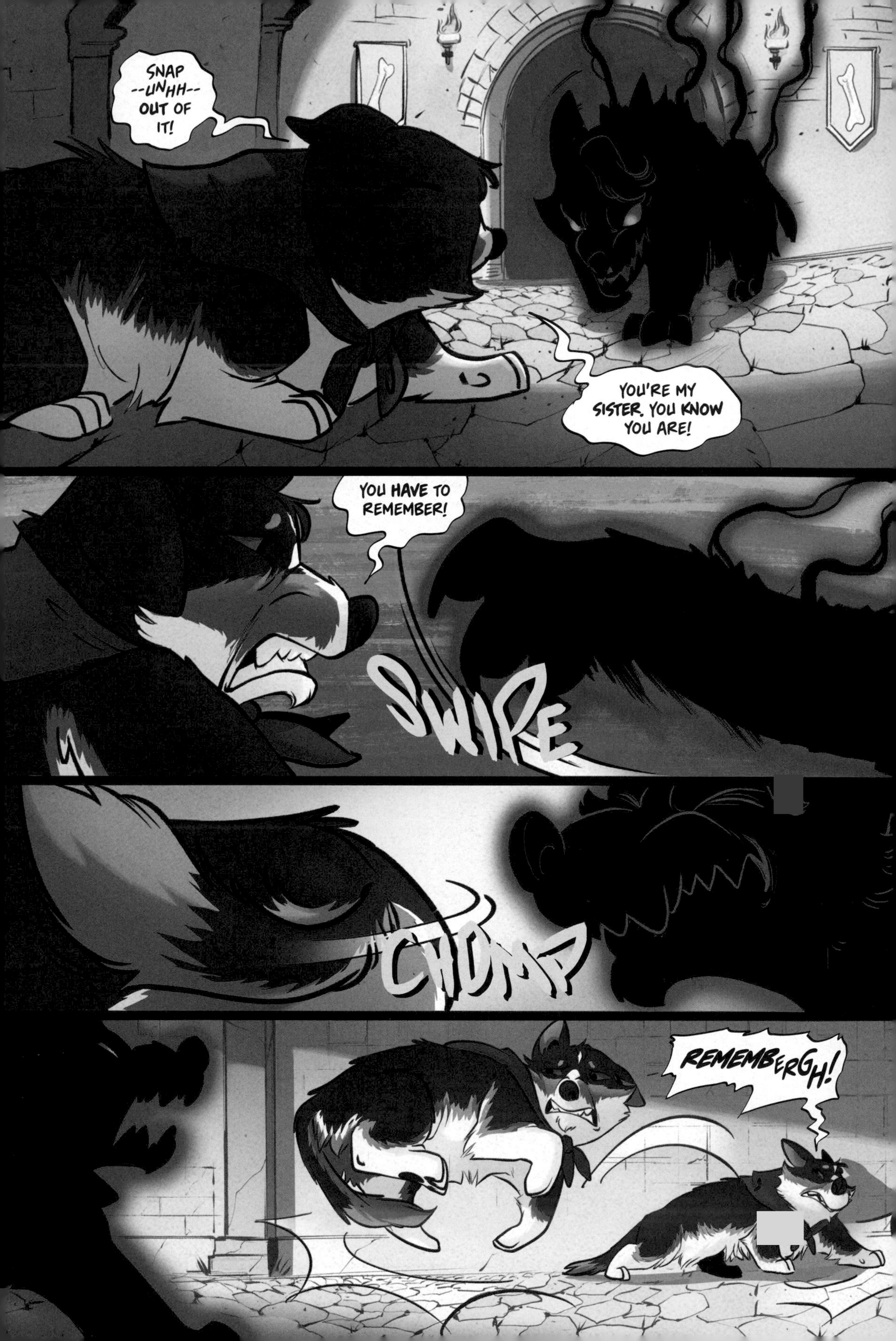
SNAP --UNHH-- OUT OF IT!
YOU'RE MY SISTER. YOU KNOW YOU ARE!
YOU HAVE TO REMEMBER!
SWIPE
CHOMP
REMEMBERGH!

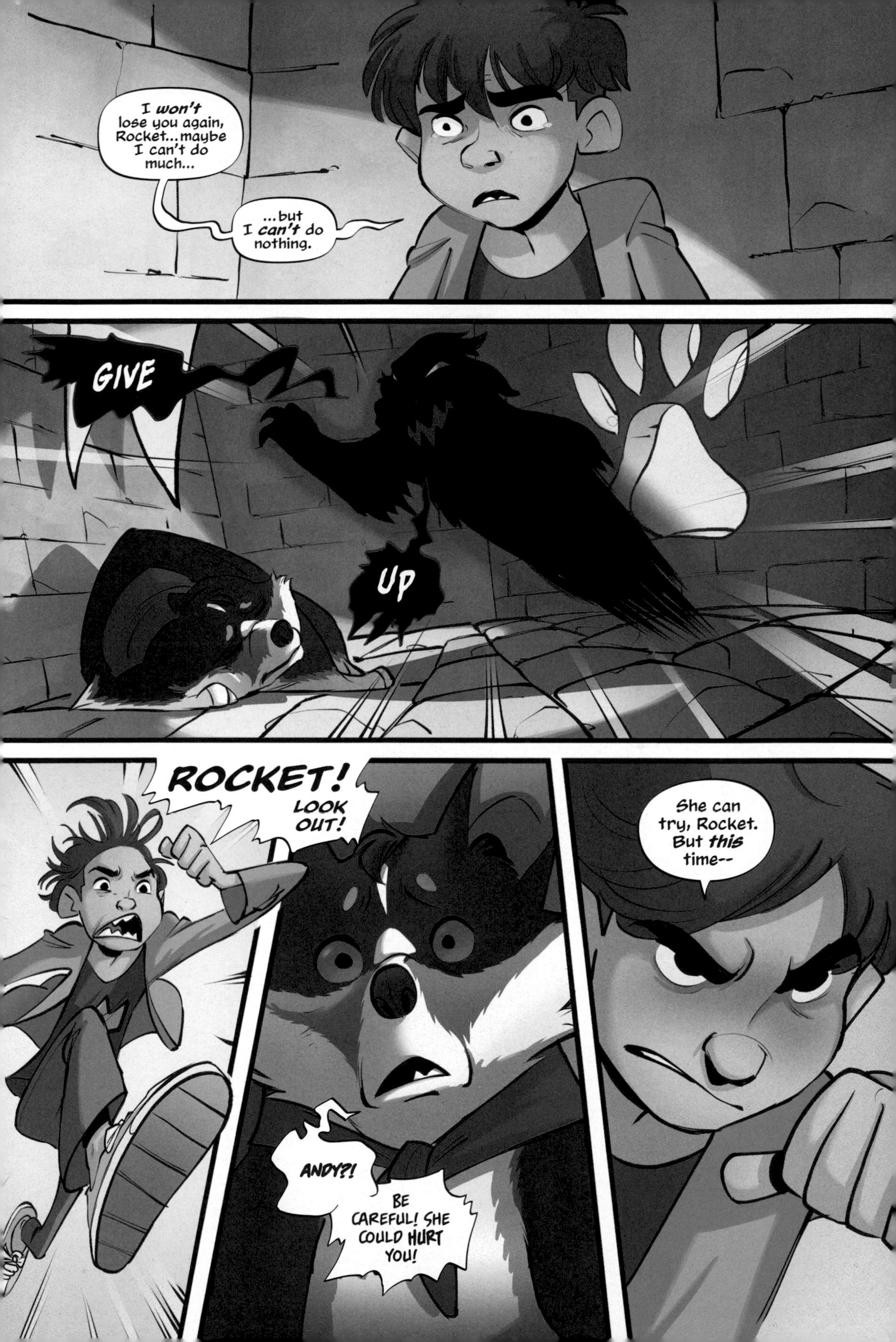
I won't lose you again, Rocket...maybe I can't do much...
...but I can't do nothing.
GIVE
UP
ROCKET! LOOK OUT!
ANDY?!
BE CAREFUL! SHE COULD HURT YOU!
She can try, Rocket. But this time--

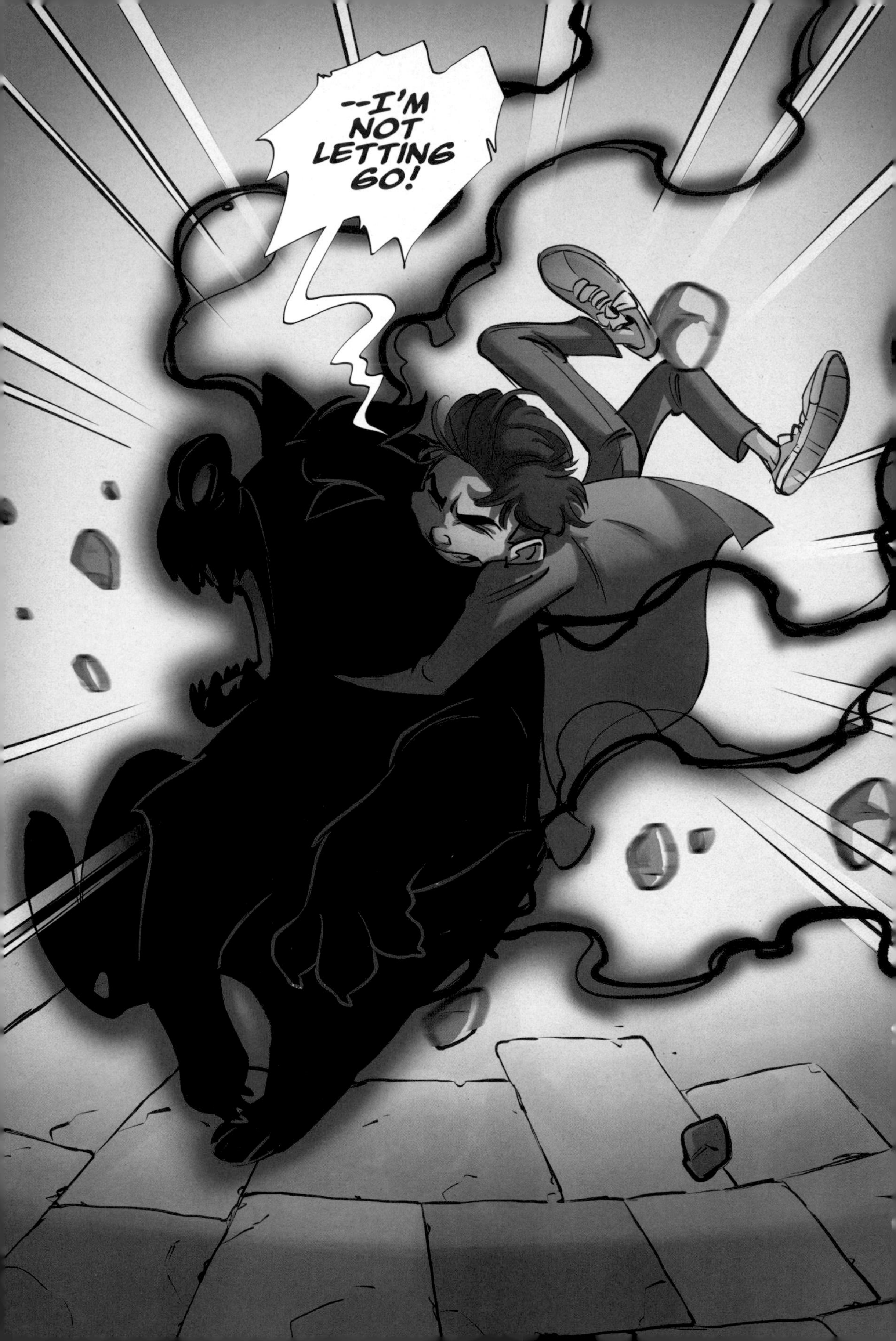
--I'M NOT LETTING GO!

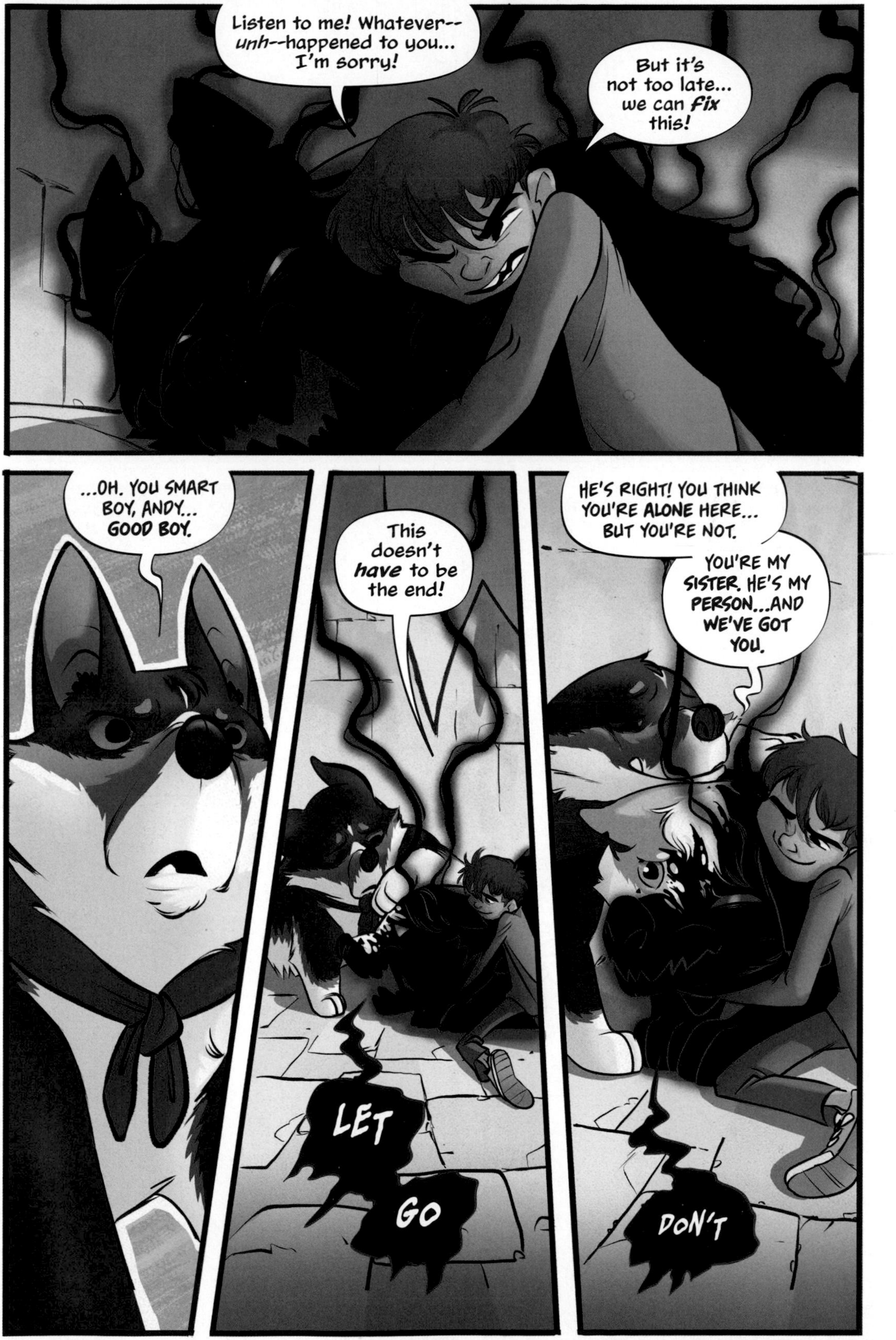
Listen to me! Whatever--*unh*--happened to you... I'm sorry!
But it's not too late... we can *fix* this!
...OH. YOU SMART BOY, ANDY... GOOD BOY.
This doesn't *have* to be the end!
LET
GO
HE'S RIGHT! YOU THINK YOU'RE ALONE HERE... BUT YOU'RE NOT.
YOU'RE MY SISTER. HE'S MY PERSON...AND WE'VE GOT YOU.
DON'T

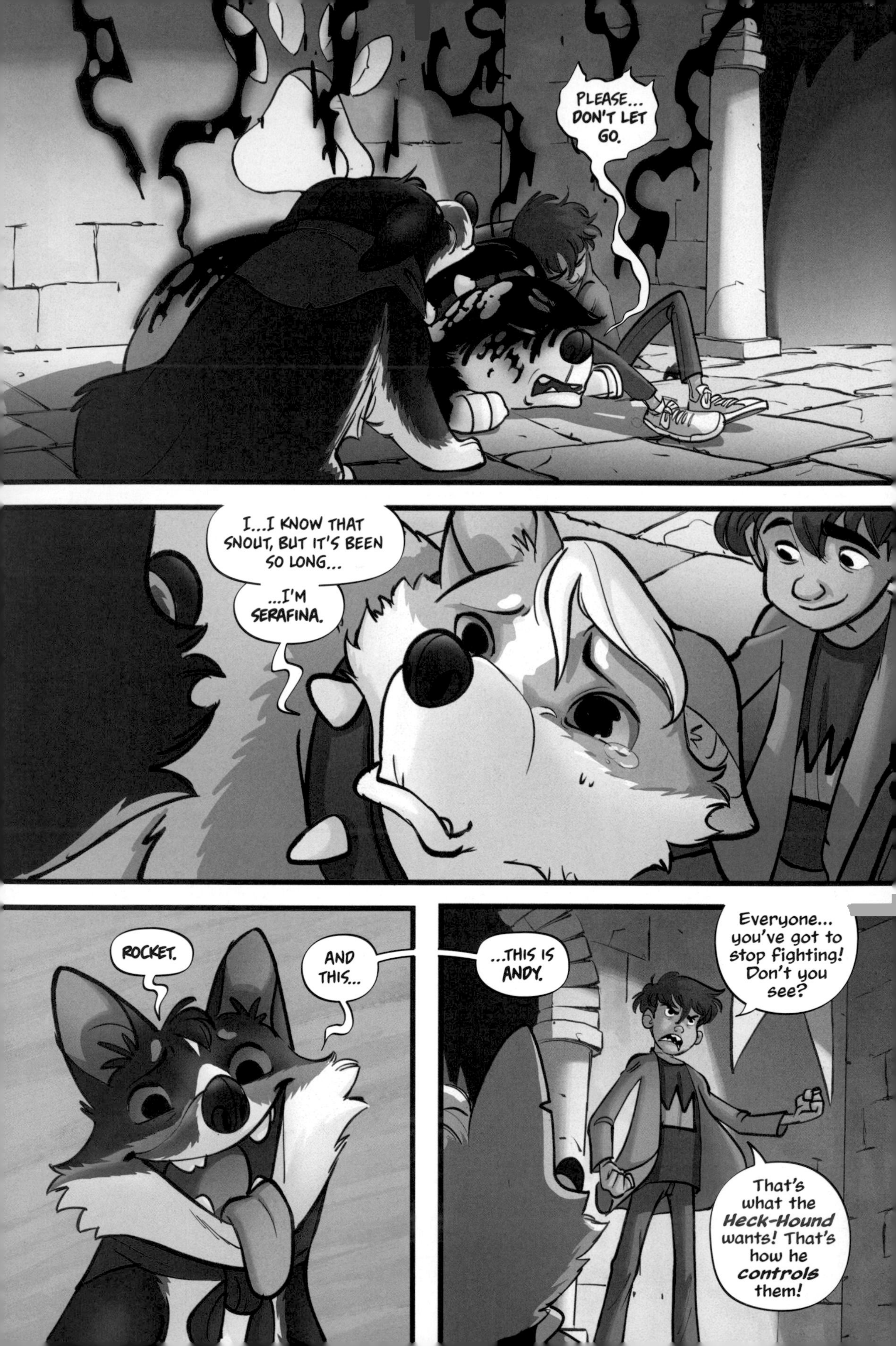

PLEASE... DON'T LET GO.
I...I KNOW THAT SNOUT, BUT IT'S BEEN SO LONG...
...I'M SERAFINA.
ROCKET.
AND THIS...
...THIS IS ANDY.
Everyone... you've got to stop fighting! Don't you see?
That's what the **Heck-Hound** wants! That's how he **controls** them!

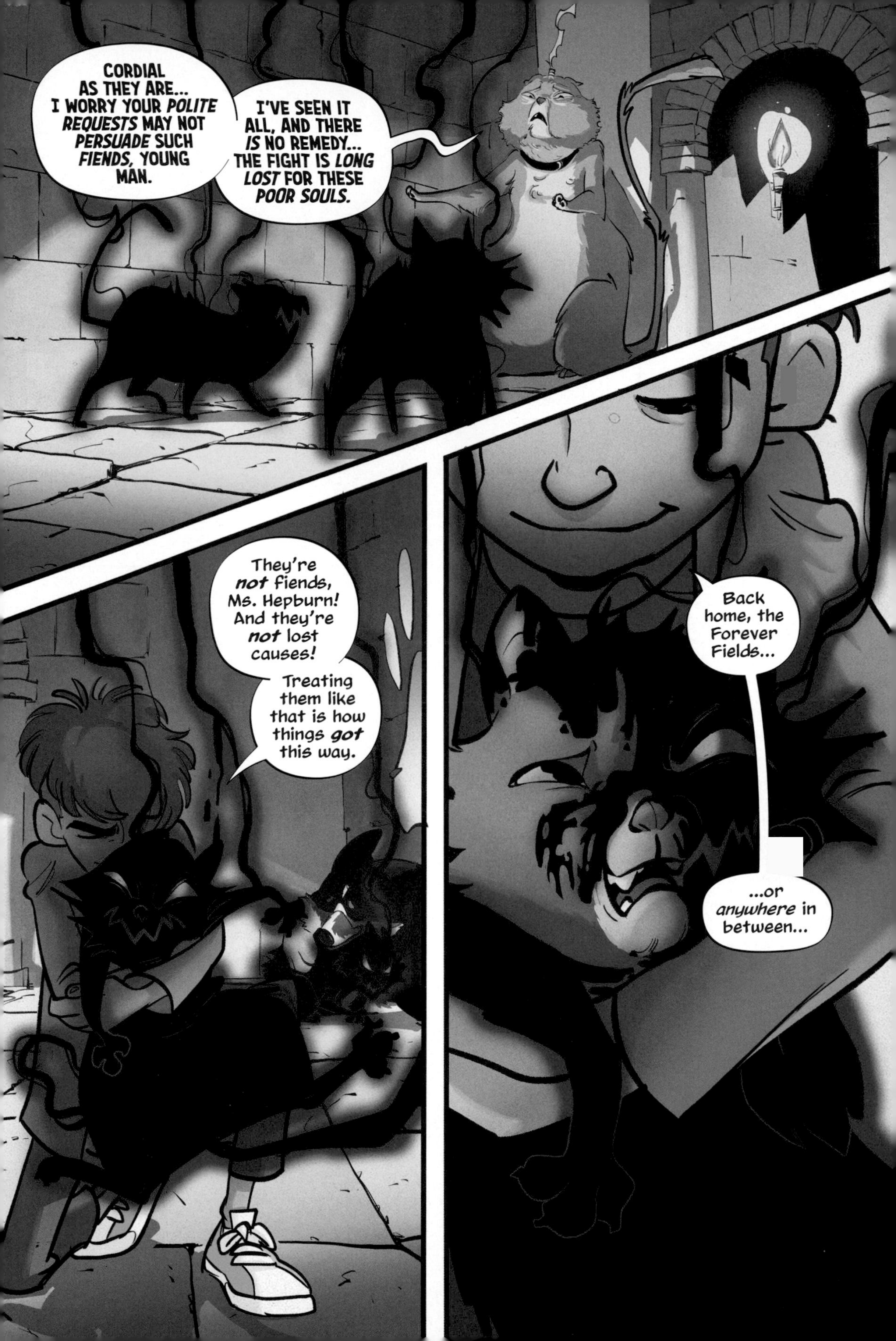

CORDIAL AS THEY ARE... I WORRY YOUR POLITE REQUESTS MAY NOT PERSUADE SUCH FIENDS, YOUNG MAN.
I'VE SEEN IT ALL, AND THERE IS NO REMEDY... THE FIGHT IS LONG LOST FOR THESE POOR SOULS.
They're not fiends, Ms. Hepburn! And they're not lost causes!
Treating them like that is how things got this way.
Back home, the Forever Fields...
...or anywhere in between...

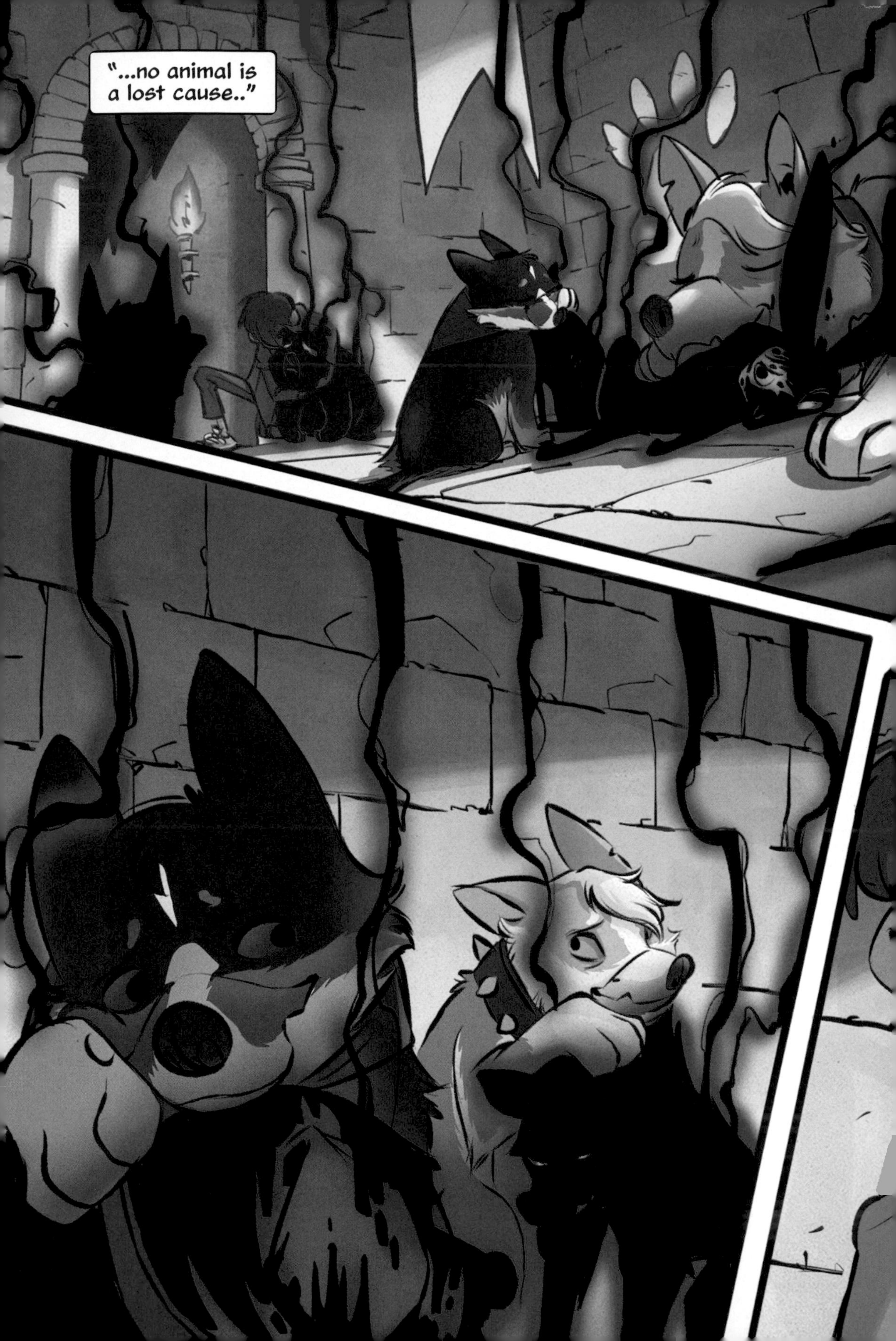
"...no animal is a lost cause.."

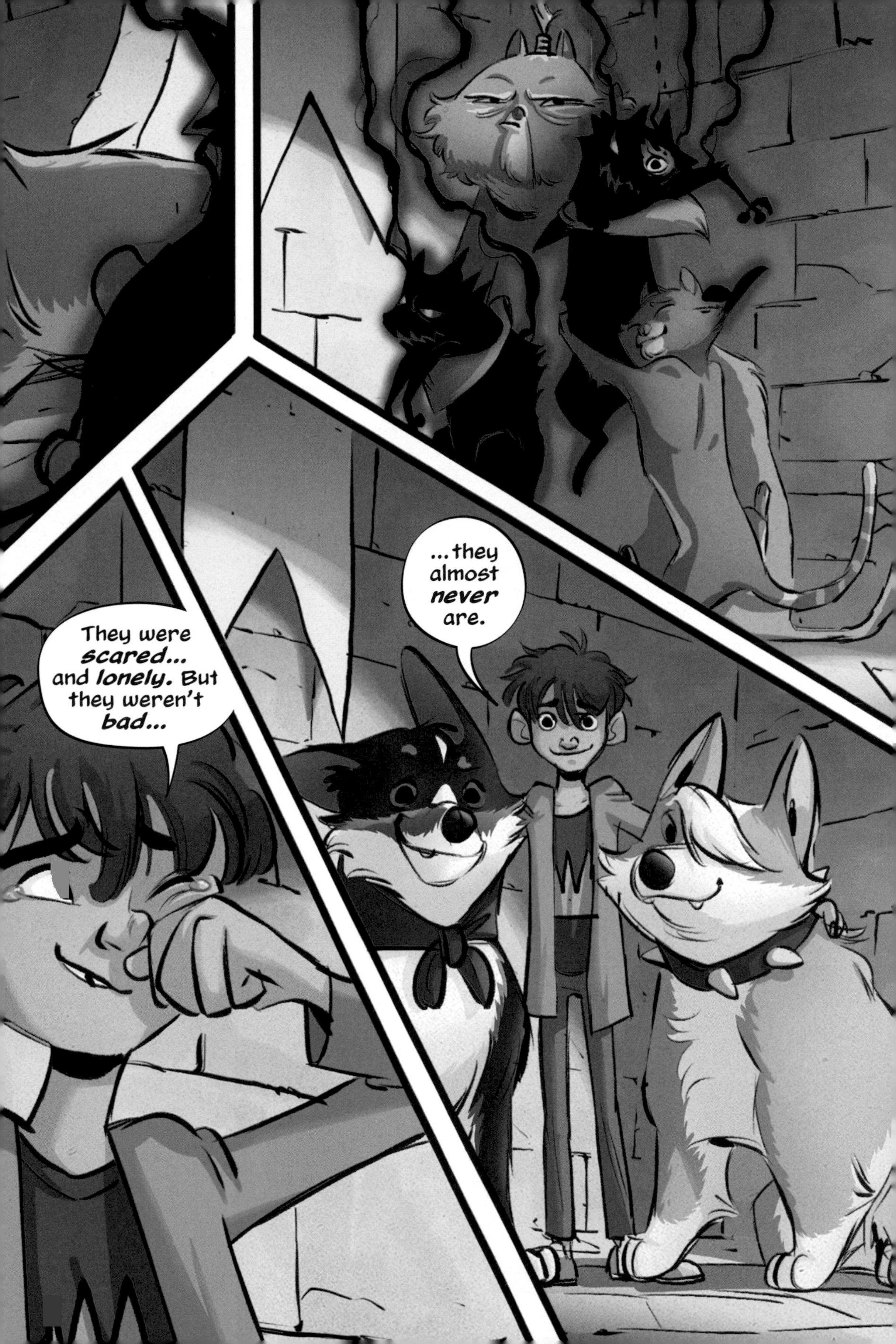
They were scared... and lonely. But they weren't bad...
...they almost never are.

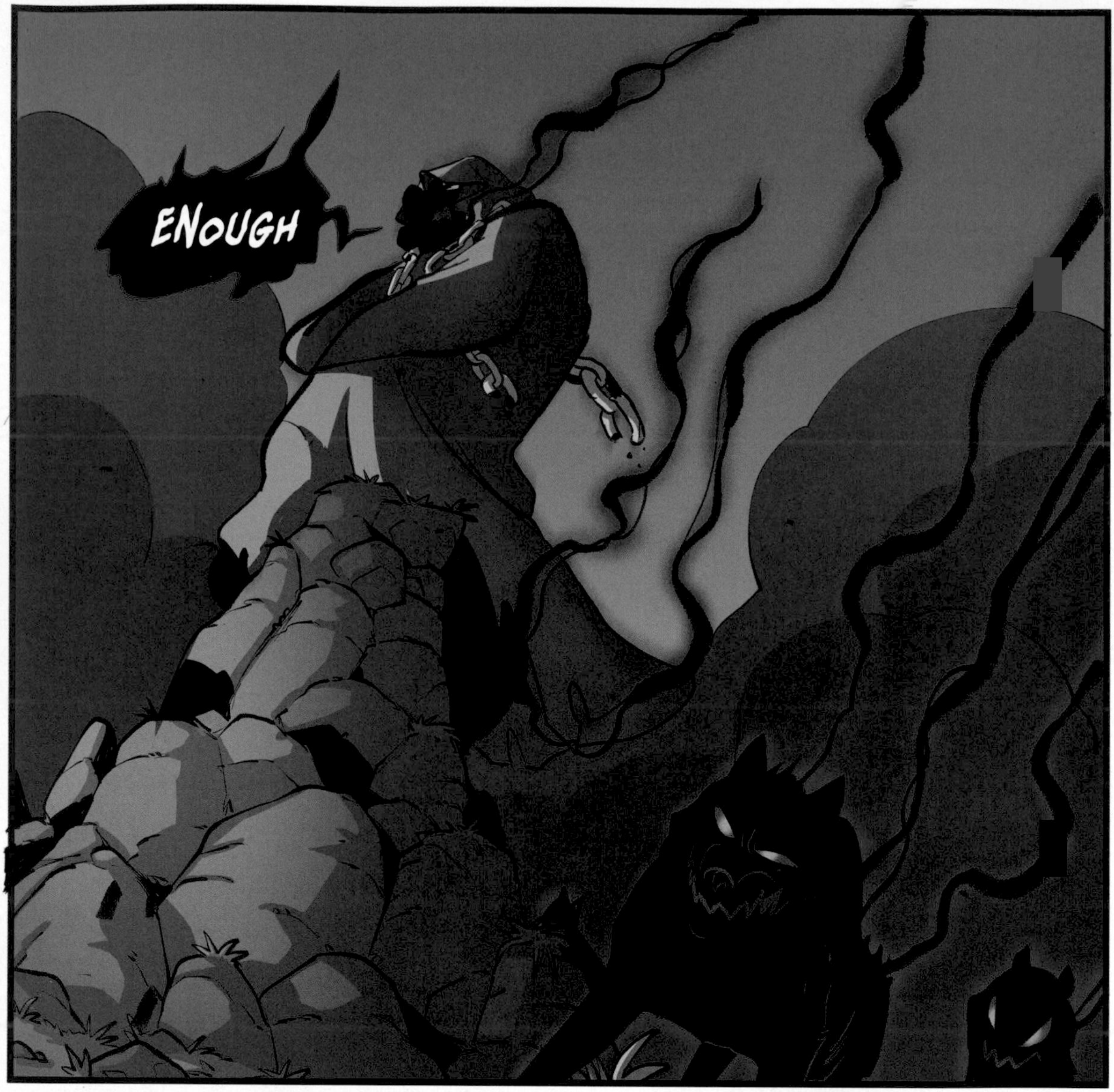
ENOUGH

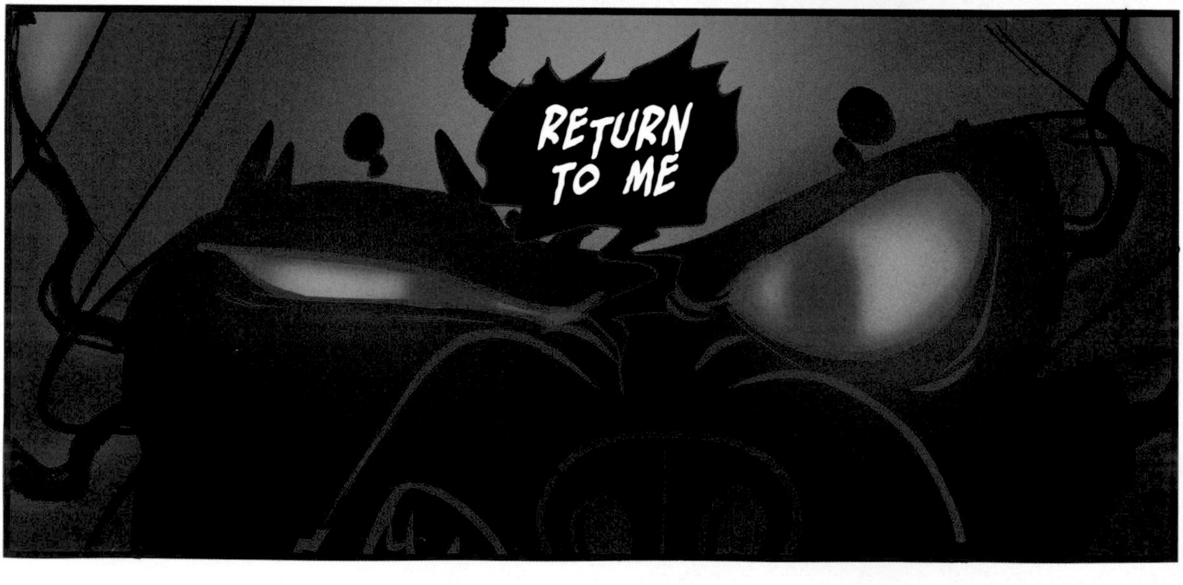
RETURN TO ME

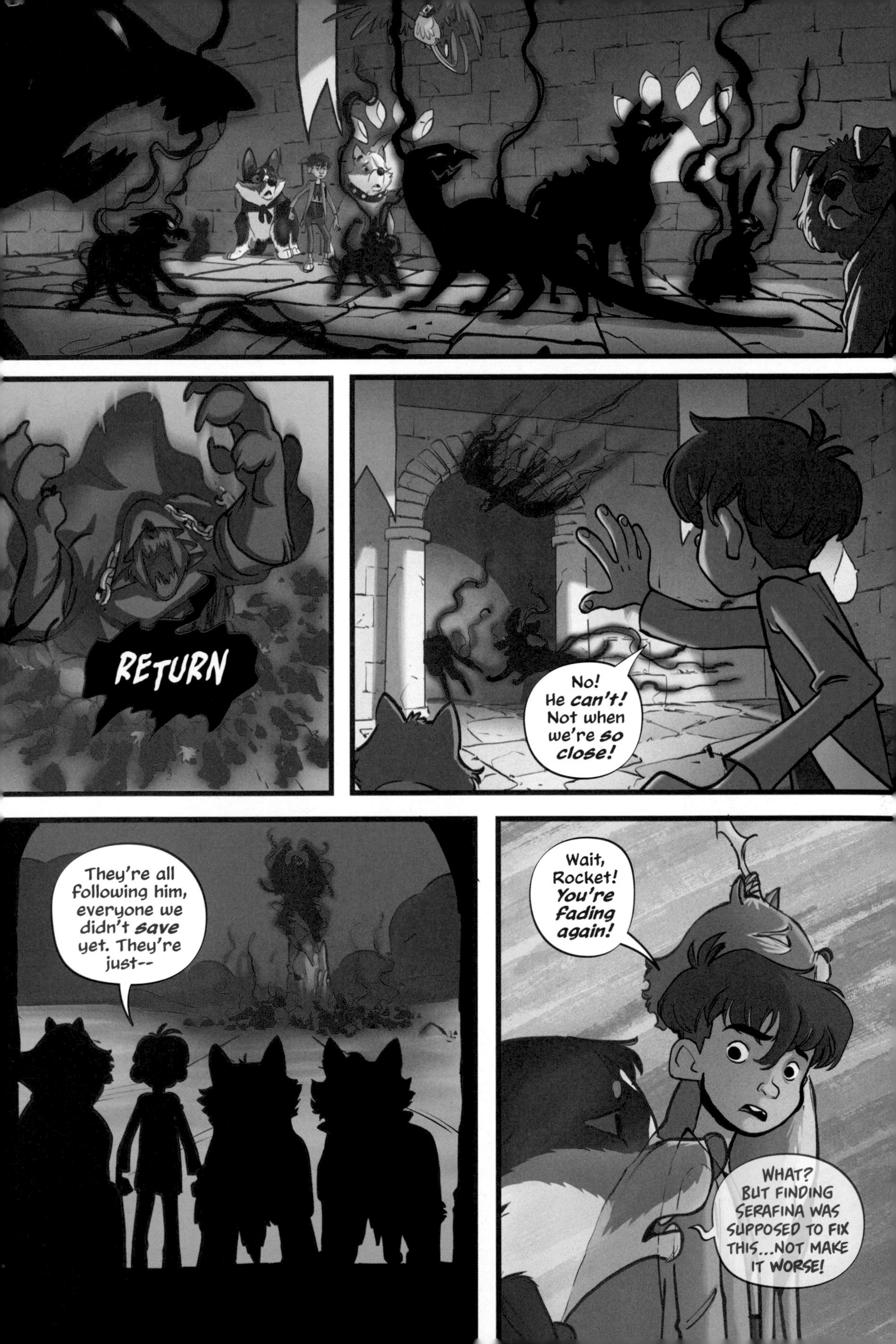
RETURN
No! He can't! Not when we're so close!
They're all following him, everyone we didn't save yet. They're just--
Wait, Rocket! You're fading again!
WHAT? BUT FINDING SERAFINA WAS SUPPOSED TO FIX THIS...NOT MAKE IT WORSE!

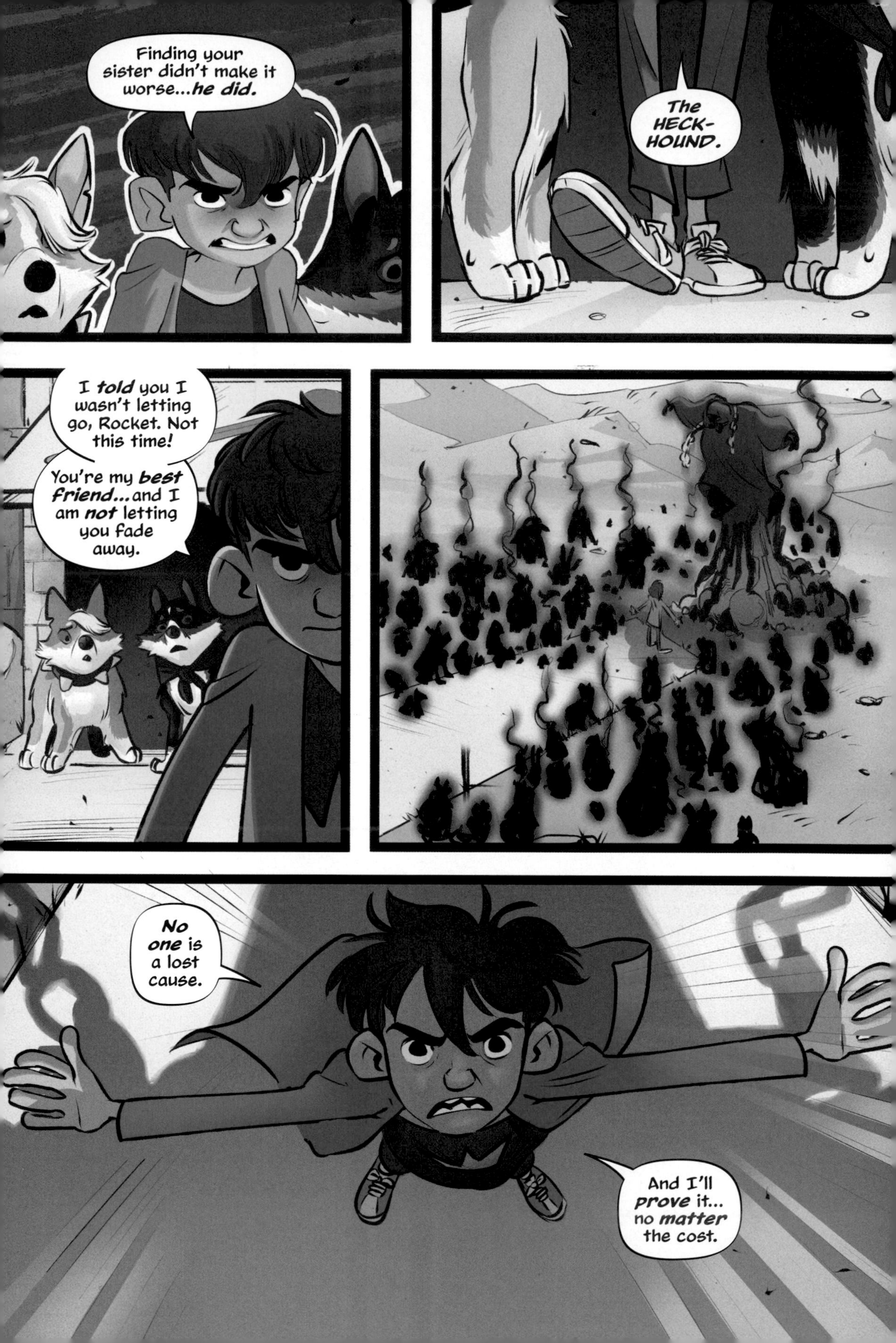
Finding your sister didn't make it worse...*he did.*
The HECK-HOUND.
I *told* you I wasn't letting go, Rocket. Not this time!
You're my *best friend*...and I am *not* letting you fade away.
No one is a lost cause.
And I'll *prove* it... no *matter* the cost.

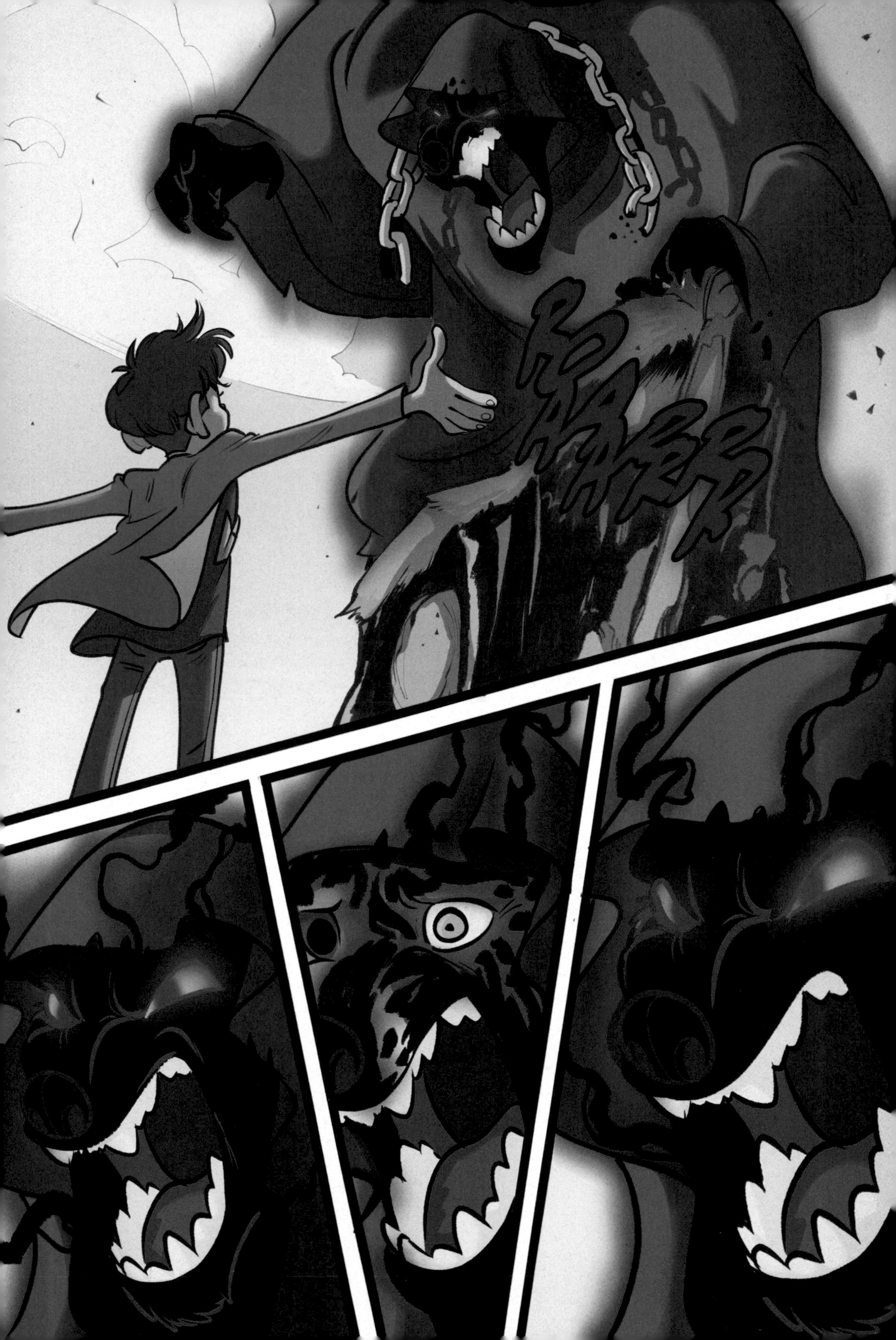

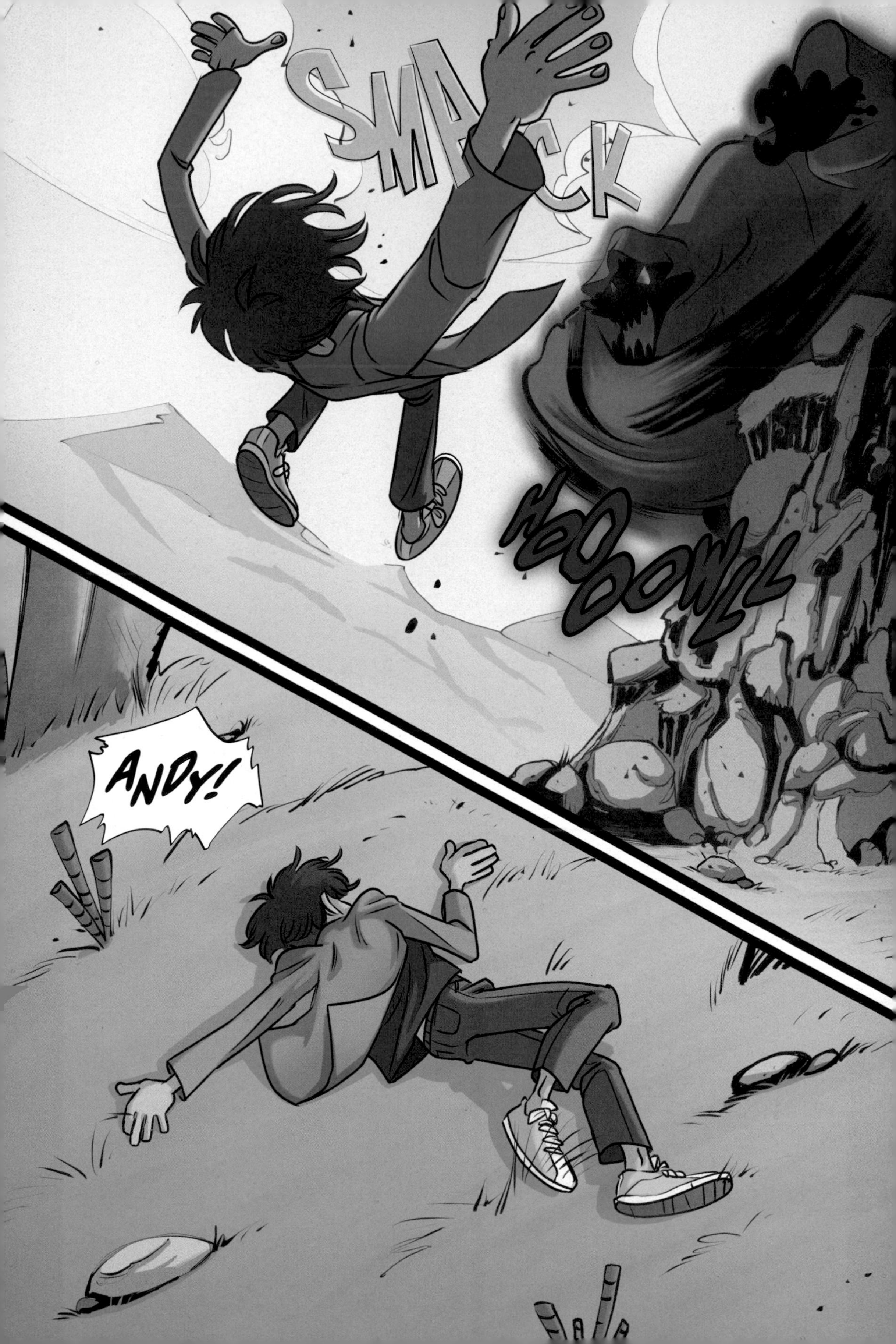
SMACK
HOOOOWLL
ANDY!

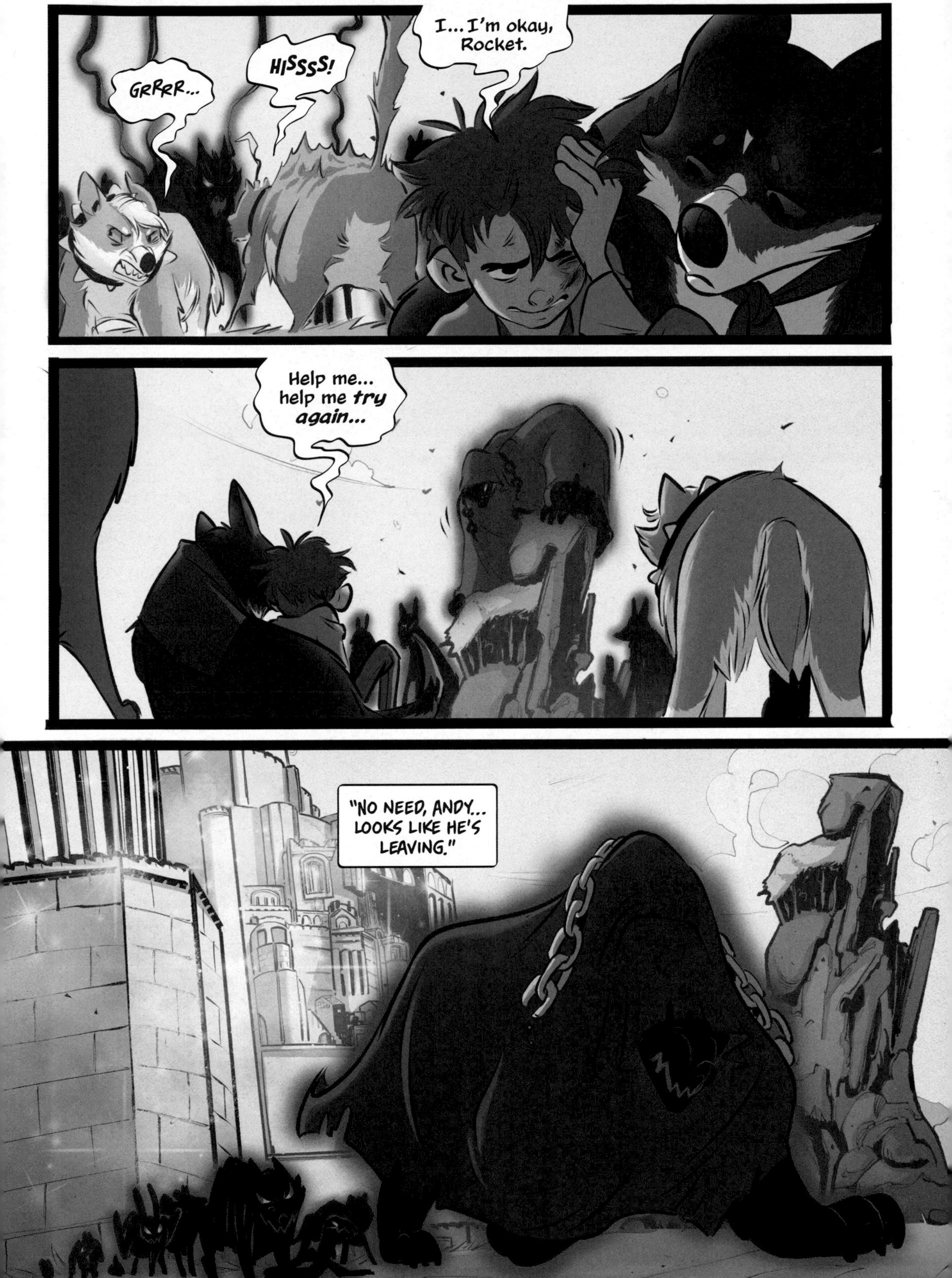
GRRRR...
HISSSS!
I... I'm okay, Rocket.
Help me... help me *try* again...
"NO NEED, ANDY... LOOKS LIKE HE'S LEAVING."

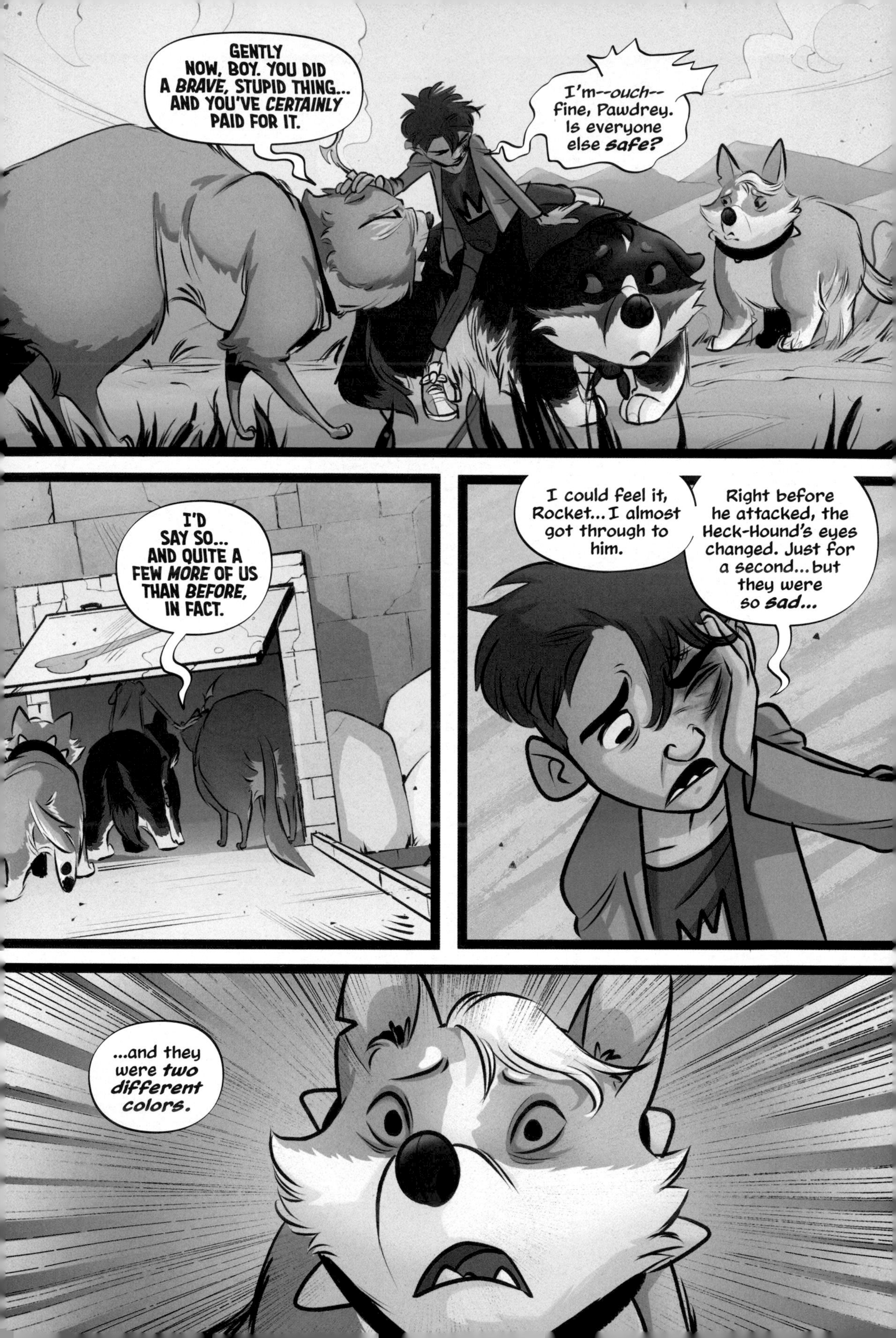
GENTLY NOW, BOY. YOU DID A *BRAVE*, STUPID THING... AND YOU'VE *CERTAINLY* PAID FOR IT.
I'm--*ouch*--fine, Pawdrey. Is everyone else *safe?*
I'D SAY SO... AND QUITE A FEW *MORE* OF US THAN *BEFORE*, IN FACT.
I could feel it, Rocket... I almost got through to him.
Right before he attacked, the Heck-Hound's eyes changed. Just for a second... but they were so *sad...*
...and they were *two different colors.*

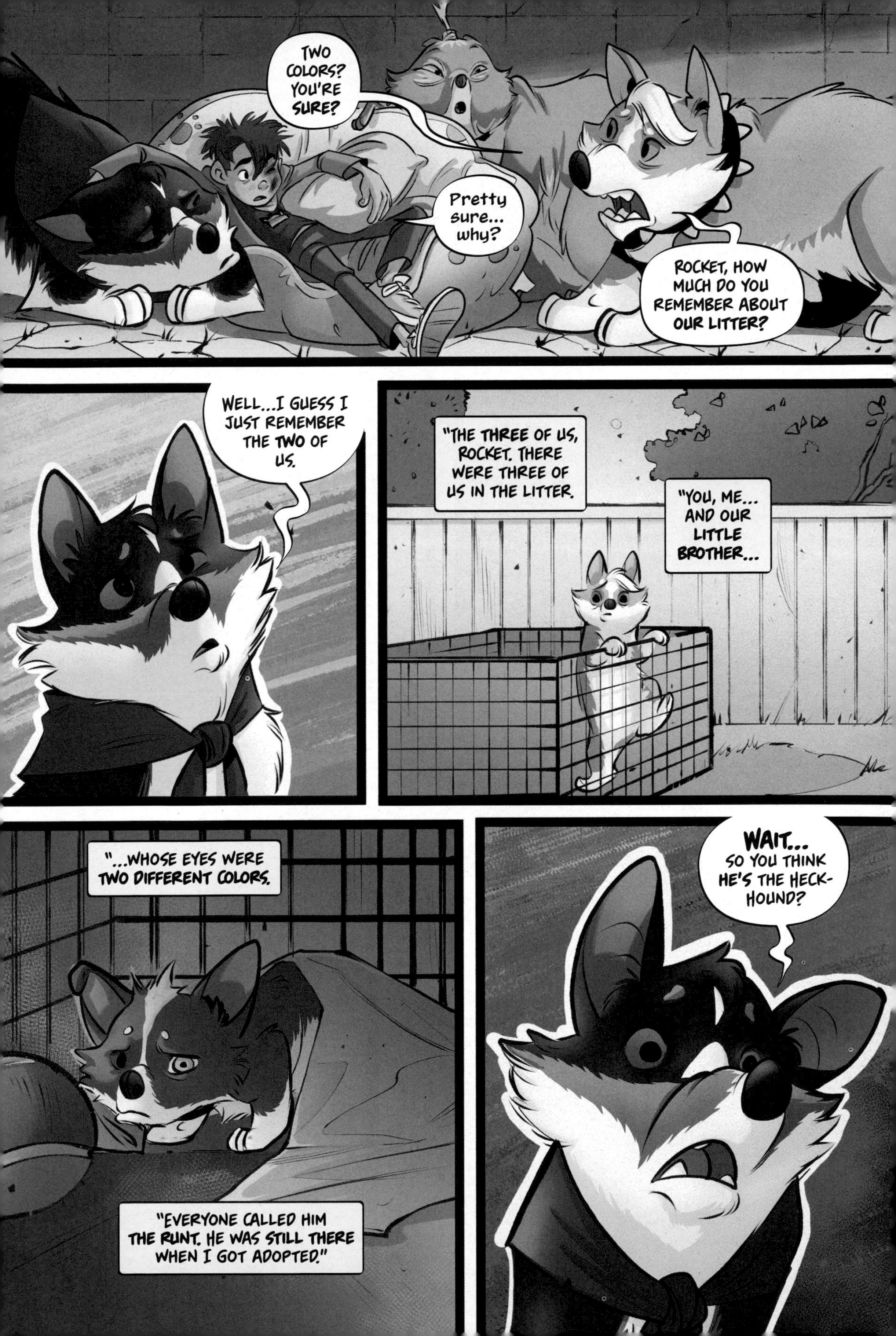
TWO COLORS? YOU'RE SURE?
Pretty sure... why?
ROCKET, HOW MUCH DO YOU REMEMBER ABOUT OUR LITTER?
WELL...I GUESS I JUST REMEMBER THE TWO OF US.
"THE THREE OF US, ROCKET. THERE WERE THREE OF US IN THE LITTER.
"YOU, ME... AND OUR LITTLE BROTHER...
"...WHOSE EYES WERE TWO DIFFERENT COLORS.
"EVERYONE CALLED HIM THE RUNT. HE WAS STILL THERE WHEN I GOT ADOPTED."
WAIT... SO YOU THINK HE'S THE HECK-HOUND?

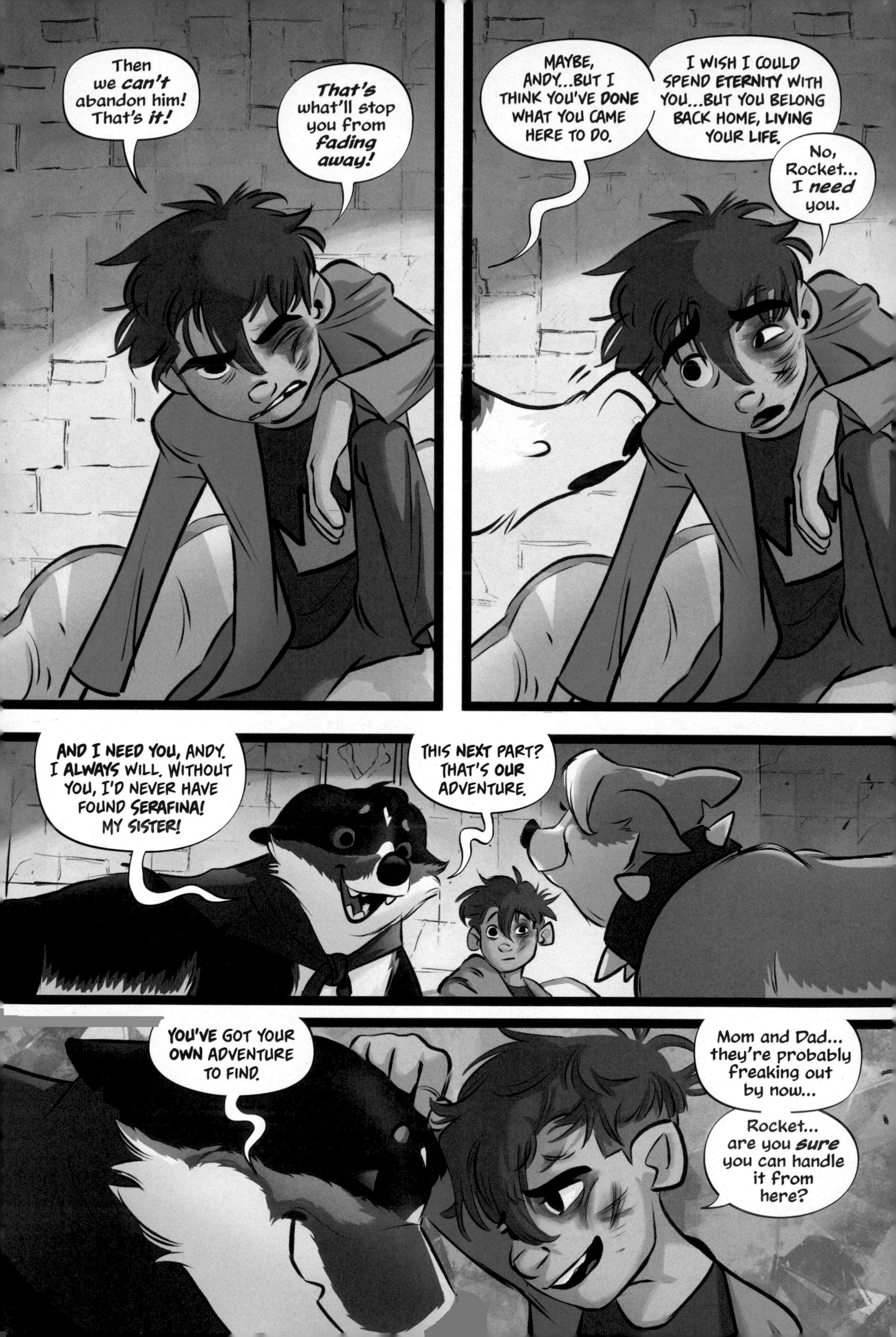
Then we *can't* abandon him! That's *it!*
That's what'll stop you from *fading away!*
MAYBE, ANDY...BUT I THINK YOU'VE DONE WHAT YOU CAME HERE TO DO.
I WISH I COULD SPEND ETERNITY WITH YOU...BUT YOU BELONG BACK HOME, LIVING YOUR LIFE.
No, Rocket... I *need* you.
AND I NEED YOU, ANDY. I ALWAYS WILL. WITHOUT YOU, I'D NEVER HAVE FOUND SERAFINA! MY SISTER!
THIS NEXT PART? THAT'S OUR ADVENTURE.
YOU'VE GOT YOUR OWN ADVENTURE TO FIND.
Mom and Dad... they're probably freaking out by now...
Rocket... are you *sure* you can handle it from here?

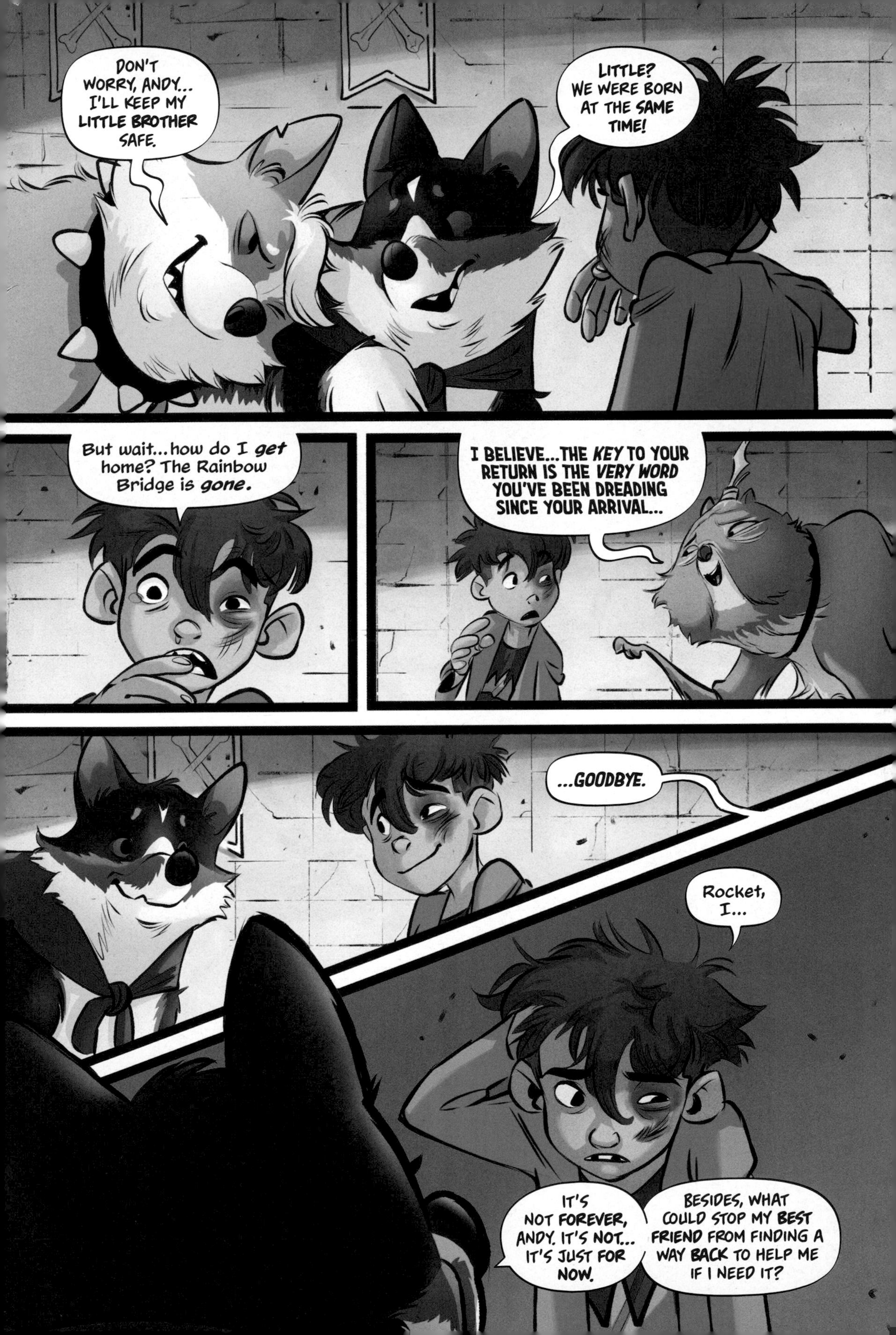
DON'T WORRY, ANDY... I'LL KEEP MY LITTLE BROTHER SAFE.
LITTLE? WE WERE BORN AT THE SAME TIME!
But wait...how do I get home? The Rainbow Bridge is gone.
I BELIEVE...THE KEY TO YOUR RETURN IS THE VERY WORD YOU'VE BEEN DREADING SINCE YOUR ARRIVAL...
...GOODBYE.
Rocket, I...
IT'S NOT FOREVER, ANDY. IT'S NOT... IT'S JUST FOR NOW.
BESIDES, WHAT COULD STOP MY BEST FRIEND FROM FINDING A WAY BACK TO HELP ME IF I NEED IT?

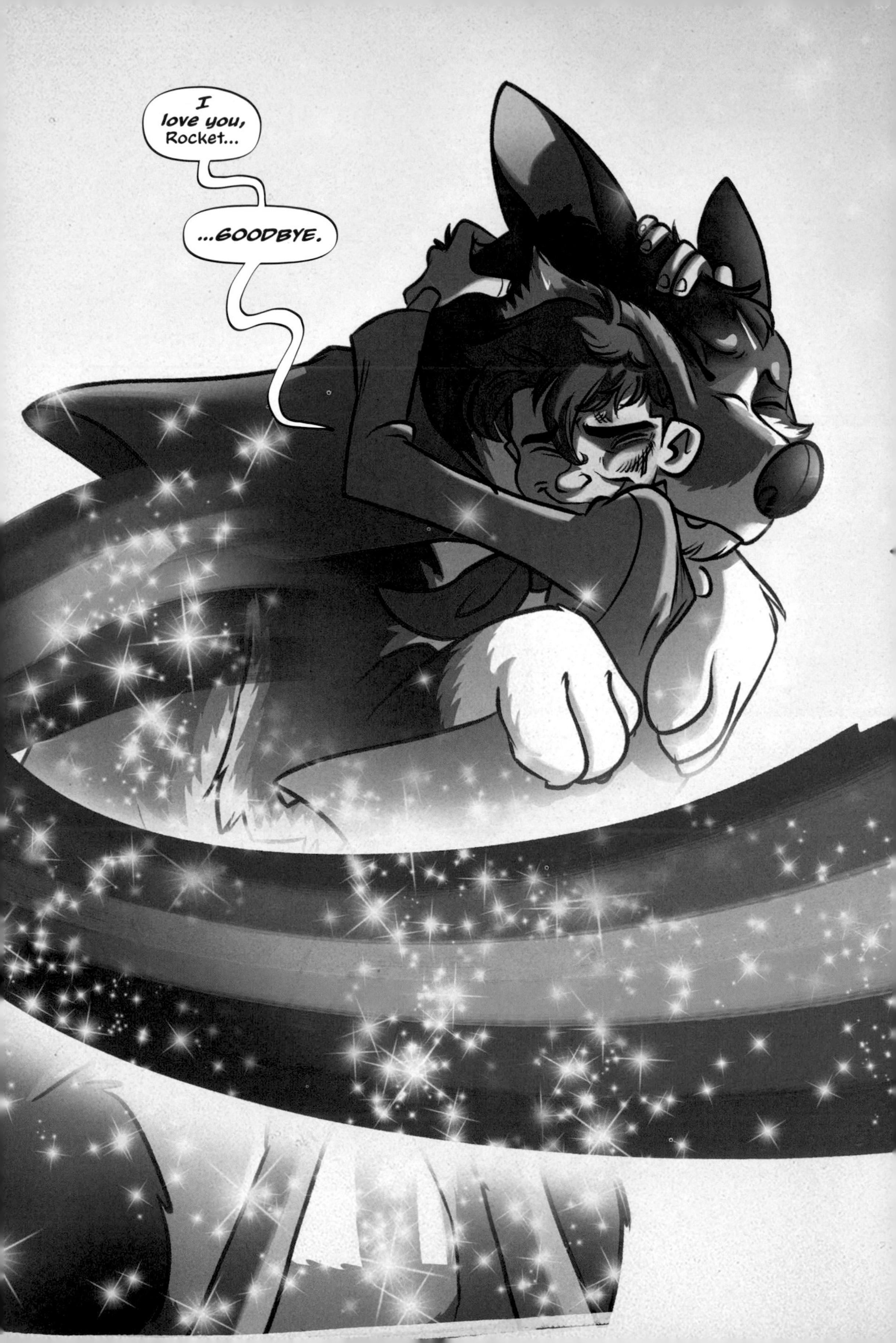
I love you, Rocket...
...GOODBYE.

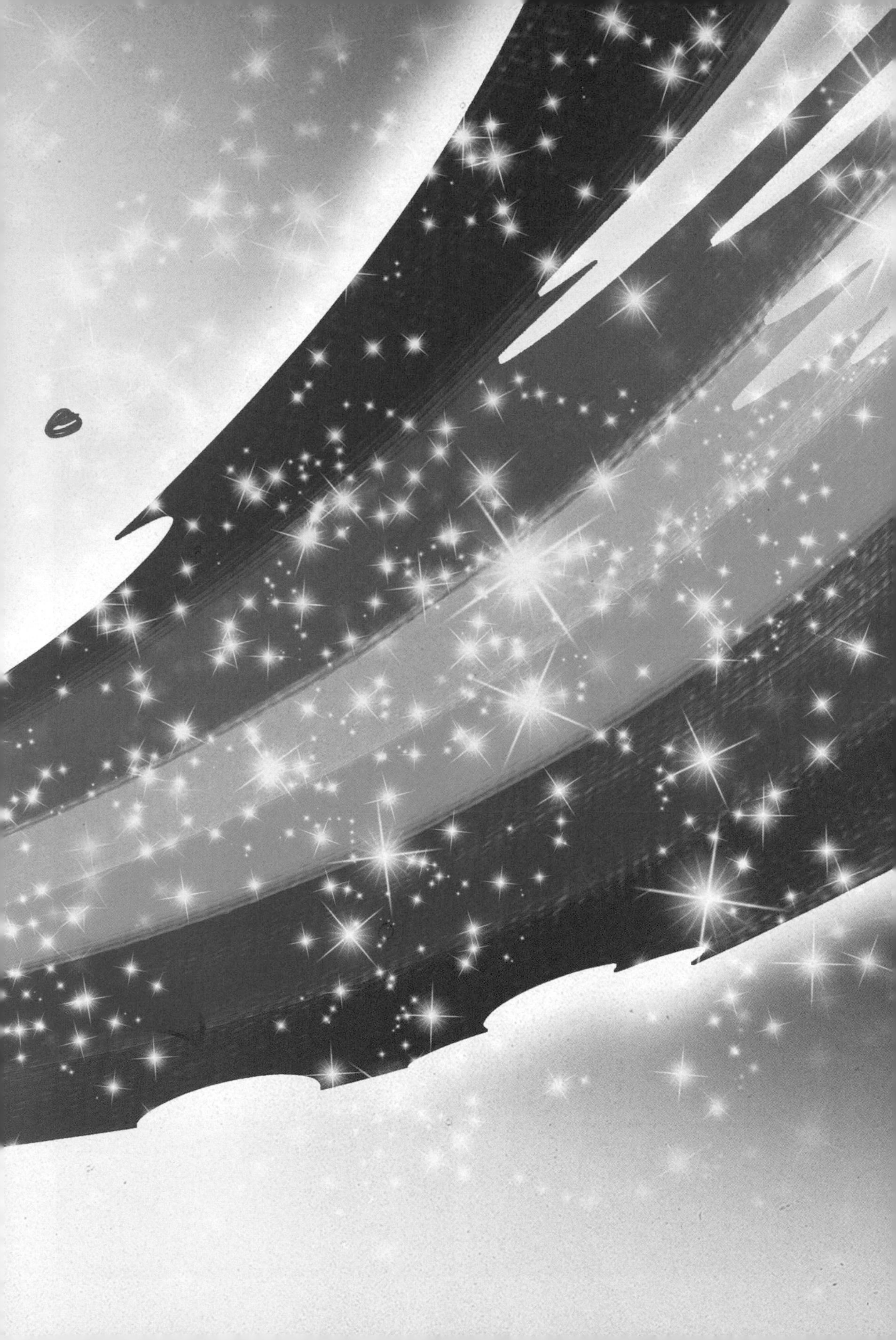

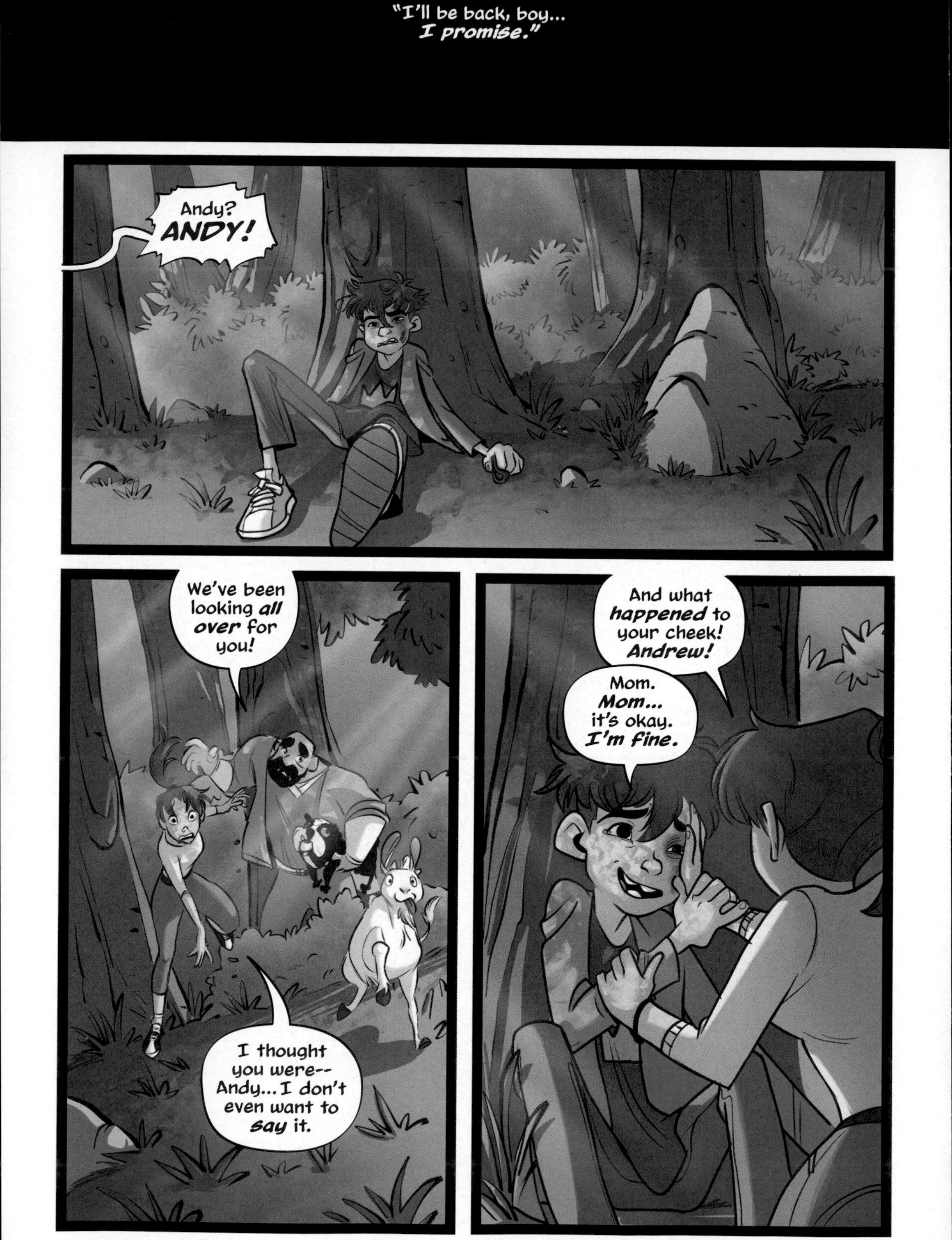
"I'll be back, boy...
I promise."
Andy? **ANDY!**
We've been looking ***all over*** for you!
I thought you were-- Andy... I don't even want to ***say*** it.
And what ***happened*** to your cheek! ***Andrew!***
Mom. ***Mom...*** it's okay. ***I'm fine.***

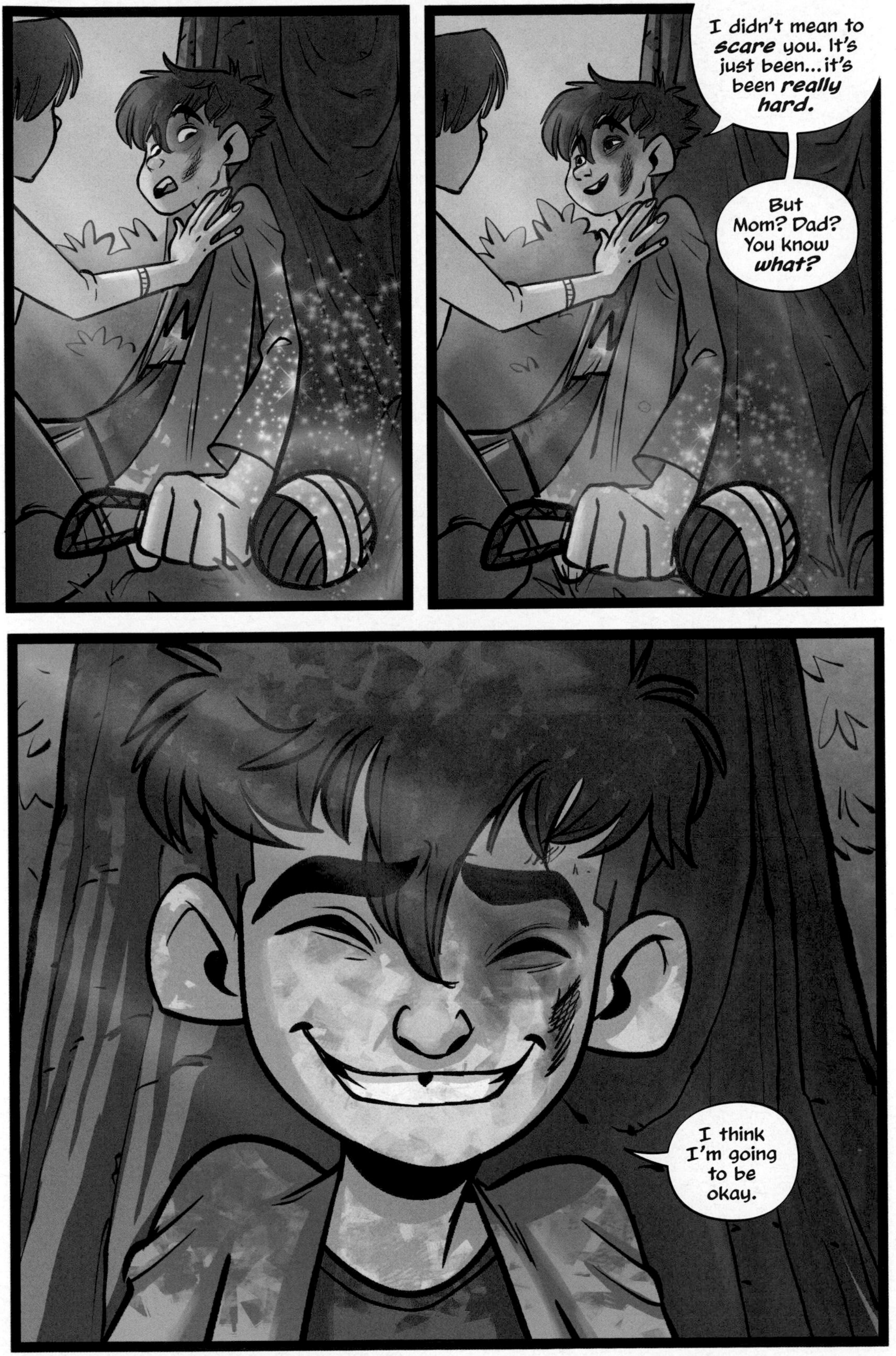
I didn't mean to scare you. It's just been...it's been really hard.
But Mom? Dad? You know what?
I think I'm going to be okay.

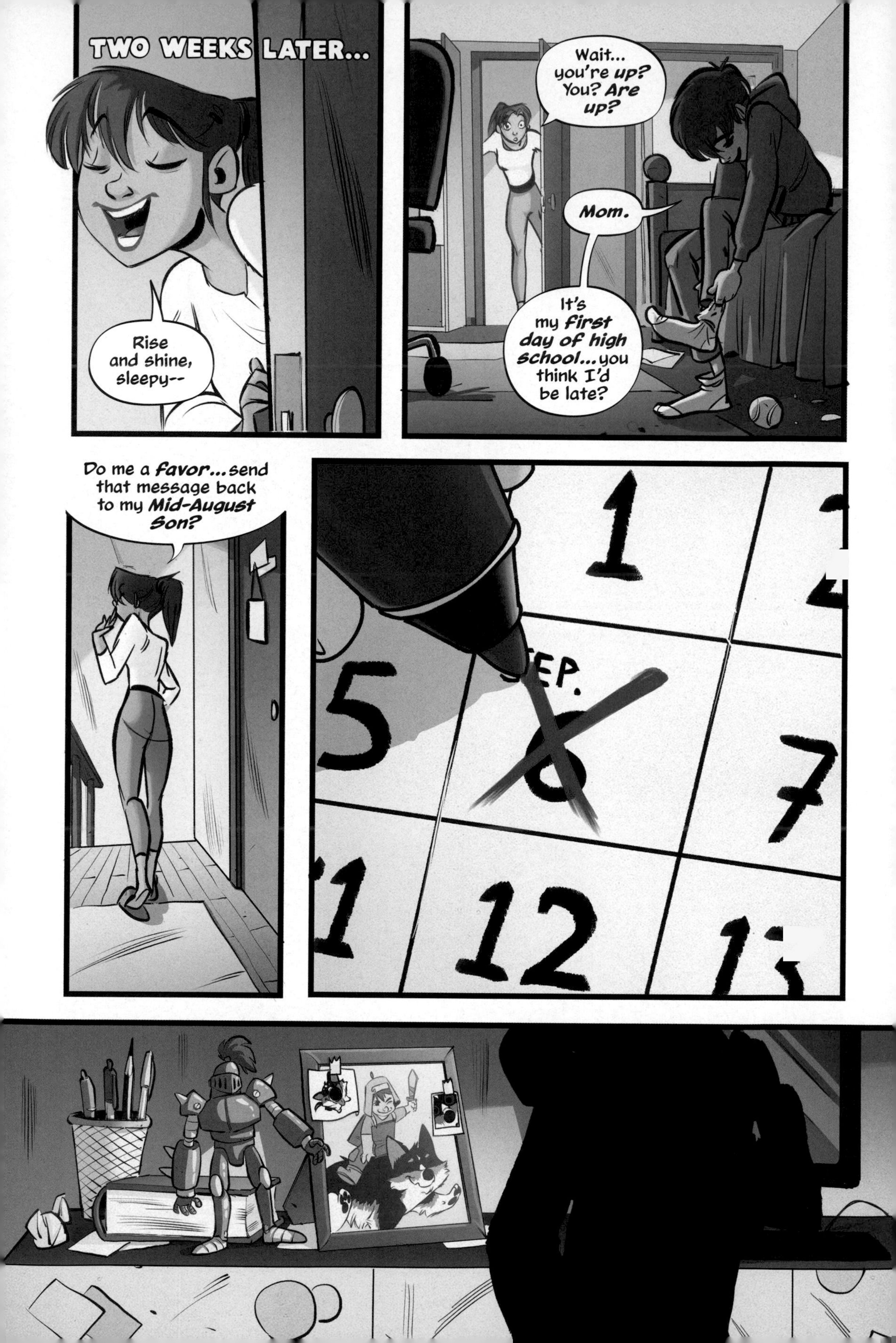
TWO WEEKS LATER...
Rise and shine, sleepy--
Wait... you're up? You? Are up?
Mom.
It's my first day of high school... you think I'd be late?
Do me a favor... send that message back to my Mid-August Son?
SEP.

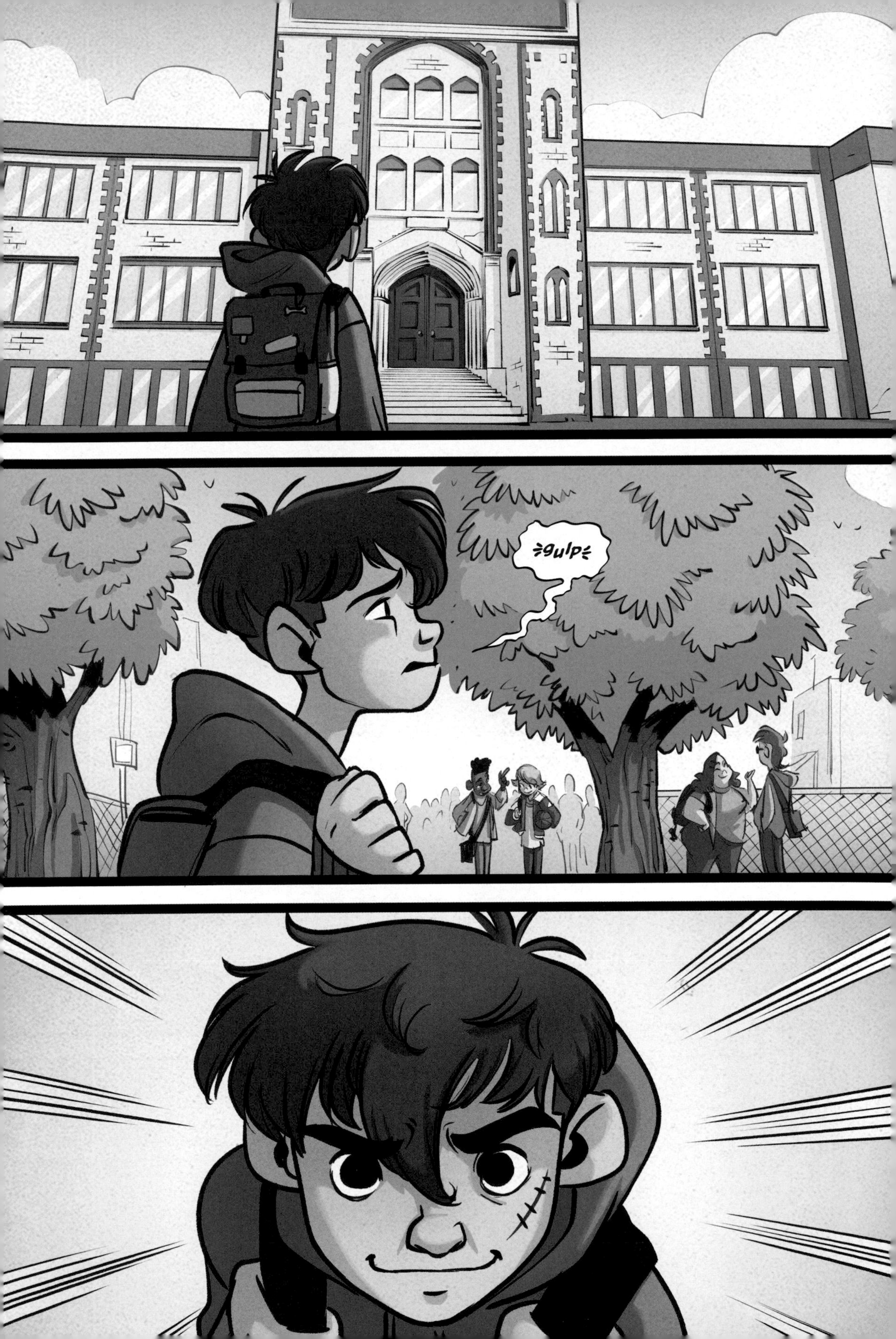
gulp

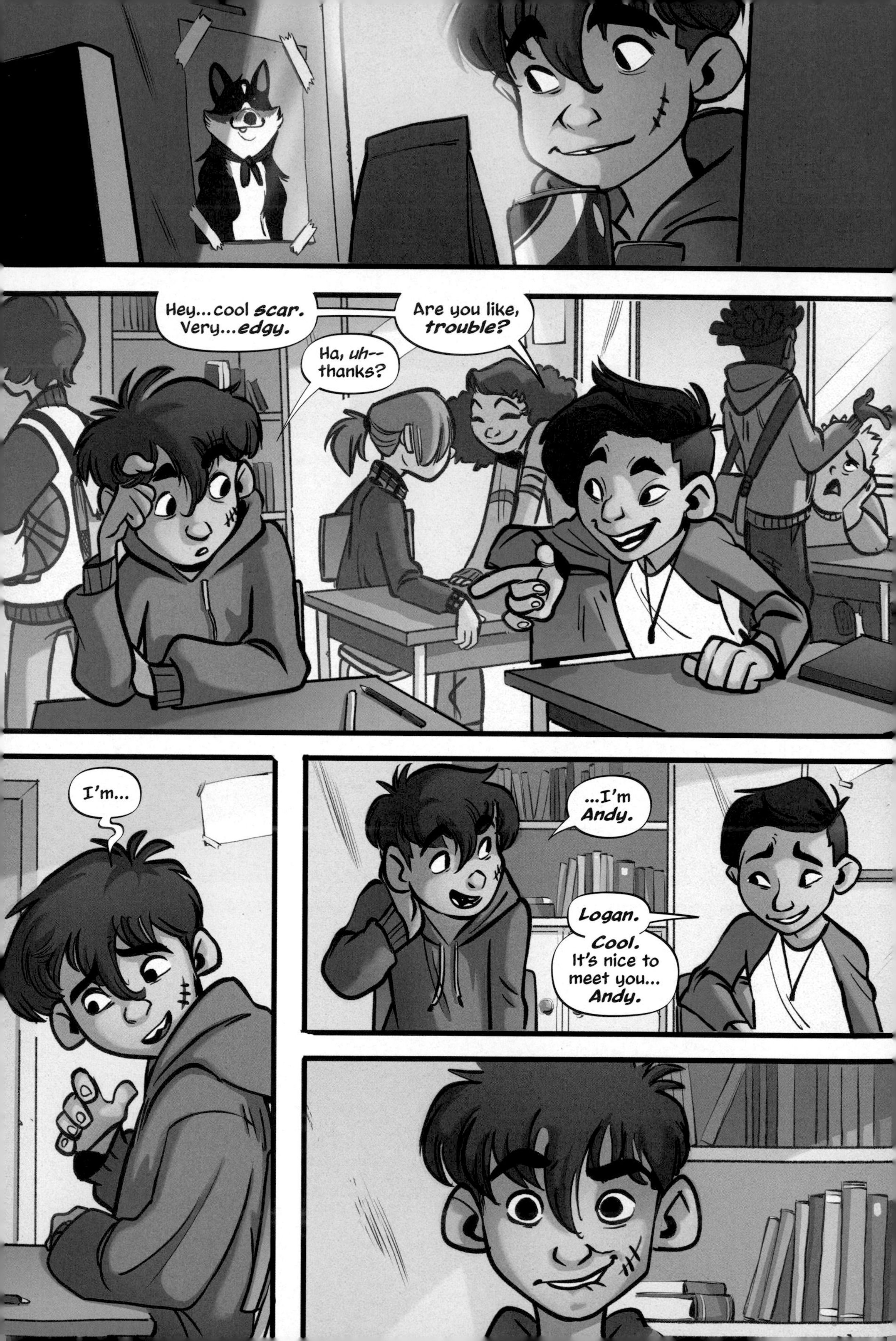
Hey...cool scar. Very...edgy.
Are you like, trouble?
Ha, uh-- thanks?
I'm...
...I'm Andy.
Logan.
Cool. It's nice to meet you... Andy.

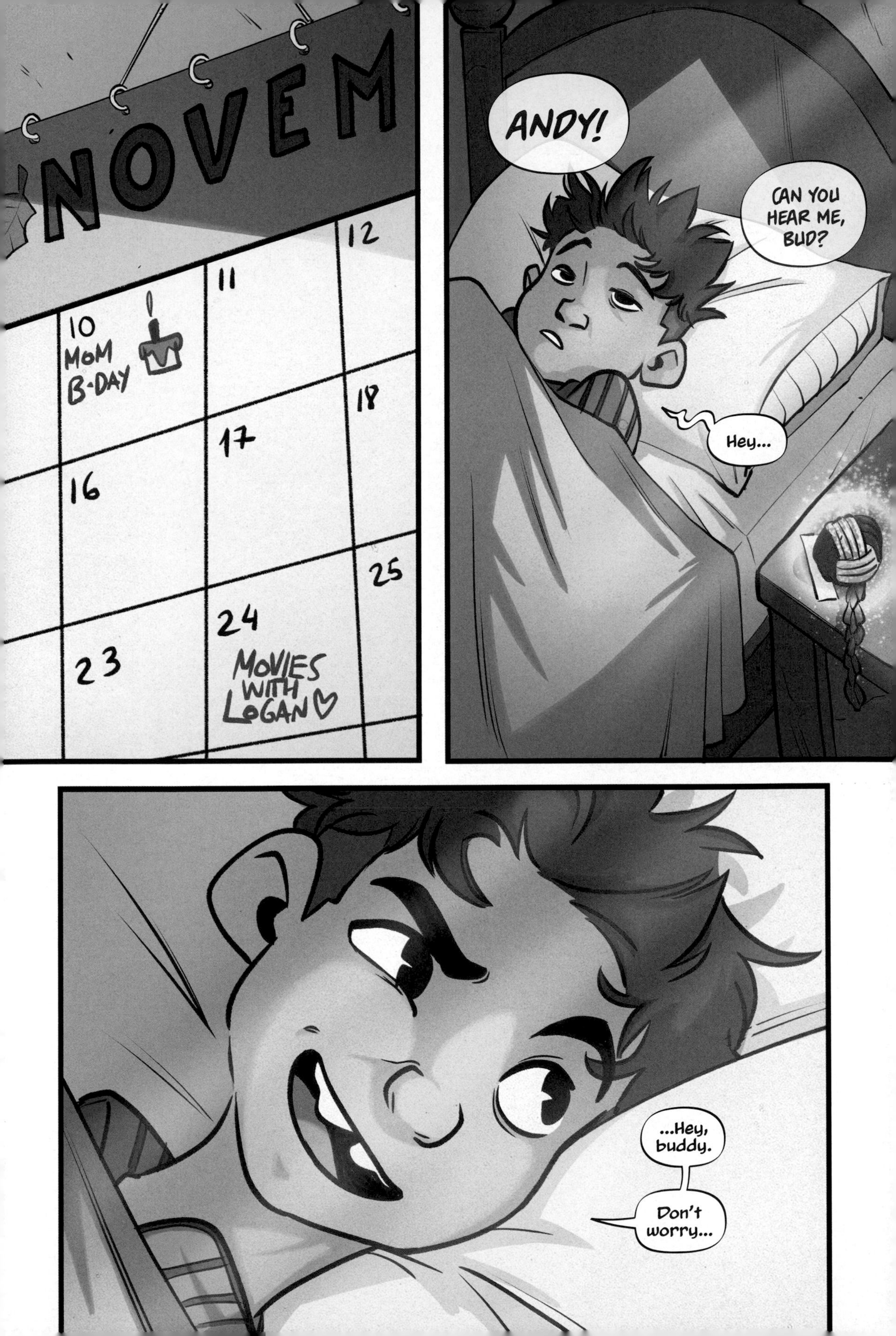
NOVEM
12
11
10
MOM
B-DAY
18
17
16
25
24
23
MOVIES
WITH
LOGAN
ANDY!
CAN YOU HEAR ME, BUD?
Hey...
...Hey, buddy.
Don't worry...

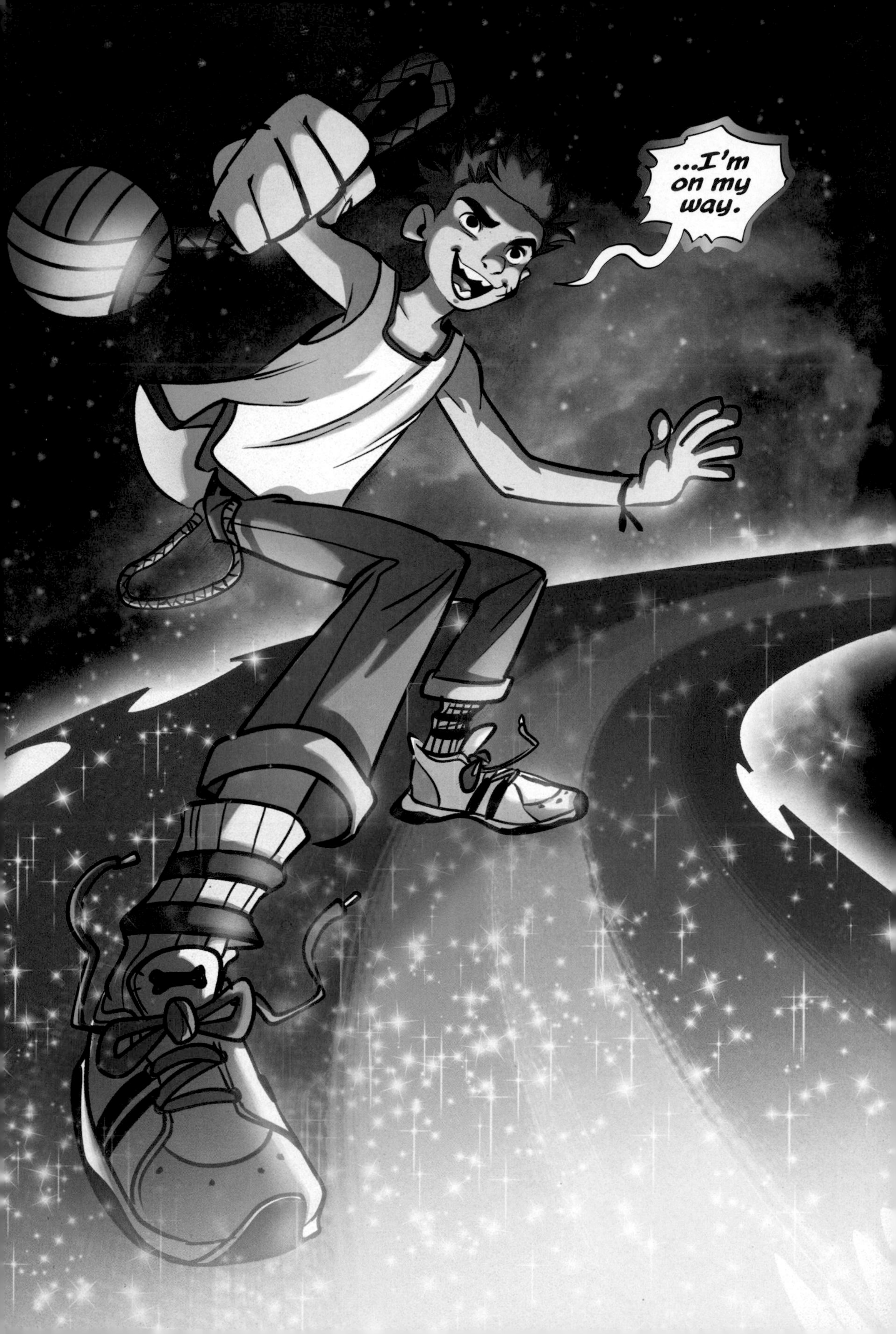
...I'm on my way.

RAINBOW BRIDGE SKETCHBOOK

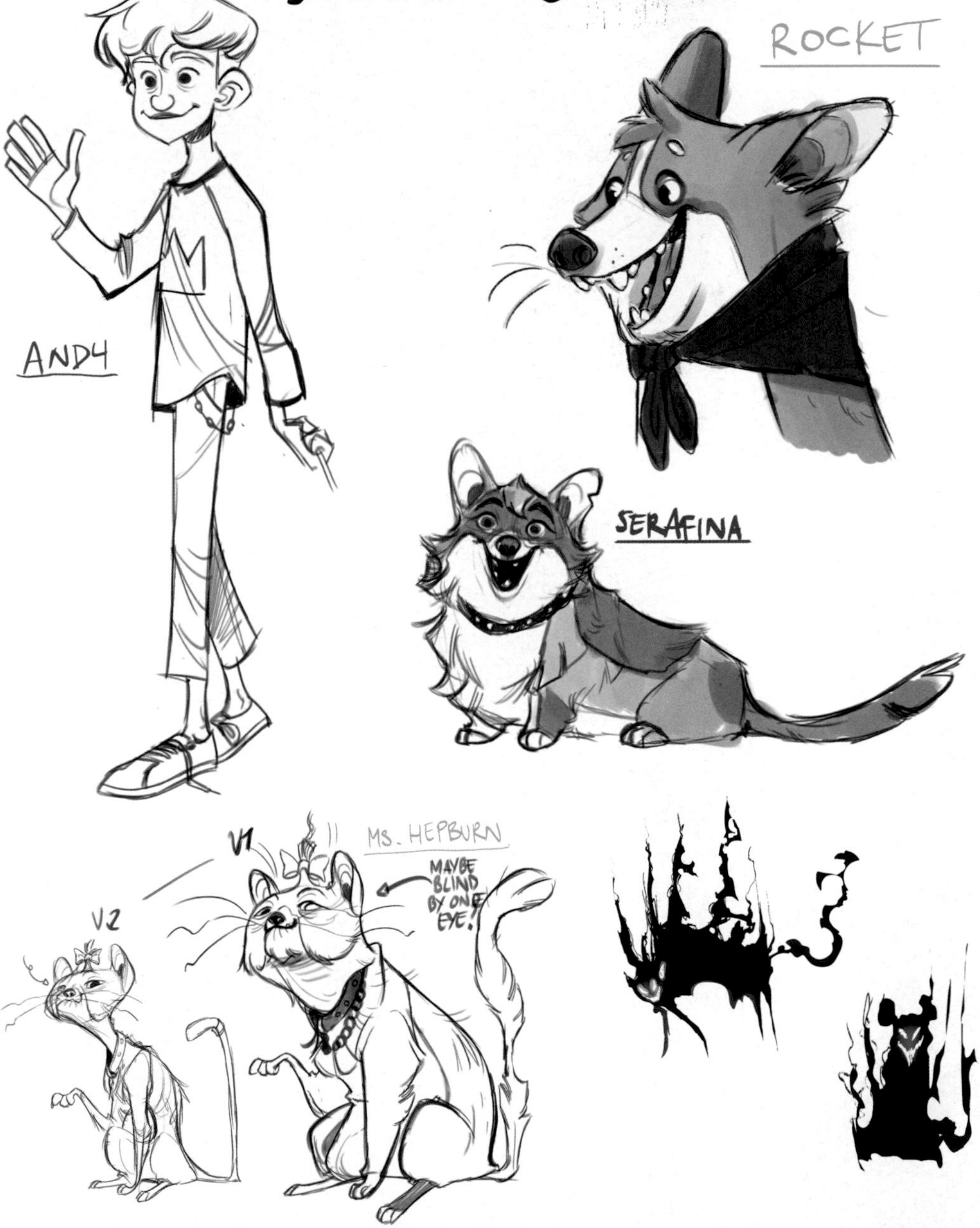
ROCKET
ANDY
SERAFINA
MS. HEPBURN
V1
V2
MAYBE BLIND BY ONE EYE!

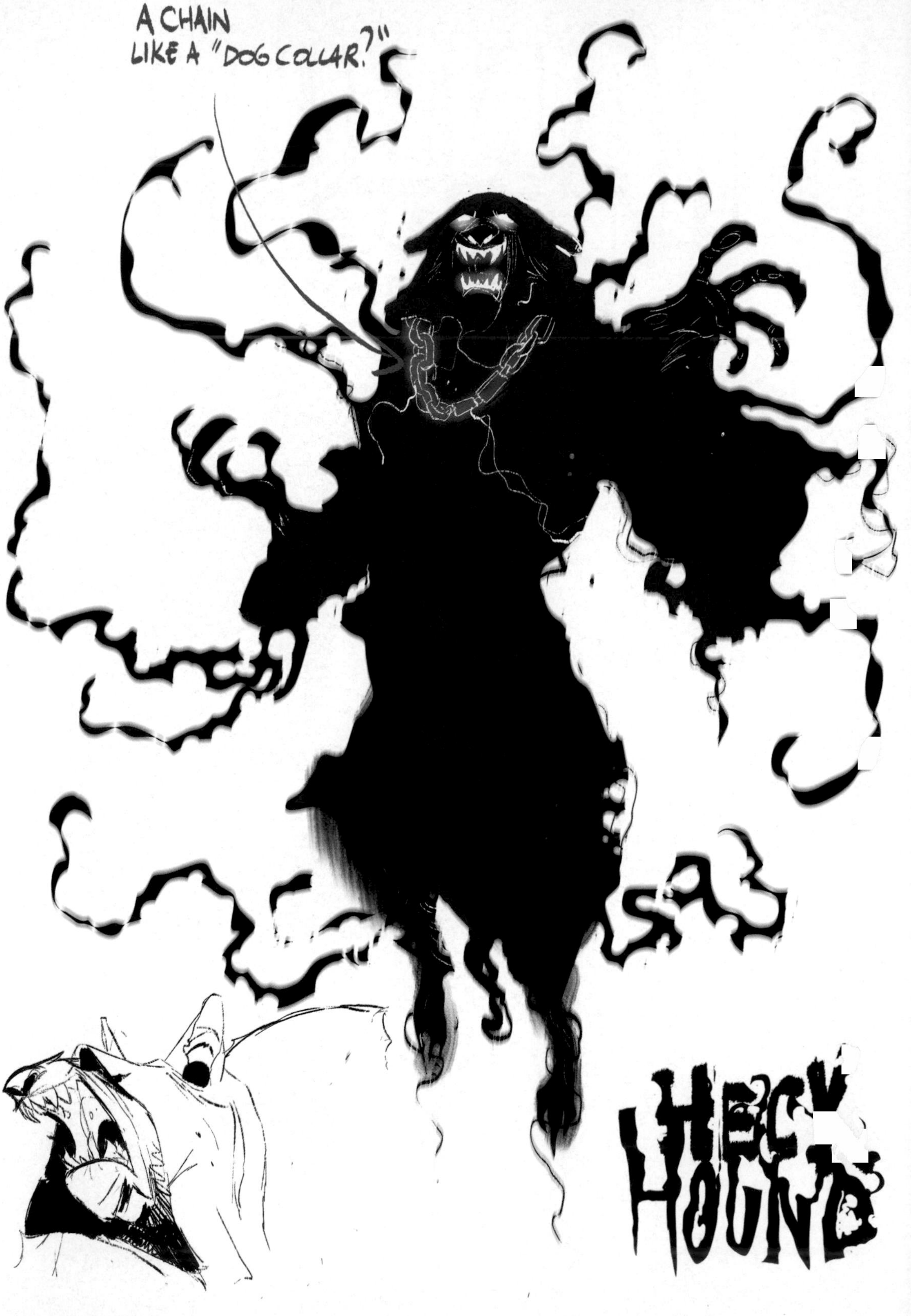
A CHAIN
LIKE A "DOG COLLAR?"
HOUND

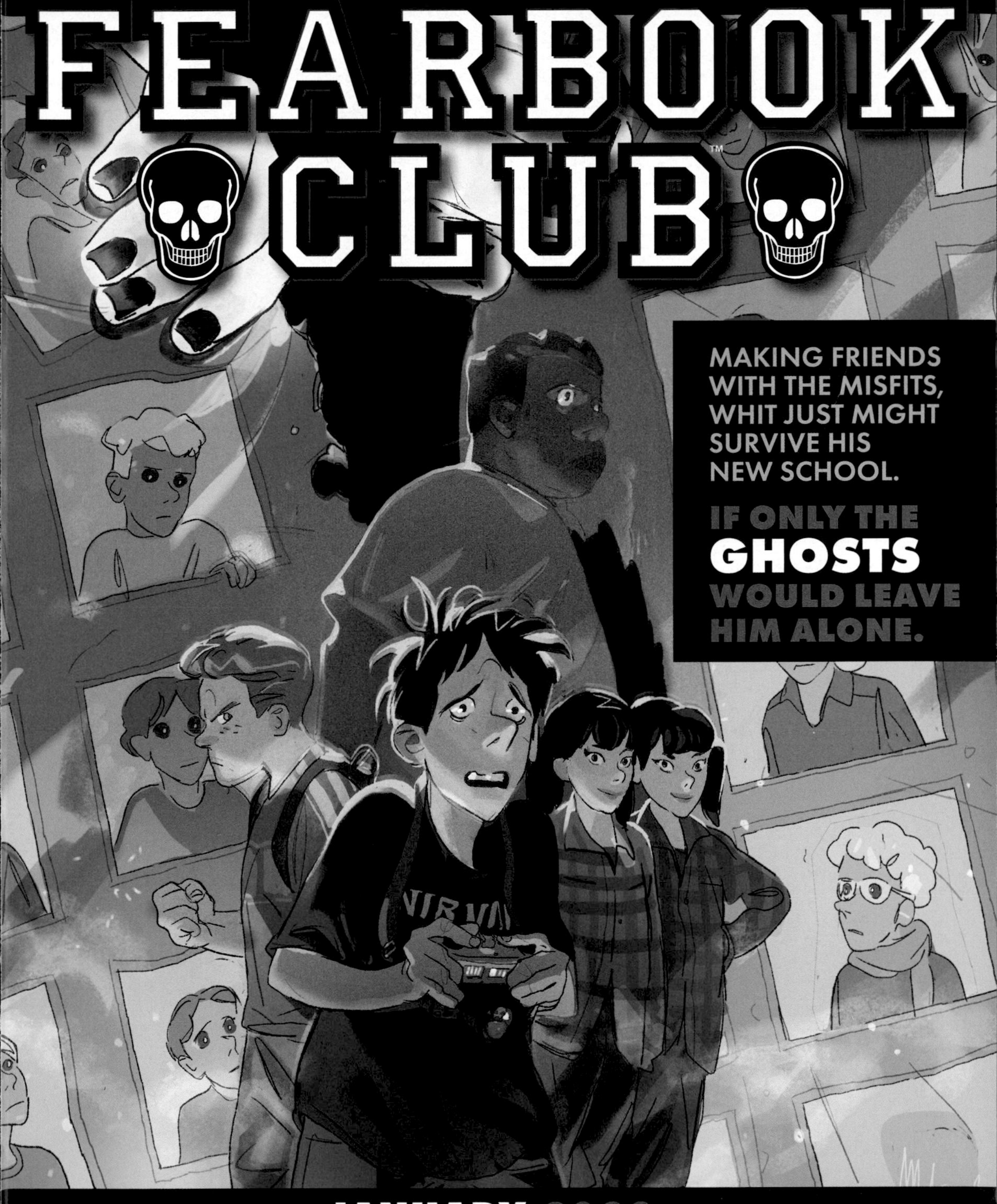
FEARBOOK CLUB™
MAKING FRIENDS WITH THE MISFITS, WHIT JUST MIGHT SURVIVE HIS NEW SCHOOL.
IF ONLY THE GHOSTS WOULD LEAVE HIM ALONE.
NIRVANA

ABOUT THE CREATORS

STEVE ORLANDO
writer

Steve Orlando is a storyteller at heart with works including *Undertow*, and stories in the Eisner Award-Nominated *Outlaw Territory* at Image Comics. Steve's other works include the GLAAD-nominated *Midnighter* and *Midnighter and Apollo*, as well as *Martian Manhunter, Wonder Woman* and *Mighty-Morphin Power Rangers*. Outside of comics, Steve has been featured in National Geographic and worked on the Cartoon Network TV show, *Ben 10*.

STEVE FOXE
writer

Steve Foxe is the author of *Spider-Ham: Great Power, No Responsibility* and over 50 other comics and children's books for properties including *Pokémon, Batman, Transformers, Adventure Time, Steven Universe* and Nintendo. He is the co-creator of *Razorblades: The Horror Magazine*, alongside James Tynion IV. He is also the editor of *The Department of Truth* from Image comics, and writes plenty of things kids shouldn't read, as well. He lives in Queens, where he tweets about comics, scary movies, his boyfriend and their dog.

VALENTINA BRANCATI
artist

Valentina Brancati is an Italian comic book artist and character designer artist who studied in Italy at the International School of Comics based in Rome. Valentina started her comic career in 2017 with the comic books *Les Ravencroft* edited by Edition Paquet (France). She has also collaborated with Walt Disney Company Italia as comic artist and for *Forge Studios* as character designer. At the moment she is working on a new project with Edition Paquet (FR) while also continuing her activity as character designer on the animated short films *Breath* (IT) and *Avyanna* (Spain), now both in the pre-production stages. She also teaches character design at IDEA Academy in Rome.

MANUEL PUPPO
colorist

Manuel Puppo is an Italian colorist and illustrator. He is one of the co-founders of ARANCIA Studio. There, he began his artistic career in the Italian market as a colorist on titles such as *Weird West Mickey* and *Donald Quest Saga* by The Walt Disney Company. He has also collaborated with publishers such as Le Lombard and Éditions Dupuis in Belgium, Éditions Glénat and Petit-à-Petit in France and Egmont in Germany and Baltic countries. He departed ARANCIA Studio in 2016, but he remains a collaborator and a friend of the Studio. In 2017, he had a sabbatical because his beautiful baby girl was born. At the moment he is hard at work on the *Mes Souvenirs en BD* Series by Belgium's Éditions Dupuis.

HASSAN OTSMANE-ELHAOU
letterer

Hassan Otsmane-Elhaou is a writer, editor and letterer. He's lettered comics like *Shanghai Red, Peter Cannon, Red Sonja, Lone Ranger* and more. He's also the editor behind the Eisner-winning publication, *PanelxPanel*, and is the host of the Strip Panel Naked YouTube series. You can usually find him explaining that comics are totally a real job to his parents.